LARGE
PRINT
EDITION

RANDOM
HOUSE

THE MARK OF THE
Assassin

A Novel

DANIEL SILVA

Published by Random House Large Print
in association with Villard Books,
a division of Random House, Inc.
New York 1998

Library of Congress Cataloging-in-Publication Data

Silva, Daniel.
The mark of the assassin : a novel / Daniel Silva.
        p.   cm.
ISBN 0-375-70227-X
1. Large type books.   I. Title.
[PR6069.I362S63   1998]
823'.914—dc21   97-40720
CIP

Random House Web Address:
http://www.randomhouse.com/
Printed in the United States of America
FIRST LARGE PRINT EDITION

This Large Print Book carries the
Seal of Approval of N.A.V.H.

For Esther Newberg,
my literary agent and friend.
And, as always, for my wife, Jamie,
who makes everything possible,
and my children, Lily and Nicholas.

And ye shall know the truth,
and the truth shall make you free.
—The creed of the Central Intelligence
Agency, taken from the Gospel of John

And ye shall know the truth,
and the truth shall piss you off.
—The staff version

THE MARK OF THE
Assassin

PROLOGUE

The Czech-Austrian Border: August 1968

THE SEARCHLIGHT PLAYED across the flat open field. They lay in a drainage ditch on the Czech side of the border: a man and woman and a teenage boy. Others had come this way on previous nights—dissidents, reformers, anarchists—hoping to escape the Russians who had invaded Czechoslovakia and crushed Alexander Dubček's experiment with freedom already known as the "Prague Spring." A few had made it. Most had been arrested; Dubček himself had been abducted and taken to the Soviet Union. According to the bristling rumor mill, some had been taken to a nearby potato patch and shot.

The three people in the ditch were not worried about making it out. They had been ordered to come at that time and had been assured their passage to the West would go smoothly. They had no reason to doubt what they had been told, for all three were officers of the Soviet Committee for State Security, better known as the KGB.

The man and the woman served in the First Chief Directorate of the KGB. Their orders were to infiltrate the dissident Czech and Russian communities in the West.

The boy was assigned to Department V, the assassins.

•   •   •

THE MAN CRAWLED on his belly to the top of the ditch and peered into the night. He put his face down in the cool damp grass as the light passed overhead. When darkness returned he rose again and watched. A half-moon hung low on the horizon, throwing off just enough light to see it all clearly: the guard tower, the silhouette of a border policeman, a second policeman walking along the gravel approach to the fence.

The man checked the luminous dial of his watch. He turned around and whispered in Czech, "Stay here. I'll see if they're ready for us."

He crawled over the top of the ditch and was gone.

The woman looked at the boy. He was no more than sixteen years old, and she had been sleepless with sexual fantasies about him since they had come to Czechoslovakia three weeks earlier. He was too pretty for a boy: black hair, deep blue eyes, like a Siberian lake. His skin was pale, almost white. He had never been operational before tonight, yet he showed no signs of fear. He noticed she was looking at him. He stared back at her with an animal direct-ness that made her shiver.

The man returned five minutes later. "Hurry," he said. "Walk quickly and don't say a word."

He reached down and pulled the woman out of the ditch. He offered a hand to the boy, who refused and climbed out himself. The border policeman met them at the fence. They walked fifty meters to the spot where the gash had been cut in the wire. The guard pulled back the flap, and one by one the three KGB agents crossed into Austria.

The control officers at Moscow Center had writ-ten the script for them. They were to proceed on foot to the nearest village and find an Austrian police officer. From past experience, they knew they would be taken to a detention center for other refugees from the East. Inevitably, they would undergo vigorous questioning from Austrian security agents to make certain they were not spies. Their Czech identities had taken months to manufacture; they were airtight. Within weeks, if all went according to plan, they would be released into the West and begin their assignments for the KGB.

Department V had other plans for the boy.

THERE WAS NO SECURITY on the Austrian side of the border. They crossed an open field. The air was thick with the stink of manure and the chatter of crickets. The landscape darkened as the wet moon slipped behind a stray cloud. The lane was exactly where the control officers had said it would be. When you reach the road, head south, they had said. The village will be there, two miles away.

The lane was pitted and narrow, barely wide enough for a horse-drawn cart, rising and falling over the gentle landscape. They walked quickly, the man and woman leading, the boy a few feet behind. Within a half hour the horizon glowed with lamplight. A few moments later a church steeple floated into view above a low hill.

It was then that the boy reached inside his coat, withdrew a silenced pistol, and shot the man in the back of the head. The woman turned quickly, eyes wide with terror.

The boy's arm swung up, and he shot her rapidly three times in the face.

October

1. Off Long Island, New York

THEY MADE THE ATTEMPT on the third night. The first night was no good: heavy cloud cover, intermittent rain, windblown squalls. The second night was clear, with a good moon, but a bitter northwest wind made the seas too rough. Even the oceangoing motor yacht was buffeted about. It would be hell in the Boston Whaler. They needed a calm sea to carry it off from the Whaler, so they motored farther out and spent a seasick night waiting. That morning, the third morning, the marine forecast was promising: diminishing winds, gentle seas, a slow-moving front with clear weather behind it.

The forecast proved accurate.

The third night was perfect.

HIS REAL NAME was Hassan Mahmoud, but he had always found it rather dull for an Islamic freedom fighter, so he had granted himself a more venturous nom de guerre, Abu Jihad. He was born in Gaza and raised by an uncle in a squalid refugee camp near Gaza City. His politics were forged by the stones and fire of the Intifada. He joined Hamas, fought Israelis in the streets, buried two brothers and more friends than he could remember. He was wounded once himself, his right shoulder shattered by an Israeli army bullet. The doctors said he would never regain full use of the arm. Hassan Mahmoud, alias Abu Jihad, learned to throw stones with his left.

THE YACHT WAS 110 FEET in length, with six staterooms, a large salon, and an aft deck large enough to accommodate a cocktail party of sixty people. The bridge was state of the art, with satellite navigation and communication systems. It was designed for a crew of three, but two good men could handle it easily.

They had set out from the tiny port of Gustavia on the Caribbean island of Saint-Barthélemy eight days earlier and had taken their time moving up the east coast of the United States. They had stayed well outside American territorial waters, but still they had felt the gentle touch of U.S. surveillance along the way: the P-3 Orion aircraft that passed overhead each day, the U.S. Coast Guard cutters slicing through the open sea in the distance.

They had prepared a cover story in the event they were challenged. The vessel was registered in the name of a wealthy French investor, and they were moving it from the Caribbean to Nova Scotia. There, the Frenchman would board the yacht, along with a party of twelve, for a month-long Caribbean cruise.

There was no Frenchman—an officer in a friendly intelligence service had created him—and there most certainly was no party of twelve.

As for Canada, they had no intention of going anywhere near it.

·   ·   ·

THAT NIGHT THEY OPERATED under blackout conditions. It was clear and quite cold. The bright half-moon provided enough light to move about the decks easily. The engine was shut down, just in case an infrared-equipped satellite or aircraft passed overhead. The yacht rocked gently on the flat sea.

Hassan Mahmoud smoked nervously in the darkened salon. He wore jeans, Nike running shoes, and a fleece pullover from L.L. Bean. He looked up at the other man. They had been together ten days, but his companion had spoken only when necessary. One warm night, off the coast of Georgia, Mahmoud tried to engage him in conversation. The man simply grunted and walked to his stateroom. On those rare occasions when he did communicate verbally, he spoke in the precise accentless Arabic of someone who has studied the language diligently but not mastered its subtleties. When Mahmoud asked his name, the man ran his hand over his short black hair, pulled at his nose, and said if names were necessary he should be called Yassim.

He most definitely was not a Yassim. Mahmoud had traveled well for a boy from the camps of Gaza; the trade of terror made that a necessity. He had been to Rome, and he had been to London. He had stayed many months in Athens and hidden with a Palestinian cell in Madrid for an entire winter. The man who wished to be called Yassim and spoke with a strange accent was no Arab. Mahmoud, watching him now, tried to assign geography and ethnicity to the cocktail of strange features possessed by his silent accomplice. He looked at the hair: nearly black and shot with gray at the temples. The eyes were a pene-trating blue, the skin so pale as to be nearly white. The nose was long and narrow—a woman's nose, he thought—the lips full and sensuous, the cheekbones wide. Maybe Greek, he thought, maybe Italian or Spanish. Maybe a Turk or a Kurd. For a mad instant, he thought he might be an Israeli.

Mahmoud watched as the man who wished to be called Yassim disappeared down the companionway and went belowdecks. He returned two minutes later, carrying a long, slender object.

Mahmoud knew just one word for it: Stinger.

YASSIM, WHEN HE SPOKE, treated Mahmoud as though he knew nothing of Stingers. Mahmoud knew them quite well, however. He knew the shoulder-launched version was five feet long and weighed precisely thirty-four and a half pounds. He knew it possessed heat-seeking, passive infrared, and ultraviolet guidance systems. He knew its effective range was about three miles. He had never actually fired one—the things were too precious and too costly to waste on a test firing—but he had drilled for dozens of hours and knew exactly what to expect.

"It's already been preset to seek out a large four-engine aircraft," Yassim was saying. "The warhead has been set to penetrate the target before exploding."

Mahmoud nodded and said nothing.

"Point the missile at the target," he said patiently, in his accentless Arabic. "When the guidance system has acquired its target and locked on, you will hear the tone in your ear. When you hear the tone, fire the missile."

Mahmoud tapped out another Marlboro and offered one to Yassim, who waved his hand and went on with his lecture.

"When the missile is away, simply lay the empty launch tube in the Whaler and return to the yacht."

"I was told to throw the launch tube into the water," Mahmoud said.

"And I'm telling you to bring it back here. When the airliner goes down, the Americans will scan the sea floor with sonar. There's a damned good chance they'll find your launch tube. So bring it back with you. We'll dispose of it farther out."

Mahmoud nodded. He had been told to do it differently, but the explanation for the change in plans was reasonable. For twenty minutes, they said nothing. Mahmoud toyed with the grip stock of the Stinger. Yassim poured coffee and drank it on the aft deck in the cold night air.

Then Yassim went to the bridge to listen to the radio. Mahmoud, still sitting in the salon, could hear the crisp commands of the air traffic controllers at JFK International Airport.

TWO SMALLER BOATS were secured to the stern of the motor yacht, a Zodiac and a twenty-foot Boston Whaler Dauntless. Mahmoud clambered down to the swim step, drew the Whaler closer to the yacht, and stepped over the rail into the forward seating area. Yassim followed him down the ladder and handed over the Stinger.

The Whaler had a dual console, split by a passage connecting the forward and aft seating areas. Mahmoud laid the Stinger on the aft deck, sat in the cockpit, and fired the engine. Yassim untied the Whaler, tossed the line onto the deck, and pushed the smaller craft away with a quick movement of his foot.

Mahmoud opened the throttle, and the Whaler sliced toward the shore of Long Island.

TRANSATLANTIC AIRLINES FLIGHT 002 departs JFK International Airport each evening at 7:00 and arrives the following morning in London at 6:55. Captain Frank Hollings had made the trip more times than he cared to remember, many times in the same Boeing 747 he would fly that night, N75639. The aircraft was the one hundred and fiftieth to roll off Boeing's 747 assembly line in Renton, Washington, and it had experienced few problems during its three decades in the air.

The forecast called for clear weather most of the way and a rainy approach to Heathrow. Hollings expected a smooth flight. At 6:55, the first flight attendant informed Captain Hollings that all passengers were on board. At precisely 7:00 he ordered the cabin doors closed, and TransAtlantic Flight 002 pushed back from the gate.

MARY NORTH TAUGHT ENGLISH at Bay Shore High School on Long Island and served as faculty adviser to the Drama Club. It had sounded like a good idea at the time—escorting club members to London for five days of theater and sightseeing. It had taken more effort than she could have imagined: endless bake sales, car washes, and raffles. Mary had paid her own way, but it meant leaving her husband and two children behind. John taught chemistry at Bay Shore, and jetting to London for a few days of theater was beyond their budget.

The students were acting like animals. It had started in the van on the way to Kennedy: the shouting, the screaming, the rap music and Nirvana blasting from headphones. Her own children were four and six, and each night she prayed they would never reach puberty. Now the students were throwing popcorn at each other and making suggestive comments about the flight attendants. Mary North closed her eyes. Maybe they'll get tired soon, she thought. Maybe they'll sleep.

A popcorn kernel bounced off her nose.

She thought, Maybe you've truly lost your mind, Mary.

As FLIGHT 002 TAXIED toward the end of the runway, Hassan Mahmoud was aboard the Dauntless, racing toward the western tip of Fire Island, the slender barrier island on the southern shore of Long Island.

The trip from the motor yacht had been uneventful. The low moon shone in the eastern sky, allowing him to navigate with no running lights. Ahead of him the borough of Queens glowed pale yellow on the horizon.

Conditions were perfect: clear skies, calm seas, scarcely a wind. Mahmoud checked the depthometer and shut down the engine. The Dauntless glided to a stop. In the distance he could hear the grumble of a freighter leaving New York Harbor. He switched on the radio and tuned it to the proper frequency.

Five minutes later, Mahmoud heard the air traffic controller give TransAtlantic Flight 002 final clearance for takeoff. He picked up the Stinger and switched on its fire and guidance systems. Then he hoisted it onto his shoulder and peered through the sighting mechanism into the night sky.

Mahmoud heard the jetliner before he could actually see it. Ten seconds later, he picked up the 747's navigation lights and tracked it across the black sky. Then the tone sounded in his ear, alerting him that the Stinger had acquired a target.

The Whaler rolled violently as the Stinger's solid rocket fuel ignited and the missile roared from the launch tube. "The Americans like to refer to their precious Stinger as a fire-and-forget weapon," his trainer had told him during one of their sessions. The trainer was an Afghan who had lost an eye and a hand killing Russians. Fire and forget, Mahmoud thought. Fire and forget. Simple as that.

The launch tube, now empty, was considerably lighter than before. He dropped it onto the deck, as Yassim had instructed him to do. Then he fired the Whaler's engine and raced away from the coast, taking just one glance over his shoulder to watch the Stinger streaking at supersonic speed across the black canvas of the night.

CAPTAIN FRANK HOLLINGS had flown B-52s over North Vietnam, and he had seen surface-to-air missiles before. For a brief instant, he permitted himself to believe it might be something else—a small plane ablaze, a meteor, stray fireworks. Then, as the missile raced relentlessly toward them at lightning speed, he realized it could be nothing else. The nightmare scenario had come true.

"Holy Mother of God," he murmured. He turned toward his copilot and opened his mouth to speak. The aircraft shuddered violently. An instant later it was ripped apart by a massive explosion, and fire rained down on the sea.

WHEN HE HEARD THE APPROACH of the Dauntless, the man called Yassim quickly flashed a powerful signal lamp three times. The smaller vessel came into view. Mahmoud reduced power, and the Dauntless glided toward the stern of the yacht.

Even in the weak light of the moon he could see it on the boy's face: the crazed excitement, the fear, the rush. He could see it in the shining deep-brown Palestinian eyes, see it in the jittery hands fumbling over the controls of the Dauntless. Left to his own devices, Mahmoud would be up all night and the next day too, reliving it, recounting every detail, explaining over and over how it felt the moment the plane burst into flames.

Yassim detested ideologues, detested the way they all wore their suffering like armor and disguised their fear as valor. He distrusted anyone who would willingly lead a life such as this. He trusted only professionals.

The Dauntless nudged against the stern of the yacht. The wind had picked up in the last few minutes. Gentle swells lapped against the sides of the boats. Yassim climbed down the ladder as Hassan Mahmoud shut down the engine and clambered into the forward seating area. He reached out a hand for Yassim to help him out of the boat, but Yassim simply drew a silenced 9mm Glock pistol from the waistband of his trousers and shot the Palestinian boy rapidly three times in the face.

THAT NIGHT HE SET THE YACHT on an easterly heading and engaged the automatic navigation systems. He lay awake in his stateroom. Even now, even after countless killings, he could not sleep the first night after an assassination. When he was making his escape, or still in public, he always managed to remain focused and operational cool. But at night the demons came. At night he saw the faces, one by one, like photographs in an album. First alive and vibrant; then contorted with the death mask or blown apart by his favorite method of killing, three bullets to the face. Then the guilt would come, and he would tell himself that he had not chosen this life; it had been chosen for him. At dawn, with the first gray light of morning leaking through his window, he finally slept.

HE ROSE AT MIDDAY and went about the routine of preparing for his departure. He shaved and showered, then dressed and packed the rest of his clothing into a small leather grip. He made coffee and drank it while watching CNN on the yacht's superb satellite television system. Such a pity: the grieving relatives at Kennedy and Heathrow, the vigil at a high school somewhere on Long Island, the reporters wildly speculating about the cause of the crash.

He walked through the yacht room by room one last time to make certain he had left no trace of his presence. He checked the explosive charges.

At 6 P.M., the precise time he had been ordered, he retrieved a small black object from a cabinet in the galley. It was no larger than a cigar box and looked vaguely like a radio. He carried it outside onto the aft deck and pressed a single button. There was no sound, but he knew the message had been sent in a coded microburst. Even if the American NSA intercepted it, it would be meaningless gibberish.

The yacht motored eastward for two more hours. It was now 8 P.M. He set each of the charges and then slipped on a canvas vest with a heavy metal clamp on the front.

There was more wind tonight. It was colder and there were high clouds. The Zodiac, cleated at the stern, rose and fell rhythmically with the three-foot swells. He climbed into the craft, untied it, and pulled the starter cord. The engine came to life on the third pull. He turned away from the yacht and opened the throttle.

He heard the helicopter twenty minutes later. He shut down the Zodiac's engine and shone a signal lamp into the sky. The helicopter hovered overhead, the night filled with the thump of its rotors. The cable fell from its belly. He attached it to his vest and pulled hard on it twice to signal that he was ready. A moment later he rose gently from the Zodiac.

He heard explosions in the distance. He turned his head in time to see the large motor yacht being lifted out of the water by the force of the blasts. Then it began its slow descent toward the bottom of the Atlantic.

2. San Francisco

PRESIDENT JAMES BECKWITH was notified of the tragedy while vacationing at his home in San Francisco. He had hoped for a few days of rest: a quiet afternoon in his study overlooking the Golden Gate Bridge, a relaxing dinner party with old friends and political supporters in Marin. Most of all, a day of sailing aboard his prized thirty-eight-foot ketch *Democracy,* even if it meant being pursued by a pack of White House pool reporters and cameramen across the waters of San Francisco Bay. The day sails on *Democracy* always provided the kind of news pictures his handlers and political advisers liked best— the President, fit and youthful despite his sixty-nine years, still able to handle the boat with only Anne aboard; the tanned face, the lean body moving easily about the deck, the smart European-style sunglasses beneath the brim of his Air Force One cap.

The private office in Beckwith's large home in the Marina District reflected his taste and image to perfection: polished, comfortable, traditional, yet with enough modern touches to convey that he was firmly in touch with today's world. The desk was glass, tinted slightly gray, his personal computer black. He took pride in knowing as much about computers, if not more, than most of his youthful staff.

He picked up the receiver of his black telephone and pressed a single button. A White House operator came onto the line. "Yes, Mr. President?"

"Unless the chief of staff telephones, hold all my calls for now, Grace. I'd like some time to myself."

"Of course, Mr. President."

He heard the line go dead. He replaced the receiver and walked to the window. It was a remarkable view, despite the dense bulletproof glass inflicted by the Secret Service. The sun had dropped low into the western sky, painting the city soft watercolor shades of purple and orange. The evening's fog was creeping through the Golden Gate. Below him, colorful kites floated over the bay shore. The view worked its magic. He had forgotten how long he had been standing there, watching the silent city, the white-capped waters of the bay, the brown hills of Marin in the distance. The last light of the afternoon retreated, and after a few minutes his own reflection stared back at him in the glass.

Beckwith disliked the word "patrician," but even he had to admit it was an accurate description of his appearance and bearing. His advisers joked that if God had created the perfect political candidate, it would have been James Beckwith. He stood out in any room he entered. He was well over six feet tall, with a full head of shimmering hair that had turned gray-white by the time he was forty. There was a strength about him, a lingering physical agility from his days as a star football and baseball player at Stanford. The eyes were pale blue and turned down at the corners, the features of his face narrow and re-strained, the smile careful but confident. His skin was permanently tanned from countless hours aboard *Democracy.*

When Beckwith assumed the presidency four years earlier, he had made one promise to himself: He would not allow the office to consume him the way it had consumed so many of his predecessors. He ran thirty minutes each day on the treadmill and spent another thirty minutes lifting weights in the White House gym. Other men had grown haggard in the office. James Beckwith had lowered his weight and added an inch of muscle to his chest.

Beckwith had not sought out politics; politics had come to him. He was the top prosecutor in the San Francisco District Attorney's office when he caught the eye of the state's Republican elite. With Anne and their three children at his side, Beckwith easily won every race he entered. His rise had seemed effortless, as if he were preordained to greatness. California elected him attorney general, then lieutenant gover-nor. It sent him to the U.S. Senate for two terms and then brought him back to Sacramento for a term as governor, the final preparation for his ascent to the White House. Throughout his political career, the professionals surrounding him had crafted a careful image. James Beckwith was a common-sense conser-vative. James Beckwith was a man the country could trust. James Beckwith could get things done. He was exactly the kind of man the Republican Party was looking for, a moderate with a pleasing face, a pre-

sentable counterbalance to the hard-line conserva-
tives in Congress. After eight years of Democratic
control of the White House, the country had been in
the mood for change. The country chose Beckwith.

Now, four years later, the country wasn't sure it
still wanted him. He turned from the window, walked
to his desk, and poured himself a cup of coffee from a
chrome-colored insulated carafe. Beckwith believed
that from all adversity good things come. The downing of an American jetliner off Long Island was an
egregious act of international terrorism, a savage and
cowardly deed that could not go unanswered. The
electorate soon would be told what Beckwith already
knew: TransAtlantic Flight 002 had been brought
down by a Stinger missile, apparently launched from
a small craft offshore. The American people would be
frightened, and if history were a guide, they would
turn to him for comfort and assurance.

James Beckwith detested the business of politics, but he was savvy enough to realize that the terrorists had handed him a golden opportunity. For
the past year his approval ratings had hovered
below fifty percent, death for an incumbent president. His acceptance speech at the Republican National Convention had been flat and lifeless. The
Washington press corps had branded his vision for a
second term "warmed over first-term." Some of its
elite members had begun writing his political obitu-
ary. With just one month before the election, he
trailed his opponent, Democratic Senator Andrew
Sterling of Nebraska, by three to five points in most
national polls.

The electoral map looked different, though. Beckwith had conceded New York, New England, and the industrial Midwest to Sterling. His support remained solid in the South, the crucial states of Florida and Texas, and California, the mountain West. If Beckwith could capture them all, he could win. If any one of them fell to Sterling, the election was lost.

He knew the downing of Flight 002 would change everything. The campaign would freeze; Beckwith would cancel a swing through Tennessee and Kentucky to return to Washington to deal with the crisis. If he managed it well, his approval ratings would rise and he would close the gap. And he could do it all from the comfort and security of the White House, not racing around the country in Air Force One or some godforsaken campaign bus, shaking hands with old people, making the same goddamned speech over and over again.

Great men are not born great, he told himself. Great men *become* great because they seize opportunity.

He carried his coffee back to the window. He thought, But do I really want a second term? Unlike most of his predecessors, he had given that question serious consideration. He wondered whether he had the endurance for one last national campaign: the endless fund-raising, the microscopic scrutiny of his record, the constant travel. He and Anne had come to detest living in Washington. He had never been accepted by the city's ruling elite—its rich journalists, lawyers, and lobbyists—and the Executive Mansion had become more like a prison than a home. But to leave office after one term was unacceptable. To lose reelection to a second-term senator from Nebraska and leave Washington in defeat . . . ?

Beckwith shuddered at the thought.

They would be coming for him soon. There was a private bathroom just off his study. An aide had left his clothes on a hook on the back of the door. The President went inside and cast his eyes over the clothing. He knew the outfit had been selected personally by his chief of staff and longtime friend, Paul Vandenberg. Paul saw to the details; Paul saw to everything. Beckwith would be lost without him.

Sometimes, even Beckwith was embarrassed by the extent to which Paul Vandenberg ran his affairs. The media routinely referred to him as "the prime minister" or "the power behind the throne." Beckwith, ever conscious of his image in history, worried he would be written off as a pawn of Paul Vandenberg. But Vandenberg had given Beckwith his word; he would never portray himself in that manner. The President trusted him. Paul Vandenberg knew how to keep secrets. He believed in the quiet exercise of power. He was intensely private, kept a low profile, and leaked to reporters only when it was absolutely necessary. He reluctantly appeared on the Sunday morning talk shows, but only when the White House press secretary begged. Beckwith thought he was a horrible guest; the confidence and brilliance he displayed in private planning and policy meetings evaporated once the red light of the television camera came on.

He removed his faded jeans and cotton pullover and dressed in the clothes Paul had chosen for him:

gray woolen trousers, blue button-down shirt, light-weight crew-neck sweater, blue blazer. Dignified yet comforting. His national security staff was meeting in ten minutes in the dining room downstairs. There would be no video cameras, just a White House still photographer who would capture the moment for the press and for history. James Beckwith, confronting the most important crisis of his presidency. James Beckwith, casting aside his reelection campaign to deal with the responsibilities of his office. James Beckwith, leader.

He looked at his reflection in the mirror one last time.

Great men are not born great. Great men become great because they seize opportunity.

3. Washington, D.C.

ELIZABETH OSBOURNE had been dreading this moment all week. She turned her silver Mercedes into the parking lot at Georgetown University Medical Center and found a space not far from the entrance. She looked at the dashboard clock. It was four-thirty; she was fifteen minutes early. She shut off the engine. A tropical storm had moved up from the Gulf of Mexico and settled over the city. Heavy rains fell all afternoon. Gusty winds uprooted trees all across Northwest Washington, shut down National Airport, and drove the tourists from the monuments and museums along the Mall.

Rain drummed on the roof and ran in rivers down the windshield. After a moment, the rest of the world vanished behind a blurry curtain of water. Elizabeth liked the sensation of being able to see nothing else around her. She closed her eyes. She liked to fantasize about changing her life, about slowing down, about leaving Washington and settling somewhere slow and quiet with Michael. She knew it was a silly, unrealistic dream. Elizabeth Osbourne was one of Washington's most respected lawyers. Her husband, while professing to be an international business consultant, was a senior officer at the Central Intelligence Agency.

Her cellular phone rang softly. She picked up the handset, eyes still closed, and said, "Yes, Max."

Max Lewis was her twenty-six-year-old executive secretary. The previous night, sitting alone in her bedroom with a glass of wine and a stack of legal briefs, Elizabeth had realized she spoke to Max more than anyone else in the world. This depressed her greatly.

"How did you know it was me?" he asked.

"Because you and my husband are the only people who have this number, and I knew it couldn't be him."

"You sound disappointed."

"No, just a little tired. What's up?"

"David Carpenter's on the line from Miami."

"Tell Mr. Carpenter I'll call him as soon as I get home. It's been my experience that conversations with David Carpenter should rarely be conducted on cellular telephones."

"He says it's urgent."

"It usually is."

"What time should I tell him to expect your call?"

"About seven o'clock, but it may slip a little bit depending on how things go here."

"Braxton's secretary telephoned."

Samuel Braxton was the managing partner at Braxton, Allworth & Kettlemen and the firm's biggest rainmaker. He had served two Republican administrations—once as deputy White House chief of staff and once as deputy secretary of the Treasury—and was on the short list to be secretary of state if Beckwith managed to win a second term. He viewed Elizabeth with suspicion because he didn't like her politics; her father was Douglas Cannon, a liberal Democrat from New York who served four terms in the Senate, and she had twice left the firm to work for Democratic senators. Braxton routinely referred to her as "our in-house lefty." At meetings, when working his way around the table on an issue, he frequently managed to break up the room by turning to Elizabeth and saying, "And now, with the view from the ACLU, Elizabeth Cannon-Osbourne."

There was a more serious side to her conflict with Samuel Braxton; he had fought to prevent her from making partner and had relented only when the other partners convinced him he would be setting the firm up for a gender-discrimination lawsuit. Now, three years later, their relationship had settled into an uneasy truce. Braxton generally treated her with respect and made a genuine effort to consult her on all major decisions concerning the future and direction of the firm. He regularly invited her to social functions, and last year, at the White House Christmas party, he referred to her as "one of our

real stars" when introducing her to Chief of Staff
Paul Vandenberg.

"What does Lord Braxton desire, Max?"

Max laughed. She would trust him with her life.
It was mutual. Six months earlier Max had told her
something he had told no one else—he was HIV-
positive.

"The Lord would like you to attend a dinner party
Thursday evening."

"Is it being held at the manor?"

"No, one of his big clients is throwing it. The
Lord's secretary made it sound as if attendance was
not optional."

"Who's the client?"

"Mitchell Elliott."

"Mitchell Elliott of Alatron Defense Systems?"

"He's the one."

"Where's the party?"

"At Elliott's home in Kalorama. California
Street, to be precise. You have a pen handy?"

Elizabeth fished a pen and her calendar from her
briefcase and jotted down the address as Max read it
to her.

"What time?"

"Seven-thirty."

"Am I allowed to bring a date?"

"Spouses are permitted. Elizabeth, you're going
to be late for your appointment."

She glanced at the dashboard clock. "Oh, shit!
Anything else?"

"Nothing that can't hold till morning."

"Where am I going tomorrow?"

"Chicago. I put the tickets in the outside flap of your briefcase."

She pulled open the flap and saw the American Airlines first-class ticket jacket.

"I'd be lost without you, Max."

"I know."

"You didn't hear from Michael, did you?"

"Not a peep."

"I'll call you from the plane tomorrow morning."

"Great," he said. "And good luck, Elizabeth. I'll be thinking about you."

She severed the connection and punched in the speed-dial code for Michael's car phone. The phone rang five times before a recorded voice announced that the customer was not available at this time. Elizabeth angrily snapped the receiver back into its cradle. She sat very still for a moment, listening to the rattle of the rain.

She whispered, "Michael Osbourne, if you don't drive into this parking lot in the next five minutes, so help me God, I'll . . ."

She waited five minutes; then she struggled into her raincoat and stepped outside the warmth of the car into the storm. She threw up her umbrella and started across the parking lot, but the wind gusted and ripped it from her grasp. She watched it for a moment, tumbling toward Reservoir Road. Something about it made her laugh helplessly. She clutched her raincoat tightly against her throat and hurried across the parking lot through the rain.

"THE DOCTOR IS RUNNING a few minutes behind schedule."

The receptionist smiled, as though it was the most interesting thing she'd said all day. Elizabeth went inside, removed her wet raincoat, and sat down. She was the last patient of the afternoon and, thankfully, she was alone. The last thing she wanted now was to make idle conversation with another woman suffering from the same problem. Rain pattered against the window overlooking the parking lot. She turned and peered out. A line of trees shed leaves to the onslaught of the wind. She looked for Michael's Jaguar but saw no sign of it.

She reached in her bag and removed one of her pocket cellular telephones—she carried two with her at all times to make certain she could conduct two conversations at once—and punched in Michael's number. Again, there was no answer. She wanted to phone his office, but if he was still at Langley he would never make it in time anyway.

She stood up and slowly paced the room. It was at times like these that Elizabeth Osbourne detested the fact that she was married to a spy. Michael hated it when she called him a spy. He patiently explained he was a case officer, not a spy. She thought it was a silly term for what Michael did. "It sounds as if you're some kind of counselor or social worker," Elizabeth had said, the night Michael tried to explain his work to her for the first time. He smiled his careful smile and replied, "Well, that's not very far from the truth."

She had fallen in love with Michael before she learned he worked for the CIA. A friend had invited her sailing on the Chesapeake, and Michael had been invited too. It was a sweltering day in late July with very little wind. As the boat drifted over the still water, Elizabeth and Michael lay in the shade of the limp sails, drinking icy beer and talking. Unlike most men in Washington, he spoke little about his work. He said he was an international business consultant, he had lived in London for a number of years, and he had just transferred to the firm's Washington office.

That night they ate crab cakes and drank cold white wine at a small waterfront restaurant in Annapolis. She found herself staring at him throughout the meal. He was simply the most beautiful man she had ever seen. The day of sailing had changed him. The sun had tanned his skin and left streaks of gold in his dark hair. His eyes were deep green, flecked with yellow, like wild summer grass. He had a long, straight nose, and several times she had to restrain herself from reaching out and touching his perfect lips. She thought he was rather exotic-looking, like an Italian or a Turk or a Spaniard.

He followed her back into the city that night along Route 50, and she took him home to her bed. She was thirty-four years old and had almost given up on the idea of marriage. But that night, taking him inside her body for the first time, she fell desperately and hopelessly in love with a man who she had met just eight hours earlier and about whom she knew next to nothing.

HE TOLD HER two months later, during a long weekend alone at her father's summer home on Shelter Island. It was late September. The days were warm, but at night when the wind came up there was a bite of autumn in the air. After dinner they put on sweaters and long pants and drank coffee in Adirondack chairs on the beach.

"I need to talk to you about my work," he said without warning, and even in the dying twilight she could see his face had gone suddenly serious. His work had been troubling her for weeks. She found it odd that he never discussed it unless she asked him. She was also troubled by the fact that he never called her during the day and never asked her to lunch. When she rang him at the office, a woman answered the phone and dutifully took down the message, but it was a different woman each time. Sometimes it was hours before he returned her call. When he did he could never speak for longer than a minute or two.

"I'm not an international business consultant, and I've never been one," he began. "I work for the CIA. I had to deceive you until I felt I could trust you enough to tell you. You have to understand, Elizabeth, I didn't want to hurt you—"

She reached out and slapped him across the face. "You bastard!" she screamed, so loudly that a group of gulls standing on the beach broke into flight over the water. "You lying bastard! I'll drive you to the ferry in the morning. You can take the bus back into the city. I never want to see you again. Damn you, Michael Osbourne!"

She stayed on the beach until the cold drove her inside. The bedroom was dark. She let herself inside without knocking and found him lying on the bed in the darkness. She undressed silently and pressed her body to his. He tried to speak, but she covered his lips with her mouth and said, "Not now. No talking allowed."

Afterward, she said, "I don't care who you are or what you do for a living." She brushed her mouth against his chest. "I love the person that's inside here, and I don't ever want to lose you."

"I'm sorry I didn't tell you sooner. I couldn't."

"Is Michael Osbourne your real name?"

"Yes."

"You've never killed anyone, have you?"

"No. We only kill people in the movies."

"Have you ever seen anyone killed?"

"Yes."

"Can you talk about it?"

"No, not yet."

"You'll never lie to me, will you, Michael?"

"I'll never lie to you, but there will be things I won't be able to tell you. Can you live with that?"

"I don't know yet, but promise me you'll never lie to me."

"I'll never lie to you."

She kissed his mouth. "Why did you become a spy?"

"We don't call ourselves spies. We call ourselves case officers."

"Fine. So why did you become a case officer?"

He laughed his quiet, controlled laugh. "I have no idea."

HER FATHER THOUGHT she was a fool to marry a CIA officer. He had served on the Senate Select Intelligence Committee, and while he detested sweeping generalizations in principle he believed the nation's spies were the biggest collection of kooks and odd-balls he had ever seen. With Michael he made an exception. The two men spent a day sailing together on Gardiners Bay, and the senator gave his enthusiastic blessing to the union. There was much about Michael's work Elizabeth loathed: the long hours, the travel to dangerous places, the fact that she *really* didn't know exactly what he did all day. She knew most women would find a marriage like hers unacceptable. She liked to think she was stronger than most women, more self-possessed, more independent. But at times like these she wished her husband had a normal job.

THE ROOM WAS QUIET except for a large television set that continuously played an infomercial hosted by a television anchorwoman Elizabeth detested. She wanted something to read, but all the magazines dealt with raising children, not a pleasant subject for a childless woman of forty.

She tried to change the channel to watch the news, but the television wouldn't change channels. She tried to turn down the volume, but the volume was preset. She thought, An airliner has just been shot down, and I'm trapped with this insipid blonde trying to sell me baby lotion. She went back to the window and looked for Michael's car one last time. It was foolish of her to expect him. One of the few things she knew about her husband's job was that it dealt with counterterrorism. She would be lucky if he even managed to come home tonight.

The nurse appeared in the doorway. "The doctor is ready for you, Mrs. Osbourne. This way, please."

Elizabeth picked up her briefcase and her rain-coat and followed the nurse down a narrow hall.

FORTY MINUTES LATER, Elizabeth took the elevator down to the lobby and stepped outside onto a cov-ered sidewalk. She turned up her collar and plunged into the drenching rain. The wind blew her hair across her face and tore at her raincoat. Elizabeth seemed not to notice. She was numb.

The doctor's words ran through her head like an irritating melody that she could not drive from her thoughts. *You're incapable of having a baby natu-rally. . . . There's a problem with your tubes. . . . In vitro fertilization might help. . . . We'll never know unless we try. . . . I'm very sorry, Elizabeth. . . .*

A car nearly struck her in the fading light. Eliza-beth seemed not to notice as the driver blared his horn and tore off. She wanted to scream. She wanted to cry. She wanted to be sick. She thought about making love to Michael. Their marriage had its minor flaws—too much time apart, too many distrac-tions from work—but in bed they were perfect. Their lovemaking was familiar yet exciting. She knew Michael's body and he knew hers; they knew how to give each other pleasure. Elizabeth had always as-sumed that when she was ready to have a baby, it would happen as naturally and pleasantly as their lovemaking. She felt betrayed by her body.

The Mercedes stood alone in the corner of the parking lot. She dug in her pocket for her keys. She pointed the remote at the car and pressed the button. The doors unlocked and the lights came on. She climbed quickly inside, closed the door, and locked it again. She tried to shove the key into the ignition, but her hands were shaking and the keys fell from her grasp to the floor. Reaching down for them, she bumped her head against the dashboard.

Elizabeth Osbourne believed in composure: in the courtroom, in the office, with Michael. She never let her emotions get the better of her, even when Sam Braxton made one of his wisecracks. But now, sitting alone in her car, her hair plastered to the side of her face, composure deserted her. Her body slowly fell forward until her head rested against the steering wheel. Then the tears came, and she sat in the car and wept.

4. Washington, D.C.

TWENTY MINUTES LATER, a black White House sedan pulled to the curb in the section of the city known as Kalorama. Black staff cars and limousines were not unusual in the neighborhood. Nestled in the wooded hills on the edge of Rock Creek Park just north of Massachusetts Avenue, Kalorama was home to some of the city's most powerful and influential residents.

Mitchell Elliott detested eastern cities as a rule—he spent most of his time in Colorado Springs or at his canyonside home in Los Angeles, near the headquarters of Alatron Defense Systems—but his $3 million mansion in Kalorama helped make his fre-

quent trips to Washington bearable. He had considered a large estate in the horse country of Virginia,
but commuting into the city along Interstate 66 was a
nightmare, and Mitchell Elliott didn't have time to
waste. Kalorama was ten minutes from National Airport and Capitol Hill and five minutes from the
White House.

It was five minutes before seven. Elliott relaxed
in the second-floor library overlooking the garden.
The wind hurled rain against the glass. It was cold
for October, and one of his aides had laid a fire in the
large fireplace. Elliott paced slowly, sipping thirty-
year-old single-malt Scotch from a cut-glass tumbler.
He was a small man, just over five and a half feet tall,
who had learned long ago how to carry himself like a
big man. He never allowed an opponent to stand over
him. When someone entered his office, Elliott always remained seated, legs crossed, hands resting on
the arms of his chair, as if the space were too small to
contain his frame.

Elliott was schooled in the art of warfare—and,
more importantly, in the art of deception. He believed in illusion, misdirection. He ran his company
like an intelligence agency; it operated on the principle of "need to know." Information was strictly compartmentalized. The head of one division knew little
of what was taking place inside another division,
only what the executive *needed* to know. Elliott
rarely conducted meetings with all his senior officers
present. He gave them orders face-to-face in private
meetings, never in written memoranda. All meetings
with Elliott were regarded as strictly confidential;

executives were forbidden to discuss them with other executives. Office gossip was a firing offense, and if one of his employees was telling tales out of school, Elliott would soon know about it. Their telephones were tapped, their electronic mail was read, and surveillance cameras and microphones covered every square inch of office space.

Mitchell Elliott saw nothing wrong with this. He believed God had given him the right—indeed, the responsibility—to take whatever steps were necessary to protect his company and his country. Elliott's belief in God pervaded everything he did. He believed the United States was God's chosen land, Americans His chosen people. He believed Christ had told him to study aeronautics and electrical engineering, and it was Christ who told him to join the Air Force and fight the godless Chinese Communists in Korea.

After the war he settled in Southern California, married Sally, his high school sweetheart, and took a job with McDonnell-Douglas. But Elliott was restless from the beginning. He prayed for guidance from the Almighty. After three years he formed his own company, Alatron Defense Systems. Elliott had no desire to build aircraft. He knew planes would always be vital to the nation's defense, but he believed God had granted him a glimpse of the future, and the future belonged to the ballistic missile—God's arrows, as he called them. Elliott did not build the missiles themselves; he developed and manufactured the sophisticated guidance systems that told them where to strike.

Ten years after forming Alatron, Mitchell Elliott was one of the wealthiest men in America and one of its most influential as well. He had been a confidant of Richard Nixon and Ronald Reagan. He had been on a first-name basis with every secretary of defense since Robert McNamara. He could reach half the members of the Senate by telephone in a matter of minutes. Mitchell Elliott was one of the most powerful men in Washington, and yet he operated permanently in its shadows. Few Americans knew what he did or even knew his name.

Sally had died of breast cancer ten years earlier, and the heady days of big defense spending were long gone. The industry had been devastated, thousands of workers laid off, the entire California economy thrown into turmoil. More important, Elliott believed America was weaker today than she had been in years. The world was a dangerous place. Saddam Hussein had proven that. So had a terrorist armed with a single Stinger missile. Elliott wanted to protect his country. If a terrorist could shoot down a jetliner and kill two hundred people, why couldn't a rogue state like North Korea or Libya or Iran kill two *million* people by firing a nuclear missile against New York or Los Angeles? The civilized world had placed its faith in treaties and ballistic-missile control regimes. Mitchell Elliott reserved faith for the Almighty, and he did not believe in promises written on paper. He believed in machines. He believed the only way to protect the nation from exotic weapons was with more exotic weapons. Tonight, he had to make his case to the President.

Elliott's relationship with James Beckwith had been cemented by years of steady financial support and wise counsel. Elliott had never once asked for a favor, even when Beckwith became a powerful force on the Armed Services Committee during his second term in the Senate. That was all about to change.

One of his aides knocked gently at the door. His phalanx of aides was drawn from the ranks of the Special Forces. Mark Calahan was like all the others. He was six feet in height—tall enough to be imposing but not so tall as to dwarf Elliott—short dark hair, dark eyes, clean-shaven, dark suit and tie. Each carried a .45 automatic at all times. Elliott had made many enemies along with his millions, and he never set foot in public without protection.

"The car is here, Mr. Elliott."

"I'll be down in a minute."

The aide nodded and silently withdrew. Elliott drifted closer to the fire and finished the last of his whiskey. He didn't like being sent for. He would leave when he was ready to leave, not when Paul Vandenberg told him. Vandenberg would still be selling life insurance if it weren't for Elliott. And as for Beckwith, he would have been an unknown San Francisco lawyer, living in Redwood City instead of the White House. They both could wait.

Elliott walked slowly to the bar and poured another half inch of whiskey into the glass. He went back to the fire and knelt before it, head bowed, eyes closed. He prayed for forgiveness—forgiveness for what he had done and for what he was about to do.

"We are your chosen people," he murmured. "I am your instrument. Grant me the strength to do your will, and greatness shall be yours."

SUSANNA DAYTON felt like an idiot. Only in movies did reporters sit in parked cars, drinking coffee from a Styrofoam cup, conducting surveillance like some private investigator. When she left the office an hour earlier, she had not told her editor where she was going. It was just a hunch, and it might lead to nothing. The last thing she wanted her colleagues to know was that she was tailing Mitchell Elliott like a B-movie sleuth.

Rain blurred her view. She flicked a switch on the steering column, and wipers swept away the water. She scrubbed away the moisture on the inside of the windshield with a napkin from the downtown deli where she bought the coffee. The black staff car was still there, engine idling, headlights off. Upstairs, on the second floor of the large house, a single light burned. She sipped the coffee and waited. It was awful, but at least it was hot.

Susanna Dayton had been White House correspondent for *The Washington Post,* the pinnacle of power and prestige in the world of American journalism, but Susanna had loathed the job. She hated filing, every day, essentially the same story that two hundred other reporters filed. She hated being herded around like cattle by the White House press staff, shouting questions at President Beckwith from rope lines at staged and choreographed events. Her writing took on an edge. Vandenberg complained regu-

larly to top management at the *Post*. Finally, her editor offered her a new beat, money and politics. Susanna took it without hesitation.

The new assignment was her salvation. She was
to find out which individuals, organizations, and in-
dustries were giving money to which candidates and
which parties. Did the contributions have an undue
effect on policy or legislation? Were the politicians
and the givers playing by the rules? Was the money
spent properly? Did anyone break the law? Susanna
thrived on the work because she loved making the
connections. A Harvard-trained lawyer, she was a
thorough and cautious reporter. She applied the rules
of evidence to virtually every scrap of information
she uncovered. Would it be admissible in a court
of law? Is it direct testimony or hearsay? Are there
names, dates, and places in the story that can be
checked out? Is there corroborating testimony? She
preferred documents rather than leaks from anonymous sources, because documents can't change their
story.

Susanna Dayton had concluded that the nation's
system of financing its politics amounted to organized bribery and shakedowns, sanctioned by the
federal government. There was a thin line separating
legal activity from illegal activity. She saw it as her
task to catch lawbreakers and expose them. Her per-
sonality suited her perfectly to the work. She hated
people who cheated and got away with it. She despised people who cut in line at the supermarket. She
went crazy on the freeway when an aggressive driver
cut into her lane. She loathed people who took short-

cuts at the expense of others. Her job was to make sure they didn't get away with it.

Two months earlier, Susanna's editor had given her a tough assignment: Chronicle the longtime relationship, financial and personal, between President James Beckwith and Mitchell Elliott, the chairman of Alatron Defense Systems. Reporters use a cliché when an individual or a group is elusive and hard to trace: shadowy. If anyone had earned the description of "shadowy," it was Mitchell Elliott.

He had given millions of dollars to the Republican Party over the years, and a watchdog group had told her that he had funneled millions more to the party through questionable or downright illegal means. The main beneficiary of Elliott's generosity was James Beckwith. Elliott had contributed thousands of dollars to Beckwith's campaigns and political action committees over the years, and he had served as a close confidential adviser. One of Elliott's former executives, Paul Vandenberg, was the White House chief of staff. Beckwith regularly stayed at Elliott's vacation homes in Maui and Vale.

Susanna had two primary questions: Had Mitchell Elliott made illegal contributions to James Beckwith and the Republican Party over the years? And did he exercise undue influence over the President?

At this point she had answers to neither question. Her editor wanted to publish the piece two weeks from now in a special section on President Beckwith and his first term. She had a good deal of work to do before it would be ready to go. Even then Susanna knew she could do little more than raise questions about Elliott and his ties to the White House. Mitchell

Elliott had covered his tracks well. He was completely inaccessible. The *Post* photo library had just one ten-year-old picture of him, and Alatron Defense Systems didn't even have a spokesman. When she requested an interview, the man at the other end of the line chuckled mildly and said, "Mr. Elliott does not make it a habit to talk to reporters."

A source at National Airport told her Elliott had come to Washington earlier that day aboard his private jet. Congress had adjourned, and most members had gone home to campaign. The President had cut short a campaign trip to deal with the downing of Flight 002. Susanna wondered what brought Elliott to town now.

That explained why she was sitting outside his Kalorama mansion in the rain. The front door of the mansion opened and two figures appeared, a tall man holding an umbrella, and a shorter silver-haired man, Mitchell Elliott.

The taller man helped Elliott into the back of the car, then walked around and climbed in the other side. The headlights came on, illuminating the street. The car pulled swiftly away from the curb, heading toward Massachusetts Avenue.

Susanna Dayton started the engine of her small Toyota and followed, keeping to a safe distance. The large black car moved quickly eastward on Massachusetts along Embassy Row. At Dupont Circle it melted into traffic in the outer lane and turned south on Connecticut Avenue.

It was early yet, but Connecticut Avenue was nearly deserted. Susanna noticed that a strange quiet had descended over the city in the forty-eight hours since the jetliner had been shot down. The sidewalks were empty, just a few drunks spilling from a tavern south of the circle and a knot of office workers rushing through the rain into the Farragut North Metro station.

She followed the car across K Street as Connecticut turned to 17th Street. She crossed Pennsylvania Avenue and swept past the ornate, brightly lit facade of the Old Executive Office Building. Susanna thought she knew where Elliott was dining tonight.

The car made a series of left turns and two minutes later stopped at the South Gate of the White House grounds. A uniformed Secret Service agent stepped forward, peered into the back of the sedan, and ordered the driver to proceed.

Susanna Dayton kept driving. She needed a place to wait. Sitting in a parked car for any length of time around the White House was not a good idea these days. The Secret Service had tightened security after a series of attacks on the mansion. She might be approached and questioned. A report might be taken.

She parked on 17th Street. There was a small café across the street from the Old EOB that stayed open late. She grabbed her bag, bulging with newspapers, magazines, and her laptop, and got out. She hurried across the street through the rain and ducked into the café. The place was empty. She ordered a tuna sandwich and a cup of coffee and made a place for herself at a window table while she waited.

She pulled the laptop from her bag, adjusted the screen, and turned on the power. Then she inserted a disk into the floppy drive and opened a file. When it came onto the screen, the file appeared as a meaning-less series of letters and characters. Susanna was cautious by nature—many of her colleagues preferred the word "paranoid"—and she used encryption software to protect all her sensitive files. She typed a seven-letter code name, and the file came to life.

The sandwich and coffee arrived. She scrolled down through the file: names, dates, places, amounts. Everything she knew about the elusive Mitchell Elliott and his links to President Beckwith. She added the events of this evening to the file.

Then she shut down the computer and settled in for a long wait.

5. London

THE FAX ARRIVED in the *Times* newsroom shortly after midnight. It remained on the machine untouched for nearly twenty minutes, until a young assistant bothered to retrieve it. The assistant read it quickly once and took it to the night editor, Niles Ferguson. A thirty-year veteran, Ferguson had seen many faxes like it before—from the IRA, the PLO, Islamic Jihad, and the crazies who simply claim responsibility anytime someone dies violently. This one didn't look like the work of a lunatic.

Ferguson had a special telephone number for situations like these. He punched it and waited. A woman's voice answered, pleasant, faintly erotic.

"This is Niles Ferguson, *The Times*. I just received a rather interesting fax in our newsroom. I'm no expert, but it looks authentic. Perhaps you should have a look."

Ferguson made a copy of the fax and kept the original for himself. He personally carried it down-stairs to the lobby and waited. Five minutes later the car arrived. A young man with pockmarked skin and a cigarette between his lips came into the lobby and took possession of the fax. Niles Ferguson went back upstairs.

The man with the pockmarked face worked for Britain's Security Service, better known as MI5, which is responsible for counterintelligence, internal subversion, and counterterrorism within the British Isles. He hand-carried the copy of the fax to MI5's glass and steel headquarters overlooking the Thames and presented it to the senior duty officer.

The duty officer quickly made two calls. The first was reluctantly placed to his counterpart at the Secret Intelligence Service, better known as MI6, which is responsible for gathering intelligence overseas and therefore considers itself the more glamorous and significant of the two services. The second call was to MI5's liaison officer at the CIA's generously staffed London Station, located across town within the U.S. embassy complex at Grosvenor Square.

Within two minutes a copy of the letter was sent to Grosvenor Square by secure fax. Ten minutes later a typist had entered it into the computer system and forwarded it to CIA headquarters in Langley, Vir-ginia. The agency's computer system automatically distributes cables based on key words and classifica-tion. The cable from London went to the offices of the director, the deputy directors for intelligence and operations, the executive director, and the duty officer on the Middle East desk. It was also routed directly to the agency's Counterterrorism Center.

Seconds later it appeared on the computer screen of the officer assigned to the Islamic extremist group called the Sword of Gaza. The officer's name was Michael Osbourne.

6. CIA Headquarters, Langley, Virginia

HEADQUARTERS, Michael Osbourne's father always said, was the place good field men went to wither and die. His father had been a case officer in the Soviet Directorate. He had recruited and run agents from Moscow to Rome to the Philippines. James Angleton, the famed CIA counterintelligence officer who engaged in a destructive mole hunt for twenty years, ruined his career, the same way he ruined the careers of hundreds of other loyal officers. He spent his final years writing useless assessments and shuffling paper, and he left the Agency bitter and disillusioned. Three years after retirement he died of cancer.

Michael's return to headquarters was as reluctant as his father's but brought on by different circumstances. The opposition knew his true name and occupation, and it was no longer safe for him to operate undercover in the field. He accepted his fate rather like a model prisoner takes to a life sentence. Still, he never forgot his father's admonition about the perils of life at Langley.

. . .

THEY WORKED TOGETHER in a single room, known affectionately as the bull pen, on Corridor F of the sixth floor. It looked more like the newsroom of a failing metropolitan daily than the nerve center of the CIA's counterterrorism operation. There was Alan, a bookish FBI accountant who tracked the secret flow of illicit money through the world's most discreet and dirty banks. There was Cynthia, a flaxen angel of British birth who knew more about the IRA than anyone else on earth. Her cramped cubicle was hung with brooding photographs of Irish guerrillas, including the boy who blew off her brother's hand with a pipe bomb. She gazed at them throughout the day, the way a girl might stare at a poster of the latest teen heartthrob.

There was Stephen, alias Eurotrash, whose task was to monitor the various terrorist and nationalist movements of Western Europe. And there was Blaze, a six-foot-four-inch gringo from New Mexico who spoke Spanish, Portuguese, and at least ten Indian dialects. Blaze focused on the guerrillas and terrorists of Central and South America. He dressed like his targets in sandals and loose-fitting Indian garb, despite repeated written warnings from Personnel. He considered himself the modern equivalent of the samurai, a true warrior poet, and he practiced martial arts with Cynthia when the work was slow.

Michael sat in the corner next to Gigabyte, a flaking, pimply boy of twenty-two who surfed the Internet all day, searching the ether world for terrorist communication. Alternative rock music blared from his headphones, and Michael had seen things on his screen that awakened him in the middle of the night. He erected a barrier of old files to shield the view, but when Gigabyte snickered, or when his rock music grew suddenly louder, Michael knew it was best to close his eyes and place his head face down on the desk.

THE WALL CLOCK hung next to a three-foot cardboard gunman in silhouette, stamped with the circular red international symbol for no. It was nearly 8 P.M., and Michael had been working since five that morning. The bull pen was far from deserted. Peru's Shining Path had kidnapped a government minister, and Blaze was pacing, working the telephones. France's Direct Action had bombed a Paris Metro station; Eurotrash was hunched over his computer terminal reading message traffic. The IRA had murdered a Protestant developer in front of his wife and children; Cynthia was on the secure line to London, feeding intelligence to Britain's MI5. Thankfully, Gigabyte had gone to a nightclub with a group of friends who believed he created Web sites for a living.

Michael had fifteen minutes before he briefed the executive director on developments in the case. The claim of responsibility for the attack on the jetliner had been forwarded to Langley an hour ago. Michael read it for the fifth time. He reviewed the preliminary forensic studies performed by the FBI lab on the Boston Whaler found adrift off Long Island that morning. He studied the photographs of the corpse found on the boat.

Ten minutes left. He could run downstairs to the swill pit and grab a bite to eat, or he could telephone Elizabeth. He had missed her appointment at Georgetown, and he knew they would very likely quarrel. It was not a conversation he wanted to conduct on an Agency telephone. He shut down his computer and stepped out of the bullpen.

The corridor was starkly lit and quiet. The Agency's Fine Arts Commission had tried to brighten the hallway with a display of Indonesian folk art, but it was still as cold and sterile as intensive care. He followed the corridor to a bank of large elevators, took one down to the basement, then followed another anonymous hall to the swill pit. It was late, the selection worse than usual. Michael ordered a fish sandwich and French fries from the bleary-eyed woman behind the counter. She punched at the cash register as if she wanted to do it harm, snatched Michael's money, and gave him the change.

Michael ate while he walked. It was dreadful—cold, cooked hours earlier—but it was better than yet another bag of chips. He finished half the sandwich and a few of the fries and tossed the rest in a trash can. He glanced at his watch: five minutes. Enough time for a cigarette. He took the elevator up one level, then walked through a glass doorway giving onto a large center courtyard. William Webster had outlawed smoking inside the building. Those still afflicted with the habit were forced to huddle like refugees in the courtyard or around the exits. After years of working undercover in Europe and the Middle East, cigarettes and smoking had become part of his tradecraft. Michael was unable and unwilling to give them up just because he was now at headquarters.

Dead leaves swirled across the expanse of the courtyard. Michael turned his back to the wind and lit a cigarette. It was cold and very dark; the only light came from the glow of office windows above him, tinted green by soundproof glass. In the old days his office was the back streets of Berlin or Athens or Rome. He was still more comfortable in a Cairo coffeehouse than Starbucks in Georgetown. He glanced quickly at his watch. Another relaxing dinner. He stuffed his cigarette into a sand-filled ashtray and went inside.

THE BRIEFING ROOM was directly across the hall from the bull pen—small, cramped, most of it consumed by a large rectangular table of cheap government-issue wood. On one wall hung the emblems of every government agency with a role in the Center. On the wall opposite the doorway was a projection screen. Michael arrived at precisely 11:45 P.M. He was straightening his tie when two men entered the room.

The first was Adrian Carter, the director of the Counterterrorism Center and an operations veteran of twenty years. He was small and pale, with sparse gray hair and bags beneath his eyes that gave him the appearance of perpetual boredom. Michael and Carter had a professional and personal friendship dating back fifteen years. The second was Eric McManus, the Center's deputy director. McManus was big and bluff with an easy smile, a thick head of ginger-gray hair, and a trace of south Boston in his voice. He was FBI and looked it: navy blue suit, crisp white shirt, red tie. When Michael's father worked for the Agency, an FBI man in such a senior role would be considered heresy. CIA officers of the old school thought FBI agents could fit everything they knew about intelligence on the backs of their gold shields. That was not the case with McManus, a Harvard-trained lawyer who worked in FBI counter-intelligence for twenty years before his assignment to the Center.

Monica Tyler, as was her habit, entered the room last and precisely five minutes late. She regarded her time as priceless, never to be wasted by others. A pair of identical male factotums trailed softly after her, each fervently clutching a leather-bound briefing book. Except for Personnel, no one within the Agency claimed to know who they were or who had spawned them. The office wits said they were conveyed with Monica from her Wall Street investment firm, along with her private bathroom and mahogany office furniture. They were slender and sinewy, dark-eyed and watchful, and silent as pallbearers. They seemed to move in slow union, like performers in an underwater ballet. Since no one knew their true names, they were christened Tweedledee and Tweedledum. Monica's detractors referred to them as Tyler's eunuchs.

McManus and Carter got to their feet without enthusiasm as Monica entered the room. She squeezed past McManus's bulky frame and took her customary seat at the head of the table, where she could see the screen and the briefer with an easy turn of her regal head. Tweedledee placed a leather-bound notebook on the table in front of her as though it were an ancient tablet and then sat behind her against the wall, next to Tweedledum.

"Monica, this is Michael Osbourne," Carter said. "Michael's dealt with counterterror most of his career and has been working on the Sword of Gaza since the group surfaced."

Tyler looked at Michael and nodded, as though she had been told something she did not know. Michael knew that was not the case. Monica was renowned for reading the files of any officer with whom she came in contact. The rumor mill said she wouldn't bump into an officer at the water cooler without first having read his fitness reports.

She turned her gaze from Michael to the blank screen. Her short blond hair was perfectly styled, her makeup fresh. She wore a black suit with a high-collared white blouse beneath. One hand lay across the table; the other held a slender gold pen. She nibbled at the tip. Monica Tyler had no life other than her work; it was the one personal trait she made no attempt to conceal from her colleagues. The Director brought her to the Agency because she had followed him to every government job he'd ever had. She knew nothing of intelligence, but she was brilliant and an extremely quick study. She usually could be found in her seventh-floor office late into the night, reading briefing books and old files. She had the corporate lawyer's gift for knowing the right question to ask. Michael had seen her reduce ill-prepared briefers to ashes.

Carter nodded at Osbourne. He dimmed the lights and began the briefing. He pressed a button on a panel at the back of the room, and a photograph appeared on the screen.

"This is Hassan Mahmoud. He was born in Gaza, grew up in a refugee camp, and joined Hamas during the Intifada. He is a committed Islamic revolutionary and is opposed to peace with Israel. He was trained in the camps of Lebanon and Iran. He is an expert bomb maker and a deadly gunman. He split from Hamas after the peace accords were signed and joined the Sword of Gaza. He is suspected of taking part in the assassination of an Israeli businessman in Madrid and the failed attempt to kill the Jordanian prime minister in Paris last year."

Michael paused. "This next photograph is rather graphic." He switched to the next image. Carter and McManus both winced. Monica Tyler's face betrayed no emotion.

"We believe this is Hassan Mahmoud now. The body was found in a Boston Whaler twenty miles off Long Island. He was shot in the face three times. The launch tube of the Stinger was found next to him. Preliminary analysis has confirmed the missile was fired from the Whaler. The stern of the craft was blackened, and the lab has discovered residue matching the type of solid rocket fuel used in Stingers."

"Who shot him and why?" Monica asked. "And how did he get away?"

"We don't know the answers to those questions yet. We have a theory, though."

Monica raised an eyebrow and turned her attention from the screen to Osbourne. She had the straight, expressionless gaze of a therapist. Michael could feel her eyes probing for weakness. "Let's hear it," she said.

Michael switched to the next image, an aerial photograph of a large oceangoing yacht towing a boat. "This photograph was taken off the coast of Florida four days before the jetliner was shot down. The yacht is registered in the name of a French national. We've checked it out, and we're fairly certain the Frenchman in question does not exist. We do know it left the Caribbean island of Saint-Barthélemy eight days before the attack. The boat on the back is a twenty-foot Boston Whaler Dauntless, the same model that the body was found on."

"Where's the Whaler now?"

"At the Bureau's lab," McManus said.

"And the yacht?"

"No sign of it," Michael said. "The Navy and the Coast Guard are looking now. Satellite photographs of that part of the Atlantic are being reviewed."

"So on the night of the attack," Tyler said, "the small craft heads close to Long Island while the yacht remains well offshore, safely outside American territorial waters."

"So it would appear, yes."

"And when the shooter returns to the yacht, his colleagues kill him?"

"So it would appear."

"But why? Why leave the body? Why leave the launch tube?"

"All very good questions, for which we have no answers at this time."

"Go on, Michael."

"Earlier this evening a claim of responsibility was faxed to the London *Times* in the name of the Sword of Gaza."

"An attack like this doesn't fit their profile, though."

"No, it doesn't." Michael pressed the button, and the next image appeared on the screen, a brief outline of the Sword of Gaza. "The group formed in 1996, after the election of Benjamin Netanyahu in Israel. Its sole aim is to destroy the peace accords by assassinating anyone who supports it, Arab or Jew. It has never operated inside Israel or the territories. Instead, it operates mainly in Europe and the Arab world. The group is small, extremely compartmentalized, and very professional. We believe it has fewer than thirty committed action agents and a support staff of about one hundred. It maintains no permanent headquarters, and we rarely know where its members are from one week to the next. It receives virtually all its funding from Tehran, but it maintains training facilities in Libya and Syria as well."

Michael changed the image. "Here are some attacks attributed to the group. The shooting death of that Israeli businessman in Madrid carried out by Hassan Mahmoud." The image changed again, a scene of carnage on a Paris street. "The failed attack on the Jordanian prime minister. He survived; six members of his party weren't so lucky." Another image, blood and bodies in an Arab capital. "A bombing in Tunis that left the Egyptian deputy foreign minister dead along with twenty-five innocent bystanders. The list goes on. An Israeli diplomat in

Rome. Another in Vienna. An aide to Yasser Arafat in Cairo. A Palestinian businessman in Cyprus."

"But never an attack on an airliner," Tyler said, when the last image vanished from the screen.

"None that we know of. In fact, we believe they've never struck an American target before."

Michael switched on the lights. Monica Tyler said, "The Director is scheduled to brief the President at eight A.M. tomorrow. During that meeting, the President will decide whether to order air strikes against those training facilities. The President wants answers. Gentlemen, in your opinion, did the Sword of Gaza shoot down that airliner?"

Michael looked first at Carter, then at McManus. Carter took it upon himself to answer the question, since he was the senior man there. He cleared his throat gently before speaking.

"Monica, for all we know as of this moment, it might have been the Sword of Gaza, or it might have been the Washington Redskins."

"THAT LAST REMARK was a thing of beauty," Michael said, as they walked out the front doors and into the night. He turned up his collar against the cold and lit a cigarette.

Carter walked next to him, one hand clutching a briefcase, the other rammed into his pocket. Carter always managed to look slightly lost and vaguely irritated. Those who did not know him tended to underestimate him, a quality that served him well both in the field and in the bureaucratic trenches of Langley. He spoke six languages and could melt into the backstreets of Warsaw or Athens or Beirut with equal ease.

Someone must have told him to spruce up his wardrobe for headquarters, because he was always immaculately turned out in costly English and Italian suits. Fine clothing did not hang naturally on Carter's short, slouching frame; a thousand-dollar Armani ended up looking like a cheap knockoff from one of the suspect boutiques along Wisconsin Avenue in Georgetown. Michael always thought he looked slightly ridiculous, like a clerk in an exclusive men's shop who wore suits he could not afford. But Carter was an obsessive who never did anything halfway— his tradecraft, his wife and family, his jazz. His newest passion was golf, and he restlessly practiced his stroke with plastic golf balls in his small glass-enclosed office. Once Michael slipped a real ball among the replicas. Carter promptly launched it through his office window during a conference call with Monica Tyler and the Director. The following day Carter received a bill for the repairs and a reprimand from Personnel.

"She drives me nuts sometimes," Carter muttered softly. He had served as Michael's control officer when Michael was working without official cover and couldn't come to embassies. Even now, walking toward the west parking lot of headquarters, they moved as though they were conducting a debriefing under hostile surveillance. "She thinks gathering intelligence is as easy as putting together a quarterly earnings report."

"She has the Director's complete trust and therefore should be handled carefully."

"Listen to you—the headquarters man all of a sudden."

Michael tossed his cigarette into the dark. "There's something about this attack that stinks."

"More than the fact that two hundred and fifty people are lying on the bottom of the Atlantic?"

"That body in the boat makes no sense."

"None of it makes sense."

"And there's something else."

"Oh, Christ. I've been waiting for this."

"The way Mahmoud was shot in the face like that."

They stopped walking. Carter turned and looked up at Osbourne. "Michael, let me give you a piece of advice. Now is not the time to go chasing after your Jackal again."

They walked in silence until they reached Michael's car.

"Why is it that you drive a silver Jaguar and live in Georgetown and I drive an Accord and live in Reston?"

"Because I have better cover than you do, and I'm married to a rich lawyer."

"You're the luckiest man I know, Osbourne. If I were you I wouldn't fuck it up."

"What's that supposed to mean?"

"It means what's done is done. Go home and get some sleep."

MICHAEL'S FATHER ended up hating the Agency, but somewhere along the line, whether it was his intention or not, he created in his son the makings of a perfect intelligence officer. Michael came to the attention of the Agency during his junior year at Dartmouth. The talent spotter was a professor of American literature who had worked for the Agency in Berlin after the Second World War. He saw in the ragged, bearded college student the makings of a perfect field officer—intelligence, leadership skills, charisma, attitude, and the ability to speak several languages.

What the professor did not know was that Michael's father had worked in the clandestine service and that Michael and his mother had followed him from posting to posting. He could speak five languages by the time he was sixteen. When the Agency came for him the first time, he turned them down. He had seen what the job had done to his father, and he had seen the toll it had taken on his mother.

But the Agency wanted him, and it kept trying. He finally agreed after graduation, because he had no job prospects and no better ideas. He was sent to Camp Perry, the CIA training facility outside Williamsburg, Virginia, known as the Farm. There he learned how to recruit and run agents. He learned the art of clandestine communication. He learned how to spot enemy surveillance. He learned the martial arts and defensive driving.

After a year of training he was supplied with a cover identity and an Agency pseudonym and given a simple assignment: Penetrate the world's most violent terror organizations.

MICHAEL DROVE ALONG Route 123, turned onto the George Washington Parkway, and headed toward the city. The road was deserted. The tall trees on either side twisted in the gusty wind, and a bright moon shone through broken clouds. Reflexively, he checked his mirror several times to make certain he was not being followed. He pressed the accelerator; the speedometer showed seventy. The Jaguar rose and fell over the gentle landscape. The trees opened to his left, and the Potomac sparkled in the moonlight. After a few minutes the spires of Georgetown appeared. He took the Key Bridge exit and crossed the river into Washington.

M Street was deserted, just a few homeless men drinking in Key Park and a knot of Georgetown students talking on the sidewalk outside the local Kinko's. He turned left on 33rd Street. The bright lights and shops of M Street vanished behind him. The house had a private parking space in the back, reached by a narrow alley, but Michael preferred to leave his car on the street in plain view. He turned left onto N Street and found a spot; then, as was his habit, he watched the front of the house for a moment before shutting down the motor. Michael enjoyed being a case officer—the seduction of a good recruitment, the payoff of a timely piece of intelligence—but this was the part of the job he didn't like, the gnawing anxiety he felt every time he entered his own home, the fear his enemies would finally take their revenge.

Michael had always lived with an element of personal risk because of the way he did his job. In the lexicon of the CIA, he was a NOC, the Agency acronym for nonofficial cover. It meant that instead of working out of an embassy, with a State Department cover, like most operations officers, Michael was on his own. He had been a business major at Dartmouth, and his cover usually involved international consulting or sales. Michael preferred it that way. Most of the CIA officers operating from an embassy were known to the other side. That made conducting the business of espionage all the more difficult, especially when the target was a terrorist organization. Michael didn't have the albatross of the embassy hanging around his neck, but he also didn't have it for protection. If an officer operating under official cover got into trouble, he could always run to the embassy and claim diplomatic immunity. If Michael got into trouble—if a recruitment went bad or the opposing service learned the true nature of his work—he could be thrown in jail or worse. The anxiety had receded gently after so many years at headquarters, but it never really left him. His overwhelming fear was that his enemies would go after the thing he cared about most. They had done it before.

He climbed out of the car, locked it, and set the alarm. He walked west to 34th Street, examining the cars, checking the tags. At 34th he crossed the street and did the same on the other side.

Curved brick steps rose from the sidewalk to the front door of their wide Federal-style house. Michael used to be sensitive about living in a two-million-dollar Georgetown home; most of his colleagues lived in the less-expensive Virginia suburbs around Langley. They kidded him relentlessly about his lavish home and his car, wondering aloud whether Michael had gone the way of Rick Ames and was selling secrets for money. The truth was far less interesting: Elizabeth earned $500,000 a year at Braxton, Allworth & Kettlemen, and Michael had inherited a million dollars when his mother died.

He unlocked the front door, first the latch, then the deadbolt. The alarm chirped quietly as he stepped inside. He closed the door softly, locked it again, and disarmed the alarm system. Upstairs, he could hear Elizabeth stir in bed. He left his briefcase on the island counter in the kitchen, took a beer from the refrigerator, and drank half of it in the first swallow. The air smelled faintly of cigarettes. Elizabeth had been smoking, a bad sign. She had given up cigarettes ten years ago, but she smoked when she was angry or nervous. The appointment at Georgetown must not have gone well. Michael felt like a complete ass for missing it. He had a convenient excuse—his work, the downing of the jetliner—but Elizabeth had an all-consuming job too, and she had changed her schedule in order to see the doctor.

He looked around at the kitchen; it was bigger than his entire first apartment. He thought back to the afternoon five years ago when they signed the papers on the house. He remembered walking through the large empty rooms, Elizabeth talking excitedly about what would go where, how the rooms would be decorated, what color they would be painted. She wanted children, lots of children, running around the house, making noise, breaking things. Michael wanted them too. He had lived an enchanted childhood, growing up in exotic places all over the world, but he'd had no siblings and he felt there was something missing in his life. Their inability to have children had taken a toll. Sometimes the place seemed empty and cheerless, far too large for just the two of them, more like a museum than a home. Sometimes he felt as though children had been there once but had been taken away. He felt they had been sentenced to live there together, just the two of them, wounded, forever.

He shut out the lights and carried the rest of the beer upstairs to the bedroom. Elizabeth was sitting up in bed, knees beneath her chin, arms wrapped around her legs. An overhead light burned softly high in the cathedral ceiling. Dying embers glowed in the fireplace. Her short blond hair was tousled; her eyes betrayed she had not slept. Her gaze was somewhere else. Three half-smoked cigarettes lay in the ashtray on her nightstand. A pile of briefs was strewn across his side of the bed. He could tell she was angry, and she had dealt with it the way she always did—throwing herself into her work. Michael undressed silently.

"What time is it?" she asked, without looking at him.

"Late."

"Why didn't you call? Why didn't you tell me you were going to be so late tonight?"

"There were developments in the case. I thought you'd be asleep."

"I don't care if you wake me up, Michael. I needed to hear your voice."

"I'm sorry, Elizabeth. The place was crashing. I couldn't get away."

"Why didn't you come to the appointment?"

Michael was unbuttoning his shirt. He stopped and turned to look at her. Her face was red, her eyes damp.

"Elizabeth, I'm the officer assigned to the terrorist group that may have shot down that jetliner. I can't walk out in the middle of the day and come to Washington for a doctor's appointment."

"Why not?"

"Because I can't, that's why. The President of the United States is making decisions based on what *we* tell him, and in a situation like this it's impossible for me to leave the office, even for a couple of hours."

"Michael, I have a job too. It may not be as important as working for the CIA, but it is damned important to me. I'm juggling three cases right now, I've got Braxton breathing down my neck, and I'm trying desperately to have a—"

Her composure cracked, just for an instant.

"I'm sorry, Elizabeth. I wanted to come, but I couldn't. Not on a day like today. I felt horrible about missing the appointment. What did the doctor say?"

She opened her mouth to speak, but no sound came out. Michael crossed the room, sat down beside her on the bed, and pulled her close. She put her head against his shoulder and cried softly.

"He's not sure what the problem is exactly. I can't get pregnant. Something might be wrong with my tubes. He's not certain. He wants to try one more thing: IVF. He says Cornell in New York is the best. They can take us next month."

Elizabeth looked up at him, her face wet with tears.

"I don't want to get my hopes up, Michael, but I'll never forgive myself if we don't try everything."

"I agree."

"It means spending some time in New York. I'll make arrangements to work out of our Manhattan office. Dad will stay on the island so we can use the apartment."

"I'll talk to Carter about working from the New York Station. I may have to go back and forth a few times, but I don't think it'll be a problem."

"Thank you, Michael. I'm sorry about snapping at you. I was just so damned angry."

"Don't apologize. It was my fault."

"I knew what I was getting into when I married you. I know I can't change what you do. But sometimes I need you to be around more. I need more time with you. I feel like we bump into each other in the morning and bump into each other again at night."

"We could quit our jobs."

"We can't quit our jobs." She kissed his mouth. "Get undressed and come to bed. It's late."

Michael rose and walked into the large master bath. He finished undressing, brushed his teeth, and washed his face without looking in the mirror. The bedroom was dark when he returned, but Elizabeth was still sitting up in bed, her arms wrapped around her knees again.

"I see it in your face, you know."

"What are you talking about?"

"That look."

"What look?"

"That look you get on your face every time someone gets killed anywhere in the world."

Michael lay down on the bed and rolled onto his
elbow to face her.

Elizabeth said, "I see that look in your eyes, and
I wonder if you're thinking about her again."

"I'm not thinking about her, Elizabeth."

"What was her name? You've never told me her
name."

"Her name was Sarah."

"Sarah," Elizabeth said. "Very pretty name,
Sarah. Did you love her?"

"Yes, I loved her."

"Do you still love her?"

"I love you."

"And you're not answering my question."

"No, I don't love her anymore."

"God, you're a terrible liar. I thought spies were
supposed to be good at deception."

"I'm not lying to you. I've never lied to you. I've
only kept things from you that I'm not allowed to
tell you."

"Do you ever think about her?"

"I think about what happened to her, but I don't
think about *her.*"

She rolled onto her side, turning her back to him.
In the darkness, Michael could see her shoulders
shaking. When he reached out to touch her, she said,
"I'm sorry, Michael. I'm so sorry."

"Why are you crying, Elizabeth?"

"Because I'm mad as hell at you, and because I
love you desperately. Because I want to have a baby

with you, and I'm terrified about what's going to happen to us if I can't."

"Nothing's going to *happen* to us. I love you more than anything in the world."

"You don't love her anymore, do you, Michael?"

"I love you, Elizabeth, and only you."

She rolled over in the darkness and pulled his face to hers. He kissed her forehead and brushed tears from her eyes. He held her for a long time, listening to the wind in the trees outside their bedroom window, until her breathing assumed the rhythm of sleep.

7. The White House

ANNE BECKWITH HAD ONE RULE about dinner: Talking about politics was strictly forbidden. Politics had ruled their lives in the twenty-five years since her husband had been sucked into the GOP machine in California, and she was determined that for one hour each evening politics would not intrude. They dined in the family quarters of the Executive Mansion: the President, the First Lady, and Mitchell Elliott. Anne revered Italian cooking and secretly believed the country would be a better place if "we were a little more like the Italians and less like Americans." Beckwith, for the sake of his political career, had asked Anne to keep such views to herself. He resisted Anne's desire to vacation in Europe each summer, choosing "more American" settings instead. That summer they vacationed in Jackson Hole, which Anne, on the fourth day, renamed "Shit Hole."

He indulged her when it came to food. That night, beneath soft candlelight, she had chosen fettuccini tossed with pesto, cream, and peas, followed by medaillons of beef tenderloin, a salad, and cheese, all washed down by a costly fifteen-year-old bottle of Tuscan red wine.

Throughout the meal, as White House stewards drifted silently in and out of the room with each new course, Anne Beckwith carefully guided the conversation from one safe topic to the next: new films she wanted to see, new books she had read, old friends, the children, the little villa in the Piedmont district of northern Italy where she planned to spend the first summer "after our sentence is over and we're both free again."

The President looked exhausted. His eyes, normally a clear pale blue, were red and tired. He had endured a long tension-filled day. He had spent the morning with the heads of the agencies investigating the attack on the jetliner: the FBI and the National Transportation Safety Board. In the afternoon he had flown to New York and met with grieving relatives of the victims. He toured the crash site off Fire Island aboard a Coast Guard cutter and flew by helicopter to the town of Bay Shore to attend a prayer service for a group of local high school students killed in the tragedy. He had a tearful meeting with John North, a chemistry teacher whose wife, Mary, was the faculty sponsor of the trip to London.

Vandenberg had scripted the events perfectly. On television the President looked like a leader, calmly in control of the situation. He returned to Washington and met with his national security staff: the secre-

taries of Defense and State, the national security adviser, the director of Central Intelligence. At precisely 6:20 P.M., Vandenberg briefed White House
reporters on background. The President was consid-
ering military retaliation against the terrorists believed to be responsible for the attack. U.S. Navy
warships were moving into place in the eastern
Mediterranean and Persian Gulf. At 6:30 the White
House correspondents from ABC, CBS, and NBC
stood side by side on the North Lawn and told the
American people that the President might take decisive action to avenge the attack.

Mitchell Elliott knew the overnight poll numbers
would be good. But now, sitting across the table from
James Beckwith, Elliott was struck by the fatigue
written on his face. He wondered whether his old
friend had the will to fight any longer. Elliott said, "If
I didn't know better, Anne, I'd say you were ready to
leave now instead of four years from now."

The remark bordered on discussion of politics.
Instead of changing the subject, the way she usually
did, Anne Beckwith met Elliott's gaze and narrowed
her blue eyes in a rare display of anger.

"Frankly, Mitchell, I don't care if we leave four
years from now or four months from now," she said.
"The President has given this nation everything he
has for the past four years. Our family has made terrible sacrifices. And if the people want to elect an
untested senator from Nebraska to be their leader, so
be it."

The remark was vintage Anne Beckwith. Anne
liked to pretend she was above politics, that a life of

power had been a burden, not a reward. Elliott knew the truth. Behind the placid facade, Anne Beckwith was a ruthless politician in her own right who exercised enormous power in private.

A steward entered, cleared away the dishes, and poured coffee. The President lit a cigarette. Anne made him quit twenty years ago but allowed him one each night with coffee. Beckwith, in an astonishing display of self-discipline, smoked his one cigarette each night and only one. When the steward was gone, Elliott said, "We still have a month before the election, Anne. We can turn this thing around."

"Mitchell Elliott, you sound like those surrogates who go on mindless television talk shows and spew spin and talking points about how the American people haven't focused on the election yet. You know as well as I do that the polls aren't going to change between now and Election Day."

"Normally, that's the case, I'll concede that. But two nights ago an Arab terrorist blew an American jetliner from the sky. The President has the stage to himself now. Sterling is out of the picture. The President has been presented with a marvelous opportunity to showcase his experience at managing a crisis."

"My God, Mitchell Elliott, two hundred and fifty people are dead, and you're excited because you think it will help us finally move the polls!"

"Mitchell didn't say that, Anne," Beckwith said. "Just listen to the media. Everything that takes place in an election year is viewed through the prism of politics. To pretend otherwise would be naïve."

Anne Beckwith rose abruptly. "Well, this naïve old lady has had enough for one evening." The President and Elliott stood up. Anne kissed her husband's cheek and held out her hand to their guest. "He's tired, Mitchell. He hasn't slept much since being presented with this marvelous political opportunity of yours. Don't keep him up long."

When Anne was gone, the two men walked downstairs and along the covered outdoor walkway to the Oval Office. A fire was burning, and the lights were dimmed. Paul Vandenberg was there, waiting. Beckwith sat in a wing chair near the fire, and Vandenberg sat next to him. That left one of the deep white couches to Elliott. When he sat down he sank into the soft cushion. He felt shorter than the other two men and didn't like it. Vandenberg, sensing Elliott's discomfort, allowed a smile to flicker across his face.

Beckwith glared, first at his chief of staff, then at Elliott. "All right, gentlemen," he said. "Suppose you tell me what this is all about."

Elliott said, "Mr. President, I want to help you win reelection—for the good of this marvelous country of ours and for the good of the American people. And I believe I know how to do it."

The President raised an eyebrow, clearly intrigued. "Let's hear it, Mitchell."

"In a moment, Mr. President," Elliott said. "First, I think a brief prayer to the Almighty is in order."

Mitchell Elliott rose from his seat, dropped to his knees in the Oval Office, and began to pray.

·   ·   ·

"DO YOU THINK he'll go through with it, Paul?"

"Hard to say. He wants to sleep on it. That's a good sign."

During the short trip from the White House they had chatted briefly or said nothing at all. Neither man liked to talk in enclosed places, including moving government cars. Now they walked side by side up the gentle grade of California Street past the grand, brightly lit mansions of Kalorama. A wet wind moved in the trees. Leaves of ruby and gold tumbled gently through the pale yellow lamplight. The night was quiet except for the wind and the soggy grumble of traffic along Massachusetts Avenue. The car pulled ahead and parked outside Elliott's house, engine dead, lights off. Elliott's bodyguard drifted a few paces behind them, out of earshot.

Elliott said, "His mood is worse than I've ever seen it."

"He's tired."

"Even if he decides to go forward, I hope he has the energy and passion to make the case to the voters and the Congress."

"He's the best performer to sit in that office since Ronald Reagan. If we give him a good script, he'll deliver his lines and hit his toe marks."

"Just make damned sure you give him a good script."

"I've already commissioned the speech."

"Jesus Christ! Then I'm sure we'll be reading about it in the *Post* in the morning."

"I've got my best speechwriter working on the drafts. She's doing it at home. Nothing on the White

House computer system, where snoopers and leakers might get their hands on it."

"Very good, Paul. I'm relieved to know your tradecraft is as sharp as ever."

Vandenberg made no reply. A car passed them, a small Toyota. It turned left on 23rd Street. The taillights vanished into the darkness. The wind gusted. Vandenberg turned up the collar of his raincoat.

"That was quite a presentation you made, Mitchell. The President was clearly moved. He'll wake up in the morning and see the wisdom of your approach, I'm sure. I'll contact the networks and arrange live coverage of a presidential address from the Oval Office."

"Will the networks go for it?"

"Of course. They've grumbled in the past, when they think we're using the privilege of an Oval Office speech for overtly political purposes. But no one can reasonably make that case at a time like this. Besides, your little initiative is going to be the second item of business. The first item will be an announcement that the United States military has just carried out a devastating attack on the Sword of Gaza and its sponsors. I doubt even the network presidents would be arrogant enough to deny Beckwith live coverage at a time like this."

"I would have thought someone with your track record would never underestimate the arrogance of the media, Paul."

"They say I'm the power behind the throne. I get blamed when things go wrong, but I get the credit when they go right."

"I suggest you make damned sure that this one goes right."

"I will. Don't worry."

"What can I do to help?"

"Leave town as quickly and as quietly as possible."

"I'm afraid I can't."

"Jesus Christ, I asked you to keep a low profile."

"Just a small dinner party tomorrow night. Braxton, a few of his senior partners, and a senator whose ass I need to kiss."

"Add me to the list."

"I would have thought you'd be busy, Paul."

"The speech will run from nine to nine-fifteen. I'll come over immediately afterward. Save me a place at the table."

Vandenberg climbed into the back of the White House car. The ignition of the engine shattered the quiet of California Street. The car pulled away, turned left onto Massachusetts, and was gone. A few seconds later a Toyota swept past the house, the same one they had seen a few minutes earlier.

Mitchell Elliott waited for Mark Calahan to accompany him to the walk to his front door.

"Did you get the license number of that car?"

"Of course, Mr. Elliott."

"Run a check on it. I want to know who owns it."

"Right away, sir."

ELLIOT WAS READING in the library when his assistant walked in twenty minutes later.

"The car's registered to a Susanna Dayton. She lives in Georgetown."

"Susanna Dayton is the *Washington Post* reporter who's doing a piece on my connections to Beckwith."

"Could be coincidence, Mr. Elliott, but I'd say she's watching the house."

"Put her under surveillance. Bring in as many men as you need to do the job right. I want to know what she's doing and whom she's seeing. Get inside her house as quickly as possible. Bug the rooms and the telephones. No fucking around on this one."

The aide closed the door behind him as he left. Mitchell Elliott picked up the telephone and dialed the White House. Thirty seconds later, the call was routed through to Paul Vandenberg's car.

"Hello, Paul. I'm afraid we have a small problem."

8. Washington, D.C.

POMANDER WALK is a touch of France hidden within the heart of Georgetown, ten small cottages off Volta Place, reached by an alley too narrow for cars. Susanna Dayton fell in love with the little street the first time she saw it: the whitewashed brick exteriors, the brightly painted window frames, the flowers spilling from pots on the front steps. Volta Park was located just across the way, a perfect place to run her golden retriever. When one of the ten houses had finally come on the market two years ago, she sold her Connecticut Avenue apartment and moved in.

She parked her car on Volta Place, grabbed her bag, and climbed out. The rain had ended, and the street was buried beneath a carpet of slick leaves. Susanna closed the door and crossed the street. Pomander Walk was quiet as usual. The soft light of a television flickered in the living room window of the house directly opposite hers.

Carson barked loudly as Susanna walked up the front steps of her house and shoved her key in the lock. He scampered into the kitchen and came back with his leash in his mouth.

"In a minute, sweetheart. Let me do a little work and change clothes."

The house was small but comfortable for one person: two bedrooms above, kitchen and living room below. When she was still married, she and her husband lived in a larger town house two blocks away on 34th Street. It was sold in the divorce settlement and the money divided between them. Jack and his new wife, an aerobics instructor at his health club, bought a house overlooking Rock Creek in Bethesda. Susanna was glad he had moved. She wanted to stay in Georgetown without having to worry about bumping into Jack and his trophy wife every other day.

She used the spare bedroom as an office. Papers and files littered the floor. Books crammed the built-in shelves. She placed her laptop on the desk and switched on the power. For five minutes she typed rapidly. Carson sat in the doorway, eyes locked on her, his leash in his mouth. It had been an amazing night. Mitchell Elliott had spent three hours inside the White House, presumably with the President. And then she had seen him walking outside his California Street home with the President's chief of staff, Paul Vandenberg. Taken in isolation, the information was not damning. If she could fit it into the rest of the puzzle, she might have a real story. There was nothing more to do tonight. She would talk to her editor in the morning, tell him what she had learned, and decide where to look next.

She encrypted the file and saved it to her hard drive and two floppy disks. She removed the second disk and carried it into her bedroom. It was late, after eleven, but she was keyed up from sitting in the car and the café all night. She removed her sweater, stepped out of her skirt, and pulled off her stockings and her underwear. From her dresser drawer she took a pair of blue Lycra running pants and a cotton turtleneck pullover and quickly put them on. A nylon jacket hung on a hook in the bathroom. She pulled it on, then bent over the sink and scrubbed off the makeup she had put on fifteen hours earlier.

She dried her face and looked at her reflection in the mirror. At forty, Susanna Dayton still considered herself a moderately attractive woman: dark curly hair that fell about her shoulders, deep brown eyes, olive skin. The hours were beginning to show on her face, though. She had thrown herself into her work since the divorce from Jack. Sixteen-hour days were normal, not an exception. She had dated a few men casually—even slept with a couple—but work came first now.

Carson paced the upstairs hallway. "Come on, boy. Let's go."

Susanna took the disk and followed the dog downstairs. While she stretched, she picked up the cordless telephone and punched in the number for her neighbor, an environmental lobbyist named Harry Scanlon.

"I'm going out for a run with Carson," she said. "If I'm not back in a half hour, send for help."

"Where are you going?"

"I don't know. Maybe Dupont Circle and back."

"Where the hell have you been?"

"Working, as usual. I'm going to drop one through the slot on my way out."

"Fine."

"Good night, darling."

"Good night, my love."

She hung up. She placed her beeper and a cellular phone in a fanny pack, put it around her waist, and let herself out. She knew it was foolish to run so late at night—her friends constantly lectured her about it—but she always carried a cellular phone and took Carson along for protection.

She walked up the steps to Harry's house and slipped the disk through his mail slot. Susanna believed in having backups to her backups, and if her house ever burned down or was robbed, at least Harry would have a copy of her notes. Harry thought she was out of her mind, but he indulged her. They had a system: When Susanna slipped a new floppy through Harry's mail slot, Harry would return the old one through hers, usually the next morning.

She slipped out Pomander Walk. Carson relieved himself against the side of a tree. Then she zipped up her jacket against the cold and started running eastward across Georgetown through the darkness, Carson at her side.

. . .

THE MAN IN THE PARKED CAR on Volta Place watched the woman leave. He knew he wouldn't have much time. It was late; she probably wouldn't run for very long. He would have to work quickly.

He climbed out, softly closed the door, and crossed the street. He wore black trousers, a dark shirt, and a black leather jacket and carried a small leather attaché in his right hand. Mark Calahan was not wasting any time. He had served in the Special Forces—Navy Seals, to be precise. He knew how to penetrate buildings quietly. He knew how to leave without a trace.

Pomander Walk was quiet. Only one of the small houses showed any signs of life. Thirty seconds after entering the street he had picked Susanna Dayton's lock and was inside the house.

He stayed there for fifteen minutes and left as quietly as he came.

AT FOUR O'CLOCK, Michael awakened with the rain. He tried to sleep again, but it was no good. Each time he closed his eyes he saw the plane hurtling down to the sea and the face of Hassan Mahmoud, blown apart by three bullets. He slipped quietly from bed and walked down the hall to the study, switched on his computer, and sat down.

The files passed before his eyes—photographs, police reports, Agency memos, reports from friendly intelligence services. He reviewed them one more time. The murder of a government official in Spain, claimed by the Basque separatist movement ETA but later denied. The murder of a French police official in Paris, claimed by the militant Direct Action, later denied. The murder of a BMW official in Frankfurt, claimed by the Red Army Faction, later denied. The murder of a senior PLO commander in Tunis, claimed by a rival Palestinian faction, later denied. The murder of an Israeli businessman in London, claimed by the PLO, later denied. All the attacks came at critical times and served to worsen tensions. All had one other thing in common—the victims received three gunshot wounds to the face.

Michael opened another file. The victim was Sarah Randolph. She was a wealthy, beautiful art student with leftist politics, and Osbourne, against all better judgment, had fallen hopelessly in love with her while he was working from London. He knew Personnel Security would get the jitters about her politics, so he broke Agency rules and chose not to declare the relationship. When she was murdered on the Chelsea Embankment, the Agency took it as a sign that Michael's cover had been blown and that he could no longer operate as a NOC in the field.

He clicked open her photograph. She was the most beautiful woman he had ever known, but an assassin had taken her beauty and her life: three bullets to the face, 9mm rounds, just like the others. Michael had seen her killer, just for an instant. He believed it was the same man who killed the others, the same man who killed Hassan Mahmoud.

Who was he? Did he work for a government, or was he a freelancer? Why did he always kill the same way? Michael lit a cigarette and asked himself something else: Does he really exist, or is he a figment of my imagination, a ghost in the files? Carter thought Michael was seeing things. Carter would have his ass if he peddled his theory now. So would Monica Tyler. He shut off the computer and went back to bed.

9. Washington, D.C.

THE FOLLOWING MORNING Paul Vandenberg leafed through a stack of newspapers as his chauffeured black sedan sped along the George Washington Parkway toward the White House. Most administration officials preferred to scan a digest of news clips prepared each morning by the White House press office, but Vandenberg, a rapid and prodigious reader, wanted the real thing. He liked to see how a story was played. Was it above the fold or below? Was it on the front page or buried inside? Besides, he distrusted summaries. He liked raw intelligence, raw data. He had a mind capable of storing and processing immense amounts of information, unlike his boss, who needed bite-size portions.

Vandenberg liked what he saw. The downing of Flight 002 dominated the front pages of every major newspaper in the country. The presidential campaign seemed no longer to exist. The *Los Angeles Times* had the big scoop of the morning: U.S. law enforcement and intelligence officials had pinned responsibility on the Sword of Gaza. The paper laid out that case in detail, complete with precise graphics on how the attack was carried out and a profile of the terrorist involved, Hassan Mahmoud. Vandenberg smiled; the idea to leak to the *Los Angeles Times* was his. It was the most important newspaper in California, and they would need a chit or two in the stretch drive before Election Day.

The rest of it was just as good. Beckwith's trip to Long Island received prominent coverage. *The New York Times* and *The Washington Post* published complete transcripts of his remarks at the memorial service. Every newspaper printed the same Associated Press photo of Beckwith consoling the mother of one of the young victims. Beckwith as father figure. Beckwith as mourner in chief. Beckwith as the avenging angel. Sterling was frozen out. His campaign swing through California received virtually no coverage. It was perfect.

The car arrived at the White House. Vandenberg climbed out and entered the West Wing. His office was large and tastefully furnished, with French doors opening onto a small flagstone patio overlooking the South Lawn. He sat down at his desk and thumbed through a stack of telephone messages. He glanced at the President's schedule. Vandenberg had cleared the decks of anything unrelated to Flight 002. He wanted Beckwith rested and relaxed when he went before the cameras that night. It was arguably the most important moment in his presidency—indeed, in his career.

One of Vandenberg's three secretaries poked her head in the office. "Coffee, Mr. Vandenberg?"

"Thanks, Margaret."

At seven-thirty the senior staff filed into his office: the press secretary, the budget director, the communications director, the domestic policy adviser, the congressional liaison, and the deputy national security adviser. Vandenberg liked meetings quick and informal. Each staff member carried a notebook, a cup of coffee, and a doughnut or bagel. Vandenberg presided. He moved quickly around the room, getting updates, giving instructions, dispensing with problems. The meeting broke up on schedule at seven-forty-five. He had fifteen minutes before his meeting with Beckwith.

"Margaret, no visitors or phone calls, please."

"Yes, Mr. Vandenberg."

Paul Vandenberg had been at James Beckwith's side for twenty years—on Capitol Hill and in Sacramento—but this would be their most crucial encounter ever. He opened the French doors and stepped out onto the sunlit patio, breathing the chill October air. The media droned on about his power, but even the jaded Washington press corps would be shocked by Paul Vandenberg's real influence. Most of his predecessors had believed it was their job to help the President arrive at decisions by making certain he saw the right people and read the right information. Vandenberg saw his job differently: He made the decisions and sold them to the President. Their meetings never strayed far from the script. Beckwith would listen intently, blink, nod, and scribble a few notes. Finally he would say, "What do you think we should do, Paul?" And Vandenberg would tell him.

He hoped this morning would go the same way. Vandenberg would write the script and choreograph the scenes; the President would deliver the lines. If they were damned lucky, and if Beckwith didn't fuck it up, they just might get a second term.

ELIZABETH OSBOURNE stood on the corner of 34th and M streets, dressed in a colorful warm-up and running shoes. It was still early, but traffic poured over Key Bridge into Georgetown. She bent over and stretched the back of her legs. A man in a passing car blew his horn and puckered his lips at her suggestively. Elizabeth ignored him, resisting the temptation to make an obscene gesture of her own. Carson arrived first, scampering down the short hill from Prospect Street. Susanna arrived a moment later.

They waited for the light to change, jogging lightly in place, then headed down to the C&O Canal. They crossed the canal over a narrow wooden footbridge and started running along the tree-lined towpath. Carson trotted ahead of them, barking at birds, chasing a pair of terrified squirrels.

"Where's Michael this morning?"

"He had to get to work early," Elizabeth said. She hated lying to Susanna about Michael's work. They had met at Harvard Law and remained close friends over the years. They lived a few blocks apart, ran together, and saw each other regularly for dinner. Their relationship had grown closer after Susanna's divorce from Jack. He was a partner at Braxton, Allworth & Kettlemen, and Elizabeth found herself in the unenviable position of serving as unofficial mediator while the two disentangled their lives.

"And how's Jack?" Susanna asked. Their conversations always got around to Jack at some point.

Susanna had been madly in love with him, and Elizabeth suspected she loved him still.

"Jack's fine."

"Don't tell me he's fine. Tell me he's miserable."

"All right, he's a lousy lawyer and a complete asshole. How's that?"

"Much better. How's his little cookie?"

"He brought her to an office cocktail party last week. You should have seen the dress. God, I'm jealous of that body, though. Braxton could barely keep his tongue in his mouth."

"Did she look cheap? Tell me she looked cheap."

"Very cheap."

"Is Jack being faithful?"

"Actually, the gossip mill says he's been having an affair with one of our new associates."

"Wouldn't surprise me. I think Jack's physiologically incapable of fidelity. I give his marriage to the cookie three years at the most."

The trees broke and they entered bright sunshine. Elizabeth removed her gloves and her headband and stuffed them in the pocket of her jacket. A mountain bike roared past them like a bullet. To their left, on the river, a Georgetown crew pulled gracefully upstream against the gentle current.

"What happened yesterday at the doctor's?" Susanna asked, broaching the subject cautiously.

Elizabeth told her everything; there were no secrets between them, only Michael and his work.

"Does he think in vitro will work?"

"He doesn't have the faintest idea. It's like throwing darts at a board. The more you learn about infertility treatment, the more you find out they really don't know too much."

"How are you doing?"

"I'm fine. I just want it over and done with. If we can't have children, I want to get it behind us and move on with our lives."

They ran in silence for a few minutes. Carson came back, dragging a three-foot-long branch he had pulled from the trees.

Susanna said, "I want to violate an unspoken rule of our friendship."

"You want to ask me about a case our firm is handling?"

"Not a case, really. A client. Mitchell Elliott."

"He's Braxton's client. As a matter of fact, I'm having dinner with him tonight."

"You are?"

"Yes, he's in town. Braxton ordered me to attend."

"I know he's in town because he had dinner at the White House last night. After dinner, Paul Vandenberg drove him back home, and the two had a long private stroll along California Street."

"How do you know this?"

"Because I was following them."

"Susanna!"

She told Elizabeth about the assignment she had been given by her editor, about what she had learned so far about Mitchell Elliott and his questionable contributions to Beckwith and the Republican Party.

"I need your help, Elizabeth. I need to know more about the relationship between Braxton and Elliott. I need to know if Braxton is helping him in any way or if he has any role in facilitating the flow of money."

"You know I can't do that, Sarah. I can't betray the confidence of one of our clients. I'd be fired. God, I'd be disbarred!"

"Elliott's dirty. And if Braxton is helping him, he's dirty too."

"I still can't help you. It's unethical."

"I'm sorry to impose on our friendship, but my editor's on my ass about the piece. Besides, people like Mitchell Elliott make me sick."

"You're just doing your job, poking your nose where it doesn't belong. You're forgiven."

"Can I call you tonight for a fill on what went down at dinner?"

"That I can manage."

They reached Fletcher's Boat House. They stopped, stretched for a moment, and headed back toward Georgetown. A tall man wearing a dark blue warm-up suit ran past them in the other direction. He wore sunglasses and a baseball cap.

THE MAN ON THE TOWPATH was no ordinary jogger. In his right hand he held a sensitive directional microphone. Strapped to his abdomen was a sophisticated tape recorder. He had been following Susanna Dayton from the moment she stepped outside her house. It was a pleasant assignment: a crisp autumn morning, beautiful scenery, and the women ran quickly enough to give him a decent workout. He ran about a hundred yards past the wooden footbridge at Fletcher's Boat House. Then he turned suddenly and increased his pace, his long strides quickly eating up the ground between himself and the two women. He slowed and settled in about thirty yards behind them, the microphone in his right hand pointed directly at the two figures ahead.

PAUL VANDENBERG always got a brief chill when he set foot in the Oval Office. The President entered the room at precisely eight o'clock. Five men followed in rapid succession. James Beckwith's predecessor strove for diversity in his cabinet, but Beckwith wanted his closest advisers to be like himself, and he made no apologies for it. The men took their places in the seating area of the office: Vice President Ellis Creighton, National Security Adviser William Bristol, Secretary of State Martin Claridge, Secretary of Defense Allen Payne, and CIA Director Ronald Clark.

The President technically presided over senior meetings like this one, but Vandenberg served as master of ceremonies. He kept the agenda, directed the flow of conversation, and made sure the discussion didn't drift.

"The first order of business is the proposed strike against the Sword of Gaza," he said. "Ron, why don't you begin."

The CIA director brought maps and enlarged satellite photographs. "The Sword of Gaza has three primary training facilities," he began. "In the Libyan desert, one hundred miles south of Tripoli; outside the town of Shahr Kord in western Iran; and here"— he tapped the map one last time—"in Al Burei in

Syria. Hit those three sites and we can deal them a serious psychological blow."

Beckwith furrowed his brow. "Why only psychological, Ron? I want to deal them a crippling blow."

"Mr. President, if I may be blunt, I don't think
that's a realistic objective. The Sword of Gaza is
small, elusive, and highly mobile. Bombing their
training sites will make us feel good, and it will give
us a modicum of revenge, but I can say with reasonable certitude that it will not put the Sword of Gaza
out of business."

"Your recommendation, Ron?" Vandenberg
asked.

"I say we hit the sons of bitches with everything
we can muster. The strike needs to be surgical as hell,
though. The last thing we need is to blow up an apartment building and provide radical Islam with five
hundred new martyrs."

Vandenberg looked at Defense Secretary Allen
Payne. "That's your job, Allen. Can we do it?"

Payne stood up. "Absolutely, Mr. President.
Right now we have the Aegis cruiser *Ticonderoga* on
patrol in the northern Persian Gulf. The *Ticonderoga*'s cruise missiles can take out those training
camps with devastating accuracy. We have satellite
imagery of the camps, and that information has been
programmed into the cruise missiles. They won't
make a mistake."

"What about the camps in Syria and Libya?" the
President asked.

"The *John F. Kennedy* and its battle group have
moved into position in the Mediterranean. We'll use
the cruise missiles against the base in Syria. Libya is

the group's main base of operations. That camp is the largest and most complex. To put it out of business will require a larger strike. Therefore, we would use Stealth fighters based in Italy for the job."

The President turned to Secretary of State Martin Claridge. "Martin, what impact will a strike have on our policy in the Middle East?"

"Difficult to say, Mr. President. It will certainly inflame Islamic radicals, and it will certainly stir things up in Gaza and the West Bank. As for Syria, it will make it more difficult to bring Assad to the peace table, but he's been in no hurry to get there in any case. It will, however, also send a powerful message to those states that continue to support terrorism. Therefore you have my support, Mr. President."

"The risks, gentlemen?" Vandenberg asked.

National Security Adviser William Bristol cleared his throat. "We must accept there is some risk that Iran, Syria, or Libya might decide to strike back."

"If they do," said Defense Secretary Payne, "they will pay a very heavy price. We have more than enough force in the Mediterranean and the Gulf to deal any one of those nations a serious blow."

"There is another threat," said CIA Director Clark. "Retaliation in the form of increased terrorism. We should certainly place all our embassies and personnel worldwide on a very high state of alert."

"Already done," said Secretary of State Claridge. "We issued a secret communication last night."

Finally, Beckwith turned to Vandenberg. "What do you think, Paul?"

"I think we should hit them and hit them very hard, Mr. President. It's a measured response, it's decisive, and it shows resolve. It demonstrates that the United States government will take steps to protect its people. And politically, it will be the equivalent of a ninth-inning grand slam. Sterling will have to support you. To do anything else would appear unpatriotic. He'll be paralyzed, sir."

A silence fell over the room as everyone waited for the President to speak. "I think the Sword of Gaza represents a clear danger to the citizens and interests of the United States of America," he said finally. "They have committed an act of cowardice and barbarism against this nation, and they need to be punished. When can we hit them?"

"Whenever you give the order, Mr. President."

"Tonight," he said. "Do it tonight, gentlemen."

Vandenberg looked down at his notes. He had orchestrated it well, and the President had reached the intended decision and was comfortable with the position. Vandenberg had done a good job.

"Before we adjourn, gentlemen, we have one other piece of business," Vandenberg said. "Mr. President, would you like to tell them about it, or shall I?"

CALAHAN PLAYED THE TAPE for Mitchell Elliott in the library of the Kalorama mansion. Elliott listened intently, his forefinger lying across his nose, his eyes fixed on the trees in the garden. The quality was good, though dropouts made parts of the conversation nearly inaudible. When it was over, Elliott sat motionless. He had planned it all so carefully, but a reporter asking too many questions could undo it all.

"She's trouble, Mr. Elliott," Calahan said, removing the tape from Elliott's elaborate stereo system.

"Unfortunately, there's not much we can do at this point except watch and wait. What kind of coverage do you have on her?"

"Room bugs in the house and one on her telephone."

"That's not good enough. I want one on her car as well."

"No problem. She leaves it on the street at night."

"And her computer, too. I want you to go in every chance you get and copy the contents of her hard drive."

Calahan nodded.

"We need to keep a closer eye on her while she's at work. Get Rodriguez on a plane right away. He's going to work at the *Post.*"

"What does Rodriguez know about journalism?"

"Nothing. That's not the kind of job I have in mind for him."

Calahan looked perplexed.

Elliott said, "Rodriguez grew up in the roughest neighborhood in Bakersfield. He speaks Spanish like a boy from the barrio. Take away his six-hundred-dollar suits and that fancy hairdo, and he'll look like a Salvadoran farmworker. Get him a false green card and find him a job on the cleaning service used by the *Post.* I want him inside by tomorrow night."

"Good idea."

"I want everything on her: financial, her divorce, everything. If she wants to play hardball, she's playing in the wrong league."

Calahan held up the tape. "What do you want me to do with this?"

"Destroy it."

10. Washington, D.C.

ELIZABETH OSBOURNE THOUGHT, If there's anything worse than a Washington dinner party, it's going to a Washington dinner party alone. She arrived at Mitchell Elliott's Kalorama mansion fifteen minutes late. She left her Mercedes with the valet, a boy who looked barely old enough to drive, and headed up the walkway. Michael had telephoned late in the afternoon to say he couldn't get away because something big was going to break. She had tried to find an escort but couldn't, on such short notice. Even Jack Dawson, Susanna's ex-husband, had turned her down.

Elizabeth pressed the button, and a solemn bell tolled somewhere inside the imposing house. A trim man in a tuxedo opened the door. He helped with her coat and glanced outside expectantly, looking for her partner. "I'm alone tonight," she said self-consciously, then immediately regretted it. She thought, I don't have to explain myself to a fucking butler.

The butler informed her that drinks were being served in the garden. She followed the center hall into the house. French doors gave onto a magnificent terraced garden. Gas heaters burned the chill from the autumn night air. Elizabeth stepped outside, and a waiter presented her with a glass of cold Chardonnay. She drank half of it very quickly.

She glanced around at the other guests and felt even more embarrassed. She was surrounded by the elite of Washington's Republican establishment: the Senate majority leader, the House minority leader, a smattering of lesser members, and the upper echelon of the city's lawyers, lobbyists, and journalists. A famous conservative television commentator was holding forth on the banks of the lap pool. Elizabeth awkwardly drifted into his orbit, clutching her wine like a shield. Beckwith was in trouble, the commentator pronounced, because he had betrayed the Party's conservative principles. His audience nodded slowly; the Oracle had spoken.

Elizabeth glanced at her watch: eight o'clock. She wondered whether she could make it through the evening. She wondered who would be the first to comment on the fact she was alone. Someone bellowed her name. She turned in the direction of the sound and saw Samuel Braxton floating toward her. He was a brilliant and ruthless lawyer, warehoused inside a lineman's body gone soft with age and prosperity. His latest acquisition, a big-breasted blonde named Ashley, hung on his beefy arm. She was wife number three or number four; Elizabeth couldn't recall for certain. They had sat next to each other at a dinner party while she was still Ashley DuPree, waiting for her divorce to become final so she could "make an honest man of Samuel." She was Huntsville rich. Her family made money from horses and from cotton, some of which was stuffed inside her head, masquerading as a brain. She suited Braxton's needs perfectly: an upper-class pedigree, money of her own, and the body of a *Playboy* centerfold despite her respectable thirty-eight years.

"Where's your husband?" Braxton asked loudly. "I wanted to show off Ashley."

The Oracle stopped speaking, and his audience turned to hear her answer.

"He was called out of town suddenly on business," Elizabeth said. She felt her face flush, despite her lawyerly effort at courtroom composure. The lying was the hardest part. It would be so much easier if she could tell the truth just once: The President is about to order air strikes against the Sword of Gaza, and my husband works for the CIA, and he couldn't exactly leave work this minute to come to this ridiculous dinner party.

Braxton made a show of looking around the garden at the other guests. "Well, Elizabeth, you do seem to be in the minority here tonight. If I'm not mistaken, you're the only card-carrying member of the Democratic Party in the room."

Elizabeth managed a careful smile. "Believe it or not, Samuel, I'm one of the few people who actually likes Republicans."

But Braxton didn't hear the crack because he was already looking past her at Mitchell Elliott, who had just entered the garden. Braxton jettisoned Ashley and floated through the guests toward his most lucrative client. For the next half hour, Ashley and Elizabeth discussed horses and the benefits of personal trainers. Elizabeth listened politely while she finished her first glass of wine and quickly drank another.

Shortly before nine o'clock, Elliott asked for everyone's attention. "Ladies and gentlemen, the President is about to address the nation. Why don't we hear what he has to say before dinner."

Elizabeth followed the crowd into the large living room. Two giant-screen television sets had been wheeled in. The dinner guests clustered around them. Tom Brokaw was chatting on one, Peter Jennings on the other. Finally, the shots dissolved and a grim-faced James Beckwith was staring into the camera.

PAUL VANDENBERG DIDN'T BELIEVE in public displays of stress, but tonight he was nervous and it showed. This one had to be perfect. He sat with Beckwith in makeup and reviewed the address one last time. He stared at the television monitors to make sure the shot was perfect. He ordered a run-through on the TelePrompTer to make sure it was working properly. The last thing he needed was a dead prompter and James Beckwith staring into the camera like a deer in the headlights.

The speech was scheduled to begin at precisely 9:01:30 P.M. Eastern. That gave the networks ninety seconds to preview the speech with their White House correspondents. Vandenberg had carefully chummed the waters. He had told reporters—on background, of course—that the President would discuss a military response to the attack on Flight 002 and a major new defense initiative. He did not go into specifics. As a result, a sense of urgency hung over Washington as the President strode into the Oval Office.

It was two minutes to air, but Beckwith calmly shook hands with every member of the network pool crew, from the executive producer to the floor director. He finally sat down at his desk. A production assistant clipped the microphone to his crimson tie. The floor director shouted, "Thirty seconds!"

Beckwith adjusted his jacket and folded his hands on the desk. A look of determined composure settled over his handsome, restrained features. Vandenberg permitted himself a brief smile. The old man was going to be just fine.

"Five seconds!" the floor director shouted. She silently pointed to James Beckwith, and the president began to speak.

MICHAEL OSBOURNE INTENDED to watch the President's speech from his desk, but shortly before nine o'clock Adrian Carter came into the bull pen and gestured for Osbourne to follow him. Five minutes later they strode through the entrance of the Operations Center.

DCI Ronald Clark reclined in a black leather executive chair, smoking a cigarette. Monica Tyler sat next to him. Tweedledee and Tweedledum drifted in an uneasy orbit.

Beckwith's face appeared suddenly on a wall of television monitors: CNN, the broadcast networks, the BBC. Ghostly infrared images flickered on three larger monitors, live satellite images of the Sword of Gaza training camps in Libya, Syria, and Iran.

Carter said, "Welcome to the best seat in town, Michael."

"GOOD EVENING, my fellow Americans," Beckwith began, pausing a beat for dramatic effect. "Two nights ago TransAtlantic Airlines Flight Double-oh-two was shot down off Long Island by a terrorist armed with a stolen Stinger missile, killing everyone on board. It was an act of cowardice and barbarism with no possible justification. The animals that carried it out apparently believed there would be no consequences for their action. They were wrong."

Again, the President paused, allowing the line to sink in. Vandenberg had gone down the hall to his office to watch the address on television. A chill ran down the back of his neck as Beckwith delivered the line perfectly.

"The law enforcement and intelligence agencies of this nation have concluded that the Palestinian terror group known as the Sword of Gaza is responsible for the attack. They will now pay the price. At this moment, the men and women of the U.S. armed forces are launching a careful and measured strike against Sword of Gaza training camps in several countries in the Middle East. This is not about vengeance. This is about justice."

Beckwith paused, breaking script. The Tele-PrompTer operator stayed with him. "Let me repeat that: This is not about vengeance. This is about justice. This is about sending a message to the terrorists of the world. The United States will not and cannot stand idly by and watch its citizens be slaughtered. To do nothing would be immoral. To do nothing would be an act of cowardice.

"I have one thing to say to the Sword of Gaza and the governments that provide them with the tools of their terrorist trade." Beckwith narrowed his eyes. "Do nothing more, and it ends here. Kill another American, just one, and there will be a very heavy price to pay. On that you have my solemn word.

"I ask for your prayers for the safe return of all those taking part in tonight's action. I also ask you to join with me in praying for the victims of this barbaric act and for their families. They are the real heroes."

Beckwith paused and shuffled the papers of his script, a sign that he was changing the subject.

"I want to be brutally honest with you for a moment. We can take steps to make certain that an attack like this is never repeated. We can keep a more careful watch on our shores. Our intelligence agencies can increase their levels of vigilance. But we can never be one hundred percent certain that something like this could never happen again. If I sat here before you tonight and told you that was the case, I would be lying to you, and I have never lied to you. But there is something this government can do to protect its citizens from terrorists and terrorist nations, and I want to talk to you about that tonight.

"The United States now possesses the technology and the ability to build a defensive shield over this country, a shield that would protect it against an accidental or deliberate missile attack. Some of the same nations that provide support to groups of savages like the Sword of Gaza are also actively trying to acquire ballistic missile technology. In short, they want missiles that are capable of striking American soil, and slowly but surely they are getting them. If just one missile, armed with a nuclear warhead, fell on a city like New York, or Washington, or Chicago, or Los Angeles, the death toll might be two million instead of two hundred.

"Together with our allies, we are trying to prevent nations such as Syria, Iran, Iraq, Libya, and

North Korea from obtaining ballistic missile technology. Unfortunately, too many countries and too many companies are willing to help these rogue nations out of greed, pure and simple. If they succeed and we are unprepared, our nation, our foreign policy, could be held hostage. We must never allow that to happen.

"Therefore, I call on the Congress to rapidly approve the funds necessary to begin construction of a national missile defense. I challenge the Congress and the Department of Defense to have the system in place by the end of my second term in office, should you grant me another chance to serve you. It won't be easy. It won't be inexpensive. It will require discipline. It will require sacrifice from all of us. But to do nothing, to give the terrorists a victory, would be unforgivable. God bless you all, and God bless the United States of America."

The camera dissolved, and James Beckwith disappeared from the screen.

SENATOR ANDREW STERLING watched Beckwith's speech from a Ramada Inn in Fresno, California. He was alone except for his longtime friend and campaign manager, Bill Rogers. The sliding glass window was open to the pleasant evening air and the sound of traffic rushing along Highway 99. When Beckwith appeared on the screen, Sterling said, "Close that, will you, Bill? I can't hear the sonofabitch."

Sterling was an avowed liberal, a Humphrey-McGovern-Mondale-Dukakis tax-and-spend bleeding-heart liberal. He believed the federal government spent too much on guns it didn't need and too little on the poor and children. He wanted to restore cuts in welfare and Medicare. He wanted to raise taxes on the wealthy and on corporations. He opposed free trade. His party agreed, and it had anointed Sterling as its nominee after a long and bitter primary fight. To the surprise of the political chattering class, Sterling roared out of the Democratic National Convention five points ahead and stayed there.

He knew his lead was fragile. He knew everything depended on holding California, where Beckwith had the home court advantage. Which explained why he was spending the night at a Ramada Inn in Fresno.

Sterling's face turned red, then something approaching purple, as Beckwith spoke. He had consistently voted against the national missile defense program. Beckwith had put him in a box and nailed down the lid. If Sterling supported Beckwith, it would look like a flip-flop. If he opposed him, the Republican attack machine would wheel out the "soft on defense" ads. There was a more important factor: California's defense industry would be rejuvenated if the missile defense system was built. If Sterling opposed it, Beckwith would jump all over him. California would slide back into the GOP's column. The election would be lost.

"Now, that's what I call an October fucking surprise," Sterling said, when Beckwith finished speaking.

Rogers rose and shut off the television. "We'll need to issue a statement, Senator."

"Fucking Vandenberg. He's one smart sonofabitch."

"We can support Beckwith on the air strikes against the Sword of Gaza. Politics stop at the water's edge and all that happy horseshit. But we'll have to oppose him on missile defense. We have no other choice."

"Yes, we do, Bill," Sterling said, staring at the blank television screen. "Why don't you go downstairs and get us a twelve-pack. Because we just lost the fucking election."

MICHAEL OSBOURNE WATCHED the first cruise missiles strike their targets while the President was still speaking. In Iran, at Shahr Kord, they must have been listening to the speech on shortwave radio, because a dozen men burst from the largest building of the compound as Beckwith announced imminent action. "Too late, boys and girls," murmured Clark. A few seconds later ten cruise missiles, fired by the Aegis cruiser *Ticonderoga* in the Persian Gulf, struck the camp simultaneously, igniting a spectacular fireball.

A similar scene played out in Syria, at Al Burei, with the same results.

The Libyan camp was the largest and most important. For that target the Pentagon chose Stealth fighters armed with laser-guided bombs, so-called SMART weapons. The aircraft had actually penetrated Libyan airspace before the President's speech began. They were over their targets when Beckwith delivered the key line of the speech. Seconds later the Libyan desert was aflame.

Ronald Clark rose and strode silently from the room, Tyler and her acolytes trailing after him. Carter looked at Osbourne, who was gazing at the monitors.

"Well," Carter said, "so much for peace in the Middle East."

THOSE WERE the very same sentiments of the trim gray-haired man seated on the top floor of a modern office block in Tel Aviv. The building served as head-quarters of the Central Institute for Intelligence and Special Tasks, better known as the Mossad or, sim-ply, the Institute. The gray-haired man was Ari Shamron, the Mossad's deputy director for opera-tions. When Beckwith finished speaking, Shamron switched off the television.

An aide knocked and entered the room. "We have reports from Syrian radio, sir. Al Burei has been at-tacked. The camp is ablaze."

Shamron nodded silently, and the aide went out. Shamron pressed his thumb and forefinger to the bridge of his nose and tried to rub away the fatigue. It was 4:15 A.M. He had been at his desk for nearly twenty-four hours straight. The way things were going, he would probably be there for another twenty-four.

He lit a cigarette, poured black tea from a ther-mos, and went to the window. Rain rattled against the thick window. Tel Aviv slept peacefully below him. Shamron could take some personal credit. He had spent his entire career in the secret services, destroy-ing those who would destroy Israel.

Raised in the Galilee, Ari Shamron entered the Israeli Defense Force at eighteen and immediately transferred to the Sayeret, the elite special forces. After three years of active duty he moved to the Mossad. In 1972 his fluent French and proficient killing skills landed him a new assignment. He was sent to Europe to assassinate the members of the Palestinian terror group Black September who took part in the kidnapping and murder of the Israeli athletes at the Munich Olympic Games. The assignment was simple. No arrests, just blood. Revenge, pure and simple. Terrorize the terrorists. Under the command of Mike Harari, the Mossad team assassinated twelve Palestinian terrorists, some with silenced guns, some by remote-detonated bombs. Shamron, deadly with a handgun, killed four himself. Then, in April 1973, he led a team of crack Israeli troops into Beirut and assassinated two more members of Black September and a PLO spokesman.

Shamron had no qualms about his work. Palestinian guerrillas broke into his family home in 1964 and murdered his parents as they slept. His hatred of Palestinians and their leaders was limitless. But now his hatred had turned to those Israelis who would make peace with killers like Arafat and Assad.

He had spent his life defending Israel; he dreamed of a Greater Israel stretching from the Sinai to the West Bank. Now the peacemakers wanted to give it all away. The prime minister was talking openly about giving back the Golan to entice Assad to the peace table. Shamron remembered the dark days before 1967, when Syrian shells rained down on the northern Galilee from the Heights. Arafat was running Gaza and the West Bank. He wanted a separate Palestinian state with Jerusalem as its capital. Jerusalem! Shamron would never allow that to happen.

He had sworn to use whatever means necessary to stop the so-called peace process dead in its tracks. If everything continued according to plan, he might very well have his wish. Assad would never come to the peace table now. Arabs in Gaza and the West Bank would boil over with rage when they awoke to news of the American strikes. The army would have to go in. There would be another round of terror and revenge. The peace process would be put on hold. Ari Shamron finished his tea and crushed out his cigarette.

It was the best million dollars he ever spent.

THREE THOUSAND MILES to the north, in Moscow, a similar vigil was being kept at the headquarters of the Foreign Intelligence Service, the successor to the KGB. The man in the window was General Constantin Kalnikov. It was just after dawn and bitter for October, even by Moscow's standards. Snow, driven by Siberian winds, swirled in the square below. Business was taking him to the Caribbean island of St. Maarten in a few weeks. He would enjoy a break from the never-ending cold.

Kalnikov shuddered and drew the heavy curtains. He sat down at his desk and began working his way through a stack of papers. A committed communist, Constantin Kalnikov was recruited by the KGB in

1968. He rose to the top of the Second Chief Directorate, the KGB section responsible for counterintelligence and crushing internal subversion. When
the Soviet Union collapsed, and with it the KGB,
Kalnikov kept a senior post in the new service, the
SVR. Kalnikov now ran Russia's intelligence operations in Latin America and the Caribbean. The job
was a joke. His budget was so small he had no money
to pay agents or informers. He was powerless, just
like the rest of Russia.

Kalnikov had watched Boris Yeltsin and his successor run the Russian economy into the ground. He
had watched the once-feared Red Army humiliated
in Chechnya, watched her tanks rusting for lack of
spare parts and fuel, watched her troops go hungry.
He had seen the vaunted KGB turned into the laugh-
ingstock of the intelligence world.

He knew there was nothing he could do to reverse
Russia's course. Russia was like a vast ship casting
about on a rough sea. She took a long time to change
course, a long time to stop. Kalnikov had given up on
his Russia, but he had not given up on himself. He
had a family, after all—a wife, Katya, and three fine
sons. Their photographs were the only personal
touches in his otherwise cold and sterile office.

Kalnikov had decided to use his position to en-
rich himself. He was the leader of a group of men—
army officers, intelligence officers, members of the
mafiya—who were selling Russia's military hardware on the open market to the highest bidder.
Kalnikov and his men had sold nuclear technology,
weapons-grade uranium, and missile technology to

Iran, Syria, Libya, North Korea, and Pakistan. They had made tens of millions of dollars in the process.

He switched on CNN and listened to a panel of experts discussing President Beckwith's speech. Beckwith wanted to build a missile defense system, a shield to protect the United States from international madmen. Those madmen would be beating down Kalnikov's door soon. They would want to grab as much hardware as they could, and quickly. President James Beckwith had just started an international arms race, a race that would make Kalnikov and his cohorts even richer. Constantin Kalnikov smiled to himself.

It was the best million dollars he ever spent.

IT WAS RAINING as Elizabeth Osbourne drove westward along Massachusetts Avenue toward Georgetown. It had been a very long night, and she was exhausted. Rock Creek passed below her. She dug through the glove compartment, found a pack of old cigarettes, and lit one. It was dry and stale, but the smoke felt good regardless. She smoked only a few a day, and she told herself she could quit anytime. She would definitely quit if she became pregnant. God, she thought, I'd give anything if I could just get pregnant.

She pushed the thought from her mind. She navigated Sheridan Circle and dropped down onto Q Street. She thought of the dinner party. Snatches of silly conversation played out in her mind. Visions of Mitchell Elliott's grand house passed before her eyes like old movies. One image remained long after she arrived home, as she lay in bed awake, waiting for Michael. It was the image of Mitchell Elliott and Samuel Braxton, huddled together like a pair of giggling schoolboys in the darkened garden, toasting each other with champagne.

November

11. Shelter Island, New York

IT WAS *THE NEW YORKER* that first christened Senator Douglas Cannon "a modern-day Pericles," and over the years Cannon did nothing to discourage the comparison. Cannon was a scholar and historian, an unabashed liberal and democratic reformer. He used his millions of inherited wealth to promote the arts. His sprawling Fifth Avenue apartment served as a gathering place for New York's most famous writers, artists, and musicians. He fought to preserve the city's architectural heritage. Unlike Pericles, Douglas Cannon never commanded men in battle. Indeed, he detested guns and weaponry as a rule, except for the bow and arrow. As a young man he was one of the world's best archers, a skill he passed on to his only child, Elizabeth. Despite his deep-seated mistrust of guns and generals, Cannon saw himself fit to oversee his nation's military and foreign policy; he had forgotten more history than most men in Washington would ever know. During his four terms in the Senate, Cannon served as chairman of the Armed Services Committee, the Foreign Relations Committee, and the Select Committee on Intelligence.

When his wife, Eileen, was alive they spent weekdays in Manhattan and weekends on Shelter Island, at the sprawling family mansion overlooking Dering Harbor. After her death the city held less and less for him, so he gradually spent more time on the island, alone with his sailboat and his retrievers and Charlie, the caretaker.

The thought of him alone in the big house troubled Elizabeth. She and Michael went up whenever she could get away for a couple of days. Elizabeth had seen little of her father as a child. He lived in Washington, Elizabeth and her mother in Manhattan. He came home most weekends, but their time together was fleeting and lacked spontaneity. Besides, there were constituents to see, and fund-raisers to attend, and bleary-eyed staff members vying for his attention. Now the roles were reversed. Elizabeth wanted to make up for lost time. Mother was gone, and for the first time in his life her father actually *needed* her. It would be easy to be bitter, but he was a remarkable man who had lived a remarkable life, and she didn't want his last years to slip away.

MICHAEL'S MEETING WITH CARTER and McManus ran late, and Elizabeth got stuck on the telephone with a client. They rushed to National Airport in separate cars, Elizabeth in her Mercedes from downtown Washington, Michael in his Jaguar from headquarters in Langley. They missed the seven o'clock shuttle by a few minutes and drank beer in a depressing airport bar until eight. They arrived at La Guardia a few minutes after nine and took the Hertz bus to pick up the rental car. The ferries were operating on the winter schedule, which meant the last boat left

Greenport at 11 P.M. That gave Michael ninety minutes to drive ninety miles on congested roads. He barreled eastward along the bleak corridor of the Long Island Expressway, expertly weaving in and out of traffic at eighty miles per hour.

"I guess that defensive driving school they put you through at Camp Perry has its applications in the real world," Elizabeth said, nails digging into the armrest.

"If you want, I'll show you how to jump from a moving car without being noticed."

"Don't we need that special briefcase you keep in your study? What's it called? A jig?"

"Jib," Michael corrected her. "It's called a jib, Elizabeth."

"Excuse me. How does it work?"

"Just like a jack-in-the-box. Throw the switch, and a spring-loaded dummy pops up. If you're being followed, it looks like two people are in the car."

"Neato torpedo!" she said sarcastically.

"It also comes in handy for the HOV lanes."

"You're joking."

"No, Carter keeps one in his car all the time. When he's running a little late he just throws the switch, and *presto!*—instant carpool."

"God, I love being married to a spy."

"I'm not a spy, Elizabeth. I'm a—"

"I know, I know, you're a case officer. Keep it under ninety, will you, Michael? What happens if we get pulled over?"

"They taught us a few things about that, too."

"Such as?"

Michael smiled and said, "I could shoot him with a tranquilizer dart from my pen." An incredulous look appeared on Elizabeth's face. "You think I'm joking?"

"You're such an asshole sometimes, Michael."

"I've been told that a time or two."

At ten o'clock he switched on the radio to catch the network hourly on WCBS.

"President James Beckwith has picked his man to head the State Department during his second term. He's longtime friend and political supporter Samuel Braxton, a prominent Washington attorney and power broker. Braxton says he's honored and surprised by the nomination."

Elizabeth groaned as Sam Braxton's tape-recorded voice came on the radio. Michael had been consumed by the case during the last days of the campaign, but like most of Washington he watched James Beckwith's remarkable victory carefully. The race changed the moment Flight 002 went down. Andrew Sterling was virtually frozen out. Nothing he said or did captured the attention of the media, which had grown bored with the interminable campaign and was thrilled to jump ship to a more exciting story. The Oval Office address sealed Sterling's fate. Beckwith had swiftly punished the Sword of Gaza for the attack, and he had done it with decisiveness and flair. The missile defense initiative buried Sterling in California. The morning after the speech, the major California newspapers all published articles describing the positive impact the program would have on the state's economy. Sterling's lead in California evaporated almost overnight. On election night James Beckwith carried his home state by seven percentage points.

Michael switched off the radio.

Elizabeth said, "He's dancing on air."

"Who?"

"Braxton."

"He should be. His man won, and now he gets to be secretary of state."

"The firm threw a party for him this afternoon when he got back from the press conference at the White House. He blathered on and on about how it was the most difficult decision of his life. He said he turned the President down the first time because he didn't want to abandon the firm. But the President asked a second time and he couldn't say no twice. God, it was such a bunch of bullshit! Everyone in town knows he's been campaigning for the job for weeks. Maybe he should have been a litigator instead of a deal-maker."

"He'll be a good secretary of state."

"I remember a president who said, 'My dog Millie knows more about foreign policy than my opponent.' I think that applies to Sam Braxton as well."

"He's smart, he's a quick study, and he's damned good on television. The professionals at Foggy Bottom can deal with the nuts and bolts of policy. Braxton just needs to make tough decisions and sell them to the American people and the rest of the world. If he does that, he'll succeed."

Elizabeth told him about her conversation with Susanna Dayton.

"She asked me for help. I told her I couldn't do it. It was unethical and I could be disbarred. She dropped it."

"You're a wise woman. Why didn't she go with the story?"

"She didn't have the goods."

"That's never stopped Susanna before."

"Michael!"

"Elizabeth, the press looks a little different when viewed from my seat."

"She thought she had the goods, but her editors didn't agree. They spiked the piece and told her to keep digging. She was furious. If the story had come out before Election Day, it would have been big news."

"Is she still working on it?"

"She says she is. In fact, she says she's making serious progress." Elizabeth laughed. "You know, the two biggest winners in this whole affair are Sam Braxton and his client, Mitchell Elliott. Braxton gets to be secretary of state; Elliott gets to make ten billion dollars building kinetic kill vehicles for the missile defense program."

"You think there's some connection?"

"I don't know what to think. You should have seen them at the dinner party after Beckwith made the announcement. My God, I thought they were going to kiss each other."

The expressway ended, and they passed through the town of Riverhead. Michael headed north along a two-lane country road bordered by immense fields of sod and potatoes. A full wet moon dangled low in the eastern sky. They turned onto Route 25 and raced eastward across the North Fork. Now and again the trees broke, and Long Island Sound shone black in the moonlight.

Elizabeth lit a cigarette and cracked the window. It was a signal that she was nervous or angry or unhappy. Elizabeth spent all her energy dissembling at work all day. When she was at home or surrounded by friends, she was pathologically incapable of concealing her emotions. When she was happy, her eyes flashed and her mouth curled into a permanent smile. When she was upset, she stalked and snapped and frowned. Elizabeth never smoked when she was happy.

"Tell me what's wrong."

"You know what's wrong."

"I know. I just thought you might want to say it out loud."

"All right, I'm nervous as hell this isn't going to work and that I'm never going to be able to have a baby for us. There, I said it. And you know what? I still feel like shit."

"I wish I could do something."

She reached out and took his hand. "Just be there for me, Michael. The one thing you can do for me is to stay at my side throughout this thing. I need you there in case it doesn't work. I need you to tell me it's all right and you'll still love me forever."

Her voice choked. He squeezed her hand and said, "I'll love you forever, Elizabeth."

He felt helpless. It was an alien sensation, and he didn't like it. By nature and training he was suited to identifying problems and solving them. Now he could do very little. His physical contribution would take place in a small dark room in a matter of minutes. After that he could be supportive and attentive and caring, but Elizabeth and her body would have to do the rest. He wanted to do more. He had asked Carter to be allowed to work out of the New York Station and to shorten his hours. Carter had agreed. Personnel was on the backs of all chiefs and supervisors about raising the Agency's dismal morale. Carter groused that the Agency should change its motto from "and ye shall know the truth, and the truth shall make you free" to "people caring about people."

"I'm going to tell you one other thing, Michael. I'm not going to get crazy about this. I'm going to try it once. If it doesn't work, I'm going to give up, and we're going to move on with our lives. Do I have your support on that?"

"One hundred percent."

"Susanna and Jack tried four times. It cost them fifty thousand dollars, and it made her crazy." She hesitated. "She's convinced Jack left her because she couldn't give him children. He's crazy about that shit. He wants a son to carry on the family name. He thinks he's an ancient king."

"I think it's fortunate she didn't have a child. Jack would have left her anyway, and she'd be a single working mother."

"What do you know that I don't know?"

"I know he was never happy, and he wanted out of the marriage for a long time."

"I didn't know you boys were so close."

"I can't stand the sonofabitch. But he drinks, and he talks. And I'm a good listener. I'm trained to be a good listener. It's made me the victim of quite a few crashing bores in my day."

"I love her to death. She deserves to be happy. I hope she finds someone soon."

"She will."

"It's not as easy as it sounds. Look how long it took me to find you. Know any good single men?"

"All the single men I know are spies."

"Case officers, Michael. They're called case officers."

"Sorry, Elizabeth."

"You're right. The last thing I want Susanna to do is marry a fucking spook."

Michael drove onto the ferry with five minutes to spare. It was windy and bitterly cold. The ferry bucked across the choppy waters of Gardiners Bay. Spray broke over the prow, washing over the windshield of the rental car. Michael got out and leaned against the rail in the frigid November night air. Across the water, on the shore of the island, he could see the Cannons' floodlit white mansion. The senator loved to leave the lights on when they were coming. Michael imagined bringing children on the ferry. He imagined spending summers with them on the island. He wanted children too—as much if not more than Elizabeth. He kept these feelings to himself. The last thing she needed was more pressure.

They arrived on the island and drove through the village of Shelter Island Heights, the streets dark, the shops tightly shuttered. It was late autumn, and the island had returned to its normal quiet state. The Cannon compound lay a mile outside the village on a finger of land overlooking the harbor on one side and Gardiners Bay on the other. As they pulled into the drive, Charlie came out of his cottage, flashlight in hand, retrievers at his heels.

"The senator turned in early," he said. "He asked me to help you inside."

"We're all right, Charlie," Elizabeth said. They kept clothing at the house so they could come up for weekends without bothering to bring luggage. "Get back inside before you freeze to death."

"All right," he said. "Good night to both of you."

They crept into the house quietly and walked upstairs to their large suite of rooms overlooking the harbor. Elizabeth opened the shades; she loved to wake up to the sight of the water and the purple-orange light of winter dawn.

A PASSING SHOWER awakened them sometime after midnight. Elizabeth rolled over in the dark and kissed the back of Michael's neck. He stirred, and she responded by taking his hand and pulling him on top of her. She wriggled out of her flowered flannel nightgown. His warm body pressed against her breasts.

"God, Michael, I wish I could have a baby with you like this."

He entered her and her body rose to his. Elizabeth was surprised at how quickly she felt her body release. The orgasm washed over her in wave after wonderful wave. She held him tightly and began to laugh.

"Be quiet or your father will wake up."

"I bet you say that to all the girls."

She laughed again.

"What's so damned funny?"

"Nothing, Michael. Nothing at all. I just love you very much."

DOUGLAS CANNON LOVED TO sail but hated taking the boat out in the summer. The waters of Gardiners Bay were jammed with big sloops, Sunfish, speedboats, and, worst of all, Jet Skis, which Cannon regarded as a sign the apocalypse was at hand. He had tried to have them barred from the waters around the island but failed, even after a ten-year-old girl was struck and killed off Upper Beach. Michael had hoped to spend a relaxing afternoon by the fire with a stack of newspapers, a book, and a good cabernet from Cannon's vast cellar. But at noon the rain ended and a weak sun shone through broken clouds. Cannon appeared, dressed in a heavy rag-wool sweater and oil-skin coat.

"Let's go, Michael."

"Douglas, you've got to be kidding. It's forty degrees outside."

"Perfect. Come on, you need some exercise."

Michael looked to Elizabeth for help. She was stretched out on the couch, working over a stack of briefs.

"Go with him, Michael. I don't want him out there alone."

"Elizabeth!"

"Oh, don't be such a whiner. Besides, Dad's right. You're getting a little soft. Come on, I'll see you boys off."

And so twenty minutes later Michael found himself aboard Cannon's thirty-two-foot sloop *Athena,*
bundled in a fleece pullover and woolen coat, pulling
on a frozen jib line like some fabled Gloucester fisherman. Cannon barked orders from the wheel while
Michael scrambled over the slick foredeck, readying
the sails and securing lines in the twenty-mile-per-
hour wind. He stubbed his toe on a cleat and nearly
fell. He wondered how long he would survive in the
frigid waters if he went overboard. He wondered
whether the seventy-year-old Cannon could react
quickly enough to save his life.

He took one last look back at the house as wind
filled *Athena*'s sails and the hull rose from the water
and heeled gently to starboard. On the lawn he could
see Elizabeth with her bow and arrow, standing 150
feet from the target, drilling one bull's-eye after another.

CANNON SET THE *ATHENA* on a broad reach across the
bay. The boat heeled hard over to stern, flying across
the surface of the gray-green water toward Gardiners
Island. Michael sat on the windward side of the boat,
hoping the sun would warm him. He struggled to light
a cigarette, succeeding after two minutes of contort-
ing his body against the wind.

"Jesus Christ, Douglas, at least put her on a beam
reach so we won't feel the wind so much."

"I like it when she heels!" he said, shouting over
the wind.

Michael looked over the boat and saw water
breaking over the bow gunwales.

"Don't you think we should *heel* just a little less?"

"No, this is perfect. She's running at top efficiency right now."

"True, but if the wind gusts, we're going to turn turtle and end up in the drink."

"This boat is incapable of capsizing."

"That's what they said about the *Titanic*."

"But in this case it's true."

"So how does that explain your little disaster at sea last year?"

The *Athena* had capsized in a sudden squall off Montauk Light the previous October. Cannon was rescued by the Coast Guard, and it cost him ten thousand dollars to salvage the boat. After that Elizabeth begged him never to sail alone.

"Defective marine forecast," Cannon said. "I called the head of the National Weather Service and gave him a piece of my mind."

Michael blew into his frozen hands. "Christ, the wind chill must be close to zero."

"Five degrees, actually. I checked."

"You're insane. If the voters knew you had a death wish, they would have never sent you to the Senate."

"Quit your bellyaching, Michael. There's a thermos of coffee below. Be useful and pour us both a mug."

Michael struggled down the companionway. The senator had been on virtually every ship in the navy, and the galley contained a collection of heavy sea mugs emblazoned with the insignia of several different vessels. Michael selected two from the *West Virginia,* a nuclear submarine, and filled them with steaming coffee.

When Michael came back up top, Cannon was smoking one of his cigarettes. "Don't tell Elizabeth," he said, accepting the coffee. "If she knew I sneaked a cigarette every now and again, she'd tell every shop on the island not to sell to me."

Cannon took a long drink of coffee and adjusted his heading.

"So what did you think about the election?"

"Beckwith made quite a turnaround."

"Bunch of bullshit, if you ask me. He played politics with Flight Double-oh-two all the way, and the American people were too bored and too distracted to notice. I supported him on the retaliation, but as for the missile defense system, I think that's payback to a lot of old friends who've backed him over the years."

"You can't deny the threat exists."

"Oh, I suppose there's some level of threat, but if you ask me, it's negligible. The supporters of missile defense say that political instability in Russia or China might lead to an accidental attack on the United States. But the Chinese went through the Cultural Revolution and the Soviets lost their empire, and no one fired anything at us by accident. And as for the so-called rogue states, I worry about them even less. The North Koreans can't even feed their own people, let alone build an ICBM capable of reaching the United States. The regional bullies like Iran and Iraq want to threaten their neighbors, not the

United States, so they're investing in shorter-range weapons. And there's something else to keep in mind: We still have the largest nuclear arsenal on earth. Deterrence worked during the Cold War, and I think it will work now. Do we *really* think the leaders of these nations are willing to commit national suicide? I don't think so, Michael."

"Why do you think it's payback?"

"Because a company called Alatron Defense Systems stands to make billions if a system is built and deployed. Alatron Defense Systems is owned by—"

"—Mitchell Elliott," Michael said.

"That's right, and Mitchell Elliott has spread more money around Washington than any other man in America. He gives as much as he can legally, and if he wants to give more, he finds a way to do it under the table. The largest benefactor of Elliott's largess has been James Beckwith. Hell, he's practically bankrolled the man's political career."

Michael thought of Susanna Dayton and the story she was working on for the *Post.*

"And remember one other thing," Cannon continued. "The White House chief of staff, Paul Vandenberg, used to work for Elliott at Alatron. Elliott sent him to work for Beckwith when he was attorney general in California. He knew how to spot talent, and he knew Beckwith had the potential to go all the way. He wanted his own man on the inside, and he got it." Cannon drew on his cigarette. The wind tore the smoke from his mouth. "Vandenberg also worked for your crowd."

Michael was stunned. "When?"

"During Vietnam."

"I thought he was in the army."

Cannon shook his head. "Nope, Agency through and through. In fact, he worked on a wonderful program known as Operation Phoenix. You remember the Phoenix program, don't you, Michael? Not one of your company's finer moments."

The goal of the Phoenix program had been to identify and eliminate communist influence in South Vietnam. Operation Phoenix was credited with capturing 28,000 suspected communists and killing 20,000 more.

"You know what they say. Once a company man, always a company man, right, Michael? Why don't you run Vandenberg's name through that fancy computer you have at Langley and see if anything comes up?"

"You think the missile defense deal is somehow corrupt?"

"I've seen the test data. The kinetic kill vehicles produced by Alatron were far superior to those built by the other major defense contractors. Elliott won the contract fair and square. But the program had only lukewarm support from the GOP and none from the Democrats. It wasn't going to be built. It took a dramatic appeal, set against a dramatic backdrop, to win the support of Congress."

Michael hesitated before uttering his next words. Finally, he said, "What if I were to tell you that I don't think the Sword of Gaza shot down that airliner?"

"I'd say you were probably onto something. Although I wouldn't say it too loudly, Michael. If the wrong person hears it, you might find yourself in a bit of hot water."

The sun disappeared behind a cloud, and it grew suddenly colder. Cannon glanced at the sky and frowned. "Looks like rain," he said. "All right, Michael, you win. Prepare to come about."

12. St. Maarten, the Caribbean

RED DUST ROSE from the narrow pitted track as the caravan of Range Rovers climbed the mountainside. The trucks were identical: black with reflective smoked windows to shield the identity of the occupants. Each man had come to the island from a different embarkation point: Latin America, the United States, the Middle East, Europe. Each would leave the following morning when the conference ended. It was the beginning of the high tourist season, and the island was jammed with Americans and rich Europeans. The men in the Range Rovers liked it that way. They liked crowds, anonymity. The caravan roared through a poor village. Barefoot children stood at the edge of the track and waved excitedly to the passing vehicles. No one waved back.

THE VILLA WAS EXTRAVAGANT even by the standards of St. Maarten: twelve master bedrooms, two large living rooms, a media room, a billiards room, a large swimming pool, two tennis courts, and a helipad. It had been commissioned just six months earlier by an unnamed European, who paid an exorbitant price to have the work completed on time.

Construction had been a nightmare, for the villa was in the middle of the island, atop a mountain, with sweeping views down to the sea on all sides. Except for the electrified fence, the forty acres of grounds were left in their natural state, covered by thick undergrowth and trees.

A security team arrived a week ahead and installed video cameras, laser trip wires, and radio-jamming devices. For their command center they appropriated the billiards room.

THE SOCIETY FOR International Development and Co-operation was a completely private organization that accepted no outside donations and no new members, except those it selected. Nominally, it was headquartered in Geneva, in a small office with a tasteful gold plaque over the austere door, though a visitor would find the office unoccupied, and a telephone call to the unlisted number would go unanswered.

To those who knew of the group's existence it was known simply as the Society. Despite its name, the Society was not interested in making the world a more peaceful place. Its membership included rogue intelligence officers, politicians, arms merchants, mercenaries, drug lords, international crime organizations, and powerful business moguls.

The executive director was a former senior officer in the British intelligence service, MI6. He was known simply as "the Director" and never referred to by his real name. He oversaw the Society's administration and operations but had no additional decision-making power. That was in the hands of the group's executive council, where each member had one vote. The Society practiced democracy internally, even though most of its members believed it was a rather cumbersome concept in the real world.

The Society's founding creed declared peace was dangerous. Its members believed constant controlled global tension served the interests of all. It prevented complacency. It maintained vigilance. It built national identity. And most of all it made them money, a good deal of money.

SOME ARRIVED ALONE, some in pairs. Some came without protection, some had a personal bodyguard. Ari Shamron came in the midafternoon and played three sets of tennis against the head of a Colombian cocaine cartel. The drug lord's black-suited, heavily armed security detail scampered after the loose balls in the scorching Caribbean sun. Constantin Kalnikov arrived an hour later. He lay by the pool for two hours, until his pale Slavic skin turned crimson with the sun, and then retired to his room for an afternoon of sex with one of the girls. The Director had flown them in from Brazil. Each had been carefully screened. Each was well schooled in the art of physical pleasure. Each had undergone extensive blood testing to make certain they carried no sexually transmitted disease.

Mitchell Elliott had no time and no taste for such activities. He detested the members of the Society. He would deal with them professionally in order to achieve his ends, but he would not frolic and whore with them on a Caribbean island.

The conference was scheduled for nine o'clock. Elliott's Gulfstream touched down at the airport at 8:30 P.M. A helicopter was waiting. He boarded it immediately with Mark Calahan and two other security men and flew up the mountainside to the villa.

FOR THE FIRST HOUR the executive council dealt with routine housekeeping matters. Finally, the Director came to the first real item of business on the agenda. He peered at Mitchell Elliott over his gold half-moon reading glasses. "You have the floor, sir."

Elliott remained seated. "First of all, gentlemen, I wish to thank you for your assistance. The operation went very smoothly, and it has had its intended results. President Beckwith was reelected, and the United States is going to build its missile defense project, a development that will prove beneficial to all of us gathered here."

Elliott paused until the polite boardroom applause died away.

"Needless to say, if a leak occurred and the Society's involvement in this matter ever came to light, the results would be disastrous. Therefore, I come before you tonight to request your permission to eliminate any operative outside this room who knows the truth."

The Director looked up, face vaguely irritated, as though disappointed by a plate of Dover sole. "By my count, that's four men."

"Precisely."

"And how do you recommend we carry out this assignment?"

"I propose using the asset who took part in the operation off New York."

"The one who's still alive, I take it?"

Elliott permitted himself a rare smile. "Yes, Director."

"Obviously, this man knows at least part of the truth—that the Sword of Gaza is not responsible for the attack."

"I agree, but he is one of the best assassins in the world, and an assignment such as this requires someone of his abilities."

"And when the job is done?"

"He will be liquidated, just like the others."

The Director nodded. He appreciated clarity and decisiveness over all else. "How do you propose to finance the liquidation? An operation such as the one you've described will be costly. You've just experienced a substantial windfall. Perhaps the expense should be borne by you."

"I agree, Director. I ask for no financial support from the Society, only its blessing."

The Director peered over his reading glasses at the other men gathered around the table.

"Any objections?"

There was silence.

"Very well, you have the support of the executive council to carry out this assignment." The Director looked down at his papers, as though slightly confused. "All right, gentlemen, item number two. Mr. Hussein of Iraq is interested in acquiring some additional real estate, and once again he'd like our assistance."

.   .   .

THE CONFERENCE ENDED at four that morning. Mitchell Elliott left the villa immediately, flew down the mountain in the helicopter, and boarded the Gulfstream at the airport. The rest of the executive committee stayed and caught a few hours of sleep. Constantin Kalnikov, desperate for a few hours of sun before his return to dreary Moscow, napped in a chaise by the pool. Shamron and the drug lord adjourned to the tennis court for a grudge match, for Shamron had beaten him handily the first time, and the drug lord, as was his habit, wanted revenge. When it was time to leave, they made the journey down the mountain in the Range Rovers. The Director left with the security team at noon. A half hour later, as he was boarding his private jet, a series of explosions ripped through the building, and the grand villa on the St. Maarten mountainside burned rapidly to the ground.

13. Brélés, France

HE HAD TAKEN THE NAME Jean-Paul Delaroche, but in the village they called him Le Solitaire. No one could quite remember exactly when he had arrived and settled himself in the stubby stone bunker of a cottage, clinging to a rocky point overlooking the English Channel. Monsieur Didier, the crimson-faced owner of the general store, believed it was the wind that had driven him mad. On the loner's isolated point, the wind was as powerful as it was incessant. It rattled the heavy windows of the cottage day and night and methodically ripped tiles from the roof. After big storms, passersby would glimpse Le Solitaire restlessly contemplating the damage. "Like Rommel inspecting his precious Atlantic Wall," Didier would whisper with a contemptuous smirk over cognac at the café.

Was he a writer? Was he a revolutionary? Was he an art thief or a fallen priest? Mademoiselle Plauché from the charcuterie believed him to be the last surviving member of the megalithic race of people who lived in Brittany thousands of years before the Celts. Why else would he spend his days in communion with the ancient stones? Why else would he sit for hours and stare at the sea beating itself against the rocks? Why else would he call himself Delaroche? He has been here before, she would conclude, knife hovering above a wheel of Camembert. He is thinking about how things used to be.

The men were jealous of him. The older ones were jealous of the beautiful women who came to the cottage one by one, stayed for a time, and then quietly left. The boys were jealous of the custom-built Italian racing bike that he rode like a demon each morning along the narrow back roads of the Finistère. The women, even the young girls and the old women, thought he was beautiful—the short-cropped hair flecked with gray, the white skin, the eyes of brilliant blue, the straight nose that might have been chiseled by Michelangelo.

He was not a tall man, well under six feet, but he carried himself like one as he moved about the village each afternoon, doing his marketing. At the boulangerie, Mademoiselle Trevaunce sought vainly to engage him in conversation each time he came into the shop, but he would just smile and politely select his bread and croissants. At the wineshop he was regarded as a knowledgeable but frugal customer. When Monsieur Rodin would suggest a more expensive bottle, he would raise his eyebrows to show it was beyond his reach and carefully hand it back.

At the outdoor market he would choose his vegetables, meat, and seafood with the fussiness of the chefs from the restaurants and resorts. Some days he would bring his current woman—always an outsider, never a local Breton girl—some days he would come alone. Some days he would be invited to join the men who passed the afternoon with red wine, goat cheese, and cards. But the loner would always gesture helplessly toward his watch—as if he had pressing matters elsewhere—and pile his things into his battered tan Mercedes station wagon for the journey back to his bunker by the sea.

As if time matters in Brélés, Didier would say, lips pulled down in his customary smirk. It is the wind, he would add. The wind has made him mad.

THE NOVEMBER MORNING was clear and bright, wind gusting from the sea, as Delaroche cycled along the narrow coast road. He was riding west from Brest toward the Pointe-de-Saint-Mathieu. He wore snug fleece pants over his cycling britches and a turtleneck sweater beneath a neon-green anorak—tight enough to avoid flapping in the wind, loose enough to conceal the bulky Glock 9mm automatic beneath his left armpit. Despite the layers of clothing, the salt-scented air cut through him like a knife. Delaroche put his head down and pedaled hard down to the point.

The road flattened out for a time as he passed the crumbled, wind-battered ruins of a sixth-century Benedictine monastery. Then he rode north for several miles into a stiff wind from the sea, the road rising and falling rhythmically beneath him. The lightweight Italian bike handled the challenging terrain and conditions well. A steep hill stood before him. He changed gears and pedaled faster. He breasted the hill and entered the fishing village of Lanildut.

In a café he purchased two croissants and filled his bottles, one with orange juice and the second with steaming café au lait. Delaroche devoured the croissant as he cycled. He passed the Presqu'Ile de Sainte-Marguerite, a rocky finger of land jutting into the sea, blessed with some of the most magnificent seascapes in all Europe. Next came the Côte des Abers, the coast of estuaries—a long flat run over a series of rivers running from the highland of the Finistère down to the sea.

He felt the first signs of leg weariness as he entered the village of Brignogan-Plage. Beyond the village, down a narrow path, lay a beach of sand so white it might have been snow. An ancient upright stone, known in Brittany as a menhir, stood like a sentinel over the entrance. Delaroche dismounted and pushed his bicycle along the pathway, sipping the remains of the café au lait as he walked. On the beach he leaned the bike against a large rock and walked along the tidal line, smoking a cigarette.

The signal site was a large outcropping of rock about two hundred meters from the place where he left the bike. He walked slowly, aimlessly, watching the sea rushing against the sand. A large wave broke over the beach. Delaroche deftly sidestepped to avoid the frigid water. He smoked the last of the cigarette, tossed the butt a few feet ahead of him, and ground it into the white sand with the toe of his cycling shoe.

He stopped walking and crouched at the base of the rock. The mark was there, two bone-white strips of medical tape, fashioned into an X. Any professional would have guessed that the person who had left the mark was trained in the tradecraft of the KGB, which indeed he was.

Delaroche tore the tape from the stone, wadded it into a tight ball, and tossed it into the gorse bordering the beach. He walked back to the bike and pedaled home to Brélés through the brilliant sun.

By MIDDAY THE WEATHER was still good, so Delaroche decided to paint. He dressed in jeans and a heavy fisherman's sweater and loaded his things into the back of the Mercedes: his easel, a Polaroid camera, his box of paint and brushes. He went back inside the cottage, made coffee, and poured it into a shiny metal thermos bottle. From the refrigerator he took two large bottles of Beck's and went back out. He drove into the village and parked outside the charcuterie. Inside he purchased ham, cheese, and a lump of local Breton paté while Mademoiselle Plauché flirted with him shamelessly. He left the shop, accompanied by the tinkle of the little bell attached to the doorway, and went next door to the boulangerie for a baguette.

He drove inland, the harsh rocky terrain of the coastline giving way to soft wooded hills as he moved deeper into the Finistère. He turned off onto a small unmarked side road and followed it two miles until it turned to a pitted track. The Mercedes bucked wildly, but after a few minutes he arrived at his destination, a quaint stone farmhouse—seventeenth century, he guessed—set against a stand of splendid trees with leaves of ruby and gold.

Delaroche did most things slowly and carefully, and preparing to paint was no exception. He methodically unpacked his supplies from the back of the Mercedes while taking in the view of the farmhouse. The autumn light brought out sharp contrasts in the stonework of the house and in the trees beyond. Capturing the quality of the light on paper would be a challenge.

Delaroche ate a sandwich and drank some of the beer while he studied the scene from several different perspectives. He found the spot he liked the best and made a half-dozen photographs with his camera, three in color, three black-and-white. The owner of the house emerged, a stout little figure with a black-and-white dog racing in circles at his feet. Delaroche called out that he was an artist, and the man waved enthusiastically. Five minutes later he came bearing a glass of wine and a plate piled with cheese and thick slices of spicy sausage. He wore a patched jacket that looked as though it had been purchased before the war. The dog, which had just three legs, begged Delaroche for food.

When they were gone, Delaroche settled in behind his easel. He studied the photos, first the black-

and-white, to see essential form and lines within the image, then the color. For twenty minutes he made sketches with a charcoal pencil until the composition of the work felt right. He worked with a simple palette—Winsor red, Winsor blue, Hooker's green, Winsor yellow, raw sienna—on heavy paper stretched over a plywood backing.

Nearly an hour passed before the message on the beach at Brignogan-Plage intruded on his thoughts. It was a summons, telling him that he was to meet Arbatov on the seawall in Roscoff tomorrow afternoon. Arbatov had been Delaroche's case officer when he worked for the KGB. For twenty years Delaroche had worked with Arbatov and no one else. Once, when Arbatov was beginning to slow, Moscow Center tried to replace him with a younger man named Karpov. Delaroche refused to work with Karpov and threatened to send him back to Moscow in a box unless Arbatov was reinstated as his handler. One week later in Salzburg, Arbatov and Delaroche reunited. To punish the grunts at Moscow Center they had a celebratory feast of Austrian veal washed down by three costly bottles of Bordeaux. Delaroche did not stand up for Arbatov out of love or loyalty; he loved no one and was loyal to nothing but his art and his profession. He wanted Arbatov back on the job because he trusted no one else. He had survived twenty years without being arrested or killed because Arbatov had done his job well.

As he painted the idyllic scene, he thought very hard about ignoring Arbatov's summons. Arbatov and Delaroche no longer worked for the KGB because there was no KGB, and men in their line of work were not absorbed by its more presentable successor, the Foreign Intelligence Service. When the Soviet Union collapsed and the KGB was abolished, Delaroche and Arbatov were set adrift. They remained in the West—Arbatov in Paris and Delaroche in Brélés—and entered private practice together. Arbatov served, in effect, as Delaroche's agent. If someone wanted a job done they came to Arbatov. If Arbatov approved he would put it to Delaroche. For his services, Arbatov was paid a percentage of the substantial fee Delaroche commanded on the open market.

Delaroche had earned enough money to consider getting out of the game. It had been more than a month since his last job, and for the first time he was not bored and restless with inactivity. The last job had paid him a million dollars, enough to live comfortably in Brélés for many years, but it had also taken something out of him. During his long career as an assassin—first for the KGB, then as a freelance professional—Delaroche had only one rule: He did not kill innocent people. The attack on the airliner off Long Island had violated that rule.

He had not actually fired the missile, but he had been a key player in the operation. His job was to get the Palestinian in place, kill him when it was done, and scuttle the motor yacht before being extracted by helicopter at sea. He had carried out his assignment perfectly, and for that he was rewarded with one million dollars. But at night, when he was alone in the cottage with nothing but the sound of the sea, he saw the burning jetliner tumbling toward the Atlantic. He imagined the screams of the passengers as they waited to die. In all his previous jobs he knew the targets intimately. They were evil people involved in evil things who knew the risks of the game they played. And he had killed each of them face-to-face. Blowing up a civilian jetliner had violated his rule.

He would keep his date with Arbatov and listen to the offer. If it was good, and lucrative, he would consider taking it. If not, he would retire and paint the Breton countryside and drink wine in his stone cottage by the sea and never speak to another person again.

One hour later he finished the painting. It was good, he thought, but he could make it better. The sun was setting, and a scarlet twilight settled over the farm. With the sun gone, the air turned suddenly cold, fragrant with wood smoke and frying garlic. He smeared paté on a hunk of bread and drank beer while he packed away his things. The Polaroids and sketches he placed in his pocket; he would use them to produce another version of the work, a better one, in his studio. He left the wineglass, the half-empty plate, and the still-damp watercolor at the door of the cottage and silently walked back to the Mercedes. The three-legged dog yelped at him as he drove away, then devoured the last of the sausage.

A HEAVY RAIN was falling the following morning as Delaroche drove from Brélés to Roscoff. He arrived at the seawall at precisely ten o'clock and found Arbatov, a picture of misery, pacing in the downpour. Delaroche parked the car and watched for a moment before making his approach.

Mikhail Arbatov looked more like an aging professor than a KGB spymaster, and, as always, Delaroche found it hard to imagine he had presided over countless murders. Obviously, life in Paris was treating him well, because he was fatter than Delaroche remembered, and his cheeks had a deceptive healthy glow about them from too much wine and cognac. He wore his customary black rollneck sweater and army-style mackintosh coat, which looked as if it belonged to a taller, thinner man. On his head he wore a waterproof brimmed hat typical of retired men everywhere. His spectacles were steel-rimmed goggles and always seemed to do more harm than good. Now they were fogged with the rain and slipping down the steep slope of his pugilist's nose.

Delaroche climbed out of the car and approached him from behind. Arbatov, the consummate professional, did not flinch as Delaroche fell into step next to him. They walked in silence for a time, Delaroche struggling to keep cadence with Arbatov's teetering waddle. Arbatov seemed forever on the verge of capsizing, and several times Delaroche resisted the impulse to reach out and steady him.

Arbatov stopped walking and turned to face Delaroche. He studied him with a straight, slightly bemused gaze, gray eyes magnified by the immense spectacles. "Jesus Christ, but I'm too old for this streetcraft bullshit," he said, in his impeccable, accentless French. "Too old and too tired. Take me someplace warm with good food."

Delaroche drove him to a good café on the waterfront. Arbatov complained about the paint mess in the

Mercedes the entire way. Five minutes later they were tucking into Gruyère and mushroom omelets and mugs of café au lait. Arbatov devoured his food and lit a wretched Gauloise before Delaroche had finished his second bite. Complaining of the cold, Arbatov ordered a cognac. He drank it in two gulps and had another cigarette, blowing slender streams of smoke at the dark-stained wood of the beamed ceiling. The two men sat in silence. A stranger might have mistaken them for a father and son who had breakfast together daily, which suited Delaroche fine.

"They want you back again," Arbatov said, when Delaroche finished eating. Delaroche did not have to ask who *they* were; they were the men who had hired him for the airliner operation.

"What's the job?"

"All they said was that it was extremely important and they wanted the best."

Delaroche did not require flattery. "The money?"

"They wouldn't tell me, except to say that it was more than the fee for the last job." Arbatov crushed out his Gauloise with the cracked fingernail of his thick thumb. " 'Substantially more' was the term they used."

Delaroche gestured for the waiter to clear away his plate. He ordered another coffee and lit his own cigarette.

"They gave you no details at all about the work?"

"Just one. It is a multiple hit, and all the targets are professionals."

Delaroche's interest was suddenly piqued. For the most part his work bored him. Most jobs required far less skill than Delaroche possessed. They took little preparation and even less creativity. Killing professionals was another matter.

"They want to meet with you tomorrow," Arbatov said. "In Paris."

"Whose turf?"

"Theirs, of course." He reached inside his jacket and withdrew a soggy slip of paper. The ink had run but the address was legible. "They want to meet with you face-to-face."

"I don't do face-to-face meetings, Mikhail. You of all people should know that."

Delaroche protected his identity with a care bordering on paranoia. Most men in his line of work dealt with the problem by having plastic surgeons give them a new face every few years. Delaroche dealt with it another way—he rarely permitted anyone who knew what he really did to see his face. He had never allowed anyone to take his photograph, and he always worked alone. He had made just one exception—the Palestinian on the airliner operation—but he had been paid an exorbitant amount of money and he had killed him when the job was done. The extraction team aboard the helicopter had not seen his face, because he had worn a black woolen mask.

"Be reasonable, my dear boy," Arbatov was saying. "It's a brave new world out there."

"I'm still alive because I'm careful."

"I realize that. And I want you to remain alive so I can continue to make money. Believe me, Jean-Paul, I wouldn't send you into a situation where I thought you could get hurt. You pay me to field offers and give you sound advice. I advise you to hear what these people have to say, on their terms."

Delaroche looked at him. Was he slipping? Was the prospect of an enormous payday clouding his judgment?

"How many people will be there?"

"I'm told just one."

"Weapons?"

Arbatov shook his head. "You'll be searched as you enter the flat."

"Weapons come in all shapes and sizes, Mikhail."

"So you'll do it?"

"I'll think about it."

Delaroche gestured toward the waiter.

"C'est tout."

14. CIA Headquarters, Langley, Virginia

MICHAEL LEFT THE HOUSE very early and drove along the deserted parkway toward headquarters in the gray half-light of dawn. He picked up coffee and a stale bagel from the swill pit and walked upstairs to the Center. The last of the shakedown night shift was there, bleary-eyed, hunched over computer screens and old paper files like medieval monks trapped in the wrong time. Eurotrash was reading the morning cables. Blaze was showing Cynthia how to kill with a piece of paper. Michael sat down at his desk and switched on his computer.

According to Belgian police, two suspected Sword of Gaza action agents were spotted aboard a train crossing into the Netherlands. Britain's security service, MI5, intercepted a phone call from an Islamic intellectual living in London that suggested a retaliatory attack somewhere in Europe was imminent. Satellite photographs of the ruined training camp in Iran revealed hasty reconstruction. The most important piece of overnight intelligence came last. Syrian intelligence officials traveled to Tehran the previous week to meet with their Iranian counterparts.

Michael had seen movements like these in the past. The Sword of Gaza was planning to strike an American target in Europe, probably soon. He picked up his internal telephone and dialed Carter's office, but there was no answer.

He hung up and stared at his computer terminal.

Why don't you run Vandenberg's name through that fancy computer you have at Langley and see if anything comes up?

Michael typed in Vandenberg's name and instructed the computer to search the database.

Ten seconds later he received a reply.

FILE RESTRICTED. ACCESS UNAUTHORIZED.

"WHAT THE FUCK do you think you were doing?"

Carter was angrier than Michael had ever seen him. He was seated at his desk, rapping a thick pen on his leather blotter, his normally pallid complexion red with exertion. McManus sat behind him, silent, as if awaiting his turn with an uncooperative suspect.

"It was just a hunch I had," Michael said weakly, and immediately regretted it, for he could see by

Carter's reaction that he had only made matters worse.

"A hunch? You had a hunch, so you decided to run the name of the White House chief of staff through Agency personnel files? Osbourne, you are a counterterrorism officer. What did you think Vandenberg was going to do, blow up the White House? Shoot his boss? Hijack Air Force One?"

"No."

"I'm waiting."

Michael wondered exactly why he was here. The geeks down in the computer room must have blown the whistle on him. Either someone was watching the activity of his computer log-in or a trip wire had been placed on Vandenberg's file. When Michael tried to read it, an alarm sounded somewhere in the system. The whole thing smelled like a Monica Tyler production. Michael had but one recourse now: tell part of the truth and hope his relationship with Carter would spare further bloodshed.

"I heard from someone I trust that he had an Agency background, and I wanted to check it out. It was a mistake, Adrian. I'm sorry."

"You're goddamned right it was a mistake. Let me make something clear to you. The Agency's files are not here for your reading enjoyment. They are not to be surfed. They are not for you to take out on a joy ride. Am I making myself clear, Michael?"

"Crystal."

"You're not in the field anymore, where you operate on your own terms. You work at headquarters, and you play by the rules."

"Understood."

Carter looked at McManus, and McManus closed the door.

"Now, between us girls, I know you're a damned good officer, and you wouldn't have tried to read that file unless it was important. Do you have something you want to tell us at this time?"

"Not yet, Adrian."

"All right. Get the fuck out of here."

15. Paris

DELAROCHE DROVE TO BREST and took a late train to Paris. He traveled with two bags, a small overnight grip with a change of clothes and a large flat rectangular case containing a dozen watercolors. His work was sold in a discreet Paris gallery, providing him with enough income to justify his unpretentious lifestyle in Brélés.

From the train station he took a taxi to a modest hotel on the rue de Rivoli and registered as a Dutchman named Karel van der Stadt—Dutch was one of his languages, and he had three excellent Dutch passports. His room had a small balcony overlooking the Tuileries Garden and the Louvre. The night was cold and very clear. To his right he could see the Eiffel Tower, ablaze with light; to his left Notre Dame, standing guard over the black shimmer of the Seine. It was late, but he had work to do, so he pulled on a sweater and a leather jacket and went out. The front desk clerk asked Delaroche if he would like to leave his key. Delaroche shook his head and, in Dutch-accented French, said he preferred to keep it with him.

The meeting was to take place in a flat in the Fifth Arrondissement on the rue de Tournefort. Spotting professional surveillance was difficult under the best of circumstances, but it was even more difficult at night in a city like Paris. Delaroche walked for a time, crossing the Seine and strolling along the Quai de Montebello. He made several sudden stops. He browsed among the book kiosks. He purchased the evening papers from a newsagent. He made a false call from a public telephone. Each time he carefully checked to see if he was being pursued but saw no signs of a tail.

For fifteen minutes Delaroche wound his way through the narrow streets of the Latin Quarter. The cold night air smelled of spice and cigarettes. Delaroche went into a bar and drank beer while leafing through a newspaper. Again, there was no visible surveillance. He finished his beer and went out.

The apartment was just the way Arbatov had described it, in an old building on the rue de Tournefort overlooking the Place de la Contrescarpe. The flat was on the third floor. From the sidewalk, Delaroche could see the front windows were dark. He could also see a small camera mounted over the doorway for tenants to check the faces of arriving guests.

There was a bistro on the corner with a good view of the flat and the entrance. Delaroche took a window table and ordered roast chicken and a half bottle of Côtes-du-Rhône. It was a good neighborhood bistro, warm and clamorous, mostly locals and students from the Sorbonne.

While he ate, Delaroche read an analysis story from the Washington correspondent of *Le Monde*. It said that the American air strikes on Sword of Gaza targets in Syria and Libya had dealt a major blow to the cause of peace in the Middle East. Syria and Libya were arming themselves with newer and more dangerous weaponry, some of it French-made. Negotiations between the Palestinians and the Israelis were at a standstill after weeks of unrest in Gaza and the West Bank. Intelligence experts warned of a new round of international terror. Western European diplomats complained that the Americans had taken their revenge with no regard for the consequences. Delaroche laid his paper on the table and ate. It always amazed him how little journalists knew of the secret world.

The man entering the apartment house caught his attention.

Delaroche looked him over carefully: short, thinning blond hair, a squat wrestler's physique gone soft with debauchery. The offensive cut of his overcoat said he was an American. On his arm was a pretty French prostitute, taller than he was, with dark shoulder-length hair and crimson lips. The American opened the door, and they disappeared into the dark entrance hall. A moment later, light burned in the third-floor flat.

Delaroche felt his spirits lift. He had feared he was walking into a trap. Alone in a strange flat, with no avenues of escape, he would be easy prey if it was one of his enemies who had actually arranged the meeting. But an operative who was so corrupt as to bring a prostitute to a safe house surely posed little threat to him. Only an amateur or an undisciplined professional would take such a risk.

Delaroche, at that moment, decided he would make the meeting.

THE FOLLOWING MORNING Delaroche rose early and went running through the Tuileries. He wore a dark blue anorak to shield himself from the gentle rain drifting over the gardens. He ran at a fast pace for forty-five minutes, the gravel of the footpaths crunching beneath his feet. He pushed himself hard for the last mile. When he finished he stood on the rue de Rivoli, doubled over and gasping for air, as Parisians hustled past on their way to work.

Upstairs in his room he showered and changed. The Glock 9mm was within easy reach the entire time. Leaving it behind was alien to him, but Delaroche would abide by the rules of the meeting. He pulled on his sweater, locked the gun away in the small room safe, and went downstairs.

He took breakfast in the hotel restaurant, a pleasant room with windows on the rue de Rivoli, and lingered over the morning newspapers. He was the last guest to leave the dining room.

From the front desk he took a Paris street map and a tourist guide. The morning clerk wondered if Delaroche would like to leave his room key. Delaroche shook his head and pushed through the doors to the street.

.   .   .

HE TOOK A TAXI to the rue de Tournefort and got out at the corner bistro where he had eaten dinner the previous night. The rain had stopped, so he sat outside. Despite the clouds, he wore Ray-Ban sunglasses with thick stems.

It was 9:45. Delaroche ordered coffee and brioche and watched the window of the third-floor flat across the street. Twice, the man with the wrestler's body appeared in the front window. The first time he wore a bathrobe and clutched a mug of coffee as though he were hung over. The second time, at 9:55, he wore a blue executive business suit, and his thinning blond hair was combed neatly in place.

Delaroche scanned the street. The sidewalk was jammed with Parisians rushing to work and students heading to the Sorbonne. On the rue de Tournefort, a pair of city workers was preparing to descend into a manhole. Another city worker was sweeping up dog droppings. The tables had filled around him. He could be surrounded by surveillance and would never know it.

At ten o'clock he left money on the table and walked across the street. He casually pressed the bell and turned his back to the camera over the doorway. The electronic lock snapped back, and he pushed through the door into the entrance hall.

There was no lift, just a broad staircase. Delaroche mounted the first step and walked quickly upward. The place was quiet, no other tenants moving about. Delaroche arrived at the third floor without being spotted. Arbatov had instructed him not to ring the bell. The door opened immediately, and the wrestler invited Delaroche inside with a wave of his thick paw.

DELAROCHE EYED HIS SURROUNDINGS while the other man conducted a slow and methodical search of his body, first by hand, then with a magnetometer. The furnishings were masculine and comfortable: black informal couches and chairs grouped around a glass coffee table, teak bookshelves filled with histories, biographies, and thrillers by American and English writers. The remaining portions of exposed wall were bare, with faint outlines where framed paintings had once hung. The books were the only personal items; no photographs of family and friends, no stack of mail, no message pad next to the telephone on the desk.

"Coffee?" the wrestler asked when he was finished.

Delaroche had been right. He was an American—from the South, by the sound of his accent.

Delaroche nodded. He removed his sunglasses, while the American went into the all-black modern kitchen and busied himself with the coffee. Delaroche sat down and scanned the rest of the flat. Next to the kitchen was a small dining area, and beyond that a short hall leading to a bedroom. On the table was a black laptop computer.

The American returned with two mugs of coffee, handing one to Delaroche and keeping the other for himself.

"The job is four hits," he began without preamble, "to be carried out before the end of January. You will be paid one million dollars in advance. For each successful hit, you will immediately be paid an additional one million dollars. That adds up to five million dollars, if I'm not mistaken."

"Who do you work for?"

The American shook his head. "I am instructed to say that I work for the same group that hired you for the airliner operation. You already know they are a professional outfit and their word is good."

Delaroche lit a cigarette. "You have the dossiers on the targets?"

The American produced a compact disk. "It's all here, but you get to see the files only if you accept the assignment. Reasons of security, Mr. Delaroche. Surely a man of your reputation can understand that."

Delaroche held out his hand for the disk.

The American smiled. "We thought you'd see it our way. The first million has already been wired to your bank in Zurich. Check it out for yourself. Phone's right over there."

Delaroche conducted the conversation in rapid German. Herr Becker, his solicitous Swiss bank manager in Zurich, confirmed that, yes, one million dollars had been wired into the account overnight. Delaroche said he would call again later with wiring instructions of his own and hung up.

"The contents are encrypted," the American said, as he handed Delaroche the disk. "Your KGB code name will unlock the files."

Delaroche was stunned. Since entering the freelance market he had never divulged his KGB credentials, and he had never used his old code name. Only Arbatov and a handful of senior officers at Moscow

Center ever knew it. The men who had just retained his services were obviously very well connected. The fact that they knew his KGB code name was proof.

"I trust you know how to run one of those," the American said, gesturing at the laptop. "You'll have to excuse me, but I'm not allowed to see the contents of the dossier. You're on your own."

Delaroche carried the disk to the dining room table and sat down. He inserted the disk into the internal drive of the laptop and typed seven letters.

The computer screen flickered to life.

THE DOSSIERS WERE THE BEST Delaroche had ever seen: personal and professional histories, sexual habits, daily routines, addresses, telephone numbers, digital voice samples, surveillance photographs, even digitized videotape.

For two hours he slowly and systematically worked his way through all the information contained on the disk. He made no notes; Delaroche had a mind capable of storing, categorizing, and recalling immense amounts of information.

The American was stretched out on the couch, enjoying the 500-channel satellite television system. First he watched an American football game, then an inane quiz show. Now he had settled on Swedish pornography. Delaroche was treated to sounds of lesbian lovemaking as he worked.

The hits would be the most challenging of his career. The targets were all professionals; one was under the periodic protection of his government. The job would also require carrying out an assassination in the United States, where Delaroche had never set foot, let alone worked. If successful, the killings would be his last for some time; the assassin who carried out this assignment would have to go into hiding for a very long time. The men who had hired him understood this, which is why the fee was a lifetime's worth of money.

Delaroche opened the last computerized dossier.

It contained only one item, a photograph of the man watching television in the next room. Delaroche closed out the file and exited the program. The screen read:

IF YOU BETRAY US WE
WILL HAND YOU OVER TO THE FBI OR WE
WILL KILL YOU.

Delaroche removed the disk and stood up.

THE AMERICAN WAS ENGROSSED in the pornography. Delaroche walked from the dining room into the sitting room and collected his coat, which was tossed over a chair.

The American stood up. This pleased Delaroche. It would make his next task easier.

"One last piece of business. How do we contact you once you've gone operational?"

"You don't. No more face-to-face meetings, no more contact with Arbatov."

"You still have your address on the Internet?"

Delaroche nodded and removed his sunglasses from his coat pocket.

"Any additional instructions will be sent there—encrypted, of course—and the same code word will serve as the key."

"I don't need to tell you that the Internet is vast but highly insecure. It should be used only in an emergency."

"Understood."

Delaroche held out the disk. Just as the American was reaching for it, Delaroche let it tumble from his fingertips. The American's eyes moved from Delaroche to the disk just for an instant, yet he realized he had made a fatal mistake.

Delaroche's left hand clamped over the American's mouth with an iron grip. He turned the man's face slightly in order to increase his chances of killing him with one strike.

Then he rammed the stem of the sunglasses through his right eye.

The search had been thorough, but the wrestler had failed to notice that the right stem of Delaroche's sunglasses had been filed to a sharp point, which allowed the blow to penetrate the brain's protective cover and sever a branch of the carotid artery behind the eye. The blood loss was rapid and catastrophic. The man quickly lost consciousness. He would be dead in a moment or two.

Delaroche placed him in front of the television and his pornography. He removed the sunglasses from the ruined eye and washed them carefully in the kitchen sink. He collected the disk from the coffee table and placed it in his coat pocket.

Then he put on the sunglasses and went out into the Paris morning.

. . .

DELAROCHE DECIDED TO KILL ARBATOV as he sat in the Musée de l'Orangerie des Tuileries, surrounded by Monet's *Nymphéas*. It was not a difficult decision, really. Once Delaroche carried out the assignment, he would be one of the most wanted men on the planet. The world's most powerful law enforcement and intelligence agencies would be searching for him. The person who could harm him most was Arbatov. If Arbatov was discovered—if pressure was applied—he might betray Delaroche to save himself. It was a risk Delaroche was no longer willing to take.

He contemplated the soft blues and greens and yellows of Monet's work and thought of the action he had just carried out. Delaroche took no pleasure from killing, yet it left him with no remorse. He was trained to carry out assassinations with brutal and mechanical swiftness. The quickness with which he killed insulated him from any guilt or remorse. It was as if someone else were performing the act. He was not the murderer; the men who ordered the death were the real killers. Delaroche was just the weapon: the knife, the gun, the blunt object. If he had not carried out the contract, someone else would have.

He spent the rest of the day relaxing. He took lunch in the hotel restaurant, transforming himself once again into Karel van der Stadt, Dutch tourist, and slept for an hour in his room. In the afternoon he went to his gallery and left the paintings. The owner pronounced them spectacular and produced a check for two hundred thousand francs, Delaroche's share of the proceeds from his last batch of work.

Late that afternoon he telephoned Zurich. Herr Becker, the fussy Swiss bank manager, confirmed that, yes, a second deposit of one million dollars had been made to the gentleman's account. That meant the body of the American operative had been found. Or, more likely, the men who had hired Delaroche had witnessed the entire scene with surveillance cameras and microphones.

Delaroche requested a current balance, and after a moment's calculation Becker announced gravely that the account now contained slightly more than three and a half million dollars.

Delaroche instructed him to prepare a withdrawal of half a million dollars, bills of various denominations, to be collected in forty-eight hours. He then instructed Becker to wire three million dollars to three separate accounts in the Bahamas.

"One million dollars for each account, Monsieur Delaroche?"

"Yes."

"Account numbers, please?"

Delaroche recited them from memory.

RERTIREMENT HAD ROBBED ARBATOV of his edge. Like most old men who live alone, he had settled into a carefully scripted daily routine from which he rarely strayed. It included walking his dog each night before dinner. The only thing more predictable than Arbatov was the dog; each night it pissed on the same tree and shit on the same patch of grass in the park near Arbatov's flat.

Delaroche waited there, hidden by darkness.

Arbatov approached right on schedule. It was cold, and a light rain was starting up again. The park was deserted. Even if there were people about, Delaroche knew he could carry out the act so swiftly and silently he would never be detected.

Arbatov passed. Delaroche fell in quietly behind him.

The dog stopped to piss, same tree, right on schedule.

Delaroche paused and resumed walking when the dog finished. He glanced around to see if he was alone. Satisfied, he closed the ground between himself and Arbatov with a few quick steps. Arbatov, alarmed by the noise, turned around in time to see Delaroche, arm raised. He swung down with brutal swiftness and struck Arbatov on the side of his neck, instantly shattering his spine.

The old man collapsed. The dog barked wildly, thrashing about on his leash, which Arbatov still clutched in his hand. Delaroche reached inside Arbatov's coat and took his wallet. Street thugs don't kill with a single blow to the neck, he told himself. Only professionals do. Street thugs maul and bludgeon. He kicked Arbatov in the face several times and walked away.

The rain fell harder. The barking of the dog faded into the wet night. Delaroche walked at a normal pace. He removed the cash and the credit cards from Arbatov's wallet and threw it into a flower bed bordering the footpath.

In the pale yellow light of the street he noticed blood on his right shoe. He wiped it away with old newspaper and caught a taxi back to his hotel. He still had time to make his train. He packed quickly and checked out.

On the platform, waiting for the train, he threw Arbatov's credit cards in a rubbish bin. The carriage was crowded. He found a seat and ordered a sandwich and a beer from the porter. Then he pillowed his head on his leather coat and slept until the train arrived in Brest.

16. Washington, D.C.

SUSANNA DAYTON WORKED all Sunday afternoon from noon until eight without a break, except to answer the door sometime late in the afternoon to take delivery of a pizza. Tom Logan, her editor at the *Post,* had demanded more, and she had found it. The piece was airtight. She had real estate and bank documents to support the most damaging charges. She had double and triple human sources to support the others. No one mentioned in the piece would be able to question her reporting. The facts spoke for themselves, and Susanna had the facts.

The day was spent writing. She worked at home because she wanted no distractions. The piece was dense with information: numbers, names, dates, places, people. Susanna's challenge was to turn it into an interesting story. She opened with a brief sketch of her central character, James Beckwith, a young district attorney, a promising talent with no personal fortune, who could earn many times more in the private sector than he could in politics. Enter Mitchell Elliott, an immensely wealthy defense contractor and Republican benefactor. Stay in politics, Elliott told the young Beckwith, and leave the rest to me. Over the years Elliott had enriched the Beckwiths through a number of real estate and other financial transactions. And the man who devised many of the schemes was Elliott's chief lawyer and Washington lobbyist, Samuel Braxton.

The rest flowed from that premise. By eight o'clock that evening she had written a four-thousand-word piece. She would show it to Tom Logan in the morning. Because of the serious nature of the charges, Logan would have to run it past the paper's managing editor and editor in chief. Then the lawyers would review the copy. She knew it was going to be a long and difficult couple of days.

The piece lacked one final element—comment from the White House, Mitchell Elliott, and Samuel Braxton. She flipped through her Rolodex, found the first telephone number, and punched it in.

"Alatron Defense Systems." The voice was male, accentless, and vaguely military.

"This is Susanna Dayton of *The Washington Post.* I'd like to speak with Mitchell Elliott, please."

"I'm sorry, Ms. Dayton, but Mr. Elliott is unavailable at this time."

"I wonder if you could give him a message for me."

"Certainly."

"Do you have a pen?"

"Of course, Ms. Dayton."

"I would like Mr. Elliott to comment on the following information contained in a piece I'm preparing." She spoke for five minutes. The man on the other end of the line never interrupted. She concluded the call was probably being recorded without her consent. "Did you get all that?"

"Yes, Ms. Dayton."

"And you'll pass it on to Mr. Elliott?"

"Certainly."

"Good. Thank you very much."

She hung up and flipped through her Rolodex. She still had Paul Vandenberg's home number from her days at the White House. She punched in the number. Vandenberg answered the phone himself.

"Mr. Vandenberg, this is Susanna Dayton. I'm a reporter for—"

"I know who you are, Ms. Dayton. I don't appreciate being disturbed at home. Now, what can I do for you?"

"I wonder if you would like to comment on the following information contained in a piece I've prepared for the *Post*." Once again Susanne spoke for five minutes without interruption. When she finished Vandenberg said, "Why don't you fax me a copy of the article so I can review the charges more carefully."

"I'm afraid I can't do that, Mr. Vandenberg."

"Then I'm afraid I have nothing to say to you, Ms. Dayton—except that you have produced a piece of shoddy journalism that need not be graced with a comment."

Susanna jotted down the quote on her note pad.

"Good evening, Ms. Dayton."

The line went dead. Susanna flipped through her Rolodex and found Samuel Braxton's home number. She was reaching for the telephone when it rang.

"This is Sam Braxton."

"Boy, word travels fast."

"I understand you're about to publish a piece that libels and defames Mitchell Elliott and myself. I want to make you aware of the consequences of your actions."

"Why don't you let me read the allegations to you before you threaten me with a lawsuit."

"I've been given a summary of the charges, Ms. Dayton. Do you intend to publish this account in tomorrow's paper?"

"We haven't decided."

"I'll take that as a no."

Susanna covered the mouthpiece and murmured, "Fuck you, Sam Braxton, you pompous bastard."

"Why don't we meet in the morning and discuss the allegations?"

Susanna hesitated. If she discussed legal issues with Braxton without a *Post* lawyer at her side, Tom Logan would have her head. Still, she wanted Braxton on the record.

"Do yourself a favor, Ms. Dayton. What harm can it do?"

"Where?"

"Breakfast at the Four Seasons in Georgetown. Eight o'clock."

"See you then."

"Good night, Ms. Dayton."

Susanna had one more call to make, Elizabeth Osbourne. She was about to publish a devastating piece about the most powerful man in her firm. Elizabeth deserved a heads-up. She dialed.

"Hello."

"Hello, Elizabeth. Listen, I think we need to talk."

MARK CALAHAN WAS SITTING in the library of the Kalorama house, turning the knobs on a bank of sophisticated audio equipment, when the call from Colorado Springs came through. Calahan knew more about the allegations contained in the piece than anyone except Susanna Dayton. He had bugged her phone at *Post* headquarters downtown on 15th Street. He had bugged her phone at home. He'd planted bugs in her living room and her bedroom. He listened to her eat. He listened to her sleep. He listened to her talking to her dog. He listened to her fuck a television reporter after dinner at the Georgetown restaurant 1789. He broke into her home regularly and raided her computer files. A former NSA codebreaker, also employed by Mitchell Elliott, had cracked her childish encryption cipher, allowing Calahan to read her files at will. He was missing one thing, the finished product.

Elliott said, "Get inside her house as quickly as you can. We need to know exactly what we're dealing with."

"Yes, sir."

"And do it yourself, Mark. I don't want any fuck-ups on this one."

Calahan hung up the phone. He returned his attention to his equipment. He turned up the audio levels on the transmitters inside Susanna Dayton's home. Something caught his attention. He pulled on a black leather jacket and rushed out into the night.

He drove rapidly across Northwest Washington, from Kalorama into Georgetown, and parked behind the surveillance van on Volta Place. He rapped his knuckle on the rear door, and the technician let him inside. Two minutes later he spotted Susanna Dayton exiting Pomander Walk, dressed in an anorak and Lycra leggings, her dog at her side.

Calahan waited until she had vanished from sight. He jumped out of the van, crossed Volta Place, and entered Pomander Walk. He had made his own copy of her front door key. A few seconds later he was inside.

SUSANNA CROSSED WISCONSIN AVENUE and ran eastward along P Street. It was late and dark, and she had a running date with Elizabeth in the morning, but she had been cooped up inside her little house all day long, and she needed to do something to relieve the stress. Her neck ached from staring at the computer monitor. Her eyes burned. But after a mile or so she felt sweat break beneath her turtleneck. The magic of the run took hold, and the tension of the day slowly leaked from her body.

She pushed herself harder, flying over the red-brick sidewalk of P Street, past large, brightly lit town houses. Carson's paws clicked rhythmically beside her. She passed a 7-Eleven, then a small coffee shop. Jack and his new wife were perched atop two stools in the window, talking closely. She stared at them like an idiot as she ran past. Jack looked up, and his gaze met hers. Then his wife spotted her.

She turned away, mortified, and ran faster. *Idiot! Fucking idiot! Why didn't you look away?* And what the hell were they doing in Georgetown anyway? That was the whole point of Jack moving to Bethesda—so they wouldn't be bumping into each other all the time. God, why couldn't she just look away? Why did she have to stare through the glass like a schoolgirl with a crush? And why was her heart beating out of control? The answer to that was simple. She still loved Jack, and she always would.

Tears filled her eyes, blurring her vision. She ran faster. Carson struggled to keep pace. She pounded her feet savagely over the bricks. *God, why did he have to be sitting there? Fuck you, Jack. Fuck you!* She didn't see the tree root that had raised a portion of the side-walk. Didn't see the jagged edge of brick that had been forced upward. She felt a sudden pain in her ankle, saw the ground rushing up at her in the darkness.

SUSANNA LAY ON THE GROUND, eyes closed, gasping for breath. She felt as though she had been kicked in the stomach by a horse. She tried to open her eyes but could not. Finally, she felt someone shaking her shoulder, calling her name. She opened her eyes and saw Jack kneeling over her.

"Susanna, are you all right? Can you hear me?"

She closed her eyes again and said, "What the hell are you doing in Georgetown?"

"Sharon and I had a dinner engagement. Jesus, I didn't know I had to call and notify you first."

"No, you just startled me, that's all."

"You remember Sharon, don't you?"

She was standing behind Jack, stunning in a black cocktail dress and short black coat that showed off a pair of extraordinary legs. She was criminally skinny. The front of her coat was unbuttoned, revealing a pair of large rounded breasts. She was Jack's type: blond, blue eyes, big breasts, no brains.

She said, "I wish I could say it's a pleasure to see you, Sharon, but I'd be lying."

"We're going your way. Why don't you let us give you a lift?"

"No, thanks. I'd rather be left on the street for dead."

Jack reached down and took hold of her hand. Carson growled deep in his throat.

"It's all right, Carson. He's evil but harmless."

She got to her feet.

"There's a cab. Be useful, Jack, get him to stop for me."

Jack stepped out into the street. He flagged down the cab, and it pulled to the curb. Susanna limped over and climbed in the back, followed by the dog.

"See you around, Jack, Sharon."

She closed the door, and the cab drove off. She slumped down in the back seat, clutching her ankle. Her head leaned back against the cold leather of the seat. She sobbed quietly. Carson licked her hand. *God, why did she have to see me like that? Of all times and places, why like that?*

The cab stopped at Volta Place and Pomander Walk. She reached inside the front pouch of the anorak, took out a five-dollar bill, and handed it to the driver.

"Need any help?" he asked.
"No, I'll be fine, thanks."

THE COMPUTER WAS STILL ON when Mark Calahan climbed the staircase and entered the second-floor bedroom that Susanna used as a study. He sat down, removed a floppy from his jacket pocket, and inserted it into the disk drive of the desktop. He knew her system well now—the directories where she kept her notes and copy. He found the slug for the article and clicked on it. The encryption software asked for a password. Calahan provided it, and the story appeared on the screen.

Calahan did not bother to read it; he could do that later when he had more time. He closed the file again and typed in the command to copy it to the floppy drive. Once again the encryption software asked for the password. Once again Calahan provided it.

Since he was already inside the house, he decided to use the opportunity to gather additional intelligence. Calahan had followed the woman on several runs, and they never lasted less than thirty minutes. He had plenty of time.

Three new notepads lay on the desk next to the keyboard. He opened the cover on the first. The pages were filled with notes in Susanna Dayton's looping left-handed scrawl. He removed a microcamera from his pocket, switched on the desk lamp, and started shooting.

He was halfway through the second notepad when he heard the scrape of a key being shoved into the barrel of the front door lock. He cursed silently, switched off the light, and drew a silenced 9mm pistol from the waistband of his trousers.

SUSANNA'S RIGHT ANKLE HURT like hell. She closed the door behind her and sat down on the couch in the living room. She removed her shoe and her sock and inspected the injury. The ankle was swollen and purple. She limped into the kitchen, filled a Ziploc bag with ice, and took a bottle of beer from the refrigerator.

The pain reliever was in the bathroom medicine cabinet. She limped up the stairs and hobbled down the hall, leaning against the banister for support. She entered the bathroom, placed the beer on the edge of the sink, and opened the medicine cabinet. She found the pain reliever and washed down two tablets with the beer. She closed the cabinet door.

In the mirror she saw the reflection of a man standing behind her.

Susanna opened her mouth to scream. A gloved hand closed around her mouth, smothering her cries.

"Shut up, you fucking bitch, or I'll kill you," the man said through clenched teeth.

Susanna only struggled more. She put her weight on her injured ankle, raised her left foot, and dragged it down his shin, just the way she had been taught in her urban self-defense class. The man groaned in pain and loosened his grip. She pivoted to her right and struck backward with her right elbow. The blow landed on her attacker's cheekbone.

He relaxed his grip, and she broke away.

She stumbled into the hallway, then into the study. Reaching for the telephone, she realized the attacker had tampered with her computer and with her note-books.

She picked up the receiver.

The man appeared in the doorway, pointing a gun at her face.

"Put down the fucking telephone."

"Who are you?"

"Put down the telephone now, and I won't hurt you."

Carson charged up the stairs, barking wildly. He crouched in the hallway, baring his teeth at the in-truder. The man calmly raised the gun and shot the dog twice. The silenced weapon emitted virtually no sound. Carson yelped once, then went quiet.

"You bastard! You fucking bastard! Who the fuck are you? Did Elliott send you? Tell me, goddammit! Did Mitchell Elliott send you?"

"Put the phone down. Now!"

She looked down and punched the nine and the one.

The first shot struck her head before she could enter the last digit. She fell backward, still clutching the receiver, still conscious. She looked up. The man stood over her and pointed the gun at her head once more.

"Not in the face," she pleaded. "Please God, don't shoot me in the face."

His mask of rage softened for an instant. He low-ered the gun a few degrees, the barrel pointed at her chest. She closed her eyes. The gun emitted two brief bursts of sound. She felt one brief instant of excruci-ating pain, then a flash of brilliant light. Then only darkness.

. . .

CALAHAN REACHED DOWN, removed the receiver from her grasp, and replaced it in the cradle. The kill had been quick, but it had not been completely silent. He needed to work quickly. The police would tear the place apart. If they discovered evidence the woman was under surveillance, there was a chance they could connect the slaying to Elliott.

The cleanup job took less than five minutes. As he walked out the front door Calahan held the notepads, the two room bugs, the bug from the telephone, her handbag, and her laptop computer.

He headed out Pomander Walk, crossed Volta Place, and climbed into the surveillance van; he'd return later for his car. As he sped away he punched Mitchell Elliott's private number into a cellular phone.

"I'm afraid we have a bit of a problem, Mr. Elliott. I'll call you on a secure line in five minutes."

Calahan severed the connection and threw the phone against the windshield.

"Goddammit, why did she come back early? Fucking bitch!"

17. Brélés, France

DELROCHE CONCLUDED he needed a woman.

He reached that judgment after reviewing the disk a second time, this time on his desktop computer at the cottage in Brélés. Two of the three remaining targets were known womanizers. Delaroche knew their routines, knew where they ate and drank, knew where they did their hunting. Still, getting close to these targets would be difficult.

A woman would make it easier.

Delaroche needed a woman.

HE HAD ONE DAY to spend in Brélés. When he finished with the dossiers he went for a bicycle ride. The weather was good: clear, for November, light winds from the sea. He knew it would be a long time before he would ride again, so he pushed himself hard. He pedaled inland several miles, into the soft wooded hills of the Finistère, then down to the sea again. He paused at the ruins on the Pointe de Saint-Mathieu, then headed north along the coast back to Brélés.

The early afternoon he devoted to preparation. He cleaned and oiled his two best guns—a Beretta 9mm and the Glock—and checked and rechecked the firing mechanisms and the silencers. He had a third gun that he kept strapped to his ankle in a Velcro holster, a small Browning automatic designed to fit in a woman's purse. In the event a gun was not appropriate, he would carry a knife, a stout six-inch double-bladed knife with automatic release.

Next he gathered his false passports—French, Italian, Dutch, Spanish, Swedish, Egyptian, and American—and saw to his finances. He had the two hundred thousand francs from the gallery in Paris, and in Zurich he would collect the half million dollars. It was more than enough to finance the job.

He went out while it still was light and walked to the village. He bought bread from the boulangerie and sausage, cheese, and paté from Mademoiselle

Plauché. Didier and his friends were drinking wine at the café. He gestured for Delaroche to join them and, uncharacteristically, Delaroche agreed. He ordered more wine and ate bread and olives with them until the sun was gone.

That evening he had a simple meal outside on the stone terrace overlooking the sea. He had agreed to kill three more men in four weeks. Only a fool would accept such an assignment. He would be lucky to survive it. Even if he did, he might never be able to return to Brélés.

Delaroche had always been dispassionate about killing, but for the first time in longer than he could remember he felt an excitement rising within him. It was not unlike the feeling he had when he was sixteen, the night he killed for the first time.

He cleared away his dishes and washed them in the sink. Then, for the next hour, he systematically worked his way through the cottage and burned anything that suggested he ever existed.

DELAROCHE TOOK THE MORNING TRAIN from Brest to Paris and a midday train from Paris to Zurich. He arrived one hour before his bank closed. He left his small grip in a locker at the station and converted some of his French francs at a *bureau de change*.

He walked along a glittering street lined with brightly lit, exclusive shops. In a Gucci boutique he used cash to purchase a simple black attaché case. He told the clerk he did not require a bag, and a moment later he was walking along the sidewalk again, the attaché dangling from his right arm.

It was snowing lightly by the time he reached the austere front entrance of his bank. The only clue as to the nature of the establishment was the small gold plaque beside the door. Delaroche pressed the buzzer and waited while the security guard inspected him through the lens of the video camera mounted over the door.

The door lock snapped open, and he was let inside a small secure entrance room. He picked up a black telephone and announced he had an appointment with Herr Becker. Becker arrived a moment later, immaculately dressed and polished, shorter than Delaroche by a bald head that shone in the fluorescent light.

Delaroche followed him down a silent, dimly lit, beige-carpeted hall. Becker led him into another secure room and locked the door behind them. Delaroche felt claustrophobic. Becker opened a small vault and withdrew the money. Delaroche smoked while Becker counted it out for him.

The entire transaction took less than ten minutes. Delaroche signed the receipt for the money, and Becker helped him stack it neatly inside the case.

In the entrance room, Becker looked out at the street and said, "One can never be too careful, Monsieur Delaroche. There are thieves about."

"Thank you, Herr Becker, I think I can handle myself. Have a pleasant evening."

"Same to you, Monsieur Delaroche."

Delaroche did not want to walk a long distance with the money, so he took a taxi back to the station. He collected his bag from the locker and purchased a first-class ticket on an overnight train to Amsterdam.

DELAROCHE ARRIVED at Amsterdam's Centraalstation early the following morning. He moved quickly through the crowded hall, eyes red-rimmed from a night of fitful sleep, and stepped outside into the bright sunlight. The sight of the bicycles struck him: thousands of them, row upon row.

Delaroche took a taxi to the Hotel Ambassade in the Central Canal Ring and checked in as Señor Armiñana, a Spanish businessman. He spent an hour on the telephone, varying his languages in case the hotel operator might be listening, speaking in the coded lexicon of the criminal underground. He slept for a time, and by late morning he was seated in the window of a smoky café a short distance from his hotel.

The bookstore was there, across a busy square. It had developed a well-deserved reputation for snobbery, for it specialized in literature and philosophy and refused to stock commercial fiction or thrillers. The hotel clerk said the manager once physically removed a woman who dared to ask for the new book by a famous American romance writer.

It was a perfect place for Astrid. Twice, he caught a glimpse of her—stacking books in the front window, giving advice to a male customer who was clearly more interested in her than in any book she might be recommending.

Astrid had that effect on men, always did.

It was why Delaroche came to Amsterdam in the first place.

. . .

SHE WAS BORN ASTRID MEYER in the town of Kassel near the East German border. When her father walked out on the family in 1967, her mother abandoned his name and reclaimed her own, which was Lizbet Vogel.

After the divorce, Lizbet settled in a lakeside cottage in the mountains of Switzerland, outside Bern. It was familiar territory. Late in the war, in July 1944, her family fled Germany and sought refuge in a nearby village. It was there, alone in the mountains with her mother, that Astrid Meyer began her lifelong fascination with her grandfather, Kurt Vogel.

A heavy smoker his entire life, Vogel died of lung cancer in 1949, ten years before Astrid was born. In the end his wife, Gertrude, had tried to bring him down from the mountains, but Vogel believed the alpine air held his salvation, and he died at home gasping for breath.

Trude Vogel knew next to nothing of her husband's wartime work, but what she did know she told to Lizbet and Lizbet told to Astrid. He had given up a promising legal career in 1935 to join the Abwehr, the German secret service. He had been a close associate of the chief of the Abwehr, Wilhelm Canaris, who was executed for treason by the Nazis in April 1945. He had deceived Trude for years, telling her that he was Canaris's legal counsel. But late in the war he admitted the truth—he had recruited agents and sent them to England to spy on the British.

Lizbet remembered the night.

Her father had moved the family to Bavaria, because Berlin was no longer safe. She remembered her father arriving at the house, very late, remembered his presence in her bedroom, framed against the faint light of the open doorway. Later, she remembered the sound of her mother and father talking softly in the kitchen, and the smell of her father's supper. And then she heard the sound of dishes shattering, the sound of her mother gasping. She and her twin sister, Nicole, crawled to the top of the stairs and looked down. Below, in the kitchen, they saw their parents and two men wearing the black uniforms of the SS. One man they did not recognize; the other was Heinrich Himmler, the most powerful man in Germany after Adolf Hitler.

For years Lizbet Vogel believed her father had been a Nazi, an ally of Himmler and the SS, a war criminal who had chosen to die in the mountains of Switzerland rather than face justice in his homeland. Her mother, she concluded, secretly believed the same. When her mother was dead, Lizbet told the story to Astrid, and Astrid grew up believing her grandfather was a Nazi.

Then, on an afternoon in October 1970, a man telephoned the cottage and asked if he could visit. His name was Werner Ulbricht, and he had worked with Kurt Vogel at the Abwehr during the war. He said he knew the truth about Vogel's work. Lizbet told him to come. He arrived an hour later—gaunt, pale as baker's flour, leaning heavily on a cane, a neat black patch over one eye.

They walked for a time—Werner Ulbricht, Lizbet, and Astrid—and then sat on the grassy bank of the lake and drank coffee from a thermos bottle. Despite the snap of autumn in the air, Ulbricht's face was bathed in sweat from the exertion. He rested for a time, sipping his coffee, and then told them the story.

Kurt Vogel was no Nazi; he hated them with a passion. He came to the Abwehr on condition he not be forced to join the Party, and Canaris had been more than happy to grant him his wish. He was not an in-house legal counsel to Canaris. He was an agent runner and a damned good one at that: meticulous, brilliant, ruthless in his own way. One of his agents in Britain was a woman. Together, they learned the most important secret of the war—the time and place of the invasion. They also learned that the British were engaged in a massive deception to conceal the truth. But in February 1944, Hitler fired Canaris and placed the Abwehr under the control of Himmler and the SS. Vogel kept his information to himself, and joined the anti-Hitler plotters of the *Schwarze Kapelle,* the Black Orchestra. When the July 20 coup attempt ended in disaster, many of the *Schwarze Kapelle* plotters were arrested and executed. Vogel fled to Switzerland.

Lizbet's eyes were damp when Ulbricht finished the story. She stared at the lake, watching the wind ripple the surface. "Who was the other man who came with Himmler to my mother's house?" she asked.

"He was Walter Schellenberg, a very senior officer in the SD. He took over the Abwehr when Canaris was fired. Your father deceived him about the invasion."

"The woman who was his agent . . . ?" Lizbet asked, voice trailing off. "Was he in love with her? Mother always thought he was in love with someone else."

"It was a long time ago."

"Tell me the truth, Herr Ulbricht."

"Yes, he loved her very much."

"What was her name?"

"Her name was Anna Katerina von Steiner. Your father forced her to become an agent. She never came back from England."

Astrid's obsessive fascination with her grandfather began that afternoon. Her own grandfather, an ally of Wilhelm Canaris, a brave *Schwarze Kapelle* resister who tried to rid Germany of Hitler! In the attic she found a chest of his things her mother had saved: old law books and a few ancient photographs, brittle with age, some clothing. She studied them for hours on end. When she was old enough she even imitated his appearance: the spiky hair that looked as though he had cut it himself, the pebble-lensed eyeglasses, the dour undertaker's suits. She tried to imagine the agent named Anna Katerina von Steiner, the woman he had been in love with. In her grandfather's papers Astrid could find no trace of her, so she painted a portrait of Anna in her imagination: beautiful, brave, ruthless, violent.

When she was eighteen, Astrid returned to Germany to attend university in Munich and immediately became involved in leftist politics. She believed Nazis were still running Germany. She believed the Americans were occupiers. She believed industrialists had enslaved workers. She imagined what her grandfather, the great Kurt Vogel, would have done. He would join the resistance, of course.

In 1979 she gave up her studies at the university and joined the Red Army Faction. The leaders said she would have to give up her real name and choose a nom de guerre. She chose Anna Steiner and vanished into the world of terrorism.

SHE WAS LIVING ON A HOUSEBOAT on the Prinsengracht. At three o'clock in the afternoon she walked out of the bookstore, freed her bicycle from the rack, and set out across the square.

Delaroche signaled the waiter for a check.

SHE WALKED FOR A TIME, pushing the bike, obviously in no hurry. Delaroche trailed softly after her. She had changed little in the years since he had seen her last. She was tall and vaguely awkward, with beautiful but graceless legs and long hands that seemed forever in search of a comfortable resting place. Her face was from another time and place: luminous white skin, broad cheekbones, a large nose, eyes the color of mountain lake water. Her hair always changed with her mood and her politics, but now, in early middle age, it had returned to its natural state: long, blond, held back by a plain black clasp.

He followed her north along the Keizersgracht. She crossed the canal at Reestraat, then headed north again along the Prinsengracht. She passed into the shadow of the Westerkerk, the site of Rembrandt's unmarked grave. Delaroche increased his pace, closing the distance between them. Hearing his footfalls, she spun quickly, hand reaching inside her handbag, alarm on her face.

Delaroche took her gently by the arm.

"It's only me, Astrid. Don't be afraid."

.   .   .

KRISTA WAS FORTY-FIVE FEET LONG with a wheelhouse aft, a slender prow, and a fresh coat of green and white paint. It was tied up next to a boxy barge, and to get aboard Astrid and Delaroche had to scamper across the neighbor's aft deck. The inside was clean and surprisingly large, complete with a galley kitchen, a salon, and a bedroom in the prow. The weak light of late afternoon trickled through a pair of skylights and a row of portholes along the gunwale.

Delaroche sat in the salon, watching Astrid as she busied herself with coffee in the galley. They spoke Dutch, for she was passing herself off as a divorcée from Rotterdam and didn't want the neighbors to hear her chattering in German. Like all Amsterdammers, she was obsessive about her bicycle. She had lost four to thieves since settling in the city. She told Delaroche about the day she was strolling along the Singel and came upon a man selling used bicycles. Among the stock Astrid spotted one of her missing bikes. She told the man it was hers and demanded he give it back. He said she was crazy. She looked beneath the seat and found the name tag she had placed there. He said she was a liar. She grabbed hold of the bicycle and announced she was taking it back. He tried to stop her. She lashed sideways with an elbow, breaking his larynx, and then shattered his jaw with a vicious roundhouse kick. She picked up the bike and strolled away to a chorus of cheers, the heroine of every Amsterdammer who had ever lost a bike to the black market.

She carried the coffee to the salon and sat down across from Delaroche. She removed the clasp from her hair and allowed it to fall about her shoulders. She was a stunningly attractive woman who had learned to conceal her beauty in order to blend into her surroundings. For a moment he enjoyed just looking at her.

"So what brings you to Amsterdam, Jean-Paul? Business or pleasure?"

"You, Astrid. I need your help."

She shook her head slowly and lit a cigarette. Delaroche anticipated she might be unwilling to work with him. She had killed often, and she had paid a very high price—a life spent underground on the run from every secret service and police force in the West. She was more settled than she had ever been, and now Delaroche was asking her to undo it all.

"I've been out of the game for a long time, Jean-Paul. I'm tired of killing. I don't enjoy it like you do."

"I don't enjoy it. I do it because I'm paid money, and it's all I know how to do. You were very good at it once."

"I did it because I believed in something. There's a difference. And look at what it's gotten me," she said, gesturing at her surroundings. "Oh, I suppose it could be worse. I could be in Damascus. Jesus, that was awful."

Delaroche had heard she'd spent two years hiding in Syria, courtesy of Hafiz al-Assad and his intelligence service, and another two years in Libya as the guest of Mu'ammar Gadhafi.

"I'm offering you a way out, a chance to put it all behind you, and enough money to live comfortably somewhere quiet for the rest of your life. Do you want to hear more?"

She crushed out her cigarette and immediately lit another. "Damn you."

He rose and said, "I'll take that as a yes."

"How many people are we going to kill?"

"I'll be back in a half hour."

HE WENT BACK to his hotel, packed, and checked out. Thirty minutes later he was climbing down the companionway of the *Krista,* clutching his small overnight bag and a nylon case holding his laptop computer. They sat in the salon again, Delaroche hunched over his computer, Astrid perched atop an ottoman. Delaroche went through the targets one by one. Astrid sat still as a statue, legs folded beneath her, one long hand cupping her chin, another holding a cigarette. She said nothing, asked no questions, for like Delaroche she had the gift of a flawless memory.

"If you help me, I will pay you one million dollars," Delaroche said, at the conclusion of the briefing. "And I will help you settle somewhere safe and a little more pleasant than Damascus."

"Who's the contractor?"

"I don't know."

She raised an eyebrow. "That's not like you, Jean-Paul. They must be paying you a great deal of money." She drew on the cigarette and blew a slender stream of smoke at the ceiling. "Take me to dinner. I'm hungry."

THEY HAD BEEN LOVERS once, a long time ago, when Delaroche assisted the Red Army Faction with a particularly difficult assassination. They went back to the *Krista* after dining in a small French restaurant overlooking the Herengracht. Delaroche lay on the bed. Astrid sat down next to him and silently undressed.

It had been many months since she had brought a man to her bed, and she took him very quickly the first time. Then she lit candles, and they smoked cigarettes and drank wine as rain rattled on the skylight above their bodies. She made love to him a second time very slowly, drawing his body into her long arms and legs, touching him as though he were made of crystal. Astrid liked to be on top. Astrid liked to be in control. Astrid trusted no one, especially her lovers. For a long time, she lay pressed against his body, kissing his mouth, staring into his eyes. Then she rose onto her knees, legs straddling his body, and it was as if Delaroche was no longer there. She toyed with her hair, she stroked the nipples of her small, upturned breasts. Then her eyes closed, and her head rolled back. She pleaded with him to come inside her. When he did she convulsed several times, then fell forward onto his chest, her body damp with sweat.

After a moment, she rolled onto her back and watched rain running over the skylight.

"Promise me one thing, Jean-Paul Delaroche," she said. "Promise me you won't kill me when you're finished with me."

"I promise I won't kill you."

She rose onto her elbow, looked into his eyes, and kissed his mouth.

"Have you seen Arbatov lately?"

"Yes, in Roscoff a few days ago."

"How is he?" she asked.

"Same as ever," Delaroche said.

18. Washington, D.C.

ELIZABETH OSBOURNE WAITED on the corner of 34th and M streets, jogging in place, blowing on her hands against the cold morning air. She looked at her watch. Susanna was five minutes late. She had many faults, but tardiness was not one of them. She walked across the street to a pay phone and punched in Susanna's home number. The answering machine picked up.

"Susanna, it's Elizabeth. Pick up if you're there. I'm waiting for you on the corner. I'll give you a few more minutes, then I have to get going. I'll try you at work."

She dialed Susanna's desk at the *Post*. Her voice mail picked up.

Elizabeth hung up without leaving a message.

She looked up 34th Street but saw no sign of Susanna or Carson.

She called home and checked her machine to see if Susanna had left a message there. The answering machine told her she had one message. She punched the access code, but it was only Max telling her a lunch meeting had been canceled.

She hung up, thinking, Dammit, where the hell is she?

She thought of the phone call from Susanna last night. She was about to break a big story about Mitchell Elliott and Samuel Braxton. Maybe she was

on the phone, working the story. Maybe she was talking to her editors.

She turned and jogged up 34th Street. At Volta
Place she turned right and then made another right
into Pomander Walk. She bounded up the steps to
Susanna's house and rang the bell.

There was no answer.

She hammered on the wooden door with the side
of her fist. Again, there was no answer and no sound
from within the house. Carson was ever vigilant; he
usually started barking *before* Elizabeth knocked on
the door. If the dog were inside he'd be barking his
head off.

She turned around and saw lights burning inside
Harry Scanlon's house. She crossed the walkway
and knocked on the door. Scanlon answered in his
bathrobe.

"I'm sorry to bother you, Harry, but Susanna and
I were supposed to go for a run, and she stood me up.
It's just not like her. I'm worried. Do you still have
her key?"

"Sure, hang on a sec."

Scanlon disappeared into the house and came
back a moment later with a single key.

"I'll give you a hand," he said.

They went back to Susanna's front door. Scanlon
shoved the key into the lock and pushed open the
door.

Elizabeth called out, "Susanna!"

There was no answer.

She looked around the living room and the
kitchen. Everything seemed normal. She started up

the stairs, calling Susanna's name, Scanlon behind her.

When she reached the landing she saw the dog.

"Oh, God! Susanna! Susanna!"

She stepped over the body of the dog and looked in the bathroom. The white tile floor was covered with glass where a beer bottle had fallen and shattered. Elizabeth walked a few more steps down the hall and looked into the study.

She turned away and screamed.

ELIZABETH SAT on the front steps of Harry Scanlon's house, a woolen blanket wrapped around her shoulders. A half-dozen Metropolitan Police cruisers, red and blue lights flashing, choked Volta Place. The crime scene truck had arrived, and the technicians were poring over the inside of Susanna's house. She tried to call Michael, but he had not answered his phone. She left an emergency message with the operator and Harry Scanlon's number.

She thought, Dammit, Michael, I need you.

Elizabeth pulled the blanket about her tightly, but the shaking wouldn't stop. She closed her eyes, but she saw Susanna's shattered body sprawled on the floor, and she saw the blood. *God, so much blood!* She realized someone was calling her name. She opened her eyes and saw a tall fair-skinned African-American with striking green eyes standing before her. His police shield hung from the pocket of his blue double-breasted suit coat.

"Mrs. Osbourne, I'm Detective Richardson, Homicide. I understand you discovered the body."

"Yes, I did."

"What time?"

"Between seven-fifteen and seven-twenty, I believe."

"You knew the victim?"

Elizabeth thought, *The victim.* Susanna had already been robbed of her name. Now she was just *the victim.*

"We were best friends, Detective. I've known her for twenty years. We were supposed to go running this morning. When she didn't show up, I came looking for her. I got the key from the neighbor and went inside."

"Anything look out of the ordinary to you?"

"Except for her body, no."

"I'm sorry, Mrs. Osbourne. Where did she work?"

"She was a reporter for *The Washington Post.*"

"I thought the name sounded familiar. Worked at the White House for a while, right? Used to be on the roundtable show on TV."

Elizabeth nodded.

"This may sound like a strange question, but do you know anyone that would want to kill her?"

"Not a soul."

"Anything unusual going on in her life?"

"No."

"Any angry boyfriends? Jilted lovers?"

Elizabeth shook her head.

"Husband?"

"He's remarried."

"How's their relationship?'

"I work with him, Detective. He's a partner at my firm. He's a shit, but he's not a murderer."

"We can't find a purse. Did she carry one?"

"Yes, she always left it on the kitchen counter."

"It's not there."

"Who did this?"

"Impossible to say. Looks like someone was inside the house and she surprised him. She had jogging clothes on, but one of her shoes had been removed. Looks like she may have twisted her ankle. Dog was wearing a leash."

"So they shot her."

"A lot of people in this town would rather kill someone than leave a witness behind who could identify them later." He said this matter-of-factly. He reached out and put a hand on her shoulder. "I'm very sorry, Mrs. Osbourne. Here's my card. If you think of anything else, let me know."

ELIZABETH HEARD THE TELEPHONE ringing inside the house. Harry Scanlon came to the door, eyes red. "It's Michael," he said.

Elizabeth rose and walked inside, unsteady on her feet. "Michael, come home quickly. I need you."

"What happened? Why are you at Harry's?"

"Susanna's dead. Someone shot her in her house. I found her. Oh, God, Michael—" Her voice choked with tears. "Please come home, Michael. Please hurry."

"Stay there. I'll come get you."

"No, meet me at home. I need to walk. I need some air."

She looked out the window and saw Susanna's body, wrapped in a white sheet, being taken from the house on a stretcher. She had maintained her composure until then, but the sight of Susanna like that broke down the last of her strength.

"Elizabeth, are you there? Elizabeth, talk to me."

"They're just taking her away. Oh, God, poor Susanna! I just keep thinking about what she must have gone through before she died. I can't stop thinking about it."

"Get out of there. Go home. It will make you feel a little better. Trust me."

"Hurry."

"I will."

She hung up the telephone. Scanlon was holding a floppy disk. "Well, I guess she won't be needing this." He paused, his eyes filling with tears. "God, I can't believe I said that."

"What is it?"

Scanlon explained their system—how Susanna always made extra copies of her work and left them through his door slot. "She was paranoid about it."

"I know. In law school, she kept her papers in the refrigerator because she read somewhere that refrigerators could withstand fire." Elizabeth smiled at the memory. "God, I miss her so much. I can't believe this is happening."

Scanlon laid the disk on the kitchen counter.

"I found it when I came home last night. She must have slipped it through my door when she went out for her run. Funny, I always told her she was a fool to run at night, but she got killed in her own home."

Elizabeth thought about the call from Susanna last night. She had been working on an important story all day. Whatever she was writing was probably on that disk.

Elizabeth said, "Can I have that?"

"Sure, but you'll never be able to read it."

"Why?'

"Because she used encryption software. Like I told you, she was paranoid about people reading her stuff."

"You don't know the password?"

"No, she never told me. I would have thought she'd tell you."

Elizabeth shook her head. "What about her editors at the *Post*?"

"No way. She distrusted everyone, especially the people she worked with."

"Let me have it," Elizabeth said. "I have a friend who knows something about these things."

ELIZABETH SHOWED MICHAEL THE DISK as they lay in bed, surrounded by tousled linen. Michael lit a cigarette and turned the disk over in his hand. Elizabeth laid her head on his tan stomach, trailing a finger through the patch of dark hair at the center of his chest. She felt guilty about making love at a time like this. When he came home she wanted to be close to him. She wanted to hold him and never let him out of her sight. She was frightened, scared to death by what had happened to her friend, and she was afraid to let go of him. She held him; she kissed his lips and his eyes and his nose. She undressed him and made love to him, slowly, gently, as if she never wanted it to end. Now she lay close to him, watching rain streaming down the bedroom windows.

"Harry says it's encrypted."

"That's not a problem. All we need to do is figure out the keyword."

"How do you intend to do that?"

"People are lazy. They use birth dates, addresses, all sorts of words and numbers that they can remember easily. You know more about Susanna than anyone alive."

"Do you need special software?"

"I have it on my computer."

"Let's go."

They put on bathrobes and walked down the hall to Michael's study. Michael sat down at the desk. Elizabeth stood behind him, hands draped over his shoulders.

"Birth date?"

"November seventeenth, 1957."

Michael typed in the numerical version: 11-17-57. The screen read:

ACCESS DENIED—INCORRECT PASSWORD.

Michael said, "Birth date backward."

The computer made the same response.

"Address. . . . Address backward. . . . Telephone number. . . . Telephone number backward. . . . Work phone. . . . Work phone backward. . . . First name. . . . First name backward. . . . Middle name. . . . Middle name backward. . . . Last name. . . . Last name backward. . . ."

Elizabeth said, "This could take forever."

"Not forever."

"I thought you said it was going to be easy."

"I said it wouldn't be a problem. Parents' names?"

"Maria and Carmine."

"Maria and Carmine?"

"She's Italian."

"She *was* Italian."

Michael worked steadily for the next two hours. He learned more about Susanna's life than he ever thought possible: boyfriends, hometown, bank, favorite movie, favorite book. He tried them all—forward, backward, and sideways—and nothing worked.

"What was the dog's name?'

"Carson."

"Why Carson?"

Elizabeth smiled. "Because she was an insomniac, and she loved *The Tonight Show.*"

Michael typed CARSON. Nothing. He tried JOHNNY. Nothing. He tried DOC and ED. Nothing.

"She had the last two shows on tape. She watched them a hundred times."

"Who was on the last show?"

"It was just Johnny, remember? He just talked to the audience."

"What about the show before?"

"Bette Midler. Jesus, she was crazy about Bette Midler."

Michael typed BETTE. Nothing. MIDLER. Nothing. He typed them backward. Nothing.

He slammed his palm on the desk.

"Move out of the way," Elizabeth said.

She leaned over his shoulder, typed THE ROSE, and struck the ENTER key. The computer hesitated for a few seconds, and then the last thing Susanna Dayton ever wrote appeared on the screen.

Michael said, "Jesus Christ."

19. Amsterdam

THE HOUSEBOAT ON THE PRINSENGRACHT had taken on the appearance of a military operations room. Delaroche briefly considered returning to Brélés, but it was a village, with a village's inclination to gossip, and he knew the presence of a tall blond woman would arouse unwelcome interest among Didier and his cohorts. Besides, the *Krista* provided a relaxing and secluded atmosphere to plan the assassinations. On the walls he hung large-scale street maps of the cities where he would carry out the killings: London, Cairo, Washington. He rose early each morning and worked while Astrid slept. Then they spent two hours together, talking and planning, before she left for the bookshop at ten o'clock.

By the afternoon the walls would close in on him, so he would borrow Astrid's appalling bicycle and pedal the narrow streets of the canal rings. He found an art supply shop, purchased a small watercolor kit, and produced several fine paintings of the bridges and the boats and the gabled houses overlooking the canals. On the fourth day a bitter cold front pushed in from the North Sea. For the next two days the *Krista* was filled with the playful screams and shouts of hundreds of skaters gliding over the frozen surface of the Prinsengracht.

Each evening he would collect Astrid from the bookshop and take her to a different restaurant. Afterward they would stroll the windswept canals and drink De Koninck beer in the cannabis-scented bars of the Leidseplein. She made love to him for two nights, then turned her back to him for the next two. Her sleep was fitful, troubled by nightmares. On the night before their departure she awoke in a panic, bathed in sweat, grabbing for the small Browning automatic she habitually kept on the floor next to the bed. She might have blown off Delaroche's head had he not wrested the gun from her grasp before she could release the safety. She made frenzied love to him and begged him never to leave her.

The following morning broke cold and gray. They packed in silence and padlocked the *Krista*. Delaroche destroyed his paintings. Astrid telephoned the bookshop. She had a family emergency and needed a few days off. She would be in touch.

They took a taxi to the Centraalstation and caught the early-morning train to the town of Hoek van Holland. They took another taxi to the ferry terminal and had a late breakfast of bread and eggs at a small waterfront café. One hour later they boarded the car ferry for Harwich, across the North Sea, in Britain.

The passage usually took six hours in good weather, eight or more when the seas turned rough. On that day a cold winter storm pushed down from the Norwegian Sea. Astrid, who was prone to seasickness, spent much of the journey in the lavatory, violently ill, cursing Delaroche's name. Delaroche stayed outside on the observation deck, in the glacier-

scented air, watching the wind-driven rollers breaking across the prow of the ferry.

Shortly before their arrival, Astrid altered her appearance. She pinned her blond hair close to her
scalp and covered her head in a black shoulder-
length wig. Delaroche put on a baseball hat bearing
the name of an American cigarette and, despite the
weather, his Ray-Ban sunglasses.

The European Community makes the life of the
international terrorist much easier because, once inside a member nation, travel to the others is almost
free of risk. Delaroche and Astrid entered the United
Kingdom on Dutch passports, posing as unmarried
tourists, enduring only a cursory inspection of their
travel documents by a bored British official. Still,
Delaroche knew the British security forces routinely
videotaped all arriving passengers, regardless of
their passport. He knew he and Astrid had just left
their first footprints.

Night had settled over the English coastline by
the time Delaroche and Astrid boarded the train at
Harwich station. Ninety minutes later they arrived in
London.

FOR HIS BASE CAMP, Delaroche chose a small service
flat in South Kensington. He rented it for a week
from a company that specialized in providing flats
for tourists. His first act was to cancel the "service"
aspect of the arrangement; the last thing he needed
was a maid poking her nose into his things. The flat
was modest but comfortable, with a fully functioning
kitchen, a large sitting room, and a separate bed-

room. The telephone line was direct, no switch-boards involved, and there were large windows look-ing down onto the street.

They wasted no time. The target was an MI6 of-ficer named Colin Yardley, a fifty-four-year-old for-mer field officer who had served in the Soviet Union, the Mideast, and lately in Paris and was now await-ing forced retirement in a dead-end head-office desk job. He fit the profile of many intelligence officers at the end of their careers—burned out, bitter, divorced. He drank too much and put himself about with too many women. MI6 Personnel had told him in no un-certain terms to knock it off. Yardley had told the flunkies in Personnel to fuck off. It was all in De-laroche's report. Killing him would be easy. The challenge would be killing him the right way.

Despite his years in the field, Yardley had grown lazy and careless now that he was back in London. Each evening he took a taxi from MI6's riverside headquarters to a restaurant and bar in Sloane Square. It was there he did his hunting: young girls attracted by his sturdy gray good looks, wealthy West End di-vorcées, bored wives looking for a night of anony-mous sex. He arrived a few minutes after six o'clock and took his usual seat at the bar.

Astrid Vogel was waiting for him.

SHE WAS NOT the same woman Delaroche had seen in the Amsterdam bookshop ten days earlier. She had spent the afternoon at Harrods and the glittering shops in Bond Street, armed with a stack of De-laroche's money. She now wore a black cocktail dress, black stockings, a gold watch, and a double strand of exquisite pearls around her throat. The simple black clasp was gone from her hair, which had been trimmed and blown out by a fussy Italian stylist at a salon off Knightsbridge. Now it fell dramatically about her face and neck. Astrid knew how to play down her natural good looks, but she also knew how to attract attention when necessary.

Delaroche sat on a bench in Sloane Square, pretending to read a copy of *The Evening Standard* purchased from a newsstand outside the Sloane Square Underground station. He watched the performance inside the restaurant as pantomime. Astrid sits at the bar alone, the eternal cigarette burning between her long, slender fingers. Yardley, tall, gray, distinguished, asks if the seat next to her is free. A drink appears before Yardley automatically—his regular— and by his expression he thinks she is impressed by this. He gestures to the bartender to bring her another glass of white wine. Astrid, grateful, turns her body to face him, one long leg crossed suggestively over the other, her skirt riding high on her thigh. She belongs to him now. The frightened, lonely woman from the houseboat in Amsterdam is gone. She is a confident and cosmopolitan Dutchwoman whose husband makes money and ignores her too much and, yes, you can light my cigarette for me, darling.

After an hour of this, she rises and puts on her coat. They shake hands formally. She allows her fingers to linger on his an instant too long. He asks her where she's staying? The Dorchester. Can he give her a lift? No, that's not necessary. Can he get her a taxi? No, I can manage. Could he see her again before she leaves London? Come back tomorrow night, and if you're very lucky, darling, I'll be here.

SHE WALKED QUICKLY across the square, passing Delaroche, who was engrossed in his newspaper. She headed north, up Sloane Street. Delaroche watched Yardley hail a taxi and disappear inside. He stood up and strolled across the square to Sloane Street. Astrid was waiting for him.

"How did it go?"

"He would have fucked me right there at the bar if I had let him."

"So he was interested?"

"He asked me to come to his place for a drink and a take-away curry. I told him my husband might be a little upset if I wasn't back at the hotel by the time his meeting was over."

"Good, I don't want him to think you're a whore. Besides, he can't be as stupid as he looks. What about tomorrow night?"

"I left the strong impression I'd be back at the bar."

"He'll be back."

"Please, Jean-Paul, I just don't want to kiss him. His breath smells like shit."

"That part of the operation is in your hands."

"God, I hope he doesn't try to kiss me. I swear if he tries to kiss me, I'll kill him myself."

YARDLEY ARRIVED FIRST the next night. Delaroche, watching from his bench in Sloane Square, stifled

laughter as the highly trained British intelligence officer cast a series of expectant glances toward the door.
After half an hour Delaroche decided Yardley had
waited long enough for his reward. He signaled Astrid,
who was sitting in the window of a wine bar across the
square. Five minutes later she was striding through the
door of the restaurant, straight into the arms of Colin
Yardley.

SHE TAUNTED him. She toyed with him. She hung on
his every word. She ran her fingers through her hair.
She allowed him to buy her too many glasses of
Sancerre. She leaned forward so he could look down
her blouse and see she was wearing no brassiere. She
stroked the inside of his calf with the toe of her expensive Bruno Magli shoe. She tried several times to
leave—*my husband will want to know where I am,
darling*—but he would signal the bartender, and another glass of Sancerre would arrive, and somehow
she just couldn't find the willpower to drag herself
away from this terribly interesting man, and be a love
and get me another pack of cigarettes please. Marlboro Light 100s. Astrid the seductress. Astrid the
needy. Astrid the silly sex-starved Dutch tart who
would do anything for the attention of a middle-aged
Englishman with a Savile Row suit and an expensive
address. Delaroche admired her work from his van-
tage point in the square. He felt something else—a
flash of tenderness. He reached inside his coat and
felt for the butt of the Glock.

THE NEXT PART went according to plan. Astrid leaned
forward and whispered in his ear. Yardley paid the

check and collected their coats. Two minutes later, they were climbing into a taxi.

Delaroche watched them go. He rose and walked slowly after them, across Sloane Square, westward along the King's Road. He was not alarmed when the taxi disappeared from sight; he knew exactly where they were going, Yardley's home in Wellington Square.

Get him inside the house, Astrid. Tell him you're in a hurry. Tell him your husband will be crazy if you're gone too long. Take him straight to bed. Don't worry about the door. I'll take care of the door.

Delaroche turned left off the King's Road and entered the stillness of Wellington Square. The noise of the rush-hour traffic faded to a pleasant drone. A gentle rain began to fall. Delaroche walked quickly across the square, collar up, hands pushed deeply into his pockets.

Yardley's house was dark, perfect. The front door lock provided little challenge, and after a few seconds he was inside. He heard the sound of voices upstairs in the bedroom. Astrid had done her job well.

When Delaroche entered the room he found Yardley resting against the headboard, stripped to his shirt and his socks, masturbating while Astrid performed a slow striptease for him at the foot of the bed. For an instant Delaroche actually felt sorry for the man. He was about to die a most humiliating death.

Delaroche removed the Glock from the waistband of his trousers and stepped inside the room. Alarm registered instantly on Yardley's face. Astrid stopped dancing and stepped aside. Delaroche took her place at the end of the bed. Then his arm swung up, and he shot Colin Yardley rapidly, three times in the face.

The body tumbled from the bed onto the floor. Astrid stepped forward, kicked Yardley's head with the toe of her Bruno Magli shoe, and spit on his face. Astrid the revolutionary.

DELAROCHE INFORMED THE MANAGEMENT COMPANY that he would have to cut short his London vacation due to a family emergency. Before leaving the flat he logged on to the laptop and sent a brief encrypted message to his employers, informing them that the job had been carried out and please wire the specified funds to the specified account in Zurich. He and Astrid took a late train to Dover and spent the night in a quaint seaside bed and breakfast. In the morning they took the first ferry to Calais, where they hired a Renault car and drove northward along the Channel coast. By nightfall, they were back aboard the *Krista,* on the quiet Prinsengracht in Amsterdam.

THE BODY OF COLIN YARDLEY was discovered early that afternoon, as Delaroche and Astrid were passing from France into Belgium. MI6 Personnel Security became alarmed when he did not arrive for work and when repeated calls to his Wellington Square residence went unanswered. An MI6 team broke into the house shortly after 1 P.M. and discovered the body in the upstairs bedroom. The Metropolitan Police, however, were not informed of the death until four-fifteen.

The BBC reported the shooting death of an unidentified man on its *Nine O'Clock News.* By the time ITN went on the air at ten, the corpse had a name and a job: Colin Yardley, a mid-level Foreign Office clerk. During the program, a telephone call arrived at the news desk. The caller said the Provisional Irish Republican Army had carried out Yardley's murder. The caller provided the special recognition code to prove the claim was authentic.

By morning BBC reporters had uncovered Yardley's true occupation—that he was a career member of the Secret Intelligence Service, MI6.

Jean-Paul Delaroche listened to the BBC aboard the *Krista.* He switched off the radio when it was over and then settled in with his maps and his computer, plotting the next killing.

He telephoned Zurich. Herr Becker confirmed one million dollars had been wired into the account that morning. Delaroche instructed him to transfer the money to four Bahamian accounts, a quarter million for each.

The sun came out at midday. He borrowed Astrid's bicycle and spent the rest of the afternoon painting along the banks of the Amstel River, until the image of Yardley's exploded face was erased from his conscience.

20. McLean, Virginia

"I DON'T KNOW WHY Carter has to send you to London. Why the hell can't someone else go?"

Elizabeth had picked Michael up at headquarters and was driving him to Dulles Airport, twenty miles from Washington on the western edge of northern

Virginia's suburban sprawl. It was 7 P.M. The rush hour was technically over, but traffic still jammed the Capital Beltway. Elizabeth tended to tailgate when she was tense. As a result they were riding two feet from the rear bumper of a hunter-green Ford Explorer, traveling forty-five miles per hour.

"I thought you talked to him about our situation, Michael. I thought he agreed to let you work from New York. I thought he was going to let you cut back for a couple of weeks."

Michael thought, Maybe I should have taken an Agency car to the airport. The last thing he wanted to do was quarrel with his wife before boarding an international flight. He was not a superstitious man— nor was he a nervous flier—just realistic.

"I'll only be a day," he said. "Over and back, with a couple of meetings in between."

"If it's so routine why can't Carter send someone else?"

Elizabeth was not a litigator—she practiced law in the quiet of corporate shadows—but she was skilled at the art of cross-examination. She hammered on the horn. Michael knew he had just been declared a hostile witness.

"A British intelligence officer was murdered in London last night," Michael said calmly. "It may have something to do with a case I've been working for a long time."

"I read about it in the *Post* this morning. The IRA claimed responsibility. Since when have you dealt with the IRA? I thought your portfolio was strictly Arab terrorism."

"It is, but we think there may be a tie-in."

Michael hoped she would let it drop. The trip to London was his idea, not Carter's. Carter wanted the liaison work handled by an officer from London Station, but Michael convinced Carter to send him instead.

"In two days I have my eggs harvested. At that time they'll be fertilized with sperm. Hopefully it will be yours, Michael."

"I'll be back. Don't worry. And if something comes up we've got an ace in the hole. On ice."

Because of the nature of his work and the possibility of sudden mandatory travel, the doctors at Cornell Medical Center had recommended that some of Michael's sperm be frozen.

Elizabeth said, "I would like you there for emotional support, Michael. I thought you case officers were supposed to be good at that kind of thing. The least you could do is be there with me."

"I'll be there. I promise."

"Be careful what you promise, Michael."

She exited the Beltway, turning onto the Dulles access road. The traffic cleared away. Elizabeth accelerated to sixty-five. A full moon hung over the Virginia countryside, shrouded behind a transparent layer of cloud. Michael lit a cigarette and cracked the window. Elizabeth drove aggressively, changing lanes without signaling, tailgating, flicking her high beams at anyone who dared to drive under seventy in the passing lane. Michael knew the real reason for Elizabeth's bad temper. He was going to London to investigate an act of terrorism, and she knew it would trigger thoughts of

Sarah's murder. Her stubborn pride would not allow her to say it aloud, but it was written in the anxious expression on her face. She would be more upset if he told her the truth: He suspected Sarah and the British officer were murdered by the same man.

Elizabeth said, "I gave Tom Logan the material from Susanna's disk."

"Is he going to publish the piece?"

"He says he can't, not without confirming all the details first. He says the allegations are too explosive to print without being reviewed by their lawyers. And since the reporter who wrote it is now dead, there can't be a thorough review."

"What's he going to do?"

"He's assigned a team of his best reporters to match the story. Unfortunately, Susanna's not going to be much help to them from the grave. Her notes don't contain many clues about the identity of her sources. So Logan's team has to basically start from scratch."

"That could take a very long time."

"It took Susanna three months to do it alone."

They arrived at Dulles. Elizabeth drove to the departure level and pulled over to the curb. Michael climbed out and collected a lightly packed garment bag from the trunk. He closed it, then walked to the driver's side of the Mercedes. Elizabeth had let down the window and was leaning her head out, waiting for a kiss good-bye.

"Be careful, Michael."

"I will."

He waited until her taillights vanished into the darkness; then he went inside the terminal.

· · ·

MICHAEL CAME AWAKE as the jetliner slipped below the cloud cover and descended into the gray London morning. London Station had offered to send a car, but Michael wanted as little to do with London Station as possible, so he took a taxi instead. He pulled down the window. The raw air felt good against his face, despite the stink of diesel fumes. London had been his home for eight years; he had made the journey from Heathrow to central London a thousand times. The dreary western suburbs sweeping past him were more familiar than Arlington or Chevy Chase.

He checked into his hotel, a modest independent establishment on Knightsbridge, overlooking Hyde Park. He preferred it because each room came with a small sitting room in addition to the bedroom. He ordered a full English breakfast and picked at it until it was late enough to phone Elizabeth. He awakened her, and they had a disjointed two-minute conversation before she drifted back to sleep.

Michael was tired, so he slept until early afternoon. When he awoke, he dressed in a waterproof jogging suit. He hung the DO NOT DISTURB sign on the door and for insurance left a telltale, a tiny piece of paper, wedged between the door and the jamb. If it was still there when he returned, it was likely the room had not been entered. If it was gone, someone had probably been there.

He set out on the footpaths of Hyde Park under clouds the color of pewter, heavy with rain. Ten minutes into the run the skies opened up. The Londoners rushing past beneath windblown umbrellas glared at him as though he was an escaped mental patient.

After fifteen minutes his breath turned ragged, and he stopped to walk. Over the years he had been able to maintain his physical fitness, despite being a moderate smoker. But now the cigarettes were taking their toll. And Elizabeth was right—he was getting thicker around the waist.

He ran back to the hotel. The telltale fell to the floor as he opened the door to his room. He showered and changed into a blue business suit. He took a taxi to Grosvenor Square and flashed his identification to the Marine guard at the entrance. Michael felt uncomfortable in embassies; he was a NOC, through and through. When he was based in London he came to the embassy only in emergencies and only "black," meaning he arrived underground in the back of a van. He wished he didn't have to come at all, but Center doctrine demanded a courtesy call to the local chief of station.

The COS in London was a man named Wheaton, an unabashed Anglophile with a pencil-thin mustache, a Savile Row chalk-stripe suit, and an annoying habit of toying with a tennis ball when he didn't know quite what to say. Wheaton was old school: Princeton, Moscow, five years as head of the Russia desk before scoring the plum career-ending assignment in London. He said he had known Michael's father, but he didn't say he liked him. He also made it clear he didn't think London Station needed any help from the CTC on this one. Michael promised to brief him on his findings. Wheaton politely told Michael he'd like him to get out of town as quickly as possible.

• • •

THE TAXI DROPPED MICHAEL at the white Georgian terrace in Eaton Place. Helen and Graham Seymour
owned a pleasant apartment, and from the street
Michael could see them like actors on a multilevel
stage—Graham upstairs in the drawing room, Helen
below street level in the kitchen. He descended the
steps and rapped on the paned-glass kitchen door.
Helen looked up from her cooking and smiled broadly.
Opening the door to him, she kissed his cheek and
said, "God, Michael, it's been too long." She dumped
Sancerre into a goblet and thrust it into his hand. "Graham's upstairs. You boys can talk shop while I finish
supper."

Graham Seymour was fidgeting with the gas fire
when Michael entered the room. It was wood-paneled
and wood-floored, with an exquisite array of Oriental
rugs and Middle Eastern decorations. Graham stood
up, smiled, and stuck out his hand. They regarded
each other as only men of identical size and shape can
do. Graham Seymour was like Michael's negative.
Where Michael was olive complected, Graham was
fair. Where Michael was dark-haired and green-eyed,
Graham was blond and gray-eyed. Michael wore a
blue business suit; Graham was dressed for safari in
khaki trousers and a khaki bush shirt.

They sat down and talked about old times. They
had lived nearly identical lives. Like Michael, Graham's father had worked in intelligence—MI5's
Double Cross operation during the war, then MI6 for
twenty-five years after that. Like Michael, Graham
followed his father from posting to posting and

joined the Secret Intelligence Service immediately after graduating from Cambridge. The two men had worked side by side over the years, though Graham always functioned under official cover. They had developed a professional respect and personal friendship. Indeed, they were closer than either of their services would prefer if they knew.

The smell of Helen's cooking drifted upstairs into the drawing room.

"What's she making?" Michael asked cautiously.

"Paella," Graham said and frowned. "Perhaps you should run to the chemist's now before it closes."

"I'll be all right."

"You say that now, but you haven't had Helen's paella."

"That bad?'

"I don't want to spoil the surprise. Perhaps you should have some more wine."

Graham went downstairs to the kitchen, returning a moment later with glasses filled with white Bordeaux.

"Tell me about Colin Yardley."

Graham grimaced. "Curious thing happened a couple of months ago. A Lebanese arms dealer named Farouk Khalifa decided to set up shop in Paris. We found out about it and notified our French friends. They put Mr. Khalifa under watch."

"That was nice of the French."

"He sells weapons to people we don't like."

"He's a bad man."

"He's a very bad man. He opens up the bazaar and starts receiving clients. The French photograph everyone who comes and goes."

"I get the picture."

"In September a man calls on Mr. Khalifa. The French are unable to identify him, but they suspect he's a Brit, so they send us a copy of the photo by secure fax."

"Colin Yardley?"

"In the flesh."

"The top floor confronted him. They demanded to know what the fuck he was doing meeting with a chap like Khalifa. Yardley made up some bullshit story about how he was bored with his desk job and was itching to do field work again. He worked in Paris for a time. Said he was freelancing. The top floor weren't happy, to say the least. Yardley got his wrists slapped in a very big way."

"Jesus Christ."

"Now, guess which weapon Farouk Khalifa has in great abundance."

"According to our files, it's Stinger missiles." Michael drank some of the wine. "I don't suppose your service passed any of this along to my service?"

Graham shook his head. "We were a little embarrassed about it. You understand, don't you, Michael? The top floor just wanted it to go away, so they made it go away."

Helen appeared at the top of the stairs.

"Dinner's ready."

"Wonderful," Graham said a little too enthusiastically. "Well, I guess the video will have to wait."

HELEN SEYMOUR COOKED elaborately but dreadfully. She believed that "British cuisine" was an oxymoron, and her specialty was the food of the Mediterranean:

Italian, Greek, Spanish, North African. Tonight she served a ghastly paella of raw fish and burned shrimp, so spicy Michael felt dampness at the back of his neck as he forced fork after fork into his mouth. He bravely finished his first helping. Helen insisted he have another. Graham choked back laughter as his wife piled two heaping spoonfuls onto Michael's outstretched plate. "It's divine, isn't it?" Helen purred. "I think I'll have a little more myself."

"Once again, you've outdone yourself, darling," Graham said. He had learned long ago how to deal with his wife's unique brand of exotic cooking. He grabbed take-away sandwiches and hamburgers on the way home from work and devoured them descending into the Underground. Three years ago he professed a sudden devotion to bread. Each night Helen brought home new and different varieties, which Graham ate in vast amounts. He had grown pudgy around the middle from eating too many carbohydrates late at night. He scheduled important telephone calls at the dinner hour and pretended they were unexpected. Like an impetuous child, he had become a master at distributing uneaten food about his plate to create the illusion of consumption. For a time Graham refused to allow Helen to cook for guests; they entertained in restaurants instead. Now he took a certain pleasure at having friends for dinner, the way the condemned take comfort from companionship in the hours before death.

Graham dragged a chunk of coarse Spanish bread through a plate of virgin olive oil and shoved it into his mouth. "Helen, Michael and I have a little more work to do. Do you mind if we take coffee upstairs?"

"Of course not. I'll bring you dessert in a few minutes." She turned to Michael, a rapturous smile on her face. "Michael, I'm so glad you enjoyed the paella."

"Helen, I can't remember the last time I had a meal like that."

Graham choked on a crust of bread.

MICHAEL CAME OUT of the bathroom. Graham said, "You all right, mate? You look a little green around the gills."

"Jesus Christ, how do you eat like that every night?"

"You ready to watch a movie?"

"Sure."

They sat down on the couch in the drawing room. Graham picked up the remote control from the coffee table. "Mr. Yardley had another problem," he said. "He liked women."

"Did the Service know about this, too?"

"Yeah, Personnel told him to cool it. He told them to go fuck themselves. He was single, and he had a few years left till retirement, and he was going to enjoy himself."

"Good attitude."

"The Service discovered the body. We went in before the police and had a go at his house. We discovered the lovely Colin Yardley had installed a secret video taping system in his bedroom so he could record his conquests and replay them at his leisure. Had quite a collection, our Yardley. The watchers have been using them to relieve the boredom between assignments."

Graham aimed the remote at the video machine and pressed PLAY. The camera was mounted somewhere above the headboard. Yardley lay on the bed, undressed, slowly masturbating, while a tall woman performed a sultry striptease. She unbuttoned her blouse, ran her hands over her breasts and inside the waistband of her panty hose.

Graham froze the image.

"Who is she?" Michael asked.

"We think she's Astrid Vogel."

"According to our information, she's living in Damascus."

"Ours too. In fact, we thought she'd left the Red Army Faction altogether, which makes her involvement in this affair all the more puzzling." Graham pressed the remote, and the image came alive again. "Here's the good part. I won't spoil the ending."

Astrid Vogel's striptease grew more intense. Her hands were between her legs, her head rolled back, feigning ecstasy. "She's good," Graham said. "Damned good."

Helen walked in bearing a tray of coffee and apple tart. "Oh, isn't this lovely. I leave you boys alone for ten minutes and you run out and rent a porno flick."

She set the tray on the coffee table, gaze fixed on the screen. "Who is that creature?"

"A former RAF assassin named Astrid Vogel."

A look of terror flashed across Yardley's face.

Graham stopped the video. "This part's a little gruesome, my dear. Perhaps you should go downstairs."

Helen sat down on the couch.

"Suit yourself," Graham said, and started the video again.

A dark figure strode into the room, appearance shrouded by a billed hat and sunglasses. He reached behind his back, drew a silenced gun, and shot Colin Yardley rapidly three times in the face. Yardley's body tumbled from the bed. The woman stepped forward, kicked the corpse in the head, and spit on him.

Graham stopped the tape.

"Christ almighty," Helen said.

"It's him," Michael said.

"How can you tell? His face was covered the entire time."

"I don't need to see his face. I've seen him handle a gun. It's him, Graham. I'd stake my life on it. It's him."

"I KNOW I NEEDN'T say this, but the usual rules apply, Michael. The information I gave you is for your background purposes only. You may not share it with any member of your service or any other service."

"I'll sign a copy of the Official Secrets Act if that would make you sleep easier."

Michael turned up the collar of his coat and shoved his hands into his pockets. The rain had ended, and he wanted to walk. Graham had agreed to accompany him halfway. They drifted through the quiet Georgian canyons of Belgravia, the distant rush of evening traffic on the King's Road the only sound.

Michael said, "I want to talk to Drozdov."

"You can't talk to Drozdov. He's off limits to you. Besides, he says he's finished talking and wants to live out his days in peace."

"I have a theory about the assassin who killed Yardley, and I want to run it by him."

"Drozdov is *our* defector. We've shared the harvest with you. If you try to talk to him, you're going to find yourself in serious trouble with both our services."

"So I'll do it in an unofficial capacity."

"What's your plan? Just sort of bump into him and say, 'Hey, wait a moment. Aren't you Ivan Drozdov, former KGB assassin? Mind if I ask you a few questions?' Come on, Michael."

"I thought I'd use a slightly more subtle approach."

"If it falls apart, I'll deny any involvement. In fact, I'll denounce you as a Russian spy."

"I would expect nothing less."

"He's living in the Cotswolds. A hamlet called Aston Magna. He takes tea and reads the newspapers every morning in a café in Moreton, a few miles away."

"I know it well," Michael said.

"He's the one with the corgis and the knotted walking stick. Looks more English than Prince Philip. You can't miss him."

GRAHAM SEYMOUR WALKED MICHAEL as far as Sloane Street before saying good night and heading back to Eaton Place. Michael should have walked north, toward Hyde Park and his hotel, but instead he went south toward Sloane Square when Graham vanished from sight.

He crossed the square and drifted through the quiet side streets of Chelsea until he came to the Embankment, overlooking the Thames. The luxury flats above burned with light. The pavement shone with river mist. Michael had the place to himself except for a small bald man, who hurried past, hands rammed inside a battered mackintosh, limping like a toy soldier no longer in good working order.

He leaned against the railing, looked out at the river, then turned and stared toward Battersea Bridge, the bright lights of the Albert Bridge beyond. He could see Sarah walking to him, through darkness and mist, coal-black hair pulled back, skirt dancing across buckskin boots. She smiled at him as though he was the most important person on earth—as though she had been thinking about nothing but him all day. It was the same smile she gave him every time he entered her flat, every time he met her for drinks at her wine bar or for espresso at her favorite café.

He thought of the last time he was with her. It was the previous afternoon, when he popped by her flat and found her sprawled on the floor in a white leotard, slender torso bent over long bare legs. He remembered how she rose to him and kissed his mouth and pulled her leotard off her shoulders so he could touch her breasts. Later, in bed, she confessed to fantasizing about fucking him to relieve the boredom of her stretching exercises. How it always left her terribly tense and how she always had to solve the problem alone because he was working.

He fell completely in love with her that moment. He made love to her one last time. She lay on her back, perfectly still, eyes closed, face passive, for as long as she could, until the physical pleasure became too much and she opened her eyes and mouth and pulled his face to hers and kissed him until they came together. It was this image of her, and the sight of her flowing toward him in the light of the Chelsea Embankment, that was shattered by the man with the gun.

He remembered her face exploding, remembered her body crumbling before his eyes. He remembered the killer—pale skin, short-cropped hair, slender nose. He saw again the way he drew the silenced pistol from his waistband at the small of his back, the way the arm swung straight out, the way he fired three times without an instant of hesitation.

Michael went to her, even though he knew she was dead. Sometimes, he wished he had chased her killer, though he realized it probably would have cost him his life. Instead, he knelt beside her and held her, pressing her head against his chest so he couldn't see her ruined face.

It started to rain. He took a taxi back to the hotel. He undressed, climbed into bed, and telephoned Elizabeth. She must have sensed something in his voice, because she choked as she said good night and hung up. Michael felt a hot flash of guilt pour over him, as though he had just betrayed her.

21. London

EARLY THE FOLLOWING MORNING, Michael checked out of his hotel and rented a silver Rover sedan from a Hertz outlet north of Marble Arch. He entered the A40 near Paddington Station and drove westward against the early-morning rush. It was still dark, a gentle rain falling. Michael switched on the radio and listened to the 6 A.M. newscast on the BBC. The A40 turned to the M40 as he flashed through the northwest suburbs of London. Dirty dawn light came up as he rose into the gentle hills of the Chilterns. The complimentary Hertz map lay unopened on the passenger seat. Michael had no need for it; he knew the roads well.

Sarah's family had owned a large cottage in the Cotswolds village of Chipping Campden. Limestone walls, covered in clematis and variegated ivy, surrounded the cottage. Michael and she spent several weekends there during the months they were together. The countryside changed her. She shed the black leather uniform of her Soho clan. She wore faded jeans and sweaters in winter and girlish sundresses in summer. In the mornings they walked the footpaths outside the village, through pastures thick with sheep and pheasant. Afternoons they made love. In summer, when it was warm, they made love in the garden, concealed by limestone and flowers. Sarah liked it best outside. She liked the sensation of Michael inside her and the sun on her fair skin. Secretly she hoped people were watching. She wanted the world to know how their lovemaking looked. She wanted everyone to be jealous.

She danced, she modeled, she read many books. Sometimes she acted; sometimes she made photographs. Her politics were atrocious and as flexible as her long body. She was Labour, she was a communist. She was Green, she was an anarchist. She lived in a Soho room above a Lebanese take-away, strewn with secondhand clothing and leotards. She listened to the Clash and the Stones. She listened to recordings of ocean and forest noises and Gregorian chant. She was vegetarian, and the smell of grilling lamb from the take-away made her want to puke. To cover the smell she burned incense and candles. The first time she took Michael to her bed he had the uneasy sensation of making love in a Catholic church.

She introduced him to a world he never knew. She took him to strange parties. She took him to experimental theater. She took him to readings and exhibitions. She picked out different clothing for him. She couldn't sleep nights unless she made love to him first. She loved to look at their bodies in candlelight. "Look at us," she would say. "I'm so white, and you're so dark. I'm good, and you're evil."

His work bored her, and she never asked about it. The idea that someone would travel the world selling things seemed to confound her. She asked only where he was going and when he was coming back.

Adrian Carter was Michael's control officer. He was obligated to tell Carter and Personnel about the relationship with Sarah, but they would dig into her past—her politics, her work, her friends, her lovers— and they might very well uncover things Michael would rather not know. He kept Sarah secret from the Agency and the Agency secret from Sarah. He feared she would leave him if he told her the truth. He feared she would tell her friends, and his cover in London would be jeopardized. He was lying to his employer and his lover. He was happy and miserable at the same time.

. . .

HE WAS NEARING OXFORD. A white commercial Ford minivan had been shadowing him for twenty miles, staying three or four car lengths behind. It was possible the Ford was simply traveling the same direction, but Michael was trained not to believe in coincidence. He slowed and allowed traffic to pass.

The Ford remained in the same place.

He approached a roadside café and petrol station. He exited the motorway and parked outside the restaurant. The Ford followed and entered the petrol station. The driver climbed out and pretended to put air in the front passenger-side tire while he watched the Rover. Michael wondered who might be tailing him. Wheaton from London Station? Graham Seymour and MI6?

He went inside the café, ordered a bacon and fried egg sandwich and coffee, and went to the toilet. He collected the food, paid for it, and went back out. The Ford was still at the petrol station; the driver was preparing to put air in the rear tire.

Michael went into a public telephone and called his hotel. He told the woman at the desk that he had left a pair of valuable cuff links in the bathroom. He gave her a false address in Miami, which she dutifully took down while Michael watched the Ford. He hung up and climbed back inside the Rover. He started the engine and drove off, slipping into traffic on the motorway. He glanced in the rearview mirror while he ate the sandwich.

The Ford was there, three car lengths behind.

THE CAR FOLLOWED MICHAEL to Moreton-in-Marsh, a large village by Gloucestershire standards, straddling the intersection of the A44 and the A429. He pulled into a carpark outside a row of shops and climbed out. The Ford parked fifty meters away. The café was next to a butcher. Dead pheasant hung in the doorway. Michael thought of Sarah, sitting across from him with a plate of rice and beans and yellow squash, glaring at him as he pulled meat from the bones of a roasted Cotswolds pheasant. He went inside the café, ordered coffee and pastry from the plump girl behind the counter, and sat down.

Michael recognized Ivan Drozdov from Agency photographs. He was bald except for a gray monkish fringe, his tall frame bent over a stack of morning newspapers. Gold reading glasses rested on the end of his regal nose, gray eyes squinted against the smoke of a cigarette poking from thin lips. He wore a gray rollneck sweater and a green field jacket with a corduroy collar. A pair of matching corgis groomed themselves next to Wellington boots caked with fresh mud.

Michael carried his food to the table next to him and sat down. Drozdov looked up briefly, smiled, and returned to his newspapers. Several minutes passed this way, Michael drinking tea, Drozdov reading *The Times* and smoking.

Finally, without looking up, Drozdov said, "Are you ever going to speak, or are you just going to sit there and annoy my dogs?"

Michael, surprised, said, "My name is Carl Blackburn, and I was wondering if I might have a word with you."

"Actually, your name is Michael Osbourne. You work for the CIA's Counterterrorism Center in Langley, Virginia. You used to be a field agent, until your lover was murdered in London and the Agency brought you inside."

Drozdov carefully folded the newspaper and fed pieces of cake to the dogs.

"Now, if you'd like to talk about something, perhaps we could take a walk," he said. "But don't lie to me ever again. It's insulting, and I don't take well to insults."

"DO YOU REALIZE you're under surveillance, Mr. Osbourne?"

They were walking along a one-lane track toward the village of Aston Magna, where Drozdov had taken up residence when the Soviet Union crumbled and the threat of assassination from his old KGB masters vanished. He was taller than Michael by a narrow head, and like many large men he stooped slightly to shrink himself. He walked slowly, hands clasped behind his back, head down as if looking for a lost valuable. The dogs walked a few meters ahead, like countersurveillance. Michael, by nature a fast walker, struggled to keep pace with Drozdov's loping disjointed gait. He wondered how the old man had spotted the surveillance, for Michael had never seen him look for it.

"Two men," Drozdov said. "White Ford van."

"I spotted them on the M-Forty, a few miles outside London."

"Does anyone know you were coming to see me?"

"No," Michael lied. "I'm not here as a representative of the CIA, and I didn't request permission from the British. It's strictly a personal matter."

"You've placed yourself in a rather difficult position, Mr. Osbourne. If you do something I don't care for, all I need do is pick up the telephone and ring my handler at MI-Six, and you'll be in a good deal of trouble."

"I know. Obviously, as a professional courtesy, I ask that you not do so."

"It must be rather important."

"It is."

"I suspect those men in the white van have a long-range microphone. Perhaps we should walk someplace they can't follow."

They turned onto a footpath bordering a field of dead winter grass. In the distance, hills rose into low cloud. A gang of sheep bleated at them along the fence line. Drozdov scratched the thick wool of their heads as they passed. The path was muddy with the night's rain, and after a few paces Michael's suede Italian loafers were ruined. He turned around and looked back. The van was heading back toward Moreton.

"I think we can speak now, Mr. Osbourne. Your friends seem to have given up the chase."

For ten minutes Michael did all the talking. He ran through the list of assassinations and terrorist attacks. The Spanish minister in Madrid. The French police official in Paris. The BMW executive in Frankfurt. The PLO official in Tunis. The Israeli businessman in London. Drozdov listened intently, sometimes nodding, sometimes grunting quietly. The dogs tore across the meadow and scattered pheasant.

"And what is it you want to know exactly?" Drozdov asked, when Michael had finished.

"I want to know whether the KGB carried out those hits."

Drozdov whistled for his dogs. "You're to be commended, Mr. Osbourne. Oh, you've missed quite a few, but you've made an excellent start."

"So they were KGB hits?"

"Yes, they were."

"Were they carried out by the same man?"

"Absolutely."

"What is his name?"

"He had no name, Mr. Osbourne. Only a code name."

"What was his code name?"

Drozdov hesitated. He had defected, betrayed his service. But revealing code names was the intelligence equivalent of breaking the Mafia's *omertà*.

Finally, he said, "October, Mr. Osbourne. His code name was October."

THE SUN APPEARED BRIEFLY between broken clouds, warming the countryside. Michael unbuttoned his coat and lit a cigarette. Drozdov followed suit, brow furrowed as he smoked, as if searching for the best place to start the story. Michael had handled many agents. He knew when it was best to push and when it was best to sit back and just listen. He had no leverage over Drozdov; Drozdov would talk only if he wanted to talk.

"We weren't very good at killing people, contrary to popular belief in the West," Drozdov said finally. "Oh, inside the Soviet Union we were very efficient. But outside the Soviet bloc, in the West, we were quite awful when it came to wet affairs. One of our top assassins, Nikolai Khokhlov, had second thoughts while attempting to kill a Ukrainian resistance leader and defected. We tried to kill him and botched that job, too. For the longest time the Politburo simply gave up assassination as a tool of the trade."

Drozdov dropped his cigarette butt in the mud and ground it out with the toe of his Wellington.

"In the late 1960s, this changed. We looked at the West and saw internal strife everywhere: the Irish, the Basques, the German Baader-Meinhof Gang, the Palestinians. Also, we had our own business to attend to—dissidents, defectors, you understand. Assassinations, as you know, were handled by Department Five of the First Chief Directorate. Department Five wanted a highly trained assassin, permanently based in the West, who could carry out killings on short notice. That assassin was October."

Michael said, "Who is he?"

"I came to Department Five after he was in place in the West. His file said nothing of his real identity. There were rumors, of course. That he was the illegitimate son of a very senior KGB officer: a general, perhaps the chairman himself. These are all rumors, nothing more. He was taken by the KGB at a very early age and given intensive schooling and training. In 1968, as a teenager, he was sent into the West through Czechoslovakia, posing as a refugee. He eventually moved to Paris. He posed as a homeless street urchin and was taken in by a Catholic orphanage. Over the years he established an airtight French identity. He went to French schools, had a French passport, everything. He even endured his mandatory service in the French army."

"And then he started killing."

"We used him primarily to promote instability in the West, to make problems for Western governments. He killed on both sides of the divide. He stirred the pot, so to speak. Blew on the flames. And he was very good at his job. He prided himself on the fact that he never botched a single assignment. He wouldn't use any of the devices we offered to make his work easier, the cyanide-tipped bullets or the weapons that dispensed poison gas. He developed his own signature method of killing."

"Three bullets to the face."

"Brutal, effective, quite dramatic."

Michael had seen his work close up; he didn't need a description from Drozdov of the effect of the assassin's chosen method. "Did he have a control officer?" Michael asked evenly.

"Yes, he would only work with one officer, a man named Mikhail Arbatov. I tried to replace Arbatov once, but October threatened to kill the man. Arbatov was the closest thing to family October ever had. He trusted no one except Arbatov, and he barely trusted him."

"A Mikhail Arbatov was murdered in Paris recently."

"Yes, I saw that. The police said street thugs probably killed him. The newspaper accounts described him as a retired Russian diplomat living in Paris. There's one thing I've learned in this life, Mr. Osbourne. You can't trust what you read in the newspapers."

"Who killed Arbatov?"

"October, of course."

"Why?"

"That's a very good question. Perhaps Arbatov knew too much about something. If October feels threatened, he kills. It's the only thing he knows how to do. Except paint. He's rumored to be quite talented."

"He's gone into private practice? He's a contract killer now?"

"Among the best in the world, very much in demand. Arbatov was his agent. They'd grown quite rich together. I hear there was a good deal of jealousy over the way Arbatov had cashed in on October's talents. Arbatov had many enemies, many people who would wish him harm. But if you're looking for his killer, I would start with October."

The sun vanished once more, and the clouds thickened, black with rain. They passed a large limestone manor house surrounded by broad green lawns. Michael told him about Colin Yardley. About the videotape of the killing. About Astrid Vogel.

Drozdov shook his head slowly. "You'd think someone in Yardley's line of work would know the pitfalls of placing a camera in a bedroom. I must say it's the one thing about growing old I don't mind. The eternal craving for female flesh has finally left me in peace. I have my dogs and my books and my Cotswolds countryside."

Michael laughed quietly.

"He worked once with the Red Army Faction. He met Astrid Vogel on that assignment. She spent many years in hiding—Tripoli, Damascus, the Shouf Mountains. She paid dearly for her idealism. Something has drawn her back into the game. I suspect it's probably money."

"Why would October kill Colin Yardley?"

"Perhaps you should pose the question this way: What did Colin Yardley do in order for someone to take out a contract on his life with the world's best assassin?"

Michael thought, Maybe he purchased a Stinger missile from a black-market arms dealer named Farouk Khalifa and supplied it to the men who shot down Flight 002.

Gentle rain fell, and the air turned cold. The dogs scampered around Drozdov's Wellington boots, eager for home and a spot next to a hot fire. The village of Aston Magna appeared ahead of them, a clump of cottages scattered about the intersection of two narrow roads. Drozdov said, "I'd offer to take you back to Moreton, but I don't drive."

"Thank you, but I'll walk."

"I apologize for the shoes," he said, jabbing his walking stick at Michael's ruined loafers. "They were a poor choice for a winter walk through the Cotswolds."

"A small price for the help you've given me."

Michael stopped walking. Drozdov continued a few feet ahead of him, then stopped and turned around. "There's one killing you haven't mentioned," he said. "The murder of Sarah Randolph. I suppose it's not related to your current case. I admire your professionalism, Mr. Osbourne."

Michael said nothing, just waited.

"She was a committed communist, a revolutionary," he said, opening his arms and gazing at the sky. "God save us please from the idealists. Your Sarah was a friend to the oppressed everywhere: the Irish, the Arabs, the Basque. She also willingly worked for my service. We knew your real identity. We knew you ran penetration agents against guerrilla organizations friendly to our cause. We wanted to know more about your movements, so we placed Sarah Randolph in your path."

Michael felt his head swimming. His heart beat faster. He felt he was losing the ability to hear. Drozdov seemed to be moving away from him, a vertical line at the end of a long dark tunnel. He tried to regain control of his emotions. He feared Drozdov would see it and shut down. He wanted to hear it all. After so many years he wanted to know the truth, no matter how painful.

"Sarah Randolph made one terrible mistake," Drozdov said. "She fell in love with her quarry. She told her handlers she wanted out. She threatened to tell you everything. She threatened to go to the police and confess. Her control officer concluded she was too unstable to continue the assignment. Moscow Center wanted her eliminated, and the job fell to me. Perhaps I should apologize to you, but you understand, it was only business, not personal."

Michael struggled to free a cigarette from his pack and stick it in his mouth. His hands were trembling. Drozdov stepped forward and lit the cigarette with a battered silver lighter.

"I felt you deserved to know the truth, Mr. Osbourne, which is why I told you everything else. But it's over. It's part of the past, just like the Cold War. Go back to your wife and forget about Sarah Randolph. She wasn't real. And whatever you do, keep your wits about you," he added, mouth close to Michael's ear. "If you go after October and you make a single mistake, he will kill you so quickly you'll never know what hit you."

MICHAEL WALKED BACK TO MORETON through driving rain. By the time he reached the village, he was soaked to the skin and numb with cold. He found the Rover in the parking lot and pretended to drop his keys trying to open the door. He got down on all fours and quickly inspected the undercarriage. Seeing nothing unusual, he climbed in and started the engine. He turned the heat on full, closed his eyes, and rested his forehead against the wheel. He didn't know whether to hate her because she lied to him or love her even more because she wanted out of it and paid with her life. Images of her flashed through his thoughts. Sarah flowing toward him, smiling, long skirt over buckskin boots. Luminous skin, gold with candlelight. Her body arched to him. Her exploded face!

He slammed his fist against the dash and drove off, tires slipping over wet pavement. The white Ford minivan followed him and remained there until Michael returned the Rover at Heathrow Airport.

MICHAEL TOOK THE RENTAL CAR BUS to Terminal Four and hurried inside. The check-in line at the TransAtlantic Airlines ticket counter was unbearable, so he found a telephone kiosk and called Elizabeth at the office. Max Lewis, her secretary, answered and asked Michael to hold while he pulled Elizabeth out of a meeting. Michael wondered what to say to her. He

decided to tell her nothing for now. It was too com-
plicated, too emotional, to discuss by phone.

She came on the line. Michael said, "I'm at the
airport. I'm getting on the plane soon, and I just
wanted to tell you that I love you."

"Everything all right, Michael? You sound upset
about something."

"Just a long morning. I'll tell you all about it
when I get home tonight. How are you doing? Are
you ready for tomorrow?"

"As ready as I'm ever going to be. I'm just trying
not to think about it too much right now. I have a ton
of work to get done today, so that helps."

Michael turned around to see if the check-in line
had grown any shorter. A hundred people stood in
line like refugees at a processing center, baggage at
their feet, exasperation on their faces. Three young
men entered the terminal. Each wore a baseball cap;
each carried an identical black leather grip bag. They
were dressed casually in jeans and athletic shoes,
dark hair beneath the caps, olive complexions.

Michael watched them. He lost track of what
Elizabeth was saying. The three men stopped walking and set down their bags. They squatted next to
the bags and unzipped the compartments.

"Hold on, Elizabeth," Michael said.

"Michael, what's wrong?"

Michael made no response, just watched.

"Michael, answer me, goddammit! What's
wrong?"

Simultaneously the men reached beneath the
brims of their caps, and their faces vanished behind
veils of black silk.

Michael yelled, "Get down! Get down!"

He dropped the receiver.

The men stood up, automatic weapons and grenades in hand.

Michael shouted, "Gun! Gun! Get down!"

The attackers tossed grenades into the crowd and started firing.

Michael ran toward them, shouting wildly.

IN DOWNTOWN WASHINGTON, Elizabeth was screaming into the telephone. She heard Michael shouting, then gunfire, then explosions. Then the line went dead. "Oh, God, Michael! Michael!"

She fumbled for the remote, turned on the television in her office, and switched to CNN. They were in the middle of some silly report about the health benefits of avocados.

She paced wildly. She chewed her nails. Max sat with her and waited, holding her hand. After ten minutes she sent him away and did something she hadn't done in twenty years.

She closed her eyes, folded her hands, and prayed.

22. London

THE DIRECTOR TELEPHONED Mitchell Elliott on a secure line from the upstairs study of his home in St. John's Wood.

"I believe Mr. Osbourne may present us with a bit of a problem, Mr. Elliott. He had an interesting conversation with a man from the Intelligence Service last night, which we monitored with a directional microphone from the street. This morning he met with one Ivan Drozdov, a KGB defector who once supervised the activities of our assassin."

Elliott sighed heavily on the other end of the line.

The Director said, "Suffice it to say he knows a good deal, and he probably suspects a good deal more. He is a very worthy opponent, our Mr. Osbourne. In my opinion, to take him lightly would be a serious miscalculation."

"I don't take him lightly, Director. You can be certain of that."

"What's happening at your end?"

"Osbourne and his wife discovered a computer disk containing Susanna Dayton's notes and a copy of her story. They apparently were able to unlock her encryption code. They've given all the material to the editors at *The Washington Post*."

"An unfortunate development," the Director said, coughing gently. "It would seem to me that Mrs. Osbourne is also in a position to do serious damage."

"I've placed her under watch."

"I hope your men conduct themselves in a more professional manner this time. The last thing we need at this stage of the game is for Susanna Dayton's best friend to end up dead also. Her husband is another story. He's made his share of enemies during his career. It might be fortuitous if one of those enemies would surface and exact his revenge."

"I'm certain that could be arranged."

"You have the Society's blessing, Mr. Elliott."

"Thank you, Director."

"As long as this remains an issue of campaign finance, I suspect you'll weather the storm. Oh, it will be embarrassing and messy. There might be a heavy fine, some uncomfortable media speculation, but your project will survive. If, however, Mr. Osbourne uncovers something approaching the truth. . . . Well, I suppose I needn't explain the consequences to you."

"Of course not, Director. What about the defector, Ivan Drozdov? Does he present us with a problem?"

"I'm not certain, but I'm not willing to take that chance. Mr. Drozdov is being dealt with at this moment."

"A wise move."

"I thought so. Good afternoon, Mr. Elliott."

IN ASTON MAGNA, Ivan Drozdov was sitting next to the fire, reading by the weak light from the French doors, when he heard the knocking. The corgis bounced out of their basket and bounded to the front door of the cottage, barking wildly. Drozdov followed after them slowly, legs stiff from sitting. He opened the door to find a young man in a blue coverall, face like an altar boy.

"What can I do for you?" Drozdov asked.

The boy pulled out a silenced gun. "Say your prayers."

Drozdov stiffened. "I'm an atheist," he said calmly.

"Pity," said the boy.

He raised the gun and shot Drozdov twice through the heart.

23. Heathrow Airport, London

THE GUNMAN NEAREST MICHAEL was firing wildly
into the crowd. He spotted Michael charging, leveled
the automatic, and opened fire. Michael dived behind
a *bureau de change* kiosk as rounds ricocheted on the
floor next to him. Two people huddled next to him, a
woman screaming in German and a French priest
murmuring the Lord's Prayer.

The gunman lost interest in Michael and once
again turned his gun on the helpless passengers.
Michael leaned out and looked. The attack had lasted
less than fifteen seconds, but to Michael, crouched
behind the kiosk, it seemed like an eternity. The floor
was covered with the dead and dying and with terrified people vainly trying to protect themselves behind luggage and ticket counters.

Michael thought, Goddammit! Where are the security forces?

One of the attackers paused to reload. He reached
inside his grip, pulled the pin from another grenade,
and lobbed it behind the TransAtlantic counter. The
building shook with the concussion. Michael saw a
pair of bodies hurled into the air, limbs blown away.
The air stank of smoke and blood. The screams of the
victims nearly masked the rattle of the automatic
weapons.

Michael wished he had a gun. He looked to his
right. Four British antiterrorist police were moving
into firing position behind another ticket counter.
Two rose, took aim, and fired. The head of one gunman exploded in a pink flash of blood and brain. The

two surviving gunmen returned fire, hitting one of the police officers. The policemen rose from behind their barrier, guns blazing. A second gunman fell, body riddled with rounds.

The last terrorist gave up the fight. He back-pedaled toward the doorway, firing wildly as he went. He crashed through the automatic door, safety glass shattering around him.

Michael could see a fourth member of the team sitting behind the wheel of the escape vehicle, a silver Audi. He rose, went through a set of parallel doors, and ran along the departure-level walkway, leaping over travelers and airport employees lying on the ground.

The terrorist behind the wheel gunned the engine nervously. A half-dozen security men were running across the terminal, guns drawn. Michael pounded his feet savagely on the pavement, hands out.

The last gunman was twenty meters from him, about to climb into the car. The driver threw open the rear door. The gunman was about to climb inside when he looked up and saw Michael rushing toward him. He turned and tried to raise the automatic.

Michael lowered his shoulder and drove the gunman to the ground.

The blow broke the attacker's hold on his weapon.

Michael grabbed the man by the throat and delivered two brutal blows to his face. The first crushed his nose, the second shattered his cheekbone and rendered him unconscious.

The terrorist behind the wheel threw open his door and was climbing out, automatic pistol in gloved hand. Michael reached out frantically and grabbed for the fallen machine gun. He took hold of it and fired through the Audi's windshield. The gunman managed to get off two wild shots before he collapsed onto the pavement, dead.

Michael, heart racing, saw a flash of dark color and what he thought was a gun. He pivoted on his knee and leveled the gun at one of the British security forces.

"Put the gun down, nice and easy, mate," the officer said calmly. "It's all over. Just put the gun down."

WHEATON, THE CIA'S LONDON STATION CHIEF, collected Michael from Heathrow Airport and took him into the city in the back of a chauffeured government sedan. Michael leaned his head against the window and closed his eyes. He had endured an hour of questioning by a senior British police official and two men from MI5. For a time Michael stayed with his cover—an American businessman returning to New York after a brief meeting in London. Finally, someone from the embassy arrived. Michael asked to speak to Wheaton, and Wheaton called the police and MI5 and told them the truth.

Michael had never killed before, and he was unprepared for his reaction. In the moments after the fight he felt a wild exhilaration, a strange thrill approaching blood lust. The terrorists were evil men who had slaughtered innocent people; they deserved to die a violent, painful death. He was glad he had blown one away and smashed the other's face. He had spent a career pursuing terrorists using only his intellect and his wits for weaponry. For once he had been able to use his fists and a gun—indeed, the gun that had been used to massacre innocent people—and it felt good.

Now, exhaustion overtook him. It pressed on his chest, squeezed his head. His hands no longer trembled; adrenaline dissipated from his veins. Nausea came and went. He closed his eyes and saw blood flying, heads exploding, screams, and the rattle of automatics. He saw the getaway driver blown backward, felt the gun surging in his grasp. He had taken a life, an evil life but a life regardless. It didn't feel good anymore. He felt dirty.

Michael was rubbing his right hand. "Perhaps you should have that looked at," Wheaton said, as if Michael were suffering from a recurring flare-up of tennis elbow.

Michael ignored him. "What was the count?"

"Thirty-six dead, more than fifty wounded, some of them quite seriously. The Brits expect the death toll to go higher."

"Americans?"

"At least twenty of the dead are Americans. Most of the people waiting at the check-in line were boarding the New York flight. The rest of the dead are British. We've spoken to your wife, by the way. She knows you're all right."

Michael remembered how he had left her. One second they were talking, the next he had dropped the telephone and was shouting. He wondered what Elizabeth had heard over the line. Had she heard the whole thing—the explosions, the gunfire, the screams—or had the line mercifully gone dead? He pictured her at the office, worried sick, and he felt awful. He desperately wanted to talk to her but not in front of Wheaton.

They had entered London and were driving east on the Cromwell Road. Wheaton said, "Obviously, the baying hounds of the media are desperate to talk to you. Witnesses have told them about the hero in the blue business suit who killed one of the terrorists and subdued another. The police are telling them that the man wishes to remain anonymous because he fears the Sword of Gaza will retaliate. They're buying it for now, but God knows how many London police officers know the truth. All it takes is one leaker, and we're going to have a serious problem."

"Did the Sword of Gaza claim responsibility yet?"

"They sent a fax to *The Times* a few minutes ago. The Brits are having a go at it, and we've sent a copy to the CTC in Langley. Smells authentic. Should be released to the media soon."

"Revenge for the air strikes on the training bases?"

"But of course."

They headed north on Park Lane, then into Mayfair toward Grosvenor Square. The car went to the front entrance of the U.S. embassy. Michael wished they could use the underground entrance, but it probably made little difference now. He climbed out of the car. He was light-headed and his knee hurt terribly. He must have injured it in the fight, but the adrenaline had masked the pain until now. The Marine guards snapped to attention and saluted as Michael entered the embassy complex, Wheaton at his side. The ambassador and his senior staff were waiting, the rest of the large embassy staff standing behind them. The ambassador broke into applause, and the others followed suit. Michael had worked in the shadows for his entire career. His commendations were awarded in secret. When he had a good day at the office, he could tell no one about it, not even Elizabeth. Now, the applause of the embassy staff washed over him, and he felt a chill at the back of his neck.

The ambassador stepped forward and put a hand on Michael's shoulder. "I know you probably don't feel like celebrating at a time like this, but I just wanted to let you know how proud we all are of you."

"Thank you, Mr. Ambassador. It means a great deal to me."

"There's someone else who wants to talk to you. Follow me, please."

WHEN MICHAEL ENTERED the communications room, sandwiched between Wheaton and the ambassador, the presidential seal was on the large monitor. The ambassador picked up a telephone, murmured a few words into the receiver, and hung up. A few seconds later the presidential seal dissolved and James Beckwith appeared, seated in a white wing chair next to a dying fire in the Oval Office, wearing an open-neck shirt and cardigan sweater.

"Michael, words cannot convey how grateful and how proud you've made us all," the President began. "At considerable risk to your own safety, you single-handedly overpowered one Sword of Gaza terrorist and killed another. Your actions may have saved countless lives, and they have dealt a serious blow to a band of ruthless cowards. I will insist that you be awarded the highest decoration possible for your actions. I only wish I could pin it on your chest *personally* in front of the entire nation, because your country would be very proud of you today."

Michael managed a smile. "I'm used to working in secret, Mr. President, and if it's all right with you I'd prefer to keep it that way."

Beckwith smiled broadly. "I didn't think you'd have it any other way. Besides, you're too valuable to waste on some photo opportunity. We have enough of those as it is, thanks to my chief of staff."

The camera pulled out wider, revealing the rest of the men seated around the President: Chief of Staff Vandenberg, CIA Director Clark, National Security Adviser Bristol. On the edge of the screen sat a small man in an ill-fitting designer suit, hands folded in his lap, face obscured, like a good spy. Michael knew at once that it was Adrian Carter.

"Excuse me for interrupting, Mr. President," Michael said. "Could the camera pan a little to the left? I can't see the tiny man on the couch there."

The camera moved, revealing Carter's face. As usual he looked sleepy and bored, even though he was sitting in the Oval Office surrounded by the President and his senior national security team.

Michael said, "Well, well, how did they let a knuckle-dragger like Adrian Carter into the Oval Office? Be careful, Mr. President. He steals hotel towels and ashtrays. I'd put a Secret Service detail on him."

"He's already taken a dozen boxes of presidential M and Ms," Beckwith said, clearly enjoying himself.

Carter finally smiled. "If you're going to start acting like some kind of American hero, I'm going to be sick. Remember, I was with you from the beginning, Michael. I know where the bodies are buried, *literally*. I'd be careful, if I were you."

When the laughter died away, Beckwith said, "Michael, there's something else we need to discuss with you. I'm going to let Adrian and Director Clark brief you on the details."

"Michael, I won't beat around the bush," Clark began.

The CIA director was a politician, a patrician former senator from New Hampshire who prided himself on the fact that he spoke like a common man. As a result, the lexicon of intelligence work forever baffled him. He was tall and thin, with undisciplined gray locks and a bow tie. He looked better suited to a well-endowed chair at Dartmouth than to the executive suite of Langley.

"As crazy as this might sound, the Sword of Gaza would like to meet with us." Clark gently cleared his throat. "Let me be more specific. The Sword of Gaza doesn't want to meet with *us,* they want to meet with *you.*"

"How did they make the request?"

"Through our embassy in Damascus, about an hour ago."

"Why me?"

"They apparently know exactly who you are and what your job is. They say they want to meet with the

man who knows the most about their group, and they
know that's you."

"How's the meeting supposed to go down?"

"Tomorrow morning on the first Dover-to-Calais
car ferry. They want you to wait on the port deck,
midship, and their man will make the approach. No
watchers, no recording devices, no cameras. If they
see anything they don't like, the meeting is blown."

"Who's their man going to be?"

"Muhammad Awad."

"Awad is the second-highest ranking member of
the organization. The fact that they want to put him
on a ferry and meet face-to-face with an officer of the
CIA is remarkable."

"Therefore it's probably too good to be true,"
Carter said, the camera panning to capture his image.
"I don't like it. It violates all our rules for meetings
like this. We control the site. We set the terms. You of
all people should know that."

Michael said, "I take it you're against going forward with it."

"One hundred and ten percent."

Beckwith said, "I'm interested in hearing your
reaction, Michael."

"Adrian is right, Mr. President. Usually, we don't
meet with known terrorists under situations like
these. Agency doctrine says we control the meeting—the time, the place, the ground rules. Having
said that, I think we should seriously consider tearing
up the rule book in this case."

Clark said, "What if their intention is to assassinate you?"

"If the Sword of Gaza wants me dead, there are much easier ways than arranging an elaborate meeting aboard the Dover-to-Calais car ferry. I'm afraid all they would have to do is send a gunman to Washington and wait outside headquarters."

"Point well taken," Clark said.

"I think they want to talk," Michael said. "And I think we'd be fools not to listen to what they have to say."

Carter said, "I disagree, Michael. This is one of the most vicious terrorist groups in the business. They speak with their actions every day. Frankly, I don't give a good goddamn what they might have to say." Carter looked at Beckwith and said, "My apologies for the rough languange, Mr. President."

Michael said, "I told you he wasn't fit for polite company, Mr. President."

National Security Adviser William Bristol waited for the laughter to die away and then said, "I think I'm going to side with Michael on this one, Mr. President. True, Muhammad Awad is a dangerous terrorist who should not be granted an audience simply because he asks for one. But quite frankly, I'd like to hear what he has to say. The meeting might pay dividends. Surely, it might provide the CIA with some valuable insight into the group's personnel and mindset. I agree with Michael on another point—if the Sword of Gaza wants him dead, there are easier ways to go about it."

The President turned to Vandenberg. "What do you think, Paul?"

"I hate to disagree with you, Bill, since foreign policy is your area of expertise and not mine, but I think we have nothing to gain by meeting with the leader of a bunch of bloodthirsty thugs like the Sword of Gaza. Adrian is right: The Sword of Gaza speaks with actions, not words. There's something else to consider. I wouldn't want to be the one to explain to the American people why we met with Muhammad Awad at a time like this. Your handling of this crisis has been exemplary, and the American people have rewarded you for it. I wouldn't want to see all that goodwill go to waste because a terrorist like Muhammad Awad wanted to have a little chat."

Beckwith fell into a long speculative silence. Michael knew it was not a good sign. He had never been in the President's presence, but he had heard stories of Paul Vandenberg's power. If Vandenberg didn't want the meeting to go forward, the meeting probably wouldn't go forward.

Finally, Beckwith looked up into the camera, addressing Michael in London rather than the men seated around him. "Michael, if you're willing to go through with this, I'm interested in hearing what Muhammad Awad has to say. I know this is not without risk, and I know you have a wife."

"I'll do it," Michael said simply.

"Very well," Beckwith said. "I wish you the best of luck. We'll talk tomorrow."

Then the image from Washington turned to black.

24. London

THE AMBASSADOR ALLOWED Michael to use his office to telephone Elizabeth in Washington. Michael dialed her private line, but it was Max, her secretary, who answered. Max expressed relief at hearing Michael's voice; then he explained that Elizabeth had left for New York already and could be reached later at her father's Fifth Avenue apartment. Michael felt a momentary flash of anger—how could she leave her office without waiting to hear his voice?—but then he felt like a complete fool. She had left work early because in the morning she was having her eggs extracted and fertilized at Cornell Medical Center in New York. In the turmoil of the attack at Heathrow, Michael had completely forgotten. And he had agreed to meet Muhammad Awad in the middle of the English Channel, which would delay his arrival in New York by another two days. Elizabeth would be furious, and rightly so. Michael told Max he would call her in New York later, then hung up.

Actually, Michael was relieved not to have reached her. The last thing he wanted was to hold a conversation like this over a monitored embassy line. He went to Wheaton's office and found him sitting at his desk, squeezing his tennis ball, a Dunhill between bloodless lips.

"I lost my bag at Heathrow," Michael said. "I need to do some shopping before the stores close."

"Actually, you can't," Wheaton said disdainfully. Wheaton didn't like Michael operating on his turf to begin with; the fact that Michael was now flavor of the day didn't help. "Carter wants you on ice somewhere nice and secure. We have a safe flat near Paddington Station. I'm sure you'll find it comfortable."

Michael groaned inwardly. Agency safe flats were the intelligence equivalent of an Econo Lodge.

He knew the flat near Paddington Station all too well; he had used it to hide several frightened penetration agents over the years. The last thing he wanted was to spend the night there as a guest instead of a baby-sitter. Michael knew there was no fighting it. He was making the meeting with Muhammad Awad against Carter's wishes, and he didn't want to alienate him further by bitching about spending a night in the Paddington safe flat.

"I still need some clothes," Michael said.

"Make a list, and I'll send someone."

"I need to get some air. I need to *do* something. If I have to spend the next twelve hours locked up in a safe flat watching television, I'm going to go fucking stir-crazy."

Wheaton picked up the receiver of his internal telephone, clearly annoyed, and murmured a few un-intelligible words into the mouthpiece. A moment later two officers appeared in the door, dressed in matching light-gray suits.

"Gentlemen, Mr. Osbourne would like to spend the afternoon at Harrods. Make sure nothing happens to him."

"Why don't you just send a few of the Marine guards in full uniform?" Michael said. "And actually, Marks and Spencer will be just fine."

THEY TOOK A TAXI to Oxford Street, one officer next to Michael on the bench, the other squeezed onto a jump seat. Michael went into Marks & Spencer and pur-chased two pairs of corduroy trousers, two turtleneck cotton pullovers, a gray woolen sweater, underwear and socks, and a dark green waterproof coat. The watchers trailed after him, picking through stacks of sweaters and rows of suits like a pair of communists on their first voyage to the capitalist West. Next he went to a chemist's shop and bought a new shaving kit: razors, shaving cream, toothbrush and toothpaste, deodorant. He wanted to walk, so he carried his things along Oxford Street, gazing in shop windows like a bored businessman killing time, instinctively checking his tail for signs of surveillance. He saw no one but the Agency men, twenty yards behind.

Gentle rain fell. Dusk descended like a veil. Michael picked his way through the crowds pouring in and out of the Tottenham Court Road tube stop. Late-autumn evening in London; he loved the smell of it. Rain on pavement. Diesel fumes. Lager and cigarettes in the pubs. He remembered nights like these when he would leave his office, dressed in a blue suit and salesman's tan overcoat, and go to Soho to find Sarah at her coffeehouse or wine bar, surrounded by her dancers or her writers or her actors. Michael was an outsider in their world—a symbol of convention and everything they despised—yet in their presence Sarah focused only on him. She flaunted the romantic regulations of her clan. She held his hand. She kissed his mouth. She shared whispered intimacies and refused to divulge them when pressed.

Michael, crossing Shaftesbury Avenue, wondered how much was real and how much was invention. Had she ever loved him? Was it an act from the first moment? Why did she tell the Russians she wanted out? He pictured Sarah in her appalling flat, body rising to him in candlelight, long hair falling over her breasts. He smelled her hair, her breath, tasted salt on translucent skin. Their lovemaking had been religious; if it was a complete lie, then Sarah Randolph was the finest agent he had ever encountered.

He wondered whether she had learned anything of value. Perhaps he should have declared her to Personnel. They would have looked into her background, put her under surveillance, spotted her meeting with her Russian controller, and the whole thing could have been avoided. He wondered what he would tell Elizabeth. *Promise you'll never lie to me, Michael. You can keep things from me, but never lie to me.* I wish I could tell you the truth, he thought, but I'm damned if I know what it is.

Michael sat down on a bench in Leicester Square and waited for his watchers to catch up. They caught a taxi to the safe flat, located in an offensive white building overlooking Paddington Station. The interior was worse than Michael remembered—stained clubhouse furniture, dusty drapes, plastic cups and dishes in a wartime kitchen. The stink of the rooms reminded Michael of his Dartmouth fraternity house. Wheaton had stocked the fridge with cold cuts and beer from Sainsbury's. Michael showered and changed into a set of his new clothing. When he emerged, his minders were eating sandwiches and watching English football on a flickering television. Something about the scene depressed him terribly. He needed to telephone Elizabeth in New York, but he knew they would quarrel, and he didn't want to do it with the Agency listening in.

"I'm going out," Michael announced.

"Wheaton says you're supposed to stay put," one of them said, through a mouthful of ham, cheddar, and French bread.

"I don't give a damn what Wheaton says. I'm not going to sit here with you two clowns all night." Michael paused. "Now, we can go together, or I can lose you both in about five minutes, and you'll have to call Wheaton at home and tell him about it."

THEY DROVE TO BELGRAVIA and parked outside the Seymours' apartment in Eaton Place. The watchers waited in the Agency sedan. The street shone with rain and light from the ivory facades of the Georgian terrace. Through the windows Michael could see Helen in her kitchen, attention focused on that evening's culinary disaster, and Graham upstairs in the drawing room, reading a newspaper. He walked down the steps, wet with rain, and rapped on the paned glass of the kitchen door. Helen opened the door and kissed his cheek. "What a wonderful surprise," she said.

"Mind if I impose?"

"Of course not. I'm making bouillabaisse."

"Have enough for one extra?" Michael asked, bile reflexively rising at the back of his throat.

"But of course, darling," Helen purred. "Go upstairs and drink with Graham. This attack at Heathrow has upset him terribly. God, what a nasty business that was."

"I know," Michael said. "Unfortunately, I was there."

"You're joking!" she exclaimed. Then she looked at his face and said, "Oh, no, you're not joking, are you, Michael? You look terrible, poor lamb. The bouillabaisse will make you feel better."

When Michael entered the sitting room, Graham looked up and said, "Well, if it isn't the hero of Heathrow." He set down his copy of *The Evening Standard*. The headline read TERROR AT TERMINAL FOUR.

A plate of brie and coarse country paté sat on the coffee table, next to a large loaf of bread. Graham had devoured half of it. Michael smeared some of the cheese on a piece of bread and looked cautiously at the paté.

"Don't worry, love. I bought it from a shop off Sloane Square. She's been threatening to learn how to make it at home. Next she'll start baking bread, and I'll be finished."

In the background Michael could hear the BBC news on Graham's fine German stereo system. Graham had a perfect ear and probably could have been a concert pianist if the service hadn't got their hooks into him. His talent had atrophied over the years, like an unspoken second language. He tinkered on his Steinway grand once or twice a week, while Helen murdered his dinner, and he listened to other men play music. Michael could hear a witness describing the blue-suited traveler who killed one terrorist and subdued another.

"I need to phone Elizabeth, and I didn't want half of London Station listening in. Mind if I use your telephone?"

Graham pointed to the telephone on the coffee table.

Michael said, "I need something a little more private. She's not going to like what I'm about to tell her."

"Bedroom's down the hall."

MICHAEL SAT DOWN on the edge of the bed, picked up the telephone, and dialed. Elizabeth answered on the first ring, voice agitated.

"My God, Michael, where have you been? I've been worried sick."

It was not the way he wanted the conversation to begin. His first instinct was to blame it on the Agency, but Elizabeth had long ago lost patience with excuses about the unique demands of his job.

"Wheaton told me he'd talked to you. By the time I was able to get to a telephone, you'd already left for New York. Besides, I wanted to use an unmonitored phone."

"Where are you now?"

"With Helen and Graham."

Elizabeth had spent a fair amount of time with the Seymours and liked them very much. Two years earlier, when Graham had come to Washington for some counterterrorism liaison work, the four of them had spent a long weekend together at the Shelter Island house.

"Why aren't you on your way home? My extraction is scheduled for ten A.M. I need you to be here."

"There are no more flights today. I won't be able to make it home in time."

"Michael, you work for the Central Intelligence Agency. They can get a plane. Tell them the circumstances. I'm sure they'll be very understanding."

"It's not that simple. Besides, it costs tens of thousands of dollars. They're not going to do that for me."

Elizabeth exhaled heavily. Michael could hear the flick of her cheap lighter, and she stopped talking long enough to light another Benson & Hedges.

"I've been watching CNN all day," she said, changing subjects abruptly. "They talked to some witnesses who said a passenger took down one of the terrorists and killed another with his own gun. The man they described sounded suspiciously like you."

"What did Wheaton tell you?"

"Oh, no, Michael, I'm not going to let you two get your story straight. What happened? The truth."

Michael told her.

"Jesus Christ! You couldn't just stay down and wait for it to end? You had to pull some stunt? Play hero and risk your life?"

"I wasn't playing hero, Elizabeth. I reacted to a situation. I did what I was trained to do, and I probably saved a few lives as a result."

"Well, congratulations. What would you like me to do?" Her voice trembled with emotion. "Stand up and lead the applause for nearly making me a widow?"

"I didn't nearly make you a widow."

"Michael, I had to listen to a stranger on television describe how one of the terrorists had a gun aimed at your head and how you were able to kill him before he killed you first. Don't lie to me."

"It wasn't that dramatic."

"So why did you kill him?"

"Because I had no other choice." Michael hesitated. "And because he deserved to die. I've been pursuing people like him for twenty years, but I've never had a chance to see them in action. Today, I did. It was worse than I ever could have imagined."

He was not playing for sympathy, but his words softened her anger.

Elizabeth said, "God, I'm sorry. How are you, anyway?"

"I'm fine. I nearly broke my hand punching him, and somewhere along the line I must have banged my knee because it hurts like hell. But otherwise I'm fine."

"Serves you right," she said, then quickly added, "but I'll still kiss you all over when I see you tomorrow."

Michael hesitated. Elizabeth, radar at full power, said, "You *are* coming home tomorrow, aren't you?"

"Something's come up. I need to spend another day here."

" 'Something's come up.' Come on, Michael, you can do better than that."

"It's the truth. I wish I could tell you what it was, but I can't."

"Why can't someone else do it, whatever it is?"

"Because I'm the only one who can." Michael paused. "There's one thing I *can* tell you—the orders come directly from the President."

"I don't give a damn where the orders come from!" Elizabeth snapped. "You promised me you'd be back in time. Now you're breaking that promise."

"Elizabeth, the situation is out of my control."

"That's bullshit! Nothing is out of your control. You do exactly what you want to do. You always have."

"It's just one extra day, then I'll be back. I'll come straight to New York. I'll be there in time for your implantation."

"Well, gosh, Michael, I wouldn't want to inconvenience you. Why don't you stay in London an extra day or two, take in some theater or something?"

"That's not fair, Elizabeth, and it's not helping the situation."

"You're goddamned right it's not fair."

"There's nothing I can do about it."

"Whatever you do, Michael, don't rush back for my sake, because I'm not sure I want to see you right now."

"What are you saying?"

"I'm not sure what I'm saying. I'm just angry and hurt and disappointed in you. And I'm scared as hell, and I can't believe you're making me go through this alone."

"It's not my choice, Elizabeth. It's my job. I don't have any choice."

"Yes, you do, Michael. You do have a choice. That's what frightens me the most."

She was quiet for a moment, the hiss of the satellite connection the only sound on the line. Michael had run out of things to say. He wanted to tell her he loved her, tell her he was sorry, but it seemed like a stupid thing to do.

Finally, Elizabeth said, "When we were on the telephone at Heathrow, before the attack, you said you had something to tell me."

Michael thought back through the confusion and violence of the terror at Heathrow and realized he was about to tell her the things he had learned about Sarah. The last thing he wanted to do now was make the situation worse by telling Elizabeth he had been investigating the murder of his former lover.

"I can't remember what we were talking about," he said.

Elizabeth sighed. "My God, you're a terrible liar. I thought all you spies were supposed to be good at deceiving people." She paused, waiting for him to say something, but he had nothing left to say. "Good luck tomorrow, whatever it is you're doing. I love you."

The line went dead. Michael quickly redialed, but when the call went through he received nothing but the annoying blare of a busy signal. He tried again, but it was the same, so he hung up the telephone and went downstairs to face Helen's dinner.

"MAYBE YOU SHOULD ASK CARTER to send someone else," Graham said.

They were seated outside in the garden, around a wrought-iron table, smoking Graham's cigarettes. The rain had stopped, and the moon shone intermittently through broken cloud.

"We can't send someone else. They asked for me. They know my face. If we try to send someone else, the whole thing will go down the drain."

"Ever consider the possibility you're walking straight into a trap? These are dicey times. The Sword of Gaza might enjoy taking down a company man, especially after the stunt you pulled at Heathrow today."

"They gain nothing by killing me. You know as well as I do that they don't kill indiscriminately. They kill for a reason, and only when they believe it will advance their cause."

"I take it Elizabeth is less than thrilled about the situation."

"That's putting it mildly. She doesn't know what I'm doing tomorrow, but she doesn't like it." Michael told him everything. While the nature of their work sometimes mandated professional discretion, there were few personal secrets between them.

"I hope you know what you're doing, mate. Sounds rather serious to me."

"I don't need a marriage counselor right now. I know I'm fucking up, but I want to hear what Awad has to say."

"My experience with these bastards suggests he won't say anything useful."

"He wouldn't be putting himself in jeopardy if he didn't have something to tell us."

"Why don't you just snatch the bastard and throw him in jail? Or better yet, see to his expedient demise."

"It's tempting, but we don't operate like that. Besides, they'll only hit back harder."

"Can't get much harder than it got today, darling."

A siren howled in the direction of Sloane Square. Michael reflexively thought of Sarah.

Graham said, "Ever find friend Drozdov?"

Michael nodded.

"He tell you anything useful?"

"He was quite helpful, actually. He knew who I was. He told me why Sarah was killed."

Michael told him the story. When he finished, Graham said, "Jesus Christ, I'm sorry, Michael. I know how much she meant to you."

Michael lit another cigarette. "You didn't tell anyone from your team that I was planning on paying Drozdov a visit, did you?"

"Are you kidding? The top floor would have my ass if they found out. Why do you ask?"

"Because a couple of clods in a white Ford mini-van followed me out there and then saw me to Heathrow."

"Not ours. Maybe Wheaton put you under watch."

"I've considered that possibility."

"He's a sonofabitch, your Wheaton. The gentlemen in the executive suite at Vauxhall Cross can't wait for the day he heads back to Langley for a victory lap round headquarters."

"Did he tell SIS about the meeting with Awad tomorrow?"

"Not that I know of, and I'd be on the notification list for something like that."

"And you're not going to tell your team about it, are you, Graham?"

"Of course not. Usual rules apply, darling." Graham tossed his cigarette into a now withered flower bed. "You're not in the market for an experienced wing man are you?"

"When was the last time you operated in the field?"

"It's been awhile; it's been awhile for you too. But some things you don't forget. If I were you, I'd want someone watching my back right about now."

25. Washington, D.C.

PAUL VANDENBERG SWITCHED ON the television monitors in his office and watched the first feeds of all
three network newscasts simultaneously. Each devoted the entire first block of the broadcast to the attack at Heathrow. There were live reports from
London, the White House, and the Middle East, and
background reports on the Sword of Gaza. The tone
of the reports was generally positive, though anonymous European diplomatic sources blamed the
United States for attacking the Sword of Gaza bases
in the first place. Vandenberg could live with criti-
cism from the Europeans. Congress was on board—
even some of the more dovish Democrats like
Andrew Sterling, Beckwith's defeated opponent, had
pledged support—and *The New York Times* and *The
Washington Post* had bestowed their editorial bless-
ings. Still, twenty American civilians coming home
from London in body bags were bound to erode
some public support for the President's actions.

The program shifted focus to the rest of the day's
news. Vandenberg rose and fixed himself a vodka
and tonic, which he drank while he tidied his desk
and locked away his important files.

At seven-ten his secretary poked her head
through the door.

"Good night, Mr. Vandenberg."

"Good night, Margaret."

"You have a call, sir. A Detective Steve Richardson from D.C. Metro Police."

"He say what it was regarding?"

"No, sir. Shall I ask?"

"No, go home, Margaret. I'll take care of it."

Vandenberg turned down the volume on the television sets, punched the blinking light on his multi-line telephone, and picked up the receiver.

"This is Paul Vandenberg," he said briskly, intentionally adding a note of authority to his voice.

"Good evening, Mr. Vandenberg. I apologize for bothering you so late, but this will just take a moment or two."

"Can I ask what this is regarding?"

"The death of a *Washington Post* reporter named Susanna Dayton. Were you aware she had been murdered, Mr. Vandenberg?"

"Of course. In fact, I spoke to her the night of her death."

"Well, that's why I'm calling. You see—"

"You checked her phone records and discovered that I was one of the last people to whom she spoke, and now you'd like to know exactly what we talked about."

"I heard you were a smart man, Mr. Vandenberg."

"Where are you calling from?"

"Actually, I'm right across the street in Lafayette Park."

"Good, why don't we talk face-to-face?"

"I know what you look like. Seen you on television over the years."

"I suppose television is good for something."

FIVE MINUTES LATER, Vandenberg was walking through the Northwest Gate of the White House, crossing the pedestrian mall that used to be Pennsylvania Avenue. His car waited on Executive Drive, inside the grounds. Night had come, and with it a cold drizzle. Vandenberg stalked across Lafayette Park in a brisk parade-ground march, collar up against the cold, arms swinging at his side. Two homeless men approached and asked for money. Vandenberg stormed past, never acknowledging their presence. Detective Richardson rose from his seat on a bench and walked toward him, hand out.

"She called me for comment on a story she was working on," Vandenberg said, immediately taking the initiative. "It was a complex investigative piece of some sort, and I referred her to the White House press office."

"Do you remember anything about the details of the story?"

So there was no tape recording, Vandenberg thought.

"Not really. It was some story about the President's fund-raising activities. It didn't strike me as terribly serious, and frankly, on a Sunday night, I didn't feel much like dealing with it. So I passed her down the line."

"Did you call the press secretary to notify him about the call?"

"No, I didn't."

"May I ask why not?"

"Because I didn't believe it was necessary."

"Do you know a man named Mitchell Elliott?"

"Of course," Vandenberg said. "I worked for Alatron Defense Systems before I entered politics, and

Mitchell Elliott is one of the President's closest political supporters. We see a good deal of each other, and we talk regularly."

"Did you know Susanna Dayton telephoned Mitchell Elliott that night as well? In fact, it was just a few moments before she spoke to you."

"Yes, I know she telephoned Mitchell Elliott."

"May I ask how you know that?"

"Because Mitchell Elliott and I spoke afterward."

"Do you remember what you discussed?"

"Not really. It was a very brief conversation. We discussed the allegations contained in Ms. Dayton's article, and we both dismissed them as baseless nonsense that did not deserve a comment."

"You spoke to Elliott but not the White House press secretary?"

"Yes, that's right."

Richardson closed his notebook to signal the interview had concluded.

Vandenberg said, "Do you have any idea who murdered the woman?"

Richardson shook his head. "Right now, we're treating it as a robbery that went wrong. I'm sorry to bother you, Mr. Vandenberg, but we had to check it out. I hope you understand."

"Of course, Detective."

Richardson handed him his card.

"If you think of anything else, please don't hesitate to call."

"I DON'T ENJOY getting calls from the Washington police at my White House office, Mitchell."

The two men walked side by side in their usual meeting place, Hains Point along the Washington Channel. Mark Calahan strolled a few paces behind, looking for signs of surveillance.

"The Washington police don't make me terribly nervous, Paul," Elliott said calmly. "I think the last time they arrested someone for murder was 1950."

"Just tell me one thing, Mitchell. Tell me you had absolutely nothing to do with that woman's death."

They stopped walking. Mitchell Elliott turned to face Vandenberg but said nothing.

Vandenberg said, "Put your hand on an imaginary Bible, Mitchell, and swear to that God of yours that Calahan or one of your other thugs didn't kill Susanna Dayton."

"You know I can't do that, Paul," Elliott said calmly.

"You bastard," Vandenberg whispered. "What the fuck happened?"

"We put her under watch—complete physical and audio coverage," Elliott said. "We went into her residence to do a little housekeeping, and she surprised us."

"She surprised you! Jesus Christ, Mitchell! Do you know what you're saying?"

"I know exactly what I'm saying. One of my men has committed an unfortunate murder. The White House chief of staff is now an accessory to murder after the fact."

"You sonofabitch! How dare you bring this upon the President!"

"Keep your voice down, Paul. You never know who's listening. And I haven't brought anything upon this president, because there is no way we'll ever be connected to the murder of Susanna Dayton. If you keep your wits about you, and refrain from doing anything stupid, nothing is going to happen."

Vandenberg glared at Calahan, who stared directly back at him, unblinking. He turned and started walking. A gentle rain drifted over the river.

"I have one other question, Mitchell."

"You want to know who *really* shot down that jetliner."

Vandenberg looked at Mitchell in silence.

"Just deliver your lines and hit your toe marks, Paul. Don't ask too many questions."

"Now, Mitchell! Tell me, now!"

Elliott turned to Calahan and said, "Mark, Mr. Vandenberg isn't feeling terribly well at the moment. See him safely back to his car. Good night, Paul. We'll talk soon."

VANDENBERG'S CHAUFFEURED CAR left Hains Point and followed the parkway around the Tidal Basin. The Jefferson Memorial glowed softly across the water, blurred by rain. The car turned onto Independence Avenue, swept past the towering Washington Monument, and turned onto the Potomac Parkway. Vandenberg glanced up at the Lincoln Memorial.

He thought, My God, what have I done?

He needed a drink. He had never *needed* a drink before in his life, but God he needed one now. He closed his eyes. His right hand trembled, so he covered it with his left and stared out at the river flowing beneath the bridge.

26. London

THE NEXT MORNING, Michael rose before dawn and dressed quietly in the appalling bedroom of the safe flat. The place was quiet except for the grumble of morning traffic near Paddington Station and the prattle of Wheaton's minders in the next room. He drank vile instant coffee from a chipped mug but ignored a plate of stale croissants. Michael was usually calm before a meeting, but now he was nervous and edgy, the way he had felt when he was a new recruit, sent into the field for the first time after his training course at the Farm. He rarely smoked before noon, but he was already working on his second cigarette. He had slept little, tossing in the sagging single bed, troubled by his fight with Elizabeth. Theirs had been a calm marriage for the most part, free from the constant fighting and tension that afflicted so many Agency marriages. Small arguments unsettled them both deeply; a battle like last night's, with threats of revenge, was unheard of.

He put on a bulletproof vest over his thin turtleneck and pulled on a gray woolen crew-neck sweater. He picked up the telephone and dialed the number of the Fifth Avenue apartment one last time. It was still busy. He replaced the receiver in the cradle and went out. Wheaton was waiting downstairs at curbside in the back of an anonymous Agency sedan. They drove to Charing Cross Station, Wheaton droning on about the rules of engagement for the meeting with the intensity of one who had spent a career strapped securely to a desk.

"If it's not Awad, under no circumstances are you to make the meeting," Wheaton said. "Just wait until the boat reaches Calais, and we'll pull you out."

"I'm not dropping behind enemy territory," Michael said. "If Awad doesn't show, I'll just take the next ferry back to Britain."

"Stay on your toes," Wheaton said, ignoring Michael's remark. "The last thing we need is for you to walk up to some Sword of Gaza true believer with a wooden key around his neck."

Members of the Sword of Gaza—and many other Islamic terrorists—usually wore a wooden key beneath their clothing during suicide missions because they believed their actions would be rewarded with martyrdom and a place in heaven.

Wheaton said, "Carter doesn't want you going in there naked."

He popped open an attaché case and removed a Browning high-powered automatic pistol with a fifteen-shot magazine, the Agency's standard-issue handgun.

Michael said, "What am I supposed to do with this?" Like most case officers he could count on one hand the times he had carried a weapon in the line of duty. A case officer could rarely shoot himself out of trouble. Drawing a gun in self-defense was the ultimate sign of failure. It meant that either the officer

had been betrayed somewhere along the line or he
had been plain sloppy.

"We're not sending you onto that ferry so you can
be assassinated or taken hostage," Wheaton said. "If
it looks like you're walking into a trap, fight back.
You'll be on your own out there."

Michael snapped the magazine into the butt and
pulled the slider, chambering the first round. He set
the safety and slipped the gun into the waistband of
his trousers beneath the sweater.

Wheaton dropped Michael at the station. Michael
purchased a first-class ticket for Dover and a stack of
morning newspapers, then found the platform. He
boarded the train with five minutes to spare and
picked his way down the crowded corridor. He found
a seat in a compartment with two businessmen who
were already hammering away on laptop computers.
As the train pulled out of the station a woman entered
the compartment. She had long dark hair, dark eyes,
and pale skin. Michael thought she looked vaguely
like Sarah.

For nearly an hour the train clattered through
London's southeastern suburbs, then entered the
rolling farmland of Kent. In the buffet Michael purchased coffee and a ham and cheese sandwich. He
returned to his compartment and sat down. The businessmen were in shirtsleeves and braces, peering at
an earnings report as though it were a sacred scroll.
The woman said nothing the entire journey. She
smoked one cigarette after the next, until the compartment felt like a gas chamber. Her attractive brown
eyes flickered over the gray-green countryside of

Kent; her long hand lay suggestively over a thigh hidden by thick headmistress stockings.

The train arrived at Dover. Michael stepped from the compartment. The girl collected a leather shoulder bag and followed. She was tall, as tall as Sarah, but possessing none of Sarah's grace and feline physical agility. She wore a black thigh-length leather coat and black combat-style boots that clattered as she walked.

Michael hurried from the platform to the ferry terminal. He purchased a ticket and boarded the vessel, a 425-foot multipurpose ferry capable of carrying 1,300 passengers and 280 cars. He entered the passenger seating area on the main deck and sat down next to a window on the port side of the boat. He looked across and saw Graham Seymour sitting in the center of the room, dressed in blue jeans and a gray Venice Beach sweatshirt, carrying a guitar case. Michael quickly looked away. The girl from the train entered, sat down directly behind Michael, and immediately started smoking.

Michael read his newspapers as the ferry set sail. Dover vanished behind a curtain of rain. Every few minutes Michael glanced at the port side rail, for it was there, midship, that Awad was to appear. Once he went to the snack counter, which allowed him to scan the faces of everyone seated in the passenger lounge. He purchased murky tea in a flimsy paper cup and carried it back to his seat. He recognized no one but Graham and the girl from the train, who was engrossed in a Paris fashion magazine.

A half hour passed. The rain stopped, but now, well into the Channel, the wind increased, and white-capped rollers raced toward the broad prow of the ferry. The girl rose, purchased coffee from the bar, then sat next to Michael. She lit another cigarette and sipped coffee in silence for a moment.

"There he is, next to the rail, in the gray raincoat," she said, a hint of Beirut in her English. "Approach him slowly. Please refer to him only as Ibrahim. And don't try playing the hero again, Mr. Osbourne. I'm well armed, and Ibrahim has ten pounds of Semtex strapped to his body."

MICHAEL FOUND THE FACE VAGUELY FAMILIAR, like a boyhood friend who materializes in middle age, fat and balding. He had seen the face many times before but never close and certainly never in person. He had seen the hazy right profile snapped by the shooters of MI5 during one of Awad's visits to London. The fuzzy full face captured by the French service during a stopover in Marseilles. The old Israeli mug shot of the young Awad: stone thrower, expert maker of Molotov cocktails, child warrior of the Intifada who nearly beat to death a settler from Brooklyn with a chunk of his beloved Hebron. The Israeli photo was of limited value, for the Shin Bet had got to him first and left him nearly unrecognizable with bruises and swelling.

For a long moment Michael and his quarry stood side by side at the rail, each fixed on his own private spot of the swirling Channel waters, like quarreling lovers with nothing left to say. Michael turned and looked at Awad once more. *Please refer to him only as Ibrahim.* For an instant he wondered if the man truly was Muhammad Awad. Wheaton's tedious ad-monitions echoed through Michael's head like boarding announcements at an airport.

To Michael, the man standing next to him looked like Awad's older, more prosperous brother. He was dressed for business in a costly gray overcoat and tasteful double-breasted suit visible beneath. The features had been altered by plastic surgery. The ef-fect was to erase his Arabness and create something of uncertain national origin—a Spaniard, an Italian, a Frenchman, or perhaps a Greek. The prominent Palestinian nose was gone, replaced by the narrow straight nose of a northern Italian aristocrat. The cheekbones had been sharpened, the brow softened, the chin squared, the deer-brown eyes washed pale green by contact lenses. The back teeth had been pulled to give him the feline cheeks of a supermodel.

Muhammad Awad's life read like a pamphlet of radical Palestinian revolutionary literature. Michael knew it well, for he had compiled Awad's biography and résumé for the Center with help from the Mossad, the Shin Bet, MI6, and half the security ser-vices in Europe. His grandfather had been driven from his olive and orange groves outside Jerusalem in 1948 and cast into exile in Jordan. He died the fol-lowing year of a broken heart, according to the Awad legend, the keys to his home in Israel still in his pocket. Another branch of the Awad clan had been massacred at Deir Yassin. In 1967 the family was driven out again, this time to refugee camps in Lebanon. Awad's father never worked, just sat in the camp and told stories of how it had been for him as a boy, tending the olives and the oranges with his own father. Paradise lost. In the 1980s, young Muhammad Awad was indoctrinated in the radical Islam of south Lebanon and Beirut. He joined Hezbollah. He joined Hamas. He trained in Iran and Syria—small arms, infiltration tactics, counterintelligence, bomb making. When Arafat shook Rabin's hand at the White House, Awad was outraged. When Arafat's security forces came after Hamas, at Israel's behest, Awad swore revenge. Together with fifty of the best Hamas guerrillas, he formed the Sword of Gaza, the most deadly Palestinian terror group since Black September.

Wind gusted over the deck. Awad put a hand inside his coat. Michael flinched but resisted reaching for the Browning. "Easy, Mr. Osbourne," Awad said. "I just had the urge to smoke. Besides, if I wanted to kill you, you'd be dead already."

The English was perfect, light accent indistinguishable to an untrained ear. The cigarettes he produced from the breast pocket of his coat were unfiltered Dunhills. "I know you smoke Marlboro Lights, but perhaps these will do, yes? Your wife smokes Benson and Hedges, doesn't she? Her name is Elizabeth Cannon-Osbourne, and she practices law for one of those large firms in Washington. You live on N Street in Georgetown. You see, Mr. Osbourne, we have our own intelligence and security service. And we get a good deal of help from our friends in Damascus and Tehran, of course."

Michael accepted one of the Dunhills and turned into the wind to light it. When Awad raised his hand to light his own cigarette, Michael could see the bomb trigger in the palm of his right hand.

"You've proved your point, Ibrahim," Michael said.

"I realize it was a tedious demonstration, but I did it only to impress upon you that I mean you and your family no harm. You are not my enemy, and I have neither the time nor the resources to engage you."

"So why the Semtex strapped to your waist?"

"One must take precautions in a business such as this."

"You've never impressed me as the suicidal type."

Awad smiled and blew smoke from his sculpted nostrils. "I've always believed I was more useful to Allah alive than dead. Besides, we have no shortage of volunteers for missions of martyrdom. I believe you spent some time in Lebanon as a child. You know the conditions in which our people live. Oppression can breed madness, Mr. Osbourne. Some boys would rather die than spend a lifetime in chains."

Michael looked to his left and saw the woman from the train, leaning against the rail twenty feet away, smoking, eyes flickering over the ferry.

"I thought you believed a woman's place was in the home, shrouded by a chador," Michael said, looking at the girl.

"It is unfortunate, but sometimes this business requires the services of a talented woman. For the purposes of this conversation, her name is Odette. She is Palestinian, and she is very good with her gun. The old West German security service issued orders to shoot the women first. In Odette's case that would be very good advice indeed."

"Now that we're all acquainted," Michael said, "why don't we get down to business. Why did you want to talk?"

"The attack at Heathrow yesterday was the work of the Sword of Gaza. We staged the attack to avenge your ridiculous air strikes against our friends in Libya, Syria, and Iran. You were quite the hero yesterday, Mr. Osbourne. Your presence was coincidence, I assure you. Frankly, I wish you had killed them both. Men in custody always make me a bit nervous."

"Actually, the interrogation is going very well," Michael said, unable to resist the opportunity to toy with Awad. "I understand he's providing a tremendous amount of information on your organizational structure and tactics."

"Nice try, Mr. Osbourne," Awad said. "Our organization is highly compartmentalized, so he can do little damage."

"You just keep on believing that, Ibrahim. It will help you sleep at night. So you asked to see me so you can claim responsibility for the terror attack at Heathrow?"

"We prefer to use the term military action."

"There's nothing military about killing unarmed civilians. That's terrorism, pure and simple."

"One man's terrorist is another man's freedom fighter, but let's not get into that silly debate now. There isn't time. Your air strikes on our bases were ridiculous because there was no justification for them. The Sword of Gaza did not fire the missile that brought down Flight Double-oh-two."

Michael suspected the same, but he was not about to let that show in front of Muhammad Awad. "The body of Hassan Mahmoud, one of your most accomplished action agents, was found on the boat from which the missile was fired," Michael said, voice low but edgy with emotion. "The launch tube was next to his body. A valid claim of responsibility was received in Brussels."

Awad's face tightened. He took a long pull at his Dunhill and tossed the butt into the water. Michael looked away from Awad and saw a motor yacht shadowing the ferry, behind a veil of mist.

"Hassan Mahmoud has not been a member of the Sword of Gaza for nearly a year. He was a fucking psychopath who would not accept the discipline of an organization such as ours. We discovered he was secretly plotting to assassinate Arafat, so we threw him out. He's lucky we didn't kill him. In hindsight we should have."

Awad lit another cigarette.

"Mahmoud moved to Cairo and fell in with the Egyptian fundamentalists, al-Gama'at Ismalyya." Awad reached into his pocket once again, this time removing an envelope. He opened the envelope, removed three photographs, and handed them to Michael. "These were provided to us by a friend inside the Egyptian security service. That man is Hassan Mahmoud. If you run this photograph through your files you will discover the second man is Eric Stoltenberg. I trust you recognize the name."

Michael did, indeed. Eric Stoltenberg used to work for the East German Ministry of State Security, better known as the Stasi. He worked for Department XXII, which ran Stasi support operations for national liberation movements around the world. His portfolio included notorious terrorists like Abu Nidal and Carlos the Jackal and groups such as the IRA and Spain's ETA. Michael examined the photographs: two men seated at a chrome-topped table at Groppi's café, one dark-haired and dark-skinned, the other blond and fair, both wearing sunglasses.

Michael held out the photographs to Awad.

"Keep them," Awad said. "My treat."

"These prove nothing."

"As you probably know, Eric Stoltenberg has had to find work elsewhere," Awad said, ignoring Michael's remark. "After the Wall came down, the Germans wanted his head because he helped the Libyans bomb the LaBelle nightclub in West Berlin in 1986. Stoltenberg has been living abroad ever since, using his old Stasi contacts to make money any way he can—security, smuggling, that sort of thing. Recently he came into a fair amount of money, and he's not done a very good job concealing it."

The motor yacht had moved closer to the ferry. Michael looked at Awad and said, "Mahmoud carried out the attack, and Stoltenberg helped with the logistics—the Stinger, the boats, the escape route." Michael waved the photographs. "This is all a lie, because you're afraid we're going to strike back again."

Awad smiled with considerable charm. "Nice try, Mr. Osbourne, but you know the Sword of Gaza better. You know we have no cause to blow up an American jetliner, and you know someone else did. You don't have the proof, though. If I were you I'd look closer to home."

"Are you saying you know who did?"

"No, I'm just saying you should ask yourself a few simple questions. Who gained the most? Who would have reason to do such a thing but keep their real identity secret? The men who did this have a great deal of money and enormous resources at their fingertips. I swear to you that we did not do this. If the United States does not retaliate for Heathrow it ends now. But if you hit us again we will have no recourse but to hit back. Such is the nature of the game."

The motor yacht had closed to within fifty yards of the ferry's port side. Michael could see two men atop the flying bridge and a third near the prow. He looked to his left, toward the woman, and found her wide-eyed, pulling a small automatic weapon from her handbag. He spun round and looked past Awad, down the port railing, and saw a squat powerfully built man, gun drawn, head shrouded by a balaclava.

Michael grabbed Awad by the shoulders and screamed, "Get down!"

Two rounds burst through Awad's chest and embedded themselves in Michael's bulletproof vest. Awad collapsed onto the deck. Michael reached inside his coat for the Browning, but the Palestinian girl was ready first, gun leveled in outstretched hands, feet apart. She fired twice quickly, blowing the hooded gunman off his feet.

Awad lay on the deck, glaring at Michael, blood in his mouth. He held up his right hand, showing Michael the bomb trigger. Michael dived through a doorway into the passenger lounge. Graham Seymour was there, weapon drawn. Michael grabbed him by the shirt and pulled him to the floor as the bomb exploded and glass shattered overhead. For a few seconds there was almost complete silence; then the wounded began to moan and scream.

Michael scrambled to his feet, shoes slipping on shattered glass, and charged onto the deck. The force of the explosion had obliterated Awad. Odette, the Palestinian girl, lay on the deck, blood streaming from a head wound. The hooded gunman must have been wearing a vest because he had managed to jump over the rail, and the motor yacht was making its way toward him. One man stood on the flying bridge, two on the aft deck. Michael raised his Browning and opened fire on the craft. The two men on the aft deck produced automatic weapons and returned fire. Michael dived for cover.

Odette had pulled herself upright and was sitting with her back to the rail. She held a gun in her outstretched hand, leveled at Michael, her face very calm. Michael rolled away as she squeezed off the first shot. The round struck the deck, missing him. She fired twice more as Michael scrambled helplessly for cover. Suddenly, her body shuddered violently and she slumped forward. Graham Seymour stepped out onto the deck, gun in hand, and knelt down beside her. He looked at Michael and shook his head.

Michael got to his feet and ran to the rail. The motor yacht was idling in the choppy seas. The two men aft were pulling the gunman from the sea. Michael raised his gun, but it was an impossible shot; the ferry's forward progress had carried it about a hundred yards past the stationary yacht. When the gunman was safely on board, the yacht turned away and disappeared behind a curtain of fog.

27. New York

THE IN VITRO FERTILIZATION PROGRAM at Cornell Medical Center had an assembly-line quality that reminded Elizabeth of the criminal courts in any big city. She sat on the scratched wooden bench in the hall outside the procedure room, surrounded by other patients, as technicians moved silently about, gowned and masked. Only Elizabeth was alone. The other four women had husbands clutching their hands, and they eyed Elizabeth as if she were some spinster who had decided to have a child with the borrowed sperm of her best friend's husband. She consciously held her left hand beneath her chin to reveal her wedding band and two-carat diamond engagement ring. She wondered what the other women were thinking. Was her husband late? Was she recently separated? Was he too busy to be with her at a time like this?

Elizabeth felt her eyes begin to tear. She was using every ounce of self-control in her possession to keep from crying. The double doors of the procedure room opened. Two technicians wheeled out a sedated woman on a gurney. Another was wheeled inside from the changing room nearby to take her place on the table. Her husband was dispatched to a small dark room with plastic cups and *Playboy* magazines.

A small television hung on the wall, silently tuned to CNN. The screen showed a live shot of a smoking ferry in the English Channel. No, Elizabeth thought, it's not possible. She stood up, walked over to the television, and increased the volume.

". . . Seven people killed. . . . Appears to be the work of the Islamic terror group known as the Sword of Gaza. . . . Second attack in two days. . . . Believed responsible for yesterday's deadly terror attack at London's Heathrow Airport. . . ."

She thought, My God, this can't be happening!

She went back to her spot on the bench and dug inside her handbag for her cell phone and her telephone book. Michael had given her a special number to be used only in extreme emergencies. She tore through the pages, feeling the stares of the other patients, and found the number.

She dialed, punching the keypad of the phone violently, as she walked to a private spot on the stairwell. After one ring a calm male voice said, "May I help you?"

"My name is Elizabeth Osbourne. My husband is Michael Osbourne."

She could hear the rattle of a computer keyboard over the line.

"How did you get this number?" the voice asked.

"Michael gave it to me."

"What can I do for you?"

"I want to speak to my husband."

"Your telephone number, please."

Elizabeth gave him the number for the cell phone, and she could hear the keyboard rattling again.

"Someone will be calling you."

One of the technicians appeared in the stairwell and said, "You're next, Mrs. Osbourne. We need you inside now."

Elizabeth said to the man on the phone, "I want to know if he was on that ferry in the Channel."

"Someone will be calling you," the voice said again, maddening in its lack of emotion. It was like talking to a machine.

"Dammit, answer me! Was he on that boat?"

"Someone will be calling you," he repeated.

The technician said, "I'm sorry, Mrs. Osbourne, but you really need to come inside now."

"Are you saying he's on that boat?"

"Please hang up now and keep this telephone free."

Then the line went dead.

A NURSE SHOWED ELIZABETH to a small changing room and gave her a sterile gown. Elizabeth was clutching the cell phone in her hand. The nurse said, "I'm afraid you'll have to leave that here."

"I can't," Elizabeth said. "I'm expecting a very important call."

The nurse looked at her incredulously. "I've seen a lot of Type-A women in this program, Mrs. Osbourne, but you certainly take the cake. You're having surgery in there. It's not a time for making business calls."

"It's not a business call. It's an emergency."

"It doesn't matter. In three minutes you're going to be sleeping like a baby."

Elizabeth changed into the gown. *Ring, dammit. Ring!*

She climbed onto the gurney, and the nurse wheeled her into the operating room. The surgical team was waiting. Her doctor's mask was lowered and he was smiling pleasantly.

"You look a little nervous, Elizabeth. Everything all right?"

"I'm fine, Dr. Melman."

"Good. Why don't we get started then."

He nodded at the anesthesiologist, and a few seconds later Elizabeth felt herself drifting into a pleasant sleep.

28. Calais, France

THE PORT BURNED with blue and red emergency lights as the ferry approached the French coast. Michael stood on the bridge, surrounded by the captain and his senior officers, smoking one cigarette after the next, watching the coastline draw nearer. He was alternately freezing cold and sweltering hot. His chest hurt like hell, as though someone very strong had punched him twice. Graham Seymour was on the other side of the bridge, surrounded by his own group of crew members. They were vaguely in custody. Michael had told the captain he and Graham were from U.S. and British law enforcement and that someone from London would meet the ferry in Calais and explain everything. The captain was dubious, as Michael would be in his place.

Michael closed his eyes, and the whole thing played out again. He saw it as news footage, with himself as an actor on a stage. He saw the gunman approaching and Odette scrambling for her weapon, eyes wild. The man with the balaclava and the gun was not from the Sword of Gaza, and Muhammad Awad had not been the target. Michael was the target. Awad was just in the way.

He closed his eyes once more and pictured the two men on the motor yacht. Slowly, their faces grew clearer, as if he were focusing on them with the long-range lens of a surveillance camera. He saw the men firing at him from the stern deck. He had the annoying feeling he had seen them in passing somewhere before—a restaurant or a cocktail party or the chemist shop in Oxford Street. Or was it a petrol station on the M40 in Oxfordshire, pretending to put air in the rear tire of a white Ford minivan?

The ferry landed at Calais. Michael and Seymour were shepherded past the news crews and shouting reporters to an office inside the terminal. Wheaton and a dozen Agency and diplomatic officers were waiting. They had flown from London by helicopter, courtesy of the Royal Navy.

"Who in God's name is this?" Wheaton asked, looking at Graham, who had forsaken his guitar case but still looked like an aging student in his jeans and Venice Beach sweatshirt.

Seymour smiled and stuck out his hand. "Graham Seymour, SIS."

"Graham who and what?" Wheaton asked incredulously.

"You heard him right," Michael said. "He's a friend of mine. By coincidence he was on the ferry."

"Bullshit!"

"Well, it was worth a try, Michael," Graham said.

"Start talking, now!"

"Fuck you," Michael said, pulling off his sweater to reveal the pair of rounds embedded in his vest. "Why don't we go back to London and do the debrief there?" he said, calmer now.

"Because the French want a go at you first."

"Oh, Christ," Graham said. "I can't talk to the bloody Frogs."

"Well, since you've just landed in their jurisdiction, I suppose you'll have to."

Michael said, "What are we going to tell them?"

"The truth," Wheaton said. "And we'll just pray that they have the good sense to keep their fucking mouths shut."

IN NEW YORK Elizabeth lay sleeping in the recovery room when her cellular phone chirped softly. A nurse stepped forward and was about to shut off the power when Elizabeth awakened and said, "No, wait."

She pressed it to her ear, eyes closed, and said, "Hello."

"Elizabeth?" the voice said. "Is this Elizabeth Osbourne?"

"Yes," she croaked, voice thick with anesthesia.

"It's Adrian Carter."

"Adrian, where is he?"

"He's fine. He's on his way back to London now."

"*Back* to London? Where has he been?"

There was only silence on the line. Elizabeth was fully awake now.

She said, "Goddammit, Adrian, was he on that ferry?"

Carter hesitated, then said, "Yes, Elizabeth. He was there on a job, and something went wrong. We'll know more when he gets back to the London embassy."

"Was he hurt?"

"He's fine."

"Thank God."

"I'll call you when I know more."

THE CHOPPER TOUCHED DOWN at dusk on a Thameside helipad in East London. Two embassy cars were waiting. Wheaton and Michael rode in the first, Wheaton's drones in the second. They turned onto the Vauxhall Bridge, past the ugly modern building that served as the headquarters for MI6. Michael thought, So much for George Smiley's veiled redbrick lair at Cambridge Circus. Now, headquarters of the Service had actually made a cameo appearance in a James Bond movie.

"Your friend Graham Seymour is going to get a rough reception in that building in a few minutes," Wheaton said. "I spoke to the Director-General from Calais. Needless to say, he's not pleased. He also gave me a piece of news that will have to wait until we're behind closed doors."

Michael ignored the remark. Wheaton always seemed to take too much pleasure at the professional misfortune of colleagues. He had come up through the Soviet directorate, when Michael's father was senior staff at Langley, and had worked overseas in Istanbul and Rome. His job was to recruit KGB officers and Soviet diplomats, but he proved so inept he quickly received a series of dismal fitness reports, one written by Michael's father. Wheaton was transferred to headquarters, where he thrived in the backstabbing, patrician atmosphere of Langley. Michael knew Wheaton resented him because of his father, even though the lousy fitness report probably ended up saving his career.

They arrived in Grosvenor Square. Wheaton and Michael entered the embassy side by side, Wheaton's men following. Michael had the strange feeling of being under arrest. Wheaton went straight to the secure teleconference room. Carter and Monica Tyler appeared on the screen as Wheaton and Michael sat down in plush black-leather chairs.

"I'm glad to see you're all right, Michael," Monica said. "You've had a remarkably harrowing couple of days. We have a lot of ground to cover, so let's begin with the obvious question. What went wrong?"

For ten minutes Michael carefully recounted what happened on the ferry: Awad, the Palestinian girl named Odette, the motor yacht, and the gunman. He described the shooting, the bullets passing through Awad's body into his vest. He described the explosion, and how the men on the boat provided covering fire for the gunman's escape. Finally, he described the last battle with Odette, and how Graham Seymour shot her to death.

"What was Graham Seymour, an officer from MI-Six, doing on that boat in the first place?"

Michael knew he could gain little at this point by lying. "He's a friend. I've known him a very long time. I wanted someone watching my back I could trust."

"That's beside the point," Monica said, with practiced impatience. Monica, as a rule, disliked field operations and the officers who carried them out. "You included an officer from the service of another country without the approval of your superiors at headquarters."

"He works for the British, not the Iranians. And if he hadn't been there, I'd be dead right now."

Monica pulled a frown of irritation that made clear she would not be swayed by arguments based on emotion. "If you were so concerned about your security," she said tonelessly, "you should have requested backup from us."

"I didn't want to go in there with some heavy squad that Awad and his team could make a mile away." That was only part of the truth; he wanted as few people as possible from London and headquarters involved in the operation. He had worked in the field, and he had worked at headquarters, and he knew Langley leaked like a sieve.

"It sounds as though Awad and his team identified your good friend Graham Seymour," Monica said contemptuously.

"Why would you assume that?" Michael asked. Wheaton fidgeted uncomfortably in his seat and Carter, four thousand miles away in Langley, did the same thing. Monica Tyler did not take well to questions from staff; even rather senior officers like Michael. She had the certainty of conviction that is an unfortunate by-product of innocence.

"Why else did one of their gunman attempt to kill you? And why else would Awad set off a bomb strapped to his body?"

"You're assuming the gunman was Sword of Gaza. I think that assumption is wrong. The shooter made no attempt to spare Awad's life. He tried to kill me by killing Awad first. The woman was standing behind me the entire time. If they wanted me dead, she could have done it, and I would have never known what hit me. And when the shooting started, she went after the gunman first, not me."

"She eventually went after you."

"Yes, but only after Awad set off the explosion. I believe she assumed the gunman was one of ours."

"Did you see his face?"

"No, his head was covered by a balaclava."

Monica leaned over and whispered in Carter's ear. Carter raised his hands and moved them about his head and face. Michael realized he was explaining to Monica exactly what a balaclava was. Monica paused for a moment, studying her hands, then said, "What did Awad say to you before the trouble began?"

Michael went through the details of the conversation in painstaking detail. He had been trained to commit large amounts of information to memory, and when he worked in the field he had a legendary ability to produce nearly verbatim transcripts of meetings with agents. Carter used to call him "the human Dictaphone." Michael told them everything Awad had said—about Heathrow, about the air strikes, about Hassan Mahmoud's expulsion from the group—with one glaring omission. He did not tell them about the photographs of Mahmoud's meeting in Cairo with Eric Stoltenberg.

"Do you believe he was telling the truth?" Monica asked.

"Yes, I do," Michael said flatly. "I've always been skeptical about the Sword of Gaza claim of responsibility. I've made no secret of that. But if it wasn't the Sword of Gaza, who was it? And why would they make a false-flag claim?"

And who the hell tried to kill Muhammad Awad and me aboard that ferry today?

Carter and Monica conferred quietly for a moment. Wheaton glared at Michael professorially over his half-moon reading glasses, as though Michael had just given the wrong answer to a critical question on an oral exam.

"There's something else we need to discuss with you, Michael," Monica said. Then she added gravely, "It's very serious in nature." There was something in her boardroom tone that immediately set Michael on edge.

"Early this morning, an officer from British SIS paid a visit to a defector named Ivan Drozdov. It seems Drozdov missed his weekly check-in, something he never does, and SIS became worried. The officer broke into his cottage and found him dead. Shot to death. SIS and local police immediately investigated. Yesterday, Drozdov was seen in a local café with a man matching your description. SIS would like to know if you went to see him yesterday. And, frankly, so would we."

"You know the answer is yes, because you had me under surveillance from the time I left London until I returned to Heathrow."

"If you were under surveillance, it was not ordered by me or anyone at headquarters," Monica shot back.

"It wasn't London Station," Wheaton said.

"What the hell were you doing meeting with Drozdov without our authorization or the authorization of SIS?" Monica asked. "And by the way, what did you talk to him about?"

"It was a personal matter," Michael said. In the video monitor he could see Adrian Carter looking at the ceiling, blowing air through pursed lips. "Drozdov worked for Department Five of the First Chief Directorate of the KGB, the assassins. I've been working on something for several months and I wanted to discuss it with him. I assure you he was alive and well when I left."

"I'm glad you think this is amusing, Michael, because we don't," Monica said. "I want you on the first flight back to Washington tomorrow morning. Consider yourself on administrative leave pending an investigation of your conduct in this affair."

The screen went blank. Wheaton wordlessly held out his hand. Michael reached beneath his sweater and handed Wheaton the loaded Browning automatic.

. . .

WHEATON HAD WANTED Michael in the safe flat for his last night in London, but Michael told him in no uncertain terms to fuck off, and he had returned to his small hotel in Knightsbridge overlooking the park. Early that evening, slipping out onto rainy pavement, he immediately spotted two of Wheaton's watchers, dozing in a parked Rover. Shopping for Elizabeth in Harrods, he spotted two more. Walking south on Sloane Street, he picked off a fifth watcher on foot.

There were also two men in a Ford, this time dark blue.

Who are you? Who hired you? If not Wheaton, then who?

Shaking surveillance was not difficult, even professionals. Michael held the advantage, for he had trained with them at the Farm and he knew their tactics. For one hour he moved about the West End in gentle rain—by foot, by bus, by taxi, the tube—through Berkeley Square, Oxford Street, Bond Street, Leicester Square, and the outer reaches of Soho. He found himself at Sarah's flat. The Lebanese take-away had gone vegetarian, a monument to Sarah, perhaps. Bob Marley throbbed through a half-open window hung with dirty drapes. Sarah's window. Sarah's drapes, probably.

Sarah Randolph made one terrible mistake, Drozdov had said. *She fell in love with her quarry.*

She had been a lie, a myth created by his enemies, tragically heroic in her boundless naïveté. She had betrayed him, but she was not real. He could not love her, nor could he hate her. He only felt sorry for her.

Wheaton's watchers were long gone, so he took a taxi to Belgravia. Field men, like thieves, develop clandestine ways of penetrating their own homes for the inevitable day when a lifetime of betrayal comes calling. Michael knew Graham Seymour's method: through a mews and over the whitewashed garden wall with the help of a rope ladder left for such an occasion. Michael used the ladder now to scale the wall, then dropped through the darkness onto Graham's stone terrace. Graham answered Michael's rap at the French doors armed with one of Helen's Swiss-made kitchen machetes. They talked upstairs in the drawing room, Michael's drenched coat steaming at the gas fire, Graham's German stereo blasting Rachmaninoff to cover the conversation.

They talked for nearly an hour. They talked about what happened on the ferry. They talked about Sarah. About Colin Yardley and Astrid Vogel and the man in the dark who fired three bullets into Yardley's face. About the men on the motor yacht and in the Fords— the white minivan and now the blue one. Michael needed money. Helen was rich, and Graham always kept a spare thousand or two in the safe for emergencies. Passports were no problem. Over the years Michael had used his contacts inside friendly services to build a collection of false travel documents. He could travel as a Frenchman or a Spaniard, a Greek or a German. Even an Israeli. Call Elizabeth, Michael said. Tell her I'll explain everything when I get back. Be careful of what you say on the line. Don't tell her where I'm going or what I'm doing. Tell her I love her. Tell her to take care.

They ate penne puttanesca and salad and drank red wine. Helen and Graham spoke as if Michael weren't there. Michael felt as if he were watching a horrid daytime drama on television. He devoured two plates of the pasta, which was surprisingly good.

After dinner, Graham announced suddenly that he wanted to see a new film showing at the Leicester Square cinema. Helen enthusiastically agreed. They cleared away the dishes and went out. Michael watched them climb into Graham's BMW from the darkened drawing room window and pull away from the curb. A car engine turned over somewhere in the darkness. Michael watched as it slipped into the quiet street, headlights doused.

He went out through the French doors, across the garden, up the wall, and down the other side on the rope ladder. On the King's Road he caught a taxi and went to Victoria Station. He purchased a ticket to Rome with the cash from Graham's safe. The train was leaving in an hour. Wheaton, if he were smart, would be watching the airports and the rail stations.

Michael purchased a waterproof hat at a kiosk and pulled it low over his brow. He went outside and waited in the rain. Five minutes before the train was due to depart he went back inside the station and walked quickly to the platform. He boarded the train and quickly found an empty compartment. He sat alone in the half-darkness for a long time, listening to the rhythmic clatter of the train, looking at his reflection in the glass, thinking about it all. Then, as the train cleared the Channel tunnel and raced southward

across France toward Paris, he fell into a light, dreamless sleep.

29. London

THE DIRECTOR WATCHED the ITN ten o'clock news as
his chauffeured silver Jaguar purred through the
streets of the West End. He had dined poorly on over-
cooked lamb at his Mayfair supper club, where the
rest of the members believed he was a successful international venture capitalist, an accurate description
of his work to a degree. A handful suspected he had
done a lap or two for Intelligence once upon a time.
One or two knew the truth—that he had actually been
the director-general, the legendary C, of the Secret
Intelligence Service. Thank God he had worked for
the Service in the old days, when the Department officially did not exist and directors had the good sense
to keep their names and photographs out of the newspapers. Imagine, the head of the Service granting an
interview to *The Guardian*—heresy, lunacy. The Director believed spies and intelligence services were
rather like rats and cockroaches. Better to keep up
the pretense they don't really exist. Helps a free society sleep better at night.

The attack on the Dover-to-Calais ferry dominated the news. The Director was furious, though
his tranquil face projected nothing but bored inso-
lence. After a lifetime in the shadows his dissembling was art. He was narrow of head and hips, with
sandstone hair gone to gray and bleached surgeon's

hands that always seemed to be holding a smoldering cigarette of a length fit for a glossy magazine advertisement. His eyes were the color of seawater in winter, his mouth small and cruel. He lived alone in St. John's Wood with a boy from the Society for protection and a pretty girl who did paperwork and looked after him. He had never married, had no children, no known parentage. The office jesters at the Service used to say he had been found in early middle age in a basket on the banks of the Thames, dressed in a chalk-stripe suit, Guards tie, and handmade shoes.

He switched off the television and looked out his window, watching the London night sweep past. He detested failure more than anything else, even betrayal. Betrayal required intelligence and ruthlessness, failure only stupidity or lack of concentration. The men he had dispatched for the job on the ferry had been given every resource needed to guarantee success, yet they had failed. Michael Osbourne clearly was a worthy opponent, a man of talent, intelligence, and ingenuity. Osbourne was good; his killer would have to be better.

The car drew to a stop outside the house. His driver, a former member of the elite Special Air Service commandos, escorted the Director to the front entrance and saw him inside. The girl was waiting, a toffee-colored Jamaican sculpture called Daphne. She wore a white blouse, unbuttoned to the ledge of her ample breasts, and a black skirt that fell midway across bare thighs. Sun-streaked brown hair lay about square shoulders.

"Mr. Elliott is on the line from Colorado, sir," she said. There was a trace of East Indian lilt in her voice that the Director had spent thousands of pounds in speech therapy to eliminate. Names were permitted inside the Mayfair residence, for it was swept for bugs regularly and the walls were impermeable to outside directional microphones.

The Director went into the study and punched the flashing light on his black multiline telephone. Daphne came into the room, poured a half inch of thirty-year-old scotch into a tumbler, and handed it to him. She remained in the room as he spoke, for there were no secrets between them.

"What went wrong?" Elliott said.

"Mr. Awad brought protection, and so did Mr. Osbourne. And on top of that, he's damned good."

"He needs to be eliminated, especially after what he learned this morning on that ferry."

"I'm well aware of that, Mr. Elliott."

"When do you plan to mount another attempt?"

"As soon as possible," the Director said, pausing for a nip of the scotch. "But I want to make a substitution. Osbourne is rather good. Therefore, the opposition needs to be very good indeed. I'd like to give the task to October."

"His price is very steep."

"So are the stakes at this point, Mr. Elliott. I hardly think now is the time to quibble over an extra million or two, do you?"

"No, you're right."

"I'll prepare a detailed dossier on Osbourne and send it to October, via encrypted electronic mail. If he chooses to accept the target, the game will be on, and I anticipate Mr. Osbourne will be eliminated in short order."

"I hope so," Elliott said.

"Count on it, Mr. Elliott. Good night."

The Director replaced the receiver. Daphne stood behind him and rubbed his shoulders. "Will there be anything else this evening, sir?" she asked.

"No, Daphne, I'll just see to a little paperwork, then turn in."

"Very well, sir," she said and went out.

The Director worked in his study for twenty minutes, finishing the scotch, watching American news accounts of the ferry explosion on his satellite system. He shut off the television and went upstairs to his bedroom suite. Daphne lay on her back on the bed, blouse unbuttoned, one long leg crossed over the other, twirling a strand of hair round a stiletto forefinger.

The Director undressed silently and put on a silk robe. Some wealthy men amused themselves with horses or motorcars. The Director had his Daphne. She had removed her clothing; it lay next to her on the bed. She was gently stroking her nipples, her stomach, the tops of her thighs. Daphne was a tease, even with herself. The Director climbed into the bed and trailed a finger at her throat.

"Anything, my love?" she asked.

"No, petal."

The Director's ability to make love to a woman had been severely impaired, the by-product, he assumed, of a lifetime of lies and betrayal. She reached beneath his robe, taking him inside her long hands.

"Nothing at all?"

"Afraid not, my love."

"Pity," she said. "Shall I?"

"If you're in the mood."

"You *are* a silly boy, sir. Want to help or just watch?"

"Just watch," he said, lighting a cigarette.

Her hand slipped between her thighs. She gasped sharply, her head rolled back, her eyes closed. For the next ten minutes he took her the only way possible, with his eyes, but after a while his mind drifted. He thought of Michael Osbourne. Of the failed assassination on the ferry. Of the man called October. It would be an interesting fight. One would not survive. If it was Osbourne who died, the Society would endure and Mitchell Elliott would make his billions. If it was October. . . . The Director shuddered at the thought. He had worked too long, too hard, for it all to fall apart. Too much at stake, too much invested, for failure now.

He turned his gaze on Daphne once more and found her brown eyes fixed on him. She had the straight, unobstructed gaze of a small child. "You went away for a few minutes," she said.

Surprise flickered across his face; Daphne robbed him of all his old defenses.

"I watch too, you know. I want to know if I'm making you happy."

"You make me very happy."

"Is everything all right, love?"

"Everything is fine."

"You sure?"

"Yes, quite sure."

30. Cairo

"MY GOD, THIS FUCKING CITY."

Astrid Vogel stood at the French doors, open to the cool winter's dusk. There was a small balcony with a rusted wrought-iron railing, but Mr. Fahmy, the desk clerk, had warned that balconies had a way of falling off these days so, please, it is best you not stand on it. They had been in the hotel two days, and the toilet had stopped working three times. Three times Mr. Fahmy appeared, in jacket and tie, armed with a roll of packing tape and a coil of copper wire. The hotel had no handyman, he explained. All the good handymen were in the Gulf—in Kuwait or Saudi Arabia or the Emirates—working for oil sheikhs. Same with the teachers and the lawyers and the accountants. The professionals and the rich had fled. Cairo was a crumbling city of peasants, and there was no one qualified to repair it. Then the toilet would flush, as if on cue, and he would smile sadly and say, "It is fixed, *inshallah*," even though he knew he would be back again the next day with his elixir of packing tape and copper wire.

The evening call to prayer started up—first a single muezzin, very far off, then another and another, until a thousand crudely amplified voices screamed in concert. The hotel was next to a mosque, and the minaret rose just outside their window. That morning, when the thing began blasting away at dawn, Astrid startled so badly she grabbed her gun from the bedside table and rushed onto the balcony nude. Astrid was a devout atheist. Religion made her nervous. In Cairo, religion was everywhere. It enfolded you, surrounded you. There was no escaping it. Her solution was to flout it. That afternoon, when the muezzin's call started up, she took Delaroche to bed and made frenzied love to him. Now she listened to the call as a marine biologist might study the mating sounds of gray whales. She realized it was vaguely musical, harmonious, like one of those simple fugues where one violin plays the same series of notes after another has finished. "Cairo's Canon," she thought.

The call died away until one voice hung on the air, somewhere in the direction of Giza and the pyramids, and then it too was gone. Astrid remained in the French doors, arms folded beneath her breasts, smoking a beastly Egyptian cigarette, drinking ice-cold champagne because the hotel was out of bottled water, and the tap water could kill water buffalo. She wore a man's galabia, sleeves rolled up, unbuttoned to her navel. Delaroche, lying on the bed, could see the faint outline of her mannequin's body through the translucent material of the white gown. She had purchased it earlier that day in a souk near the hotel, drawing attention the way only a five-foot-eleven German blonde can in the sexually repressed streets of Cairo. For a while Delaroche thought he had made a mistake letting her loose, but it was winter, and there were thousands of Scandinavian tourists in town, and no one would remember the tall German woman who insisted on buying a peasant gown in the souk. Besides, Delaroche liked walking the throbbing streets of Cairo. He always had the sensation of moving through other cities—now a corner of Paris, now an alley of Rome, now a block of Victorian London—all covered with dust and crumbling like the Sphinx. He wished he could paint, but there was no time for it this trip.

The night wind drifting through the open doors smelled of the Western Desert. It mixed with the stink that is unique to Cairo: dust, rotting garbage, burning wood, donkey shit, urine, exhaust from a million cars and trucks, toxic fumes from the cement works of Helwan. But it was cool and dry, wonderful on the bare, damp skin of Astrid's breasts. Dust collected on her face. It was everywhere, gray, fine as flour. It worked its way inside her suitcase, her books and magazines. Delaroche was constantly cleaning the Beretta left for him in a Cairo bank safety deposit box. "The dust," he would groan, working an oiled rag over the barrel. "The goddamned dust."

Astrid liked the window open—the air conditioner was broken, and nothing in Mr. Fahmy's bag of tricks could fix it—but the maids always sealed the room tight as a sarcophagus. "The dust," they would say, by way of explanation, rolling their eyes at Astrid's open window. "Please, the dust."

She ventured onto the balcony, ignoring Mr. Fahmy's dire warning. Below her, men pushed silent cars around a choked, narrow street. A million cars in Cairo, and Astrid had not seen a single real parking garage. Cairenes had developed a perfectly insane stopgap measure: They simply left their cars in the middle of the street. For a handful of crumpled piasters, clever entrepreneurs would watch over a car all day, rolling it about, making room for others. Many downtown side streets were impassable because they had been turned into makeshift parking lots. Across the street, next to the mosque, an office building was slowly collapsing. Rather than take the furniture out in an orderly fashion, workers were simply throwing things out windows. Twenty soldiers, peasant boys from the villages, sat at the foot of the doomed building, cooking over small fires.

"Why do they put soldiers outside the building, Jean-Paul?" she asked, watching the spectacle.

"What?" Delaroche shouted from inside the room.

Astrid repeated herself, louder. Conversation, Cairo style. Because of the deafening cacophony of street noise, most conversations were conducted by shouts. This made planning Eric Stoltenberg's assassination difficult. Delaroche, for reasons of security, insisted they talk on the bed, face-to-face, so they could speak softly, directly into each other's ears.

"They put soldiers there to keep pedestrians away from the building, in case it goes without warning."

"But if the building goes without warning, the *soldiers* will be killed. That's insanity."

"No, that's Cairo."

A cart entered the street, pulled by a lame donkey. The driver was a small boy, blond, green eyes, dressed in a filthy robe. Garbage spilled from the bed of the cart. The soldiers taunted the boy and threw scraps of bread at the donkey. For an instant Astrid thought of getting her gun and shooting one of the soldiers. She said, "Jean-Paul, come here, quickly."

"*Zabbaleen,*" Delaroche said, stepping onto the balcony.

"What?"

"*Zabbaleen,*" he repeated. "It means the rubbish collectors. Cairo has no sanitation, no official system of trash removal. For years the garbage was simply thrown into the streets or burned to heat water in the baths. In the thirties, the Coptic Christians migrated to Cairo from the south. Some of them became the *zabbaleen.* They earn no money, only the garbage they collect. They live in a village of garbage in the Mokattam hills, east of Cairo."

"Jesus Christ," she said softly.

"Time to get dressed," Delaroche said, but Astrid remained on the balcony, watching the boy and his garbage.

"I don't like him," she said, and for a moment Delaroche wasn't certain if she were talking about the *zabbaleen* or Eric Stoltenberg. "He's a cruel bastard, and smart too."

"Do it just the way we planned it, and everything will be fine."

"Don't let him hurt me, Jean-Paul."

He looked at her. She had killed a dozen people, lived her life on the run, and yet she still became as frightened as a small girl at times. He touched her face, kissed her forehead softly.

"I won't let anyone hurt you," he said.

They looked up. A large wooden desk teetered on a tenth-floor balcony of the condemned office building. It hung there a moment, like a passenger clinging to the rail of a sinking ocean liner, then crashed to the street, shattering into a hundred pieces. The *zabbaleen*'s donkey bolted. The soldiers scattered. They looked up and began shouting in rapid Arabic, shaking their fists at the men on the balcony.

"Cairo," Delaroche said.

"My God," Astrid said. "What a fucking city."

THE HOTEL ELEVATOR was an old-fashioned lift, threaded through the center of a spiral staircase. It was broken again, so Delaroche and Astrid had to wind their way down from the seventh floor. Fahmy, the eternal desk clerk, shrugged his shoulders in apology. "Tomorrow, the repairman comes, *inshallah,*" he said.

"*Inshallah,*" Delaroche repeated, in a perfect Cairene accent, which Fahmy acknowledged with a formal nod of his bald head.

The lobby was quiet, the dining room deserted except for two aproned waiters silently pursuing the dust. Delaroche found it depressing and vaguely Russian, with its long tables, curled meat, and warm white wine. Astrid had wanted to stay in one of the big Western hotels—the Inter-Con or the famous Nile Hilton—but Delaroche insisted on something more secluded. The Hotel Imperial was the kind of place guidebooks recommend for adventuresome travelers who want to get a taste of "the real Cairo."

Delaroche had stolen a motorbike: small, dark blue, the kind of scooter young Italians use to race round the streets of Rome. He felt slightly guilty, for he knew some Egyptian boy had worked three jobs and saved years in order to buy it. He put Astrid in a cab and in rapid, precise Arabic told the driver where to take her. Delaroche roared off on his motor scooter, Astrid behind him in the cab.

. . .

ZAMALEK IS AN ISLAND, long and narrow, which the Nile surrounds like a moat. It is an enclave of Cairo's wealthy: the residue of the aristocracy, the young rich, a clique of Western journalists. Dusty apartment houses rise above the corniche and stare disapprovingly across the river toward the noise and chaos of downtown. Below the corniche, along the water, is an embankment where the liberated youth of Zamalek screw into the early morning. At the northern tip of the island lie the cricket fields and tennis courts of the Ghazira Sporting Club, the playground of the old British elite. In the shops and boutiques of Zamalek one hears the French brought to Cairo by Napoleon. The inhabitants wear Western clothes, eat Western food in restaurants and cafés, and dance to Western music in discotheques. It is the other Cairo.

Eric Stoltenberg lived on the top floor, the ninth, of a building overlooking the river. His neighbors complained about his loud parties and the mating sounds of his constant conquests. He ate dinner each night in one of Zamalek's fashionable restaurants, then stopped at a nightclub called Break Point to do his late-night drinking and hunting.

It was all in Delaroche's dossier.

The Break Point had a doorman and a statutory line, like a New York club. The doorman selected important clientele and pretty girls for quick entry. Eric Stoltenberg fell into the first category, Astrid Vogel the second. Delaroche, single male, attractive, midforties, had to wait ten minutes. He immediately went to the bar. In Cairene-accented Arabic he ordered Stella beer, the Egyptian brew. In the nightclub, with its murky lights and pall of smoke, he could pass for a certain kind of upper-class Egyptian.

He paid for his beer and turned around to face the room. The place was filled as usual: scantily clad Egyptian girls who would sleep with strangers, boys who would do the same, a few high-class tarts, a smattering of adventurous tourists who couldn't stand another evening in the dreary bar at the Nile Hilton. A pretty girl asked Delaroche to dance. He politely refused. A moment later her guardian angel appeared, a rough boy with a leather jacket and tight-fitting shirt to prove he lifted weights. Delaroche murmured something in his ear that made the boy immediately leave the bar, pretty girl in tow.

Astrid was dancing with Stoltenberg. She wore one of the black skirts purchased in London and a tight-fitting black pullover. She was a tourist named Eva Tebbe, born in the East, who spoke German with a Saxon accent. Astrid and Stoltenberg met the previous night, when she had come with Delaroche, who posed as a Frenchman from her tour group. Stoltenberg flirted with her relentlessly. She had two days left in Cairo; then it was off to Luxor. Stoltenberg had tried to pick her up, but she sadly declined, saying the little Frenchman would be furious. Tonight she was supposed to be alone, which is why Delaroche didn't want to dance and why he remained at the bar in shadows.

Stoltenberg had been good-looking once, but he had gone fleshy with alcohol and rich food. He had short-cropped iron-gray hair and ice-blue eyes. He wore black—black jeans, black turtleneck, black leather jacket. He was touching Astrid as she danced, and by her expression she enjoyed it very much. After three songs they adjourned to Stoltenberg's regular table. They talked, close.

After ten minutes they stood and sliced their way across the dance floor toward the door, Stoltenberg pulling Astrid by the hand. Her eyes flashed across Delaroche but did not linger on him.

Astrid the professional.

He looked carefully at her face, and he realized she was frightened.

BUSINESS WAS OBVIOUSLY GOOD for Eric Stoltenberg. He had a large black Mercedes and a driver. He opened Astrid's door, then walked behind the car and got in next to her. The car roared through the narrow streets, then turned onto the corniche and headed south along the river. Delaroche followed on the motorbike, lights doused, head covered by a helmet. He eased off the throttle as they approached Stoltenberg's riverfront apartment house. Just like London, he thought. Take him inside, get him into bed, leave a door open if you can. No problems. The Mercedes accelerated suddenly, sweeping past the building. Delaroche swore aloud, then opened up the throttle and chased after them.

"YOUR NAME is not Eva Tebbe," Stoltenberg announced, as the car accelerated. "It is Astrid Vogel. You are a former member of the Red Army Faction."

"What the hell are you talking about? My name is Eva Tebbe, and I am a tourist from Berlin. Take me back to the club now, you crazy bastard, or I'm going to scream for the police!"

"I knew it was you five minutes after we met. That crazy Saxon accent of yours wasn't good enough to fool a professional."

"Professional what? Take me back to the club now!"

"I worked for the Stasi, you idiot! I handled the RAF. You were never in the East, but plenty of your comrades were. We had photographs and complete dossiers on every RAF member, including one Astrid Vogel."

"My name is Eva Tebbe," she repeated like a mantra. "I am a tourist from Berlin."

"I had an old associate fax me this photograph. You're older now, your hair's different, but it's you."

He reached inside his leather jacket and thrust the photograph before her. Astrid was looking out the window. They had crossed the river into Western Cairo and were moving south toward Giza.

"Look at it," he screamed, "it's you—look at it!"

"It's not me. Please, I don't know what you're talking about."

Her voice was beginning to lose conviction; she could hear it. So could Stoltenberg, apparently, for he slapped her hard across the mouth with the back of his hand. Her eyes teared, and she tasted blood on her lips.

She looked at the photograph, an old West German identification picture. She was revolutionary gaunt, a how-dare-you-take-my-fucking-picture expression on her face. Kurt Vogel's spiky haircut, Kurt

Vogel's pebble-lensed spectacles. She always thought it was a bloody awful picture, but when the police put it on a wanted poster she became the sex symbol of the radical Left.

The pyramids lay ahead of them, silhouetted against the deep blue of the desert night. A bone-white three-quarter moon hung low in the sky, shining like a torch. She thought, Where the hell are you, Jean-Paul? She resisted the impulse to turn around and look for him. What was it he had said? *I won't let anyone hurt you.* You'd better do something quickly, darling, she thought, or this man is going to make a liar of you. For some reason he had not searched her body or her handbag. Her gun was there, a small Browning automatic, but she knew she could never get it out in time in the confined space of the back seat. She had no choice but to wait and stall and hope to God that Jean-Paul was there somewhere in the darkness.

The pyramids disappeared. They turned onto a narrow unpaved track, stretching into the desert. Astrid said, "Where are you taking me? If you want to fuck, we can fuck right here. You don't have to take me to the desert and play these stupid games."

He slapped her again and said, "Shut up."

The Mercedes bucked and pitched wildly.

"Who hired you?"

"No one hired me. I'm not who you say I am. I want to go back to my hotel. Please, don't do this."

He slapped her again, harder. "Answer me! Who hired you?"

"No one, please."

"Who's the man? Your partner, the Frenchman?"

"He's just a silly man from my tour group. He's no one."

"Did you kill Colin Yardley in London?"

"I didn't kill anyone."

"Did you murder Colin Yardley in London? Did the Frenchman?"

"I don't kill people. I work for a magazine in Berlin. I do graphic design. My name is not Astrid Vogel. It's Eva Tebbe. Please, this is insane. Where are you taking me?"

"A place where no one will hear you scream, and no one will find you after I've killed you." He reached inside his coat again and this time brought out a gun. He pushed the barrel against her neck and pulled her hair. "Now, one more time," he said. "Who's the Frenchman? Who hired you?"

"My name is Eva Tebbe. I am a graphic designer from Berlin."

She thought of her old RAF indoctrination lectures. If you are arrested give them nothing. Defy them, berate them, but give them nothing. They will play games with you, fuck with your head. That's what policemen do. Give them nothing. In this case the advice had a very practical application, because the moment she told Stoltenberg the truth he would certainly kill her.

He pulled her hair violently, then released her. Her handbag lay on the seat between them. He opened the flap and dug through the contents until he found the Browning. He displayed it for her, as proof of her treachery, and placed it inside his coat.

"He's very sloppy, this Frenchman of yours, Astrid. He sent you into a very dangerous situation.

He knew I worked for the Stasi. He should have realized I might recognize a former Red Army Faction killer. It takes a cold bastard to send a woman into a situation like that."

The car came to a sliding stop on a desert escarpment overlooking the city. Below them Cairo spread like a giant fan, narrow in the south, broad in the north at the base of the Nile delta. A thousand minarets stretched toward the sky. She wondered which was hers. She wanted to be back in her horrid hotel room, with her toilet that didn't work, next to her building that was about to crash down.

"You love this man, obviously. That's why you are willing to endure physical pain for him. He does not feel the same for you, I assure you. Otherwise, he would never have allowed you to approach me. He's using you, just like those bastards in the RAF used you."

Stoltenberg said something to the driver in rapid Arabic that Astrid did not understand. The driver opened the door and got out. Stoltenberg shoved the gun into her throat again.

"All right," he said. "Let's try this one more time."

DELAROCHE KILLED THE BIKE'S ENGINE when he saw the brake lights of the Mercedes flare red. He silently coasted to a stop, pushed the bike off the track, and approached the car on foot. The moon threw shadows. Cairo murmured in the distance. He froze when he heard a car door open and close. The car remained dark; Stoltenberg, like any decent officer, had disabled his interior light. In the moonlight Delaroche could see the driver, gun in hand, checking the perimeter. Delaroche crouched behind a jagged outcropping of rock and waited for the man to draw nearer. When the driver was about ten yards away, Delaroche stood and leveled his Beretta in the darkness.

STOLTENBERG WAS SLAPPING her again, her face, the back of her head, her breasts. She felt he was beginning to enjoy it. She thought about something else, anything else. She thought of her houseboat on the Prinsengracht, and her little bookstore, and she wished to God that Jean-Paul Delaroche had never come into her life. The front driver's-side door opened and closed. In the darkness Astrid could barely make out the silhouetted figure of a man behind the wheel. She realized it was not the same man who had been there before.

Stoltenberg was pressing the gun into Astrid's throat again.

"Anything back there?" Stoltenberg said in Arabic.

The man behind the wheel shook his head.

"*Yallah,*" Stoltenberg said. Let's go.

Delaroche spun around and pointed the Beretta at Stoltenberg's face.

The German was too stunned to react.

Delaroche fired three times.

"HE COULD HAVE KILLED ME, Jean-Paul."

She lay on the bed at the Hotel Imperial, dressed in her galabia, smoking one cigarette after the next in the half-darkness. Delaroche lay next to her, dismantling his guns. Her hair was damp from the shower; she had rubbed herself raw, trying to wash away Stoltenberg's blood. Wind drifted through the open French doors. She shuddered with a chill. The toilet had stopped working again. Delaroche called the front desk and asked someone to fix it, but Mr. Fahmy, the keeper of the secret knowledge, was off that night. "*Bokra, in-shallah,*" the clerk said. Tomorrow, God willing.

Delaroche regarded her statement; the professional in him could not dispute it. Eric Stoltenberg had had ample time and opportunity to kill her. He had chosen not to because he needed more information.

"He could have killed you," Delaroche said, "but he didn't because you behaved perfectly. You stalled, you told him nothing. You were never alone. I was right behind you the entire time."

"If he wanted to kill me, you couldn't have stopped him."

"This work is not without risk. You know that."

Stoltenberg's words ran through her head.

He's very sloppy, this Frenchman of yours. He sent you into a very dangerous situation.

"I'm not sure I can go on, Jean-Paul."

"You took the assignment. You took the money. You can't back out now."

"I want to go back to Amsterdam, to the Prinsengracht."

"That door is closed to you now."

She took inventory of her injuries once more: split lip, bruised cheekbone, a mark like a handprint on her right breast. She had never been in a situation where she was helpless, and she didn't like it.

"I don't want to die like an animal in the desert."

"Nor do I," he said. "I won't let that happen to either of us."

"Where will you go, when this business is finished?"

"Back to Brélés if I can. If not, the Caribbean."

"And where will I go, now that the door to Amsterdam has been closed to me?"

He put down his guns and lay on top of her.

"You can come with me to the Caribbean."

"And what will I do there?"

"Whatever you like, or nothing at all."

"And what will I be to you? Will I be your wife?"

Delaroche shook his head. "No, you will not be my wife."

"Will there be other women?"

He shook his head again. "No, there will be no other women."

"I'll be whatever you want me to be, but you mustn't humiliate me with other women."

"I would never humiliate you, Astrid."

He kissed her mouth gently, so as not to hurt the cut on her lip. He unbuttoned her galabia and kissed her breasts and the ugly mark left by Stoltenberg's hand. He slid down her body and pushed up the galabia. The terror she had felt hours earlier melted with the exquisite sensation of what he was doing between her thighs.

"Where will we live?" she asked softly.

"By the sea," he said, and resumed.

"Will you do this to me by the sea, Jean-Paul?"

She felt his head nod between her legs.

"Will you do this to me *often* by the sea, Jean-Paul?"

But it was a silly question, and he did not answer it. She took his head and pulled him tightly against her body. She wanted to tell him she loved him, but she knew such things would never be said aloud. Afterward, he lay next to her, softly breathing.

"Do you sleep at night, Jean-Paul?"

"Some nights are better than others."

"Do you see them?"

"I see them for a while, and then they go away."

"Why do you kill them that way? Why do you shoot them in the face three times?"

"Because I want them to know I exist."

Her eyes closed, and she drifted toward sleep.

"Are you the Beast, Jean-Paul?"

"What are you talking about?"

"The Beast," she repeated. "The Devil. Perhaps you leave your mark on their faces because you're the Beast."

"The people I kill are wicked men. If I don't kill them, someone else will. It's just business, nothing more."

"It's more than business with you, Jean-Paul. It's—" She hesitated, and for a moment he thought she was finally asleep. "It's *art,* Jean-Paul. Your killing is like art."

"Go to sleep, Astrid."

"Wait for me to fall asleep before you do, Jean-Paul."

"I'll wait," he said.

She was quiet for another moment; then she said, "When you retire, what will become of Arbatov?"

"I suppose he'll have to retire too," Delaroche said. "He's an old man anyway."

"Are you the Devil, Jean-Paul?" Astrid said, but she was asleep before he could answer.

SHE DUG IT FROM HER BAG in the moments before dawn, the little item from *Le Monde* about a retired Russian diplomat killed by street thugs in Paris. Delaroche was sleeping—or pretending to sleep, she was never sure.

She carried the clipping to Fahmy's treacherous balcony and read it once more in the beige dawn. Perhaps it wasn't Jean-Paul, she thought. Perhaps it really was just a robbery.

Cairo stirred beneath her. A *zabbaleen* entered the alley, a little girl, dressed in rags, sleepily flicking an ass with a switch. The muezzin screamed. A thousand more joined in.

She touched a match to the clipping and held it aloft until flame engulfed it. Then she released it and watched it drift downward, until it came to rest on a pile of garbage and turned to gray ash.

31. Cairo

THE TAXI RIDE from the airport had taken nearly as long as the flight from Rome. It was hot, even for November, and there was no air-conditioning in the well-worn little Fiat. Michael sat back and tried to relax. He knew getting agitated would only make matters worse; Cairo was like a trick knot that became tighter the more you struggled.

The driver assumed Michael was a rich Egyptian back from a Roman holiday, and he prattled on about how bad things had become. He had the modest robe and unkempt beard of a devout Muslim. The road was choked with every conceivable type of transport: cars, buses, and trucks belching diesel fumes, donkey carts, bicycles, and pedestrians. A wispy boy shoved a live chicken in Michael's face and asked if he wanted to buy it. The driver shouted him away. A colossal image of the Egyptian president smiled down benevolently from a roadside billboard. "He wouldn't be smiling if he were stuck in this traffic with the rest of us," the driver murmured.

Michael had never lived in Cairo, but he had spent a great deal of time there. He had served as the control officer for an important agent inside the Mukhabarat, the all-pervasive Egyptian security service. The agent didn't want to be debriefed by an officer from Cairo Station—he knew the embassy and the CIA residents were well monitored—so Michael slipped into Egypt from time to time, posing as a businessman, and did the debriefing himself. The agent provided valuable intelligence on the state of radical Islam in Egypt, the most important U.S. ally in the Arab world. Sometimes the information flowed the other way. When Michael learned of a plot to assassinate the Egyptian interior minister, he passed the information to this agent. The plot was foiled, and several members of the al-Gama'at Ismalyya were arrested. Michael's man received a big promotion that gave him access to better intelligence.

The Nile Hilton is located on Tahrir Square, overlooking the river. *Tahrir* means liberation in Arabic, and Michael always thought it was the most inappropriately named place on earth. The immense square was jammed with traffic well into the night. The taxi hadn't moved an inch in five minutes. The blare of traffic horns was unbearable. Michael paid the fare and walked the rest of the way.

He checked into the room, showered and changed, and went out again. The Mukhabarat had one of the most extensive monitoring operations on earth. Michael knew his room telephone was certainly bugged, even though he was traveling as an Italian businessman in town for a round of meetings. He went into the Tahrir Square metro station and found a telephone kiosk. He spoke quietly into the receiver for two minutes, raising his voice once to shout over the clatter of a train entering the station.

He had two hours to kill. He would put the time to good use. He boarded the next train, got off at the first station, and doubled back. He walked. He went to the Egyptian Museum. He was lured into a tourist shop that specialized in fragrant oils. The shop boys plied him with tea and cigarettes while he sampled several oils. Michael rewarded their hospitality by purchasing a small bottle of vile sandalwood oil, which he tossed in the nearest rubbish bin as soon as he left. He was clean, no surveillance.

He flagged down a taxi and climbed inside.

. . .

CAIRO IS A CITY of lost elegance. Once there were fine cinemas and an opera house and walled villas that spilled chamber music into the warm nights. Little is left, and what remains has the quality of newspaper left too long in the sun. Many of the villas have been deserted, the opera house is gone, and the theaters stink of urine. The restaurant Arabesque has the feel of old Cairo, rather like an old man who putters around the house all day dressed in a suit and tie.

It was midafternoon, the quiet time between lunch and dinner, and the dining room was nearly deserted. Michael actually had to strain to hear the din of traffic noise, so thorough was the restaurant's insulation. Yousef Hafez was seated at a corner table, far from anyone else. He looked up and smiled as Michael approached, flashing two rows of perfect white teeth. He had the look of an Egyptian film star, the fleshy type in his fifties with thick graying hair who attracts younger women and beats up younger men. Michael knew it was not far from the truth.

They ordered cold white wine. Hafez was a Muslim, but he thought strict adherence to Islamic law was for "the crazies and the peasants." They clinked glasses and talked about old times for an hour while the waiters brought plate after plate of Lebanese-style appetizers.

Michael finally got around to business. He told Hafez he was in Cairo on a personal matter. He hoped Hafez would help him out of friendship and professional courtesy. Under no circumstances could he discuss this matter with his current control officer. He would be paid for his help, directly from Michael's pocket.

"You can buy me lunch, and another bottle of this wine, but keep your money."

Michael signaled the white-jacketed waiter to bring more wine. While the waiter poured, Hafez talked about a pizza he had eaten in Cannes that summer. The Mukhabarat employed tens of thousands of informants; it was always possible the waiter was one of them. When he was gone, Hafez said, "Now, what can I do for you, my friend?"

"I want to talk to a man named Eric Stoltenberg. He's former Stasi, living in Cairo doing freelance work."

"I know who he is."

"You know where to find him?"

"Actually, I do."

Hafez set down his wineglass and signaled for the check.

THE BODY was in a warm room with a hundred others, covered in a gray sheet. The attendant's coverall was spotted with blood. Hafez knelt next to the body and looked to Michael to make certain he was ready. Michael nodded, and Hafez drew back the sheet. Michael looked quickly away and retched once, the lunch at Arabesque rising in his throat.

"Where did you find him?" Michael asked.

"Near the pyramids on the edge of the desert."

"Let me guess—shot three times in the face."

"Exactly," Hafez said, lighting a cigarette to cover the smell. "He was last seen in a nightclub in Zamalek. A place called Break Point."

"I know it," Michael said.

"He was dancing with a European woman—tall, blond, German, maybe."

"Her name is Astrid Vogel. She used to be a member of the Red Army Faction."

"She did this?"

"No, I suspect she had some help. You have videotapes of all arriving passengers at Cairo airport?"

Hafez pulled a face that showed he found the question mildly amusing.

"Mind if I have a look?"

Hafez covered the body and said, "Let's go."

THEY PLACED MICHAEL in a room with a videotape deck and monitor. A pair of factotums moved silently in and out, bringing new tapes in one direction, taking the old ones in the other. They brought him tea, Russian style, in a glass with an ornate metal holder. They brought him Egyptian tobacco when his Marlboros were gone. He worked backward, beginning twenty-four hours before the murder. October would be meticulous. October would plan it carefully.

He found her sometime after midnight. She was tall and erect, and her hair was drawn back tightly, accentuating her long nose. Her large hands seemed to struggle with the passport as she handed it across to the customs officer.

October appeared five minutes later, short, light on his feet, like a fencer. The brim of a baseball cap, pulled low over his brow, obscured much of the face, but Michael could see enough of it. He froze the two images and called for Hafez.

"Here are your killers," Michael said, when Hafez came into the room. "This one is Astrid Vogel, the German woman whom Stoltenberg was dancing with at the nightclub."

Hafez pointed at the second image. "And that one?"

Michael stared at the screen. "I wish to Christ I knew."

32. Amsterdam

IT WAS A BITTERLY COLD DAWN when Delaroche and Astrid returned to the houseboat on the Prinsengracht. For twenty minutes Delaroche inspected the vessel carefully to make certain no one had been aboard. He checked his telltales. He tore through the cabinets in the galley and the drawers in Astrid's bedroom. He prowled the frozen deck. Astrid was no help to him. Content to finally be aboard her beloved *Krista,* she collapsed fully clothed on the bed and watched him with one eye as if he were mad.

Delaroche felt alert and refreshed, despite the long journey. The previous morning they had flown from Cairo to Madrid, having first explained to Mr. Fahmy that they were cutting short their stay at the Hotel Imperial because madam was very ill. Fahmy feared it was the toilet that had driven them away— he offered the hotel's best suite to entice them to remain—but Delaroche assured him it was the water, not the toilet, that had forced them to leave. From Madrid they had taken the train to Amsterdam. Delaroche spent the journey hunched over his laptop like a businessman, planning his next assassination. Astrid slept fitfully next to him, reliving the last.

The canal had frozen again, and once more the *Krista* was filled with the joyous shouts of skaters. Astrid took sleeping pills and covered her head with a pillow. Delaroche was too wired to sleep, so at midmorning, when the sun burned away the clouds, he went onto the foredeck and painted, bundled in a heavy sweater and fingerless gloves. The light was good and so was the subject matter—skaters on the canal, gabled houses in the background—and when it was done he thought it was the best work he had produced in Amsterdam.

He had a curious desire for Astrid's approval, but when he went below and tried to wake her, she just mumbled that her name was Eva Tebbe, and she was a graphic artist from Berlin, and to please stop slapping her.

He left her in the early afternoon, pedaling her bicycle through Amsterdam with his laptop computer slung over his back. He locked the bike outside a telephone center near the Rijksmuseum and went inside. He entered a booth, hooked up his computer, and worked the keys for a few moments. He had one piece of electronic mail. He opened the mail, and it came onto the screen as gibberish. He entered his code name, and the message appeared in clear text.

CONGRATULATIONS ON THE SUCCESSFUL COMPLETION OF YOUR MISSION IN CAIRO. PAYMENT HAS BEEN WIRED INTO YOUR NUMBERED ACCOUNT. WE HAVE

322 *Daniel Silva*

ONE ADDITIONAL ASSIGNMENT FOR YOU. IF YOU AC-
CEPT YOU WILL BE PAID ONE AND A HALF MILLION DOL-
LARS, HALF IN ADVANCE. TO ACCEPT, PRESS THE
ENTER KEY. PAYMENT WILL AUTOMATICALLY BE FOR-
WARDED TO YOUR ACCOUNT AND A DOSSIER AND OP-
ERATIONAL DETAILS WILL BE DOWNLOADED ONTO
YOUR COMPUTER. THE FILE WILL BE ENCRYPTED, OF
COURSE, AND YOUR CODE NAME WILL UNLOCK IT. IF
YOU WISH TO DECLINE, PRESS ESCAPE.

Delaroche looked away from the screen and
thought for a moment. With that fee, he would have an
extraordinary amount of money, more than enough to
guarantee comfort and security the rest of his life. He
knew it was not without risk, though. The assassinations would grow more difficult—Eric Stoltenberg
was proof of that—and now he was being asked to
carry out another killing. He wondered too whether
Astrid could go on; the confrontation in Cairo with
Stoltenberg had taken a heavy toll on her. Delaroche
realized, however, that Astrid's life was now tied inex-
orably to his. She would do what he wanted her to do.

He pushed the ENTER key. The file downloaded
onto his laptop over the high-speed modem. He
glanced at the dossier and shut down the computer.
He knew the man; he had confronted him once before.

He put away the computer and dialed his bank in
Zurich. Herr Becker came on the line. Yes, two de-
posits had been made to the account: one for a million dollars, a second for three-quarters of a million
moments ago. Delaroche instructed Becker to wire
the money to the Bahamian accounts.

He left the telephone center and went out to collect Astrid's bicycle. A thief was working the lock. Delaroche politely informed him that the bicycle was his. The thief told Delaroche to fuck off. Delaroche drove a foot into his kidney. As he rode off on the bicycle, the thief still lay on the ground, writhing silently.

ASTRID SLEPT until after sunset. They had coffee in a café near the *Krista* and walked the canals until dinner. Astrid inhaled the cold clear air of Amsterdam, trying to cleanse her lungs of the dust and smoke of Cairo. Her nerves were brittle from sleeping pills and coffee. A man with gray-blond hair bumped into her. Astrid was reaching inside her bag for her gun before Delaroche put a hand on her arm and whispered that it was nothing, just a stranger in a hurry.

They ate like spent lovers in the restaurant on the Herengracht where Delaroche had taken her the first night. She had eaten nothing in Cairo, so she devoured her own food and most of Delaroche's. Her complexion, bone-white with exhaustion and nerves, took on color with the food and the wine and the night air. He told her over dessert. Her face registered nothing more than mild annoyance, as if Delaroche had informed her he would be working late at the office that evening.

"You don't have to do it," he said.

"I don't want to be without you."

They made love beneath *Krista*'s skylight to the screams of skaters on the Prinsengracht. Afterward, Delaroche confessed he had shot down the airliner off New York, along with a Palestinian boy whom he had killed. He told her he believed the men they had killed were involved in the attack as well, or that they somehow knew the truth.

"Who are the men that hired you?" she asked, touching his lips.

"I honestly don't know."

"You *must* know they will kill you, Jean-Paul. When you finish the contract they'll come after you. And me, too."

"I'm aware of that."

"Where will we go?"

"To our house on the beach."

"Will it be safe there?"

"It will be as safe as anywhere else."

She lit a cigarette and blew a slender stream of smoke at the skylight. He reached for his laptop, turned on the power, and punched a few keys. The hard drive whirred, then the image of a dark-haired man appeared on the screen.

"Why does this man have to die?"

"I suspect he knows too much."

Another image appeared, Elizabeth Osbourne.

"His wife is beautiful."

"Yes."

"A pity."

"Yes," Delaroche said, and he closed the laptop.

33. Shelter Island, New York

MICHAEL MADE THE LAST FERRY of the night. For a few moments he stood at the rail in the cold air, but the wind and sea spray drove him back inside the rented Buick from JFK. He had called Adrian Carter from the Long Island Expressway and told him he was back in the country. Carter wanted to know where the hell he had been. Michael said he would come to headquarters tomorrow afternoon and explain everything. When Carter demanded an explanation now, Michael lied and said the cellular connection was bad and hung up. The last thing he heard was Adrian Carter uncharacteristically screaming obscenities as he replaced the phone in its cradle.

Rollers broke over the prow, dousing the windshield. Michael flicked the wipers. The lights of Cannon Point burned across Shelter Island Sound. The images of the last weeks played out in his mind— Flight 002, Colin Yardley, Heathrow, Drozdov, Muhammad Awad, Eric Stoltenberg, Astrid Vogel, October. They were like pieces of a melody he could not complete. He was certain the Sword of Gaza had not carried out the attack. He believed it was the work of another group, or individual, which did it in the name of the Sword of Gaza. But who? And why? October was a contract killer only; if he were involved it would be at the behest of others. The same was true of Astrid Vogel; the Red Army Faction had neither the resources nor the motive for staging the attack. Michael suspected he knew the truth, or at least part of it: The man called October had been hired to eliminate the team that carried out the attack.

The ferry docked at Shelter Island. Michael turned over the engine and drove off. Shelter Island Heights was deserted, shops and Victorian cottages dark. He sped along Winthrop Road, through a tunnel of leafless trees, and skirted the edge of Dering Harbor. In the summer the harbor was filled with sailboats; now it was deserted except for the *Athena,* bobbing at her mooring in the whitecaps off Cannon Point.

Michael also suspected he had been the target on the Channel ferry, not Muhammad Awad. Who was the man beneath the balaclava? Was it October? He had seen October use his gun, in person on the Chelsea Embankment and on videotape, and it didn't appear to be the same man. He had to assume he was still a target, and he had to consider the possibility they now would send October, one of the world's best assassins, to do the job. He would have to tell Carter and Monica Tyler everything; he needed their protection. He would tell Elizabeth everything too, but for very different reasons. He loved her more than anything else and he desperately wanted to regain her trust.

Cannon Point appeared before him. Michael stopped at the security gate, lowered his window, and entered the code. The gate rolled open, and lights came on in the caretaker's cottage. Michael drove slowly up the long gravel drive. A clan of white-tailed deer, snacking on the dead grass of Cannon's broad lawn, looked up and eyed Michael warily. He saw a shaft of light and heard dogs barking. It was only Charlie, the caretaker, walking toward him, retrievers yapping at his heels.

Michael shut down the engine and got out. Lights came on in the main house, and the door swung open.

He saw Elizabeth framed in the light, shrouded in one of the senator's old coats. She stepped outside, watching him, arms folded beneath her breasts. Wind blew hair across her face. Then she came to him in a few careful steps and hurled herself against his body.

"Don't ever leave me again, Michael."

"I won't," he said. "God, I'm so sorry."

"I want to talk. I want you to tell me everything."

"I'll tell you everything, Elizabeth. There are things you need to know."

THEY TALKED for hours. Elizabeth sat on the bed, knees beneath her chin, fidgeting with an unlit Benson & Hedges. Michael roamed and paced, now sitting at her side, now staring out the window at the waters of the Sound. True to his word, he told her everything. He felt the tension release with the unburdening of each secret. He wished he had never kept things from her in the first place. He always told himself it was for Elizabeth's protection, but he realized now that was only part of the truth. He had lived a life of secrets and lies so long he knew no other way. Secrecy was like a disease, an affliction. His father had caught it, and it had driven his mother mad. Michael should have avoided the same mistakes.

She was silent for a long time after he finished. Finally she said, "What do you want from me?"

"Forgiveness," he said. "Forgiveness and understanding."

"You have that, Michael." She put the unlit cigarette back in the pack. "What's going to happen tomorrow at Langley?"

"They're probably going to put a loaded forty-five in front of me."

"What are you talking about?"

"I'm going to be in serious trouble. I may not survive it."

"Don't toy with me, Michael."

"There isn't a lot of work out there for disgraced spooks."

"We don't need the money. You can take some time off and do something normal for the rest of your life." She saw the impact of her words on his face and said, "God, Michael, I'm sorry. I didn't mean that."

"There's just one thing I want to do before I go. I want to know what really happened to that jetliner. I want the truth."

"And ye shall know the truth, and the truth shall set ye free, eh, Michael?"

"Something like that."

"Is she gone?"

"Is who gone?"

"Sarah. Is she gone?"

"She was never there to begin with."

"That's clever, Michael, but answer my question."

"Sometimes, I'll think about what happened to her. But I don't love her, Elizabeth, and I don't wish she were lying there instead of you."

A tear rolled down her face. She punched it away and said, "Come here, Michael. Come to bed."

She lay in his arms for a long time, crying. He held her until the shaking stopped. She looked up at him, face damp, and said, "Mind if I tell you a little about my day now, darling?"

"I'd love to hear about your day."

"Four of the eggs fertilized. They implanted them this morning. I'm supposed to take it easy for a couple of days. They'll do a pregnancy test and see if it worked."

He laid the palm of his hand on her stomach. She kissed his mouth.

"Michael Osbourne, that's the first time I've seen you smile in weeks."

"It's the first good news I've had in weeks."

She trailed a finger through his hair. "Will they come for you?"

"I don't know. If I'm out, I'm no threat to them anymore."

"Will you quit tomorrow? For me?"

"I don't think I'm going to be given a choice."

"And the truth shall set ye free," she said.

"Amen."

34. Cyprus

THE SMALL GULFSTREAM jet sat on the isolated runway, engines whining in the darkness. The pilot was named Roger Stephens, a former officer of the Royal Navy's Fleet Air Arm who was decorated in the Falklands War. He now worked for the Transport Section of the Society. As he mechanically went through the preflight checks, Stephens was missing one crucial piece of information: a flight plan. The passengers, a man and a woman, were supposed to supply that on boarding. He assumed it would be a long flight, though; he had been ordered to take on a full complement of fuel.

Thirty minutes later a black Range Rover turned onto the runway and headed toward the Gulfstream at high speed, headlights dark. It stopped at the foot of the stairway, deposited two people, and sped quickly away. Stephens had flown several missions for the Society, for which he was well compensated, and he knew the rules. He was not to look at the faces of the passengers, nor was he to speak to them. The arrangement suited Stephens fine. The Society and the men they employed were a rough lot, and he wanted as little to do with them as possible.

The passengers boarded the plane and took their seats. A black nylon duffel bag had been left on board for them, and the refrigerator was well stocked with food and wine. Stephens heard the rip of a zipper, the metallic crack of an experienced gunman checking the action of an automatic weapon, the pop of a champagne cork, the murmur of a woman speaking German-accented French.

A moment later the man entered the cockpit and stood behind Stephens.

"The flight plan," he said simply.

The language was English with a vague accent Stephens could not quite place. The flight plan was thrust before his face, along with a silenced Beretta handgun.

Stephens took the flight plan.

Delaroche said, "Stay in the cockpit, and don't look at either one of us. If you look at us, I'll kill you and land the plane myself. Do you hear me?"

Stephens nodded. A chill ran down the back of his neck. Delaroche left the cockpit and took his seat in the passenger compartment. Stephens reached back, without turning around, and closed the cockpit door.

A moment later the engines fired and the Gulfstream lifted into the Mediterranean night.

35. CIA Headquarters, Langley, Virginia

MICHAEL ALWAYS THOUGHT environmentalists would have a field day with Monica Tyler's office. Perched on the seventh floor, it was large and airy and over-looked the trees along the river. Monica had scoffed at the idea of decorating her lair with government furniture and had brought her own from her New York office instead: a large mahogany desk, mahogany file cabinets, mahogany bookshelves, and a mahogany conference table surrounded by cozy leather chairs. Trinkets of ivory and silver were scattered about, and fine Persian rugs covered much of the ugly gray-blue government carpeting. One wall was dedicated entirely to photographs of Monica with famous people: Monica with James Beckwith, Monica with Director Ronald Clark, Monica with a famous actor, Monica with Princess Diana. In the notoriously camera-shy world of intelligence, Monica was a veritable cover girl.

Entering the room, Michael smelled coffee brewing—a rich dark Italian or French roast—and from somewhere he could hear quiet orchestral music.

Adrian Carter arrived next, looking very hung over. He sniffed at the air, smelled the coffee, and frowned. Monica arrived last, five minutes late as usual, followed by Tweedledee and Tweedledum, each clutching a leather folder.

They sat at the conference table, Monica at the head, the factotums at her right hand, Michael and Carter at her left. A secretary brought a tray of coffee and cream and a plate of dainty cookies. Monica gaveled the proceedings to order by tapping the tip of her stiletto gold pen on the polished surface of the table.

"Where's McManus?" Carter asked.

"He had to go downtown to the Hoover Building on an urgent matter," Monica said tonelessly.

"Don't you think the FBI's representative to the Counterterrorism Center should be sitting in on this meeting?"

"Anything the FBI is required to know will be passed on to them in due course," she said. "This is an Agency matter and will be dealt with as such."

Carter, unable to hide his anger, gnawed on the nail of his forefinger.

Monica looked at Michael. "After the incident on the ferry you were ordered to return from London immediately and report to headquarters. You disobeyed that order and went to Cairo instead. Why?"

"I believed I could uncover valuable information concerning an active investigation," Michael said. "I didn't go because I wanted to see the pyramids."

"Don't be a smartass. You're in enough trouble as it is. What did you learn in Cairo?"

Michael placed the photographs given to him by Muhammad Awad on the table and turned them so Monica could see. "Here's Hassan Mahmoud, the man found dead in the Whaler, meeting with a man named Eric Stoltenberg in Cairo a few weeks before the attack on the jetliner. Stoltenberg is former Stasi. He worked in the department that supported national liberation and guerrilla groups around the world. He's freelance now. Muhammad Awad, before he was shot on the ferry, said Mahmoud had joined forces with Stoltenberg."

"Two men having coffee in a Cairo café is hardly proof of a conspiracy, Michael."

Michael held his temper. Somewhere during her ascent to the top, Monica had mastered the art of derailing her opponent in mid-thought with a barb or a shallow contradiction.

"I went to Cairo because I wanted to talk to Stoltenberg."

"Why didn't you pass on the information to Carter at the Center and let someone from Cairo Station handle it?"

"Because I wanted to handle it myself."

"At least that's honest. Continue."

"By the time I got to Cairo, Stoltenberg was dead." Michael dropped a photograph of Stoltenberg's ruined face on the table. Carter looked away and winced. Monica's face remained placid. "He was shot three times in the face, just like Hassan Mahmoud, just like Colin Yardley."

"And just like Sarah Randolph."

Michael looked down at his hands, then at Monica.

"Yes," he said. "Just like Sarah Randolph."

"And you believe these killings are all the work of the same man?"

"I'm certain of it. He's a former KGB assassin, code-named October, who was inserted into the West as a young man and planted deep. He's a contract killer now, the world's most expensive and proficient assassin."

"And this you learned from Ivan Drozdov?"

"That's correct."

"Your theory, Michael?"

"That Muhammad Awad was telling the truth: The Sword of Gaza did not carry out this attack. It was the work of some other group or individual, done in the name of the Sword of Gaza. And now October has been hired by this group or individual to liquidate the team that carried out the attack." Michael paused for a moment, then said, "And eventually he will come after me."

"Would you like to explain that?"

"I think they tried to kill me once already, on the ferry during the meeting with Awad. They failed. I think they'll try again, and this time I think they'll give the job to October."

There was a long pause. Conversations with Monica were always punctuated by moments of silence, as though she were receiving her next lines from a stage prompter in the wings.

"Who's they, Michael? What they? Where they? How they?"

"I don't know. Someone blew up that jetliner, and did it for a very good reason. Look what's happened in the interim. The Mideast peace process has collapsed; arms are pouring into the region like never before."

Michael thought, And a wounded president came from behind and won reelection, and this country is about to build a costly missile defense system.

"Good God, Michael! Surely you're not suggesting any kind of linkage."

"I don't know all the answers. What I'm suggesting is that we seriously consider the possibility other forces were involved in the attack and broaden our investigation accordingly."

Adrian Carter finally spoke. "I thought Michael was off the mark when he raised this with me the first time, but now I believe I was mistaken. I think the Agency should do as Michael suggests."

Monica hesitated a moment. "I reluctantly concur, Michael, but I'm afraid the investigation will go forward without your involvement." She treated herself to a long sip of her coffee. "You have uncovered potentially valuable intelligence, but your means and methods have been inexcusable and, frankly, unbefitting an intelligence officer of your experience. I'm afraid I have no choice but to place you on suspension, pending the outcome of a disciplinary review. I'm sorry, Michael, but you've left me no other option."

Michael said nothing. He had expected it, but still a shock wave shot through him when Monica spoke the words.

"As for your concerns about your personal safety, you can be certain that the Agency will take every step necessary to protect you and your family."

"Thank you, Monica," Michael said, and immediately regretted it. Assurances from Monica Tyler had the permanance of a sonnet written on the surface of a lake.

THE CHAUFFEURED CAR bearing Mitchell Elliott arrived at his town house on California Street shortly after 8 P.M. It had been a very long day, much of it spent on Capitol Hill twisting arms. Elliott had been around politics long enough to realize euphoria has a tendency to wear off rather quickly in Washington. Promises made by presidents often die the death of a thousand cuts in committee. It would be many months before the national missile defense came before Congress for a vote. The tragedy of Flight 002 would be a distant memory by then, and Beckwith would be a lame-duck president. It would be left to Elliott to make sure the program didn't fall by the wayside. He had spread millions of dollars around Capitol Hill; half the members of Congress were indebted to him. Still, he realized it was going to take every ounce of his influence and imagination to see the project through to the end.

The car stopped at the curb. Mark Calahan got out and opened the door. Elliott went inside the house and walked upstairs to the library. He poured himself a glass of scotch and went into the bedroom. The bathroom door opened and a woman entered the room, dressed in a terry-cloth robe, hair damp from the shower.

He looked up. "Hello, Monica darling, tell me about your day."

· · ·

"HE UNDERESTIMATES ME," she said, lying next to him in bed. "He plays me for the idiot. He thinks he's smarter than me, and I detest people who think they're smarter than me."

"Let him underestimate you," Elliott said. "It's a fatal mistake, in this case literally."

"I had to reopen the investigation today; I had no other choice. Osbourne has managed to uncover quite a lot of your little game."

"He's only scratched the surface, Monica. You know that as well as I do. And besides, there's no way he'll ever see the whole picture. Osbourne is trapped in a house of mirrors."

"He knows the identity of your assassins, and he thinks he knows why they're killing."

"He doesn't know who's behind them, and there's no way he ever will."

"I had to put out a worldwide alert for them, Mitchell."

"Who controls the distribution at Langley?"

"Everything comes to me eyes only," she said. "Theoretically, no one else in the building will see it. And I sent McManus out on an errand, so the Bureau is completely in the dark."

"And Michael Osbourne will never know what hit him. Good girl, Monica. You just earned yourself a nice bonus."

"I had something else in mind, actually."

December

36. Northern Canada

THE GULFSTREAM DROPPED below radar cover over the Davis Strait and landed on a remote flare-lit road along the eastern shores of Hudson Bay. Astrid and Delaroche ambled down the stairway, Delaroche with the nylon duffel slung across his back, Astrid with her hands over her face against the cruel Arctic air. Stephens never shut down the engines. As soon as Astrid and Delaroche were clear of the aircraft, he raced down the road once more, and the Gulfstream lifted into the clear Canadian morning.

A black Range Rover waited for them on the shoulder of the road, filled with cold-weather outdoor gear—snowshoes, backpacks, parkas, and dehydrated foods—and a packet of detailed travel instructions. They climbed in and closed the doors against the bitter air. Delaroche turned the key. The engine groaned, struggled, then died. Delaroche felt his heart sink. The jet was gone. They were completely alone. If the truck didn't start they could not survive long.

He turned the key once more, and this time the engine started. Astrid, typically German for an instant, said, "Thanks God."

"I thought you were a good communist atheist," Delaroche cracked.

"Shut up and turn the heat on."

He did as she asked. Then he opened the packet and tried to read the instructions, but it was no good. He removed a pair of half-moon reading glasses from the breast pocket of his coat and thrust them onto his face.

"I've never seen you wear those before, Jean-Paul."

"I don't like to wear them in front of people, but sometimes it can't be helped."

"You look like a professor instead of a professional killer."

"That's the point, my love."

"How do you kill people so well if you can't see?"

"Because I'm shooting them, not reading them. If there were words written across their foreheads, I'd need my glasses."

"Please, Jean-Paul, drive the bloody car. I'm freezing to death."

"I have to know where I'm going before I drive."

"Do you always read the instructions first?"

He looked at her quizzically, as if he found the question mildly offensive.

"Of course you do. That's why you're so bloody good at everything you do. Jean-Paul Delaroche, methodical man."

"We all have our vices," he said, putting away the instructions. "I don't ridicule yours." He dropped the Range Rover into gear.

"Where are we going?" Astrid asked.

"A place called Vermont."

"Is it near our beach?"

"Not quite."

"Shit," she said, closing her eyes. "Wake me when we're there."

37. Washington, D.C.

THE FIRST DAY of Michael's exile was appalling. At dawn, when the alarm awakened him, he rushed into the shower and turned on the water before realizing he had nowhere to go. He went downstairs to the kitchen, made toast and coffee for Elizabeth, and brought it up to her. She had breakfast in bed and read the *Post.* A half hour later, Elizabeth was letting herself out the front door, dressed for work with her two briefcases and two cell phones. Michael stood in the front window, waving like an idiot, as she drove off in her silver Mercedes. All he needed was a cardigan and a pipe to complete the picture.

He finished the newspaper. He tried to read a book but couldn't concentrate on the pages. He tried to put the time to good use by checking all the door locks and replacing batteries in the alarm system. That took a total of twenty minutes. Maria, the Peruvian housekeeper, came at ten o'clock and chased him from room to room with her industrial-strength vacuum and toxic furniture polish. "It is a beautiful day outside, Señor Miguel," she said, shouting at him in Spanish over the roar of the vacuum. Maria spoke to him only in her native language. "You should go out and do something instead of sitting around the house all day."

Michael understood his own housekeeper had just dismissed him. He went upstairs, dressed in a nylon warm-up suit and running shoes, and went back downstairs. Maria thrust a piece of paper into his hand, a list of cleaning supplies she needed from the store. He stuck the list in his pocket and went out the front door onto N Street.

It was a warm day for early December, the kind of afternoon that always made Michael think there was no neighborhood in the world more beautiful than Georgetown. The sky was clear, the air breezy and soft and scented with wood smoke. N Street lay beneath a blanket of red and yellow autumn leaves. They crunched beneath Michael's feet as he jogged lightly along the redbrick sidewalk. Reflexively, he looked through the windows of the parked cars to see if anyone was sitting inside. A van bearing the name of a Virginia kitchen supply store was parked on the corner. Michael committed the name and number to memory; he would call later to make certain the place was real.

He ran down the hill to M Street and crossed Key Bridge. Wind gusted high on the bridge and made rippled patterns on the surface of the river below. It was like two different rivers. To Michael's right a wild river stretched northward into the distance. To his left lay the waterfront of Washington: the Harbor Place complex, the Watergate, the Kennedy Center beyond. Reaching the Virginia side of the river, he looked over his shoulder for any sign of surveillance.

A thinly built man in a Georgetown baseball hat was a hundred yards behind him.

Michael put his head down and ran faster, past Roosevelt Island, through the grass along the George Washington Parkway. He climbed up onto the Memorial Bridge and looked over his shoulder down the parkway. The man with the Georgetown cap was still there. Michael stopped and stretched, looking down from the bridge at the footpath below. The hatted man continued running south along the river, toward National Airport. Michael stood up and resumed running.

During the next twenty minutes he saw six men with caps and three men he thought might be October. He was jittery, he knew. He ran hard the rest of the way back to Georgetown. He stopped in Booeymongers, a sandwich shop popular with students from the university, and ordered a coffee to go. He sipped it as he walked along N Street and let himself into the house. He showered and changed and went out. He telephoned Elizabeth at the office from his car.

"I'm going to Langley," he said. "I have a little housekeeping I need to take care of." There were a few seconds of silence on the line, and Michael said, "Don't worry, Elizabeth, I wouldn't miss this afternoon for anything in the world."

"Thank you, Michael."

"See you in a couple of hours."

Michael crossed Key Bridge once more and turned onto the George Washington Parkway. He had made this drive thousands of times before, but now,

as he headed to Langley to clean out his desk, he saw
it all as if for the first time. There were giant poplars,
tributaries leaking from the rocky hills of Virginia,
sheer bluffs overlooking the Potomac.

At the front entrance the guard punched in
Michael's identification, frowned, and told him to
pass. Michael felt like a leper as he walked through
the harshly lit corridors toward the CTC. No one said
a word to him; no one looked in his direction. Intelligence services are nothing if not highly organized
cliques. When one member contracts a disease, the
others stay away, lest they catch it too.

The bull pen was quiet as Michael stepped
through the door and walked to his desk. For an hour
he picked through the contents of his drawers, separating the personal from the official. A week earlier
he had been fêted because of his actions at Heathrow.
Now he felt like the kicker who had just missed a
game-winning field goal. Every once in a while
someone would come forward, lay a hand on his
shoulder, and move quickly away. But no one spoke
to him.

As he was leaving, Adrian Carter poked his head
into the bull pen and gestured for Michael to come
into his office. He handed Michael a gift-wrapped
box.

"I thought it was only a suspension pending an
inquiry," Michael said, accepting the package.

"It is, but I wanted to give you this anyway,"
Carter said. His drooping eyes made him look more
morose than ever. "Open it at home, though. Some
people around here might not understand the humor."

Michael shook his hand. "Thanks for everything, Adrian. See you around."

"Yeah," Carter said. "And Michael, take care of yourself."

Michael walked outside and found his car in the parking lot. He tossed Carter's gift in the trunk, climbed inside, and drove off. Passing through the gates, he wondered if he would ever be back again.

MICHAEL MET ELIZABETH at the Georgetown University Medical Center. He left the Jaguar with the valet and took the elevator to the doctor's office. When he walked into the waiting room there was no sign of Elizabeth. For an instant he had the sinking feeling that he had missed the appointment, but a moment later she walked through the door, clutching her briefcases, and kissed him on the cheek.

A nurse showed them to the examination room and left a gown on the table. Elizabeth unbuttoned her blouse and skirt. She looked up and noticed Michael staring at her.

"Close your eyes."

"Actually, I was thinking about locking the door."

"Animal."

"Thank you."

Elizabeth finished undressing, slipped into the gown, and sat down on the examination table. Michael was fooling with the knobs of the sonogram machine.

"Would you knock that off?"

"Sorry, just a little nervous."

The doctor came into the room. He reminded Michael of Carter: sleepy, disheveled, a look of perpetual boredom on his face. He wrinkled his face as he read Elizabeth's chart, as though torn between the mahi mahi and the grilled salmon.

"The beta count looks very good," he said. "In fact, it's a little high. Why don't we have a look with the sonogram."

He raised Elizabeth's gown and covered her abdomen with a lubricating jelly. Then he pressed the wand of the sonogram against her skin and began moving it back and forth.

"There it is," he said, smiling for the first time. "That, ladies and gentlemen, is a very nice-looking egg sac."

Elizabeth was beaming. She reached out for Michael and grasped his hand tightly.

The doctor manipulated the wand for another moment. "And here is a second very nice-looking egg sac."

Michael said, "Oh, God."

The doctor shut down the machine. "Get dressed and meet me in my office. We need to talk about a few things. And by the way, congratulations."

"AT LEAST WE WON'T NEED to buy a bigger house," Michael said, trailing Elizabeth upstairs to the bedroom. "I always thought a six-bedroom Georgetown Federal was too big for just the two of us."

"Michael, stop talking like that. I'm forty years old. I'm beyond high risk. A lot of things could go wrong." She lay down on the bed. "I'm starving."

Michael lay beside her. "I can't get the image of you covered with lubricant out of my mind."

She kissed him. "Go away. You heard the doctor. I need to stay off my feet and rest for a few days. I'm at my most vulnerable right now."

He kissed her again. "I won't argue with that."

"Go downstairs and make me a sandwich."

He climbed off the bed and went down to the kitchen. He made Elizabeth a sandwich of turkey and Swiss cheese and poured her a glass of orange juice. He placed the sandwich and drink on a tray and carried it upstairs to her.

"I think I could get used to this." She took a bite of the sandwich. "How was it at work today?"

"I've obviously been declared an untouchable."

"That bad?"

"Worse."

"Who gave you that?" she asked, gesturing at the gift-wrapped box.

"Carter."

"Aren't you going to open it?"

"I thought I could live without another set of Cross pens."

"Gimme," she said, tearing at the wrapping while she chewed an enormous bite of the sandwich. Beneath the wrapping paper was a rectangular box, and inside the box was a sheath of documents stamped MOST SECRET.

Elizabeth said, "Michael, I think you need to take a look at this."

She thrust it at Michael, and he flipped through the pages quickly.

"What is it?"

He looked up at her.

"It's the CIA case file on a KGB assassin code-named October."

38. The U.S.–Canadian Border

DELAROCHE WAITED for first light. He had found a secluded spot in the woods, well off the highway south of Montreal, about three miles from the border. Astrid slept next to him in the back of the Range Rover beneath a heavy woolen blanket, body hunched against the cold. She had begged Delaroche to run the heater from time to time, but he refused because he wanted silence. He touched her hands as she slept. They were like ice.

At six-thirty he rose, poured coffee from a thermos flask, and made a large bowl of oatmeal. Astrid came out ten minutes later, swaddled in a down parka and fleece hat. "Give me some of that coffee, Jean-Paul," she said, taking the oatmeal and finishing the rest.

Delaroche placed their supplies into a pair of small backpacks. He gave the lighter one to Astrid and shouldered the other himself. He placed the Beretta in the front waistband of his trousers. He quickly went through the vehicle from end to end to make certain they had left nothing that might identify them. The Range Rover would be left behind; another was supposed to be waiting on the American side of the border.

They walked for an hour through the mountain ridges above Lake Champlain. They could have made the crossing by staying to the frozen lakeshore, but Delaroche deemed it too exposed. Two pairs of snow-shoes had been left in the Range Rover, but Delaroche thought it was best to use only hiking boots since the ground lay beneath only a few inches of hard frozen snow. Astrid struggled up and down the hillsides and through the dense trees. She was slightly awkward and ungainly in the best of circumstances; her long body was thoroughly unsuited to the rigors of winter mountain hiking. Once, she slipped down a hillside and came to rest flat on her back with her legs propped against a tree.

Delaroche was not certain exactly when they left Canada and entered the United States. There was no border demarcation, no fence, no visible electronic surveillance of any kind. His employers had selected the spot well. Delaroche remembered a night a long time ago, when as a young boy he had crossed into the West from Czechoslovakia to Austria accompanied by two KGB agents. He remembered the warm night, arc lights and razor wire, the thick scent of manure on the air. He remembered raising his gun and shooting his escorts. Even now, walking through the freezing Vermont morning, he closed his eyes at the thought of it, his first assassinations.

He had been acting on orders from Vladimir. To describe Vladimir as his case officer would be an understatement. Vladimir was his world. Vladimir was everything to Delaroche—his teacher, his priest, his tormentor, his father. He taught him to read and to write. He taught him language and history. He taught him tradecraft and killing. When it was time to go to the West, Vladimir handed Delaroche to Arbatov the way a parent entrusts a child to a relative. Vladimir's last order was to kill the escorts. The act instilled something very important in Delaroche: He would never trust anyone, especially someone from his own service. When he was older he realized that was exactly what Vladimir had intended.

The terrain softened as they came down from the ridge. Delaroche, using the map and a compass, guided them to the outskirts of a village called Highgate Springs, two miles south of the border. The second Range Rover was waiting for them, parked in a stand of pine bordering a snow-covered cornfield. Delaroche placed the gear in the back, and they climbed inside. This time the engine started on the first try.

Delaroche drove carefully along the icy two-lane road. Astrid, exhausted from the hike, immediately fell into a deep, dreamless sleep. Forty minutes later Delaroche came to Interstate 89 and headed south.

39. Washington, D.C.

"WHY WOULD ADRIAN LIE to you about the existence of October?"

Elizabeth's question sounded strange to Michael. It was like a child asking about sex for the first time. Their new openness was alien to him, and he felt awkward discussing agency matters candidly with his wife. Still, he did enjoy it. Elizabeth, with her lawyer's intellect and secretive nature, would have made a good intelligence officer if she had not chosen the law.

"All intelligence services run on the concept of need to know. The argument could be made that I had no need to know about October's existence, and therefore I was never told of it."

"But, Michael, he murdered Sarah in front of your eyes. If anyone should be allowed to see what the Agency had on him, it's you."

"Good point, but information is kept from intelligence officers all the time for all kinds of different reasons."

"The Soviet Union has been dead and buried for ages. Why would his file still be so restricted?"

"We give up our dead slowly in the intelligence community, Elizabeth. There's nothing an intelligence service likes more than a good pile of useless secrets."

"Maybe someone wanted it restricted."

"I've considered that possibility."

Michael stopped in front of the *Washington Post* building on 15th Street. Tom Logan, Susanna Dayton's editor, had asked to meet with Elizabeth. Michael had planned to wait in the car but now said, "Mind if I tag along?"

"Not at all, but we have to hurry. We're late."

"Where are you supposed to meet him?"

"In his office. Why?"

"I'm just not crazy about enclosed places, that's all."

"Michael, this isn't East Berlin. Cut it out."

But Michael had already snatched the cell phone from its cradle. "What's his extension?"

"Fifty-six eighty-four."

The telephone rang, and Logan's secretary answered. "This is Michael Osbourne. May I speak to Mr. Logan, please."

Logan came on the line and said, "Hello, Mike."

"Elizabeth and I are downstairs. Mind if we change the venue?"

"Of course not."

"We're on Fifteenth Street, silver Jaguar."

"I'll be down in five minutes."

Michael snapped the handset back into place. Elizabeth said, "What's the problem?"

"You know that feeling you get when someone's looking at you?"

"Sure."

"I have it right now. I can't find him, but I know he's out there." Michael stared into the rearview mirror for a moment. "I have good instincts," he said distantly, "and I always trust my instincts."

Five minutes later Logan walked out the front door of the *Post* building. Logan was tall and bald, and the wind was playing havoc with his fringe of overgrown graying hair. He wore no overcoat, just a crimson scarf wrapped around his thin neck, and his hands were jammed in the pockets of wrinkled gray flannels. Osbourne reached back and threw open the rear door. Logan climbed in and said, "God, I love the weather in this town. Seventy degrees yesterday and forty today."

Michael pressed down hard on the accelerator, and the Jaguar leaped from the curb into the heavy traffic of downtown Washington. Logan buckled his seat belt and clutched the armrest.

"What do you do for a living, Mike?"

"I sell computer equipment to large clients overseas."

"Ah, sounds interesting."

Michael turned left on M Street and sped west across downtown. He turned right on New Hampshire, raced around Dupont Circle, and accelerated west along Massachusetts Avenue. He expertly weaved in and out of traffic and spent more time looking in his rearview mirror than at the road ahead of him.

Logan had by now nearly torn the armrest from the rear door. "I didn't catch the name of the company you work for, Mike."

"That's because I didn't tell you. And I prefer Michael, Tom."

Elizabeth turned around and took a long look over her shoulder. "Anything?" she asked.

"If anyone was there, they're gone now."

He slowed down and fell into pace with the rest of the traffic. Logan let go of the armrest and relaxed.

"Computer salesman, my ass," he said.

HENRY RODRIGUEZ HAD BEEN ASSIGNED to watch Elizabeth Osbourne that day, but he broke off the chase along M Street. Michael Osbourne, a former field officer, was trained to recognize sophisticated physical surveillance. One person crudely disguised as a Chinese food deliveryman could be spotted in a matter of minutes. He pulled to the curb and telephoned Mark Calahan at the command post in Kalorama.

"He was definitely trying to shake a tail," Rodriguez said. "If I tried to hang with him, he would have made me."

"Good call. Go back to Georgetown. Wait for them to show."

Calahan walked into the library to break the news to Mitchell Elliott.

"Logan must need help," Elliott said. "Why else would he be meeting with her now?"

"She's in a position to do serious damage. Perhaps we should tighten things up a bit."

"I agree," Elliott said. "I think it's time Henry went back to work."

"He's not going to like being a janitor again. He feels we're discriminating against him because of his Hispanic heritage."

"If he doesn't like it, let him file a complaint with the EEOC. I pay him well to do what he's told."

Calahan smiled. "Yes, sir, Mr. Elliott."

MICHAEL FOUND A PARKING SPOT on East Capitol Street. He dug an old windbreaker from the trunk for Tom Logan, and they walked in Lincoln Park beneath cold, slate-gray skies.

Logan said, "How much of Susanna's original material did you read?"

"Enough to get the picture," Elizabeth said.

"Let me refresh your memory," Logan said. "In the early eighties, Beckwith wanted out of politics. More specifically, Anne Beckwith wanted out of politics. She wanted her husband back in the private sector, where he could earn some serious money before he was too old. Both of them had a little family money, but not much. Anne likes nice things. She wanted more than what they could get on a government paycheck. He'd done two terms in the Senate, and she told him it was politics or her."

A pair of joggers approached them from behind, each with a dog straining at the end of a leash. Logan, like a good field man, waited for them to pass out of earshot before resuming.

"Beckwith is a lot of things, but he's totally devoted to Anne, and the last thing he wanted was to lose her. But he also enjoyed politics and wasn't particularly thrilled about practicing law again. He called his advisers and money boys together in San Francisco one night and broke the news. Needless to say, Mitchell Elliott was apoplectic. He'd invested a lot of time and money in Beckwith over the years, and he didn't want that investment to go to waste. He telephoned Anne the next morning and asked to meet privately with her. That night over dinner, Anne took it all back and encouraged Beckwith to run for governor. He won, of course, and the rest, as they say, is history."

Michael said, "What happened in that meeting between Anne Beckwith and Mitchell Elliott?"

"Elliott assured Anne that if her husband remained in politics, they both would be well cared for financially. The first stage was simple stuff, and in the overall scheme of things it was chump change. Elliott got his powerful friends in the business community to place Anne on more than a dozen boards of directors. She earned money as a consultant, even though she had almost no business experience. She also invested very wisely, with help from Elliott, we suspect, and she made a killing in the financial markets.

"Within three years, Anne had a substantial war chest, a few million dollars. She took almost all of that money and bought several hundred acres of what was then worthless desert south of San Diego. Two years later a developer announced plans to build a new community of condominiums, single family homes, and a strip mall right on Anne's land. Suddenly, her worthless land was worth a great deal of money."

"Mitchell Elliott was behind it all?" Elizabeth asked.

"We think so, but we can't prove it, and therefore we can't print it. Elliott needed help to devise all these schemes. He had big plans for Beckwith, and he didn't want him tarnished by scandal. He needed someone who understood Washington and, more importantly, understood how to circumvent campaign finance laws. He turned to a high-powered Washington lawyer."

"Samuel Braxton," Elizabeth said.

"That's right," Logan said. "And finally, after years of waiting, Elliott's investment paid off big this year. The national missile defense was dead in the water. But twenty-four hours after Flight Double-oh-two went down, Elliott was inside the White House for a meeting with Beckwith. Susanna saw it. She also saw Elliott and Vandenberg together later that same night. The next evening Beckwith goes before the nation, announces strikes against the Sword of Gaza, and proposes building a national missile defense. Capitol Hill is suddenly all for missile defense. Andrew Sterling is pinned to the wall because he's on record against it. Beckwith pulls out the election, and Elliott's Alatron Defense Systems is in line to earn several billion dollars."

"So why haven't you gone with Susanna's story?" Michael asked.

"Like I told your wife before, on a story like this we go over every fact, every quote, every piece of information, with the reporter before publication. In this case, the reporter is dead, and we had to start over, using her original copy as a road map. We've got most of it, but we're missing a very important piece of the puzzle. Somehow, Susanna got hold of original financial and real estate documents. We suspect she had a source inside Braxton, Allworth & Kettlemen who gave her the documents. We've been through Susanna's files, and we can't find them. We've tried to find our own source inside the firm, but we haven't been successful."

Logan shivered and tied his scarf more tightly around his neck. "Elizabeth, obviously you can answer this question any way you see fit, but I have to ask it. Were you the source for those documents?"

"No," Elizabeth said quickly. "Susanna asked me, and I told her I wouldn't do it. I told her it was unethical, and if it ever became known that I leaked the documents my career would be destroyed."

Logan hesitated a moment, then said, "Will you do it now?"

"No, I won't."

"Elizabeth, Samuel Braxton is a dishonest lawyer and criminal who's about to be rewarded by being made secretary of state. I don't know about you, but that pisses me off, and as a journalist I'd like to do something about it. But I can't, not without your help. Now, if you're concerned about whether you'll be protected, I assure you we will do nothing that will endanger you in any way. You can trust me."

"Tom, I've lived in Washington most of my life, and there's one thing I've learned. You can't trust anyone in this town."

Logan stopped walking and turned to face Michael. "You don't work for a computer company that sells to overseas buyers. You work in the Counter-terrorism Center at the Central Intelligence Agency. You were the hero in that attack at Heathrow Airport, and you were involved in the bombing on that Channel ferry. I know you may find this hard to believe, Michael, but even people in your outfit like to talk to reporters. We didn't publish the information, because we didn't want to place you in any danger."

Logan turned and looked at Elizabeth.

"I won't do anything that will get you hurt. You can trust me, Elizabeth."

40. Bethesda, Maryland

DELAROCHE BECAME NERVOUS for the first time when he left Interstate 95 and headed onto the Capital Belt-way. He had driven some of the most demanding roads of Europe—winding highways in France and Italy, deadly mountain roads in the Alps and the Pyrenees—but nothing had prepared him for the madness of the Washington evening rush hour.

The trip from Vermont had gone smoothly. The weather had been good, except for a brief snowstorm in upstate New York and a patch of freezing drizzle along the New Jersey Turnpike. The temperatures warmed the farther south they traveled, and the rain had ended at Philadelphia. Now it was the other drivers Delaroche feared most. Cars were roaring by him at 85 miles per hour—thirty miles above the speed limit—and the truck behind him was riding six feet from his bumper.

Delaroche thought how easy it would be to have a collision under circumstances like these. The results would be disastrous. Because he was a foreigner the police would want to see his passport. If the officer was alert and knew anything about passports, he would notice that Delaroche's bore no entrance visa. He would probably be taken into custody and questioned by immigration authorities and the FBI. His identity would crumble and he would be arrested, all because of some nut trying to get home from work.

The cars in front of him braked suddenly. The traffic came to a standstill. Delaroche found an all-news station on the radio and listened to the traffic update. Somewhere ahead of him a tractor-trailer rig had overturned. Traffic was snarled for miles.

Delaroche thought of his home in Brélés. He thought of the sea smashing against the rocks and of pedaling his Italian racing bike along the quiet back roads of the Finistère. He must have been daydreaming, because the man in the car behind him blared his horn and waved his arms frantically. The driver changed lanes, pulled alongside Delaroche, and made a vulgar gesture with his hand. "Please, Jean-Paul," Astrid said. "Let me get my gun from the back and shoot him."

Thirty minutes later they approached the scene of the accident. A Maryland state trooper stood in the roadway, directing traffic around the overturned truck. Delaroche tensed reflexively in the presence of a police officer. The fire trucks and ambulances disappeared behind them, and the traffic began moving again. Delaroche exited at Wisconsin Avenue and headed south.

He sped through downtown Bethesda, past the exclusive shops of the Mazza Galleria, the towering spires of the National Cathedral. Wisconsin Avenue fell away into Georgetown. Shoppers moved quickly through the cold evening air, and the bars and restaurants were beginning to fill. He turned left at M Street, drove a few blocks, and turned into the entrance of the Four Seasons Hotel.

Delaroche checked them in, refusing the bellman's offer to help with the bags. He closed the door and they both fell onto the bed, exhausted from the two long drives and the hike across the border.

Delaroche awoke after two hours, ordered coffee from room service, and sat down at his laptop computer. While Astrid slept, he opened Michael Osbourne's dossier and began planning his death.

41. Washington, D.C.

ELIZABETH TELEPHONED MAX LEWIS at the office late in the afternoon.

"How are you feeling?" he said over the rustle of papers. It was after 5 P.M., and he was preparing to leave the office for the day, which is why Elizabeth called then.

"I'm fine, but the doctor says I really have to stay off my feet as much as possible during the next week or so. Actually, that's why I'm calling. I was wondering if you could bring me some papers on your way home tonight."

"No problem. What do you need?"

"The McGregor case file. It's on my desk."

"Actually, it's back in your file room. I took the liberty of cleaning off your desk today. Honestly, Elizabeth, I don't know how you get any work done in there. I also threw out all your cigarettes."

"Don't worry, I've given them up. No more Chardonnay in the bathtub after work, either."

"Good girl," he said. "I'll be there in fifteen minutes. Need anything else? Want me to pick up your cleaning? Do some shopping for you at Sutton Place? Command me, my queen."

"Just bring me the McGregor file. I'll reward you with food and wine."

"In that case, I'll be there in five minutes."

"I'm flat on my back in bed, so use your key."

"Yes, my queen."

Max hung up. Michael was on a chair and ottoman at the foot of the bed, listening to the conversation on the cordless phone. He looked at Elizabeth and said, "Perfect."

IT TOOK MAX more than a half hour to fight his way through traffic to Georgetown from the firm's Connecticut Avenue office. He stuck his key in the Osbournes' lock, opened the door, and stepped inside the entrance hall.

"Elizabeth, it's me," he called.

"Hey, Max, come on up. There's cold wine in the fridge. Grab a glass and a corkscrew."

He did as he was told and walked up the stairs. He found Elizabeth sprawled on the bed, surrounded by stacks of briefs and legal pads. "My God," he said. "Maybe I should work here instead of downtown."

"That might not be such a bad idea."

He placed the McGregor files on the bedside table and instinctively began straightening papers and organizing her things. Michael walked into the room. Max said, "Hey, Michael, how are you?"

Michael said nothing. Max said, "Something wrong?"

Elizabeth touched his arm and said, "Max, we need to talk."

"SUSANNA CAME TO ME after you turned her down," Max said. He was sitting in the chair in the bedroom, legs sprawled across the ottoman. Michael had opened the wine, and Max drank half the bottle very fast. The initial shock of the confrontation had worn off, and now he was relaxed and talking freely. "She asked me to help her. I slept on it, and then I agreed to do it."

"Max, if you had been caught, they'd have fired you and probably prosecuted you. Law firms can't tolerate theft and violation of attorney-client privilege. It doesn't make clients feel good, and it makes it damned hard to attract new ones."

"I was willing to take the risk. When you're in my position, Elizabeth, you tend not to take a real long view of things."

"I don't want to be judgmental, Max, but you should have come to me first," Elizabeth said. "I hired you. You work for me. The firm would have fallen on me like a ton of bricks."

"And what would you have said?"

"I would have told you not to do it."

"That's why I didn't come to you."

"Why, Max? Why go after Braxton like that?"

Max looked at Elizabeth as though he found the question offensive. "Why Braxton? Because he's a dirty, crooked asshole who's about to become secretary of state. I'm surprised you even have to ask the question. I've heard the way he talks to you in the partners' meetings, and I've heard the way he talks about you when you're not around."

He hesitated a moment, looked at Michael, and said, "Can I bum one of those from you?" Michael handed him the pack and a lighter. Max smoked for a moment and drank more of the wine.

"It's personal, too," he said finally. "Someone told Braxton I was HIV-positive. He was working behind your back to get me fired as one of his last acts before leaving the firm. I wanted to make his final weeks so fucked up he wouldn't have time to deal with me, and Susanna gave me the opportunity to do it."

Michael said, "How did you get the documents?"

"I stole one of the keys to his file room and copied it. That night I went into the office on the pretense that I had some work to do. I went into the file room, took the documents, and headed over to Susanna's place. I laid down only one ground rule: She wasn't allowed to photocopy the files. I stayed at her house all night while she worked; then I went into the office early and put the files back in their original place. Nothing to it, really."

"You still have the key?" Elizabeth asked.

"Yeah, I thought about throwing it off Memorial Bridge, but I kept it instead."

"Good."

"Why?"

"Because we're going to go in there tonight to get those files again."

42. Washington, D.C.

OFFICIALLY, THERE WAS a lid in place at the White House, which meant the press office expected no more news that day and the President and First Lady had no public events and no plans to leave the residence. But at 8 P.M. a single black sedan slipped from the South Gate of the White House and entered the evening traffic of downtown Washington.

Anne Beckwith sat alone in the back seat. There was no bombproof presidential limousine, no black Chevy Suburban chase vehicles, no police escort. Just a White House driver and a single Secret Service agent seated in the front seat. For years Anne had been escaping the White House in this manner at least once a week. She enjoyed getting out into the real world, as she liked to put it. For Anne, the *real* world was not far removed from the opulence of the Executive Mansion. Usually she took a short ride to the wealthy enclaves of Georgetown or Kalorama or Spring Valley for drinks and dinner with old friends or important political allies.

The car headed north up Connecticut Avenue, then turned west onto Massachusetts after navigating the heavy traffic of Dupont Circle. A moment later it turned onto California Street and slowed outside the large brick mansion. The garage door opened, and the black sedan slipped silently inside.

The Secret Service agent waited for the garage door to close again before getting out of the car. He walked around the back and opened the First Lady's door. Her host was waiting when she stepped out of the car. She kissed his cheek and said, "Hello, Mitchell, so good to see you."

ANNE BECKWITH DID NOT COME for an evening of pleasant conversation and good food. This was business. She accepted a glass of wine but ignored the plate of cheese and paté one of Elliott's drones placed on the coffee table between them.

"I want to know if the situation is under control," she said coldly. "And if it's not under control, I want to know just what in the hell you're doing to *get* it under control."

"If Susanna Dayton had lived to publish that article, it could have been very damaging. Her unfortunate murder bought us some time, but I don't think we're in the clear yet."

"*Unfortunate* murder," Anne repeated, derision in her voice. "Why hasn't the *Post* published her story?"

"Because they're trying to reconfirm all her reporting, and they're not quite there yet."

"Are they going to get there?"

"Not if I can help it."

Anne Beckwith lit a cigarette and exhaled a slender stream of smoke sharply between her tense lips.

"What are you doing to prevent it?"

"I think it would be unwise for you to know about any of this, Anne."

"Don't bullshit me, Mitchell. Just tell me what I want to know."

"We think Susanna Dayton's best friend is working with the *Post* now, a lawyer named Elizabeth Osbourne."

"Isn't she Douglas Cannon's girl?"

"Yes, she is."

"Cannon hates Jim. They were on Armed Services together. Cannon was the chairman, and Jim was the ranking Republican. They were barely on speaking terms at the end of it."

Anne finished her wine. "Aren't you going to offer me another glass? California, isn't it? God, we make wonderful wine."

Elliott poured more wine. Anne said, "Mitchell, we go way back. Jim and I owe you a great deal. You've been very generous over the years. But I will not let Jim be tarnished by this in any way. He's run his last campaign. He has nothing to lose now except his place in the history books."

"I understand that."

"I don't think you do. If this becomes public in a bad way, I will use every ounce of power and influence I possess to make sure you're the one who takes the fall. I won't let Jim be hurt, and I don't give a damn about you at this point. Do I make myself clear?"

Elliott poured down the rest of his scotch. He didn't appreciate being lectured by Anne Beckwith. If it hadn't been for Anne's greed and Anne's insecurities, Elliott would never have been able to establish his special financial relationship with her husband. Anne always called the shots, even when it came to graft. He stared at her coldly for a moment, then nodded and said, "Yes, Anne, you've made yourself quite clear."

"If this thing blows up, Jim will survive it. But your little missile project will go down the crapper. It won't be built, or they'll award the contract to a less controversial company. You'll be finished."

"I know the stakes."

"Good." She stood up and collected her coat. Mitchell Elliott remained seated. "I just have one question for you, Mitchell. Did the same people who killed the reporter shoot down the airliner?"

Elliott looked at her, astonishment on his face. "What the hell are you talking about?"

"Answering a question with a question. That's a bad sign. Good night, darling. Oh, and don't bother to get up. I'm only the First Lady. I'll see myself out."

ELIZABETH DRESSED THE PART of a busy Washington lawyer returning to the office for some late-night work: jeans, urban cowboy boots, a comfortable beige cotton sweater. Max Lewis lived near Dupont Circle, and his daily work attire reflected the trends of his neighborhood: black jeans, black suede loafers, black turtleneck shirt, dark gray jacket. The law offices of Braxton, Allworth & Kettlemen stood on the corner of Connecticut Avenue and K Street. Michael waited in the car. Elizabeth and Max walked into the lobby together, checked in with the security guard, and took the elevator up to the eleventh floor.

Elizabeth's office was on the north end of the floor, overlooking Connecticut Avenue. Samuel Braxton had the largest office in the firm, a series of rooms along the corner of Connecticut Avenue and K Street, with a magnificent view of the White House and the Washington Monument. Elizabeth unlocked her office, switched on the lights, and went inside. She spoke to Max in a loud, clear voice; she wanted everything to appear normal. Max loaded some extra paper in the copier and made a pot of coffee. Elizabeth could hear the distant drone of vacuum cleaners from somewhere on the floor.

She took the keys and walked down the length of the hall to Braxton's office. She knocked once gently, received no answer, and unlocked the door with the duplicate key. She stepped inside and quickly closed the door. She took a small flashlight from her handbag and switched it on.

Elizabeth was in the exterior office where Braxton's two secretaries worked. The file room was at the far end of the office, through a heavy door. Elizabeth switched keys and opened the door. She closed it behind her and switched on the light.

Max had told her where to find the Elliott and Beckwith files: on the far wall, top left. The top shelf was beyond her reach. Braxton's secretaries kept a library-style stepstool inside the room for just such occasions. She carried the stool across the room, stepped up on it, and began picking her way through the files.

She went through the entire row once and found nothing. She started from the beginning, forcing herself to go slowly, but once again found nothing. She tried the shelf below, but it was the same thing. Nothing. She swore softly beneath her breath.

Braxton had removed the files.

ELIZABETH CLIMBED DOWN off the stool and moved across the room toward the door. She heard sounds in the office outside the door—a key being shoved in a lock, the click of a light switch, the scrape of a metal cart. Then she heard the crunch of a key shoved forcefully into the door lock a few feet from her. The lock gave way, and the door pushed back.

ELIZABETH CAREFULLY EXAMINED THE MAN standing before her and realized immediately something was wrong. Most of the cleaning staff were small dark-skinned Central Americans of Indian origin who spoke almost no English. This man was tall, about six feet, and fair-skinned. His dark hair obviously had been cut and styled by an expensive professional. His coverall was new and unsoiled, his fingernails clean. But it was the ring on his left hand that caught Elizabeth's attention. It bore the insignia of the Army Special Forces, the Green Berets.

"Can I help you?" Elizabeth said. She thought it was best to take the offensive.

"I heard a noise," the man said in thickly accented English. Elizabeth knew he was lying, because she had been very careful not to make any sound.

"Why didn't you call security?" she shot back.

The man shrugged and said, "I thought I'd check it out myself first. You know, catch a thief, be a big hero, get a reward or something."

She made a show of looking at the name tag on his coverall. "Are you an American, Carlos?"

He shook his head. "I am from Ecuador."

"Where did you get that ring?"

"Pawnshop in Adams Morgan. *Muy bonito,* don't you think?"

"It's lovely, Carlos. Now, if you'll excuse me."

She walked past him and entered the exterior office.

"Find what you're looking for?" he said to her back.

"Actually, I was just putting something back."

"Okay. Good night, señora."

"MAYBE HE WAS TELLING the truth," Michael said. "Maybe he really is Carlos from Ecuador, and he got the ring at a pawnshop in Adams Morgan."

"Bullshit," Elizabeth said.

Max had taken them to a restaurant in Dupont Circle called The Childe Harold. It was popular with journalists and young congressional staff. They sat at a corner table in the cellar bar. Elizabeth desperately wanted a cigarette but chewed her nails instead.

"I've never seen him before," Max said. "But that doesn't mean much. The people in those jobs come and go all the time."

"You've never seen him before, Max, because he's not a fucking janitor, and he's not Carlos from fucking Ecuador. I know what I saw." She looked at Michael. "Remember what you said about that feeling you get when someone's watching you? Well, I have that feeling right now."

"SHE'S NOT AN IDIOT," Henry Rodriguez reported over the phone. "She's a big-time lawyer. I tried to talk my way out of it. Did my best Freddie Prinze from *Chico and the Man,* but I know she made me."

"Why the fuck were you wearing the ring?" Calahan said.

"I forgot. Shoot me."

"Don't give me any ideas. Where are they now?"

"Restaurant called The Childe Harold. Twentieth Street, north of Dupont Circle."

"Where are you?"

"Pay phone on the other side of Connecticut Avenue. I can't get any closer."

"Stay put. I'll have someone there in five minutes."

Calahan hung up and looked at Elliott. "We have another small problem, sir."

43. Washington, D.C.

THE FOLLOWING MORNING DELAROCHE sat on a bench in Dupont Circle, watching the crowd of bicycle couriers taking their morning coffee. He found them vaguely amusing—the way they laughed and joked and threw things at each other—but he was not watching them simply to pass the time. He carefully noted the way they dressed, the kinds of satchels they carried, the manner in which they walked. Shortly after nine o'clock the couriers began receiving calls over their radios, and each reluctantly mounted a bike and pedaled off to work.

Delaroche waited until the last was gone, then flagged down a taxi, and gave the driver an address.

The taxi took Delaroche along M Street into Georgetown and deposited him at the base of Key Bridge. He entered the shop. A salesman asked if he needed help, and Delaroche shook his head. He started with the clothing. He selected the most flamboyant and colorful jersey and riding britches he could find. Next he selected shoes, socks, a helmet, and a backpack. He carried everything to the front of the store and stacked it on the checkout counter.

"Anything else?" the salesman asked.

Delaroche pointed to the most expensive mountain bike in the store. The attendant lifted it from the display rack and wheeled it toward the service counter.

"Where are you taking that?" Delaroche asked quietly, conscious of his accented English.

"We need to check out the bike, sir. It's going to take an hour or so."

"Just put air in the tires and give it to me."

"Suit yourself. Will this be cash or charge, sir?"

But Delaroche was already counting out hundred-dollar bills.

· · ·

THE NEXT HOUR, Delaroche spent shopping along Wisconsin Avenue in Georgetown. In a clothing store, he purchased a bandanna for his head; in an electronics store, a small battery-powered tape player with headphones. In a jewelry store he purchased several gaudy gold chains for his neck and had both his ears pierced and hoop earrings inserted.

He changed in a gas station toilet. He removed his street clothing and put on the long cycling britches and winter-weight jersey. He tied the bandanna over his head and put the gold chains around his neck. He attached the tape player to the waistband of his britches and placed the headphones around his neck. He stuffed his street clothes into the backpack, along with the silenced Beretta, and looked at himself in the mirror. Something was missing. He put on his Ray-Ban sunglasses, the same glasses he had used to kill the man in Paris, and looked at his reflection once more. Now it was right.

He stepped outside. A man in a leather jacket was about to steal his bike.

"Hey, motherfucker," Delaroche said, mimicking the dialect of the couriers on Dupont Circle, "the last thing you want to do is mess with my ride."

"Hey, be cool. I was just checkin' it out," the man said, backing rapidly away. "Peace and love and all that bullshit."

Delaroche climbed on the bicycle and pedaled toward Michael Osbourne's home.

DELAROCHE REVIEWED HIS PLAN to kill Osbourne one last time as he pedaled along the leafy streets of west Georgetown. Killing him would be difficult. He was a married man with no serious vices; he would not succumb to a sexual advance from Astrid. He was a professional intelligence officer who had spent many years in dangerous situations; instinctively, he would be personally vigilant at all times. Delaroche considered simply knocking on Osbourne's door, on the pretense of delivering a package, and shooting him when he answered. But there was a chance Osbourne would recognize Delaroche—he had been on the Chelsea Embankment, after all—and shoot him first. He considered trying to enter Osbourne's home by stealth, but surely a large, expensive home in a crime-ridden city like Washington was protected by a security system. He decided he would have to kill him by surprise, somewhere in the open, which was why Delaroche was dressed as a bicycle courier.

N Street presented Delaroche with his first serious problem. There were no shops, no cafés, and no telephone booths—no place for Delaroche to kill time inconspicuously—just large Federal-style brick homes set tightly against the sidewalk.

Delaroche waited on the corner of 33rd and N streets, outside a large home with a grand pillared porch, thinking about what to do. He had but one option: ride back and forth along N Street and hope he spotted Osbourne entering or leaving the house. This was alien to Delaroche—whenever possible he preferred to kill by being in exactly the right place at exactly the right time—but he had no other choice.

He mounted the bicycle, pedaled to 35th Street, turned around, and pedaled back to 33rd Street, watching Osbourne's house as closely as possible.

After twenty minutes of this a man emerged from the house, dressed in a gray and white tracksuit. Delaroche looked carefully at the face. It was the same face as the photograph in the dossier. It was the same face he had seen that night on the Chelsea Embankment. It was Michael Osbourne.

Osbourne bent over and stretched the back of his legs. He leaned against a lamppost and stretched his calf muscles. Delaroche, watching him from two blocks away, could see Osbourne's eyes flickering over the street and the parked cars.

Finally, Osbourne stood and broke into a light run. He turned left on 34th Street, right on M Street, and headed across Key Bridge toward Virginia. Delaroche dialed Astrid at the Four Seasons and spoke to her as he pedaled steadily in Osbourne's wake.

MICHAEL REACHED THE VIRGINIA SIDE of the Potomac and headed south on the Mount Vernon Trail. His muscles were stiff and sore and the cold December weather wasn't helping, but he quickened his pace and lengthened his stride, and after a few minutes of fast running he felt sweat beneath his tracksuit.

It was good to be free of the house. Carter had called earlier and informed Michael that Monica Tyler had formally ordered Personnel to begin an investigation into his conduct. Elizabeth had finally acceded to her doctor's wishes and was working from home. Their bedroom had been turned into a law office, complete with Max Lewis.

The clouds broke, and a warm winter's sun shone along the banks of the river. Michael passed the entrance to Roosevelt Island. A wooden footbridge stretched before him, running over several hundred yards of marsh and reed grass.

Michael increased his pace, feet thumping on the cross boards of the bridge. It was a weekday, and he was alone on the trail. He played a game with himself, running an imaginary race. He broke into a sprint, driving his arms, lifting his knees. He rounded a corner and the end of the bridge appeared, about two hundred yards away.

Michael forced himself to run still faster. His arms burned, his legs felt like dead weight, and his breath was raspy with the cold air and too many cigarettes. He reached the end of the footbridge, stumbled to a stop, and turned around to see the ground he had covered with his dash.

Only then did he see the man pedaling toward him on a mountain bike.

44. Washington, D.C.

ASTRID VOGEL TELEPHONED DOWNSTAIRS and asked the valet to have the Range Rover waiting. She left the hotel room and took the elevator down to the lobby. She carried a handbag, and inside the bag was a silenced Beretta pistol. The Range Rover stood beneath the covered entrance of the hotel. Astrid gave the valet the claim ticket and a five-dollar bill. She climbed inside and drove off. Delaroche had kept her up half the night memorizing street maps. Five minutes later she was backing into a parking space a few blocks away on N Street. She shut down the engine, lit a cigarette, and waited for Delaroche to call.

MICHAEL STOOD BOLT UPRIGHT as adrenaline shot through his body. Suddenly his arms and legs didn't ache any longer, and his breath came in short, quick bursts. He stared at the man approaching on the bicycle. A helmet covered the head, sunglasses the eyes. Michael stared at the exposed portion of his face. He had seen it before—in Colin Yardley's bedroom, on the Cairo airport video, on the Chelsea Embankment. It was October.

The assassin was reaching inside a nylon bag mounted on the handlebars of the bike. Michael knew he was reaching for his gun. If he turned and tried to run away, October would easily overtake and kill him. If he stood his ground, the result would be the same.

He sprinted directly toward the oncoming bicycle.

The move took the gunman by surprise. He was twenty yards away; the two men were approaching each other rapidly on a collision course. October frantically dug through the nylon bag, grabbing for the butt of the gun, trying to get his finger inside the trigger guard. He took hold of the gun, ripped it from the bag, and tried to level it at Michael.

Michael arrived as the silenced Beretta emitted a dull thud. He lowered his shoulder and drove it into October's chest. The blow knocked October from the bike, and he landed on the wooden footbridge with a heavy thump. Michael managed to stay on his feet. He turned around and saw October, lying on his back, still holding the gun.

Michael had two options—rush October, try to disarm and capture him, or run away and get help. October was a ruthless assassin, trained in the martial arts. Michael had gone through rudimentary training at the Farm, but he realized he would be no match for someone like October. Besides, he was holding one gun and probably had a second hidden somewhere on his body.

Michael turned, ran a few yards along the footbridge, then leaped over the side into the mud and reed grass at the river's edge. He scrambled across a hillside slick with wet autumn leaves and disappeared into a stand of trees.

DELROCHE SAT UP and collected his bearings. The blow had knocked the breath from him, but he had escaped serious injury. He stuck the Beretta inside the waistband of his riding britches and pulled his jersey over the butt. Two men with army sweatsuits rounded the corner as Delaroche was bending to pick up his bike. For an instant he considered shooting them both; then he realized the Pentagon was nearby, and the soldiers were simply out for a harmless midday run.

"You all right?" one of them asked.

"Just a ruffian who tried to rob me," Delaroche said, allowing his French accent to come through. "When I explained to the man that I had nothing of value he knocked me from my bicycle."

"Maybe you should see a doctor," the other said.

"No, a bruise, perhaps, but nothing serious. I'll find a police officer and file a report."

"Okay, be careful."

"Thank you for stopping, gentlemen."

Delaroche waited for the soldiers to vanish from sight. He took hold of the bike by the handlebars and brought it upright. He was angry and excited. He had never blown an assassination, and he was angry with himself for not reacting better. Osbourne had proven himself a worthier opponent than Delaroche expected. His dash toward Delaroche demonstrated both bravery and cunning. His second decision, to escape rather than fight, also demonstrated intelligence, for Delaroche surely would have killed him.

That was why Delaroche was excited. Most of his victims never knew what hit them. He appeared unexpectedly and killed without warning. Most of the time his work was less than challenging. Obviously, that would not be the case with Osbourne. Delaroche had lost the element of surprise. Osbourne was aware of his presence, and he would never allow Delaroche to get near him again. Delaroche would have to bring Osbourne to him.

Delaroche remembered the night on the Chelsea Embankment. He remembered shooting the woman named Sarah Randolph three times in the face and hearing the anguished screams of Michael Osbourne as he slipped away. A man who lost a woman in that manner would do almost anything to prevent it from happening again.

He mounted the bicycle and pedaled north toward Key Bridge. He dialed Astrid's number. She answered on the first ring. Delaroche calmly told her what to do as he cycled over the bridge toward Georgetown.

· · ·

MICHAEL REACHED the shoulder of the George Washington Parkway. At midday there was little traffic. He crossed the parkway and ran up another hillside. The glass and steel office buildings of the Rosslyn section of Arlington stood before him. He found a public telephone outside a convenience store and rapidly dialed his own number.

Max Lewis answered the phone.

"Get me Elizabeth, now!"

She came on the line a few seconds later. "Michael, what's wrong?"

"They're here, Elizabeth," Michael said, gasping for air. "October just tried to kill me on the Mount Vernon Trail. Now, listen very carefully and do exactly as I say."

45. Washington, D.C.

ELIZABETH RUSHED INTO MICHAEL'S STUDY and threw open the closet door. The briefcase was on the top shelf, a brown rectangular box so ugly it could only have been created by the Agency's Office of Technical Services. The shelf was beyond her reach, so she ripped Michael's chair away from his desk and rolled it into the closet. She stood on the chair and pulled down the briefcase.

Max was in the bedroom. Elizabeth sat at the foot of the bed, pulled on a pair of brown suede cowboy boots and then went to the closet and put on a thigh-length leather jacket. For some reason she looked at

her face in the mirror and ran a hand through her un-
combed hair.

Max looked at her. "Elizabeth, dammit! What the
hell's going on?"

Elizabeth forced herself to be calm. "I can't explain everything now, Max, but a man just tried to
kill Michael while he was running. Michael thinks
that man is coming here, and he wants us to get out
now."

Max looked at the briefcase. "What the hell is
that?"

"It's called a jib," she said. "I'll explain in a few
minutes. But right now I need you to help me."

"I'll do anything, Elizabeth, you know that."

"Now, listen to me carefully, Max," she said, taking his hand. "We're going to walk out the front door
very slowly, very calmly, and we're going to get in
my car."

TWO MINUTES AFTER HANGING UP with Delaroche,
Astrid Vogel saw the front door of the Osbournes'
house swing open and two figures emerge into the
December sunlight. The first was Elizabeth Osbourne—Astrid recognized her photograph from Delaroche's dossier—and the second was a white man
of medium height and build. The woman carried a
man's attaché case, the man nothing. They climbed
into a silver E-class Mercedes-Benz—the woman in
the passenger seat, the man behind the wheel—and
started the engine.

Astrid considered what to do. Delaroche had told
her to wait for him to return; then they would enter

the house and take the woman hostage. She couldn't allow the woman to escape. She decided to follow them and tell Delaroche where they were going.

The Mercedes pulled away from the curb and entered the quiet street. Astrid started the engine of the Rover and followed them. She punched in Delaroche's number and quickly brought him up to date.

"HE'S HERE!" Michael yelled into the phone.

"Who's here?" Adrian Carter said.

"October's here. He just tried to kill me on the Mount Vernon Trail."

"Are you sure?"

"Adrian, what kind of fucking question is that? Of course I'm sure!"

"Where are you?"

"Rosslyn."

"Give me the address. I'll send a team to collect you."

Michael looked for a street sign and gave Carter his location.

"Where's Elizabeth? I'll pick her up too."

"She was at the house, but I told her to get out."

"Why the hell did you do that?"

"Because October and Astrid Vogel have been working as a pair throughout this thing. She's probably here too. If I didn't get Elizabeth out of there, Vogel would have gone in and grabbed her. I'm sure of it."

"What's your plan?"

Michael told him.

"Jesus Christ! Who's the driver?"

"Her secretary. Kid named Max Lewis."

"Goddammit, Michael. Do you know what October's going to do to that guy when he finds out?"

"Shut up, Adrian. Just hurry up and bring me in."

ELIZABETH PULLED DOWN her sun visor and glanced into the vanity mirror as they headed south on Wisconsin Avenue. The black Range Rover was there, a woman behind the wheel, talking on a cellular telephone.

Max said, "Who are we running from?"

"You wouldn't believe me if I told you."

"At this point I'd believe just about anything."

"Her name is Astrid Vogel, and she's a terrorist from the Red Army Faction."

"Jesus Christ!"

"Make a left, and drive normally."

Max made a left onto M Street. At 31st Street the light changed from green to yellow when he was fifty feet from the intersection.

Elizabeth said, "Go through it."

Max punched the accelerator. The Mercedes responded, dropping down a gear and gaining speed rapidly. They swept through the intersection to the angry blare of horns. Elizabeth glanced at the mirror and saw that the Range Rover was still there.

"Shit!"

"What do you want me to do?"

"Just keep driving."

At 28th Street, Max had no choice but to stop at a red light. The Range Rover pulled directly behind them. Elizabeth watched the woman in the vanity mirror, and Max did the same in the rearview mirror.

"Who do you think she's talking to?"

"She's talking to her partner."

"Is her partner Red Army Faction too?"

"No, he's a former KGB assassin code-named October."

The light turned green. Max pressed the accelerator so hard the tires squealed on the pavement.

"Elizabeth, the next time you ask me to come to your house to work, I think I'll decline, if that's all right with you."

"Shut up and drive, Max."

"Where?"

"Downtown."

Max headed east on L Street, the Range Rover shadowing them. Elizabeth toyed with the handle of the briefcase. She remembered Michael's words. *Get out of the car, then throw the latch. Make sure the case is right side up. Walk calmly away. Whatever you do, don't run.* The traffic thickened as they moved deeper into downtown Washington.

"You sure that thing is going to work?" Max asked.

"How the hell should I know?"

"Maybe it's been in the closet too long. See if it has an expiration date on it or something."

Elizabeth looked at him and saw he was smiling.

"It's going to be all right, Elizabeth. Don't worry."

He turned right on Connecticut Avenue. The midday traffic was heavy, cars rushing at high speed along the broad street, big trucks double-parked outside the exclusive shops. A half-dozen cars had slipped between them and Astrid Vogel.

Elizabeth said, "I think this is our spot. Make the right onto K Street. Use the service lane."

"Got it."

He punched the accelerator and turned the wheel hard to the right.

ASTRID SAID TO DELAROCHE, "They just made a right on K Street. Dammit, I can't see them!"

She made the turn and spotted the Mercedes slipping from the service lane into the heavy traffic on K Street.

"I have them. They're heading west on K Street. Where are you?"

"Twenty-third Street, heading south. We're very close."

Astrid followed the Mercedes westward, across 20th Street and then 21st Street.

"I'm getting close, Jean-Paul. Where are you?"

"M Street. Wait for me at Twenty-third."

She crossed 23rd Street and stopped on the northwest corner. The Mercedes drew away. She looked north on 23rd Street and saw Delaroche pedaling at high speed, legs churning like pistons. He stopped, leaned the bike against a lamppost, and climbed into the Range Rover.

"Go!"

ELIZABETH SETTLED into the back of a taxi for the ride to the Hertz rental car outlet. Michael's gadget had worked just the way he said it would. Max stopped the car; Elizabeth climbed out and pulled the latch. A figure rapidly inflated, amazingly lifelike. Max drove quickly away, and Elizabeth walked into the lobby of her building. She was tempted to walk upstairs and hide in her office, but she remembered the janitor with the expensive haircut and Special Forces ring and knew her office was no longer safe. She waited behind the glass until the Range Rover sped past, and then she stepped out and flagged down the taxi.

The taxi dropped her outside the Hertz outlet. She walked quickly inside and went to the rental counter. Five minutes later an attendant brought a gray Mercury Sable to the front of the garage. Elizabeth climbed in and pulled out into the downtown traffic.

She drove west across Washington through Georgetown, then onto Reservoir Road. She took Reservoir down to Canal Road and followed it north along the banks of the C&O Canal. After ten miles she came to the Beltway. She followed the signs north to Baltimore.

Her purse rested next to her on the passenger seat. She pulled out her cell phone and dialed the Mercedes. After five rings a recorded voice informed her that the cellular phone she was trying to reach "was not in service at this time."

MAX LEWIS DROVE ACROSS Key Bridge and turned north onto the George Washington Parkway. He had lost the Range Rover somewhere in Georgetown. He looked across at the figure seated next to him, a tall rather attractive man with dark hair and a clean shave. He realized the figure looked something like Michael Osbourne. He glanced up into the rearview mirror. Still no sign of the Range Rover. For a mad instant he was actually enjoying himself. Then he thought of Elizabeth and how frightened she had been, and he regained a healthy dose of nerves.

Elizabeth had told him to drive straight to the main entrance of the CIA. Someone would meet him there and take him inside. He pressed down on the accelerator, and the speedometer needle jumped to seventy-five. The Mercedes flowed easily over the rolling hills and gentle turns of the parkway. The Potomac sparkled below in the brilliant December sunlight.

Max looked at the mannequin again. "Listen, Mr. Jib, since we're going to be spending some time together, I think now would be a good opportunity to get to know more about each other. My name is Max and, yes, I'm gay. I hope that doesn't bother you."

He looked into the rearview mirror and saw the flashing blue light of a Virginia state trooper. He looked at the speedometer and saw he was driving nearly eighty miles per hour.

"Oh, shit," Max said, gently pressing the brake and pulling into a scenic river overlook.

The trooper climbed out of the car and put on his hat. Max lowered the window. The trooper said, "You were driving well over seventy back there, sir, and probably closer to eighty. May I see your driver's license please." Then he noticed the inflatable figure on the passenger seat. "What's that, sir?"

"It's a very long story, officer."

"Your driver's license, please."

Max beat the breast pockets of his coat. He had rushed out of the Osbournes' house so quickly he had forgotten his briefcase and his wallet. He said, "I'm sorry, officer, but I don't have my license on me."

"Shut off the engine and step out of the car, please," the officer said in a dull monotone, but at that moment he was distracted by the sight of a black Range Rover pulling into the overlook.

Max said, "Officer, you're going to think I'm nuts, but you'd better listen to what I have to say."

DELAROCHE CLIMBED OUT OF THE Range Rover and walked toward the trooper. Astrid got out and stepped to the front of the Mercedes. The trooper unsnapped his holster and was reaching for his weapon. "Get back in the car, sir, now!"

Delaroche reached beneath his cycling jersey and took hold of the silenced Beretta. His arm swung up, and he fired twice. The first shot struck the officer in the shoulder, spinning him around. The second struck him in the back of the head, and he collapsed onto the shoulder of the road.

Astrid stood in front of the Mercedes, gun in outstretched hands. She looked first at the man behind the wheel, then at the mannequin sitting where Elizabeth Osbourne had been. She was overcome with rage. She had been taken in by one of the oldest tricks in the book.

The engine started, and the Mercedes dropped into gear. Astrid calmly fired three shots through the windshield. The glass shattered and was instantly red with blood. The body collapsed forward onto the steering column, and the afternoon was filled with the blaring of the car's horn.

MICHAEL MAINTAINED A TENSE VIGIL in Adrian Carter's office, pacing and smoking cigarettes. Carter putted golf balls to relieve his nerves. One of Monica Tyler's factotums waited outside Carter's office like a schoolboy in detention. Michael closed the door so they could talk.

"Why was I never allowed to see the file on October?"

"Because it was restricted," Carter said tonelessly, head bowed in concentration. He stroked the ball, but missed the target by six inches. "Shit," Carter murmured. "Pushed it."

"Why was it restricted?"

"This is an intelligence agency, Michael, not a Christian Science reading room. During the time October was an active KGB agent, you probably had no need to know of his existence."

Carter stroked another putt. This one landed on the mark.

Michael said, "Why was the information on October so tightly held?"

"To protect the identity of the source, I assume. That's usually the case."

"Dammit, he killed Sarah Randolph right in front of me. Why couldn't someone in this fucking place just show me the file at some point and help me put it to rest?"

"Because that would have been the sensible thing to do. But sensibility and intelligence work rarely go hand in hand. Surely, you've learned that by now."

"How did you get it?"

"We had some evidence a couple of years ago that October was working again on a freelance basis," Carter said. "The file was dusted off and put back into circulation on a very limited basis."

"Were you allowed to see it?"

Carter nodded.

"Dammit, Adrian! While I was trying to piece Sarah's murder together with half clues and conjecture, you had the answer all the time. Why didn't you tell me?"

Carter pulled a face that said sometimes intelligence work required lying to one's friends. "These are the rules by which we live, Michael. They protect the people who risk their lives by betraying their own country. They protect people like you who work undercover in the field."

"So why did you break the rules now and give me October's file?"

"Because in this case the rules sucked. It made no sense."

"Who wanted October's file to remain restricted?"

Carter jerked a thumb at the factotum outside his door and whispered, "Monica Tyler."

Elizabeth finally telephoned, and the emergency switchboard put the call through to Carter's office.

"What happened? Are you all right?"

"I'm fine," she said. "I did everything you told me. That suitcase of yours worked perfectly. It even looked a little like you. I'm in the car now. I'm going where you told me to go."

Osbourne smiled in utter relief.

"Thank God," he said.

"Have you heard from Max yet?"

"No, not yet. He should be here any minute."

Carter's secretary poked her head in the door and said there was another call. Carter took it on an extension outside. Osbourne said, "Elizabeth, I'm so proud of you. I love you so much."

"I love you too, Michael. Is this nightmare over yet?"

"Not quite, but soon. Keep driving. We'll figure out how and when to bring you in."

"I love you, Michael," she said, and the connection was broken.

Carter came into the office, face ashen. Michael said, "What's wrong?"

"Max Lewis and a Virginia state trooper were just shot to death on the George Washington Parkway."

Michael slammed down the telephone.

46. Washington, D.C.

DELAROCHE CROSSED KEY BRIDGE and headed back into Georgetown. He drove quickly along M Street and pulled into the drive of the Four Seasons Hotel. He waited outside in the Rover while Astrid went to get their things from the room. It gave him a moment to collect his thoughts and plan their next move.

The easiest thing to do was abort—call for an extraction and get out of the country before they were captured. Delaroche felt confident the shootings on the parkway had gone unwitnessed; the killings took seconds, and they were gone before another car passed the scene. But he had tried once to kill Michael Osbourne, and Osbourne obviously knew he was here. The stunt his wife pulled with the inflatable dummy was proof of that. Fulfilling the terms of his contract—killing Osbourne—would be very difficult now.

Delaroche wanted to continue, though, for two reasons. One was money. If he failed to kill Osbourne he would forfeit three quarters of a million dollars. Delaroche wanted to live out his days with Astrid free from financial and security concerns. That would require a great deal of money: money to buy a large house with property and sophisticated surveillance systems, money to bribe local law enforcement officials so he could remain hidden from the security services of the West. He also wanted to live a comfortable existence. He had lived like a monk in Brélés for years, unable to spend his money for fear of attracting attention. It had been even worse when he was with the KGB; Arbatov had made him live like a pauper in Paris on the little bit of money he earned from his paintings.

The second reason—indeed, the important reason—was pride. Osbourne had beaten him on the footpath along the river, outsmarted Delaroche at his own game. He had never blown an assignment, and he didn't want to end his career with a failure. Killing was his job—he had been born and bred to do it—

and failure was unacceptable. Osbourne was the first target to fight back successfully, and Delaroche had bungled the hit. He had reacted like an amateur on his first job. He was embarrassed and angry with himself, and he wanted another chance.

He thought of Osbourne's dossier. He recalled that Elizabeth Osbourne's father, a United States senator, had a home on a secluded island in New York. He thought, If I were scared, I would go somewhere I felt safe. Somewhere far away. Somewhere the authorities could provide the illusion of security. I would leave Washington as quickly as possible and go to a secluded island.

Astrid came out of the hotel. Delaroche started the engine as she climbed in. He left the hotel and parked beneath an elevated freeway along the river's edge. Then he shut down the engine and switched on his laptop computer.

He scrolled through his files until he found the Osbourne dossier. He read it quickly and found the location of the senator's house. Yes, he thought. Even the name was perfect. They'll go there, because they'll believe it's safe.

He exited the dossier and clicked on his database, where he had stored digital road maps of nearly every nation on the planet. He typed in his starting point and his destination, and the software quickly provided him with a route: the Beltway, I-95, the Verrazano Bridge, the Long Island Expressway.

He started the engine again and dropped the Range Rover into gear.

Astrid said, "Where are we going, Jean-Paul?"

He tapped the screen of the laptop.

She looked down and read, "Shelter Island."

He picked up the cellular phone, dialed the number given to him by the contractors, and spoke quietly into the mouthpiece as he drove out of Washington.

THE HELICOPTER TOUCHED DOWN at the Atlantic City airport. Elizabeth had taken I-95 north, then cut across to the Jersey shore. Airport security officers were waiting when she pulled into the Hertz rental car return area. They took her into protective custody and kept her in a small holding room inside the terminal for ten minutes.

When the helicopter's rotor had safely stopped, Elizabeth was taken in an airport van from the holding room to the tarmac. A heavy rain was falling. The last thing she wanted to do on a night like this was fly in a helicopter. But she wanted to be home. She wanted to feel safe. She wanted to smell familiar bedding, see cherished things from her childhood. For a while she wanted to pretend that none of it had ever happened.

The van door opened, and a blast of cold rain beat against her face. She climbed out and walked toward the helicopter. The door opened, and Michael stood there. She ran into his arms and held him tightly. She kissed him and said, "I'm never going to let you out of my sight again."

Michael said nothing, just held her. Finally she asked, "Where's Max? Somewhere safe, I hope."

He held her more tightly. She read something in his silence and pulled away, staring wide-eyed. "Dammit, Michael, answer me! Where's Max?"

But she knew the answer; he didn't have to say the words.

"God, no!" she screamed, and beat her fists against his chest. "Not again! God, no! Not again!"

"IT SEEMS OUR MAN made quite a mess of things in Washington," the Director said.

"He failed to kill Osbourne, and in the process he managed to kill a secretary and a Virginia state trooper," Mitchell Elliott said. "Perhaps his reputation as the world's finest assassin was undeserved."

"Osbourne is a very worthy opponent. We always knew eliminating him would be difficult."

"Where's our man now?"

"On his way north. He believes Osbourne and his wife will seek safety at Senator Cannon's home on Shelter Island."

"Well, he's correct."

"Your source inside Langley confirms this?"

"Yes."

"Very well."

"So this unfortunate business will all be over soon. October will finish what he started. I have an extraction team on standby. When he's finished, he'll contact me, and I'll pull him out."

"October had one other target in Washington."

"Yes, I realize that, but he's quite incapable of carrying out that job now. If you want that target eliminated, I suppose we'll have to hire someone else to do the job."

"I think it would be wise. I don't like loose ends."

"I quite agree."

"And October?"

"A few minutes after his extraction, October will be killed. You see, Mr. Elliott, I dislike loose ends more than you do."

"Very well, Director."

"Good evening, Mr. Elliott."

MITCHELL ELLIOTT HUNG UP the telephone and smiled at Monica Tyler. She carried her drink to bed and lay down beside him. "It will all be over by morning," he said. "Osbourne will be gone, and you'll be rich beyond your wildest imagination."

She kissed him. "I'll be rich, Mitchell, but will I be alive to enjoy it?"

Elliott shut out the light.

"I'M GLAD MY FATHER'S not here to see this," Elizabeth said, as the helicopter set down on the lawn of Cannon Point. "He always tries to act like one of the islanders when he's out here. The last thing he would ever do is land a helicopter on his lawn."

"It's the dead of winter," Michael said. "No one will ever know."

Elizabeth looked at him incredulously. "Michael, every time someone hits a deer on this island, it gets written up in the local newspaper. Believe me, people will know."

Adrian Carter said, "I'll take care of the newspaper."

The helicopter's rotors stopped turning. The door opened, and the three of them climbed out. Charlie came out of the caretaker's cottage, flashlight in hand, retrievers scrambling at his ankles. Sea wind tore at the leafless trees. An osprey screamed and broke into flight over their heads. Fifty yards from shore, the *Athena* clung to her mooring in the wind-tossed waters of the bay.

"Where's the senator?" Carter asked as they walked the gravel drive toward the main house.

"In London," Michael said. "He's taking part in a panel discussion on Northern Ireland at the London School of Economics."

"Good. One less person to worry about."

"I don't want to turn this place into an armed camp," Elizabeth said.

"I don't intend to. I'll have two security officers on the lawn all night. They'll be relieved in the morning by two more from New York Station. Shelter Island police have agreed to watch the north and the south ferries. They have a good description of October and Astrid Vogel. They've been told they're wanted in connection with the murder of two people in Virginia, but nothing more."

"Let's keep it that way," Elizabeth said. "The last thing I want is for the people of Shelter Island to think we've brought terrorists to this place."

"The truth won't come out," Carter said. "Go inside, get some sleep. Call me at Langley in the morning, Michael. And don't worry—October is long gone by now."

Carter shook Michael's hand and kissed Elizabeth's cheek. "I'm so sorry about Max," he said. "I wish there was something we could have done."

"I know, Adrian."

Elizabeth turned and walked toward the house. Carter looked at Michael and said, "Any weapons in there?"

Michael shook his head. "Cannon hates guns."

Carter handed Michael a high-powered Browning automatic and a half-dozen fifteen-shot magazines. Then he turned and climbed aboard the helicopter. Thirty seconds later it lifted off Cannon Point, turned, and disappeared over the bay.

"CARTER GAVE YOU A GUN, didn't he?" Elizabeth said, as Michael entered the bedroom. She was standing before an open armoire, choosing a flannel night-gown. The room was dark except for a small reading lamp burning on a bedside table. Michael displayed the Browning. He snapped a magazine into the butt and clicked the safety. "God, I hate that sound," she said, undressing.

She slipped on the nightgown and lay down on the bed. Michael was standing at the window, smoking a cigarette, watching the bay. Rain dashed against the glass. One of the security men was inspecting the bulkhead along the point by flashlight.

Elizabeth placed her hands on her lower abdomen. She wondered if the babies were all right. She thought, Listen to you, Elizabeth. Already calling them babies when they're nothing more than a cluster of cells. Her doctor had told her to take it easy, to stay off her feet. She had hardly done that. She had spent the day on the run from a pair of terrorists, driving for hours and flying on a helicopter through a buffeting storm. She pressed her hands tighter to her abdomen and thought, Please, God, let them be well.

She looked at Michael, standing straight as a sentinel in the window.

"You know, Michael, I think you actually want him to try again."

"After what he did to Max—"

"He tried to kill you today, too, Michael."

"Believe me, I haven't forgotten."

"And Sarah?" she said.

He was silent.

"It's healthy to want revenge, Michael. But trying to *get* revenge is something altogether different. It's a dangerous thing. People get hurt. And in this case they could get killed. For all our sakes I hope he's far away."

"It's not in his makeup. It's not in his training."

"What's not?"

"To give up. To run away. I've read his file. I probably know more about him than he knows about himself."

"You think he's out there, Michael?"

"I know he's out there. I just don't know where."

47. North Haven, Long Island

DELAROCHE CLIMBED OUT OF THE RANGE ROVER and stared across the narrow channel toward Shelter Island. It was nearly midnight. It had taken eight hours to make the drive from Washington, because Delaroche had meticulously kept to the speed limit the

entire way. He turned up the collar of his coat against
the cold windblown rain. A ferry plowed toward him,
two cars on the deck, beating against the heavy current rushing through Shelter Island Sound toward the
open water of Gardiners Bay. Outside the small ferry
office was a tan four-wheel-drive vehicle with police
markings. It was possible the officer was just making
rounds or had stopped for a cup of coffee. Delaroche
doubted that was the case, though. He suspected the
police were watching the ferry because Michael and
Elizabeth Osbourne were on the island.

He walked back to the Range Rover, climbed inside, and drove away from the ferry landing. Twice
he had to swerve to avoid small herds of white-tailed
deer. He turned onto a small dirt and gravel road that
ran into a stand of trees. There, hidden from view, he
slipped on his reading glasses and unfolded a large-
scale Long Island road map that he purchased at a
gas station along the way. Astrid peered over his
shoulder. North Haven was a small thumb of land jutting into Shelter Island Sound. To the southeast lay
the historic whaling port of Sag Harbor.

"The police are watching the ferry landings," Delaroche said. "That means the Osbournes are probably on the island. The South Ferry shuts down at one
A.M. The police will go home because they'll conclude we haven't tried to make the crossing."

"If the ferries are shut down, how do we get onto
the island?"

Delaroche tapped the map at Sag Harbor. "There
will be boats in the harbor and on the docks. We can
steal one and make the crossing after the ferries stop
running."

Astrid said, "The weather is terrible! It's not safe to go out in a boat on a night like this."

"This isn't so bad," Delaroche said, removing his eyeglasses and slipping them back into his pocket. "In Brélés they would consider this a fine night for fishing."

DELAROCHE ENTERED SAG HARBOR and parked along the marina. He climbed out of the Range Rover, leaving Astrid behind. The town was quiet, the shops and restaurants along the waterfront closed. After five minutes, Delaroche found what he was looking for, a twenty-six-foot Boston Whaler with a large Johnson outboard motor. He walked quickly back to the Range Rover and collected the things he needed: the cellular phones, the Berettas, the waterproof clothing. He locked the doors and pocketed the keys.

They walked along the marina and along a wooden dock, slick with rain. Delaroche climbed into the Whaler and helped Astrid onto the deck. There was a standing bridge and seating compartments forward and aft. Delaroche worked a lock pick inside the ignition and started the engine.

He leaped onto the dock and untied the lines, then jumped in the boat again and backed out of the slip. He cruised slowly through the harbor, boat throbbing beneath his feet. Twenty minutes later they entered the waters of Gardiners Bay.

FIVE MINUTES INTO THE JOURNEY Delaroche feared Astrid had been right. On the bay the wind was ferocious, beating down from the northwest at forty miles per hour with stronger gusts. The temperature was forty degrees, but the rain and wind made it feel much colder. The cockpit of the Whaler was open, and within minutes Delaroche and Astrid were soaked. Delaroche's hands were frozen to the wheel, despite his gloves. Astrid clung to his arm and buried her face in his shoulder against the rain.

The night was pitch-black, no moon, no starlight, nothing by which to navigate. Delaroche kept his own running lights doused to avoid being spotted from shore. Swells of four to five feet beat against the port side of the Whaler, tossing the shallow-draft little boat about.

Delaroche moved to within two hundred yards of the shoreline and headed due north. The seas calmed slightly. Off the port side he could see the very faint outline of trees and land. Delaroche knew from his maps that it was Mashomack Preserve, a giant nature conservancy. He continued north, past Sachem's Neck and Gibson's Beach. He nearly ran aground at Nichols Point, so he turned a few degrees to stern and moved farther offshore. After a few minutes he spotted Reel Point, a thin finger of land at the mouth of Coecles Harbor. He knew he was getting closer.

They rounded Ram Head and set the Whaler on a northwest heading toward Cornelius Point. The course change placed them directly into the path of the wind. Their speed slowed to a walking pace as the rollers grew larger. The little boat rose skyward as each wave passed beneath the hull; then the prow would slam down into the next trough, and seawater would crash into the seating compartments. Once

Astrid lost her grip and fell forward onto the dash. She regained her footing and stood up, blood on her forehead.

Delaroche could make out Cornelius Point off the port side: a rocky headland, the faint outline of a large summer cottage. He rounded the point and turned a few degrees to port. Off the starboard side he could see the lights of Greenport, blurry with sea fog and rain. A few moments later he passed Hay Beach Point. Delaroche turned to the southwest and ran along Hay Beach for about a quarter mile. Then he turned sharply to port and reduced power, running toward the shoreline.

Cannon Point was about four hundred yards farther down. Delaroche knew he could approach the shoreline in virtual silence because the high winds would carry all sound in the opposite direction. He killed the engine and raised the propeller. A few seconds later the boat grounded itself on a shoal a few yards from the beach.

Delaroche leaped into the icy knee-deep water and waded ashore. He pulled back the sleeve of his jacket and glanced at the luminous face of his watch. It was just two o'clock. The Whaler had made the journey from Sag Harbor in about ninety minutes, but as Delaroche tied the bowline to the limb of a fallen tree, he felt as though he had been behind the wheel fighting the sea for half the night. He waded back to the Whaler, collected the backpack, and helped Astrid over the side into the water. On the beach he unzipped the backpack, dug out the silenced Berettas, and gave one to her.

The rain beat down on them as Delaroche took his bearings. The beach ran directly to Cannon Point. It was rocky and narrow, only a few feet wide in spots. Beyond the high-water mark rose a sheer bluff, about twenty feet high, tangled with brush and dune grass.

Delaroche pulled the slider on the Beretta, chambering the first round. Astrid did the same. Then he took her by the hand and led her down the beach toward the house.

MATT COOPER AND SCOTT JACOBS had both worked in CIA security for nearly twenty years. Their government sedan was parked just inside the main gate of the compound on Shore Road. They took turns walking the perimeter of the grounds every half hour. Matt Cooper handled the 2 A.M. round.

DELAROCHE AND ASTRID LAY ON THE BLUFF overlooking the water, hidden behind the thick, thorny brush. Delaroche took in the layout of the compound: the large main house close to the water, two guest cottages, a separate three-car garage. Lights burned in the main house and in one of the cottages. Delaroche assumed that the Osbournes were in the main house and the security detail or a caretaker was in the cottage. He studied the layout of the grounds: a flat well-tended lawn dotted with tall trees, a gravel drive leading from the buildings to the front gate. Just inside the gate, Delaroche glimpsed the outline of a sedan.

The security man appeared a few minutes later. He carried a powerful flashlight in his right hand and played it across the grounds as he walked. As the man approached their position, Delaroche took Astrid firmly by the upper arm and held a finger to his lips. She nodded. A shaft of light shone over their heads, then played across the bulkhead and the beach below.

Delaroche stood suddenly, rattling brush. The beam of light played frantically for several seconds before it settled on him. His Beretta was drawn and leveled. Using the light as a target, Delaroche adjusted his aim to the right an inch or two in order to compensate for the fact that the security man held the light in his right hand.

He fired rapidly three times.

The security man collapsed onto the sodden turf.

DELAROCHE CREPT FORWARD and knelt beside the fallen man. The shots had struck his chest. Delaroche reached down, felt the neck for a pulse, and found none. He gestured for Astrid to join him. They walked along the eastern edge of the property, keeping to the trees, until they were about thirty yards from the front gate and the security car. Delaroche could see the second man inside the car, sitting behind the wheel, rainwater streaming down the windows. Certainly the man could see very little. It would be an easy kill. The challenge would be killing him silently. He crossed the lawn passing behind the car, and approached from the rear passenger side.

COOPER HAD BEEN TOO LONG in checking in. Usually, each man gave continuous updates of his progress by radio. Cooper had checked in from the west guest cottage and from the back of the main house, but Jacobs had not heard from him since he started toward the bulkhead and the beach.

Jacobs snatched up his radio and tried to raise Cooper, but there was no response. He was about to get out and go look for him when he heard the passenger door open. He turned and said, "What the hell happened to you?"

Then he looked at the face: short-cropped hair, very pale skin, two pierced ears. Jacobs didn't even attempt to go for his gun, just said softly, "Oh, Jesus Christ."

Delaroche raised his Beretta and shot him three times in the face. Then he reached across the seat and took the radio from the dead man's hand.

ASTRID STAYED in the trees. Delaroche climbed out of the car and softly closed the door. They retraced their route along the eastern boundary of the property, keeping to the trees once more. Delaroche ejected his half-spent ammunition clip and inserted a full one.

There were two entrances to the main house, a front door overlooking the gravel drive and a large screened porch overlooking the water. Delaroche planned to use the rear entrance.

The trees twisted in a gust of sea wind. Delaroche used the loud rushing noise to cover the sound of their approach. He took Astrid's hand and hurried through the treacherous ground between the trees.

They passed behind the cottage, where a porch light burned. Delaroche considered entering the cottage and killing the occupants. But there had been no activity on the grounds, no sign that their presence had been noticed, so he passed behind the cottage and started across the rear lawn.

A dog barked, then another. He turned and saw a pair of large golden retrievers running toward them. He chambered the first round in his Beretta and raised the gun at the advancing dogs.

THE DOGS awakened Michael. His eyes opened wide, and he was suddenly alert. He heard the first dog, then the second. Then both fell silent. He sat up in bed and swung his feet to the floor. On his bedside table were the Browning automatic, a portable radio, and a multiple-line telephone. He snatched up the radio and said, "This is Osbourne. Anyone there?"

Elizabeth stirred.

"This is Osbourne. Is anyone there? I heard dogs barking."

The radio crackled and a voice said, "The dogs are fine, sir. No problem."

Osbourne set down the radio, picked up the telephone, and dialed the number in the caretaker's cottage. He let the phone ring five times before slamming the receiver back into place.

Elizabeth sat up in bed.

Osbourne quickly dialed a special emergency number at Langley.

A calm voice answered.

"This is Osbourne. Shelter Island security detail is off the air. Call the local police and get some more men out here now! Move it!"

He hung up the phone.

Elizabeth said, "Michael, what's wrong?"

"He's here," Osbourne said. "He's killed the security team and he's got their radio. I just spoke to the bastard. Get some warm clothes on. Hurry, Elizabeth."

CHARLIE GIBBONS HAD BEEN THE CARETAKER at Cannon Point for twenty years. He was born and raised on Shelter Island and could trace his ancestry to the whalers who worked from Greenport three centuries earlier. He lived only ninety miles from New York City but had been there just once.

Charlie could hear the telephone ringing in his cottage as he walked across the lawn in his bathrobe, shotgun in one hand, flashlight in the other. He spotted the dogs a moment later and ran clumsily toward them. He knelt beside the first and saw his yellow coat was soaked with blood. He turned the beam of his flashlight on the second and saw it was in the same condition.

He rose and shone his flashlight toward the bulkhead. He played the beam back and forth for a few seconds and spotted something bright blue. The security men had been wearing blue waterproof jackets. He ran toward the fallen figure and knelt beside him. It was the man named Matt Cooper, and he was clearly dead.

He had to wake Michael and Elizabeth. He had to telephone the Shelter Island police. He had to get help quickly. He got to his feet and turned to run back to the cottage.

A tall blond woman stepped from behind a tree, a gun in outstretched hands. He saw the muzzle flash but heard no sound. The rounds tore through his chest.

He felt an excruciating pain, saw a flash of brilliant white light.

Then darkness.

48. McLean, Virginia

"THE SECURITY TEAM is off the air," the duty officer said. "Osbourne believes October is on the premises."

Adrian Carter sat up in bed. "Goddammit!"

"We've alerted local police, and another detail is en route."

"They'd better fucking hurry."

"Yes, sir."

"I'll be at headquarters in five minutes."

"Yes, sir."

"Now, connect me with Monica Tyler."

"Stand by, sir."

MICHAEL HAD SLEPT with his clothes on. Elizabeth pulled on a pair of gray cotton sweatpants and a beige woolen sweater. Michael slipped on his shoes and collected the Browning, the radio and cellular phone, and the keypad for the home's security system. The system was activated. The alarm would sound if October tried to enter the house. A number would read out on the keypad's digital display, showing which door or window the intruder had breached. If October tried to break inside the house, Michael would instantly know where he was.

Michael shut off the bedroom lights and led Elizabeth into the darkened hallway. They followed the stairs down to the entrance hall. Another light burned there. Michael quickly killed it.

The stairway to the basement was just off the large kitchen. Michael took Elizabeth's arm and led her through the darkness. He opened the doorway to the stairs and led her down to the basement.

DELAROCHE AND ASTRID crouched next to the door of the screened porch. Delaroche worked a knife inside the crude latch. It gave way after a few seconds. They picked their way across the veranda, around overstuffed rattan furniture and low tables, to a set of French doors. He tried the latch. It was locked. He crouched and worked his lock pick in the keyhole. The lock mechanism snapped. Delaroche pushed back the doors, and they slipped inside.

THE HOUSE, IN FACT, HAD three entrances—the main front doorway, the rear sun porch, and a small basement doorway on the north side of the house, hidden behind a set of recessed steps. Michael and Elizabeth moved through the finished rooms of the basement until they reached the doorway.

The alarm sounded in his hand. Michael quickly killed the tone and reset it. October had entered the house through the French doors off the living room.

A few seconds later the alarm sounded again, then a third time. Two motion detectors had been triggered, one in the dining room, one in the living room. The detectors were several feet apart. Unless October was moving through the house very rapidly it was unlikely that he set off both; the house was dark and unfamiliar to him. Michael assumed Astrid Vogel was in the house too. He turned to Elizabeth and said, "Go to the guest cottage and wait there until the police come."

"Michael, I don't want to leave you in—"

"Just do it, Elizabeth," Michael snapped. "If you want to live, just do what I say."

She nodded.

"The police will be here in a few minutes. When you see them, run for them. It's me he wants, not you. Do you understand me?"

She nodded. Michael said, "Good."

He punched in the disarm code and opened the door. Elizabeth kissed his cheek and started up the stairs. At the top she paused and looked in all directions. The night was pitch-black; she could barely make out the faint outline of the guest cottage overlooking the water.

She ran across the lawn, windblown rain beating against her face, until she reached the door of the cottage. She opened the door, stepped inside, then turned and took one last look at Michael.

The basement door closed, and he was gone. She closed the door and locked it, leaving the lights off. Then she went to the window and looked in the direction of the front gate.

IT WAS ASTRID VOGEL, standing in the living room, who spotted something moving across the lawn toward the guest cottage—a light-colored sweater, a woman, judging by the slightly awkward stride.

"Jean-Paul," she whispered, and gestured toward the lawn. "The woman."

"Take her," Delaroche whispered. Then he laid a hand on her arm and said, "Alive, Astrid. She's no good to us dead. And hurry. We don't have much time."

Astrid slipped out the French doors, crossed the veranda, and set off across the lawn.

MICHAEL RESET THE ALARM SYSTEM. He found a rechargeable flashlight plugged into an outlet—the senator had flashlights positioned throughout the house because of the island's frequent power outages. Michael switched on the light and played the beam back and forth across the walls until he found the fuse box. He opened it and shone the light inside. The master switch was the largest. He threw the switch and killed power to the entire house. The alarm system ran on batteries, so it would remain functional. He set the alarm on silent.

He followed the beam of light up the stairs and returned to the kitchen. On the wall, next to the telephone, was an intercom box for the front gate. The intercom operated on the telephone system, and the gate had a separate power source. He pressed a button and went quickly to a living room window overlooking the lawn. Outside, at the head of the property, he could see the metal gate rolling open on its track.

THE GUEST COTTAGE felt like an icehouse. Elizabeth couldn't remember the last time someone had stayed in the place. The thermostat was set to the lowest level to keep the pipes from bursting in a hard freeze. The wind tore at the shingled roof and beat against the windows overlooking Shelter Island Sound. Something scratched against the side of the house. Elizabeth emitted a short scream, then realized it was only the old oak tree that she had climbed countless times as a child.

It wasn't the *guest* cottage; in the lexicon of the Cannon family it was known as *Elizabeth's* cottage. The place was comfortable and modestly furnished. There were light-finished hardwood floors and, in the living room, rustic furniture arranged around the large picture window overlooking the harbor. The kitchen was tiny, just a small refrigerator and a stove with two burners, the bedroom simple. When she was a child, the cottage had been hers. When the main house was filled with her father's staff, or some delegation from a strange country, Elizabeth would come here to hide among her possessions. She adored the cottage, cared for it, spent summer nights in it. She smoked her first dope in the bathroom and lost her virginity in the bedroom.

She thought, If I could chose a place to die it would be here.

She blew on her hands and wrapped her arms tightly around herself against the cold.

Reflexively, she touched her lower abdomen.

She again thought, Are the babies all right? God, let them be all right!

She went to the window and looked out. A tall woman was running toward the cottage, gun in hand.

She could see enough of the face to realize it was the same woman who had pursued her in Washington. She walked backward from the window and nearly toppled over an armchair.

It's me he wants, not you.

She knew Michael was lying to her. They would use her to get to Michael, but they would kill her too. Just the way they killed Max. Just the way they killed Susanna.

She heard the scrape of boots on the wooden steps to the front door. She heard the metallic clicking of Astrid Vogel trying the doorknob. She heard a loud thud as Astrid Vogel tried to kick the door down, and she summoned every ounce of self-control she had to keep from screaming. She moved to the bedroom and closed the door. She heard a series of low thuds—three or four, she couldn't be certain—and the sound of splintering wood: Astrid Vogel, shooting her way through the lock. Another kick, and this time the door crashed open, slamming into the adjoining wall.

It's me he wants, not you.

And you're a liar, Michael Osbourne, she thought. They were merciless and sadistic. There would be no reasoning with them and certainly no negotiating.

She backpedaled into the corner, eyes on the closed door. God, how many times had she been here before? On beautiful summer mornings. On chilly autumn afternoons. The books on the shelves were hers, and so were the clothes in the closet. Even the threadbare rug at the foot of the bed. She thought of the afternoon she and her mother bought it together at an auction in Bridgehampton.

She thought, I can't let her take me. They'll kill us both.

She heard the woman walking through the cottage, the footfalls of her boots on the hardwood floors. She heard the wind rushing through the trees, the screaming of gulls. She stepped forward and put the hook on the door.

Hide in the closet, she thought. Maybe she won't look.

Don't be silly, Elizabeth. Think!

Then she heard the woman call out. "I know you're in here, Mrs. Osbourne. I don't want to hurt you. Just come out now."

The voice was low and strangely pleasant, the accent German.

Don't listen to her!

She opened the closet door and slipped inside. She closed the door halfway—she couldn't bear the thought of being sealed in the tiny dark room. Finally, she heard the wail of sirens, far off, carried by the wind. She wondered where they were—Winthrop Road, Manhanset Road if they were coming from mid-island. Either way, Elizabeth knew she would be dead before they arrived.

She backed away from the door. Something sharp dug into her shoulder blade—an arrow, sitting on the shelf. She groped along the wall; she knew it was here somewhere, the bow her father had given her when she turned twelve. It was hanging from a hook on the wall, next to an ancient set of golf clubs.

The woman tried the bedroom door and discovered it was locked.

Elizabeth thought, Now she knows I'm in here.

Panic shot through her. She forced herself to breathe.

Softly, she beat her palms along the wall until she touched something cold and hard.

ELIZABETH TOOK DOWN the bow. It was five and a half feet long, standard length. She reached up and grabbed hold of the arrow. The shaft was aluminum with feather fletchings. She took the arrow between the first two fingers on her right hand and with her thumb felt for the string notch behind the fletchings. She had done this countless times, so doing it in the dark was not a problem, even with shaking hands.

The woman kicked the door, but the old hook held.

Elizabeth fixed the arrow to the string and braced the shaft against the fingers of her left hand, which was clutching the bow. She pulled the arrow back halfway, then took a deep breath. The bowstring was old and brittle; it might simply snap when she pulled it to the tension required to shoot an arrow. Please, Elizabeth thought, fingering the string. I need one more shot from you.

But could she really do this? She had never killed a living thing, never dreamed of hunting. Her father wouldn't hear of it, in any case. Once he caught one of her boyfriends stalking a deer with her bow and arrow and banished him from the house for the rest of the summer.

The woman kicked the door. The latch broke and the door crashed open.

Elizabeth's body went rigid. She felt as if she were made of stone. She forced herself to breathe slowly. Do it for Michael, she thought. Do it for the children inside you.

She drew the arrow back hard on the string and pushed open the door with her foot. She saw Astrid Vogel, framed against the doorway, both hands on her gun, near her face. Astrid turned toward the sudden noise and leveled the gun with outstretched arms.

Elizabeth released the arrow.

The arrowhead struck Astrid in the base of her throat and drove her back, pinning her to the open door. Elizabeth screamed. Astrid's eyes opened wide and her lips parted.

Somehow, she managed to hold on to the gun. She raised the weapon and started firing. The silencer damped the explosions to a dull thud. Elizabeth threw herself back into the closet. The shots splintered the door, shattered the bedroom window, and tore plaster from the walls. She fell to the floor and curled herself into a ball.

Then it stopped. The room was quiet except for the wind and the clicking of Astrid Vogel attempting to fire an empty gun. Elizabeth got to her feet, took down another arrow, and stepped out of the closet.

Astrid had ejected the spent cartridge and was digging in her coat pocket for another clip of ammunition. Blood pumped from the wound in her throat. She managed to pull the new clip from her pocket.

Elizabeth said, "No, please don't. Don't make me do it again."

Astrid looked at her, then at the arrow in her throat. The clip fell from her grasp; then the gun tumbled to the floor. She breathed deeply twice. Blood gurgled in her throat.

Finally, her gaze went blank.

Elizabeth fell to her knees and was violently sick.

MICHAEL, BACK DOWNSTAIRS IN THE BASEMENT, could hear October's footsteps above him, picking his way through the living room furniture. Michael knew October would be methodical and careful. He would search the house, room by room, until he found his target. To survive, Michael would have to outsmart October once again, the way he did on the footpath in Virginia. October was operating in alien territory. Michael could find his way through the house with his eyes closed. He would use that to his advantage.

October had moved from the living room to the kitchen. He called out, "I have your wife, Mr. Osbourne. If you come down now, unarmed, with your hands in the air, no harm will come to her. If you make me hunt you down like an animal, I'll kill her too."

Michael said nothing, just listened to October's progress through the first level of the house.

After a moment October said, "I remember that night in London too, Mr. Osbourne. I remember the sound of your screams along the river. She was a beautiful woman. You must have loved her very much. It was a pity she had to die. She was the first and only woman I ever killed, but I will not hesitate to kill your wife if you persist in this nonsense. Give yourself up, or she dies with you."

Michael felt anger rising within him. Just hearing the man's voice after all these years filled him with horror. He tried to suppress it; he knew that was exactly the reaction October was trying to incite. If he lost his composure—if he acted with emotion instead of intelligence—he would die. He also knew October had no intention of allowing Elizabeth to live.

"It must have hurt very badly to lose your lover like that, shot down like a dog, right before your eyes," October said. "I heard they had to pull you from the field. Send you back to headquarters. I heard it ruined you. Just think how you'll feel if I kill another one of your women. You won't want to live after that, I assure you. So just give yourself up, Mr. Osbourne. Make it easy for both of us."

Michael heard a scream from the guest cottage: Elizabeth's scream.

"Sounds like things are getting interesting outside, Mr. Osbourne. Pick up the telephone, call the cottage. Tell your wife to give herself up, and she won't be harmed. You have my word on that."

Michael walked across the room and pressed the TALK button on the intercom. Very calmly he said, "Your word means nothing to me, Nicolai Mikhailovich."

"What did you call me?" October yelled back, after a moment's hesitation.

"I called you Nicolai Mikhailovich. It's your real name, or did the wonderful people of the KGB keep

that information from you? Nicolai Mikhailovich
Voronstov. Your father was General Mikhail Voronstov, head of the First Chief Directorate of the KGB.
You were his bastard child. Your mother was his mis-
tress. As soon as you were old enough, your father
gave you to the KGB to raise. Your mother ended up
in the gulag. Would you like me to continue, Nicolai
Mikhailovich?"

Michael released the button and waited for October's reaction. He heard a door being kicked open, a
ceramic lamp crashing to the floor, the dull *thump* of
a silenced weapon being discharged. Michael was
getting to him.

"Your teacher was a man you knew only as
Vladimir. You treated him like a father. For all intents
and purposes, he *was* your father. When you were
sixteen you were infiltrated into the West through
Czechoslovakia. You were ordered to kill your escorts. One of them was a woman, which makes you a
liar as well as a murderer. You buried yourself in the
West. Ten years later, when you were a man, you
started killing. I could name most of your victims if
you'd like, Nicolai Mikhailovich."

Michael heard a window shatter and more rounds
embedding themselves in the wall. He heard an
empty cartridge fall to the floor and a fresh one
rammed into place. Then he heard sirens a long way
off and another scream from the cottage.

He pressed the intercom again and said, "Who
hired you?"

More shots.

"Who hired you, goddammit? Answer me!"

"I don't know who hired me!"

"You're lying. Your entire life is a lie."

"Shut up!"

"You're trapped here. You'll never get off this island alive."

"Neither will you, and neither will your wife."

"Astrid's been gone a long time. I wonder what's keeping her."

"Call the cottage. Tell your wife to give herself up."

Michael set down his cellular telephone and picked up the receiver of the regular hard-line phone. He heard October pick up an extension. The telephone rang once and Elizabeth answered, breathless.

"Michael! My God, she's dead. I killed her. I shot her with an arrow. Michael, God, I don't want to be here with her. Oh, Michael, it's horrible. Please, I don't want to stay here with her."

"Go to the dock. Take the dinghy out to the *Alexandra*. Wait there until the police arrive."

"Michael, what are you—"

"Just do what I say. Go to the *Alexandra*! Now!"

ELIZABETH SET DOWN THE TELEPHONE and walked to the window. She had known Michael more than ten years. He had sailed on the boat countless times with her father. He knew it was called the *Athena,* not the *Alexandra*. It was possible he made a mistake because of the pressure of the situation, but she doubted it. It was intentional. It was for a reason. He wanted her to stay in the cottage, but he wanted October to think she was heading for the boat.

She watched the main house through the window. She listened to the sirens draw nearer. She wanted to get out. She wanted a cigarette to mask the smell of Astrid Vogel's blood. She wanted this nightmare to be over. A few seconds later she saw the screened door of the veranda swing open and the man called October running across the lawn toward the dock.

DELAROCHE PLUNGED through the darkness. Wind ripped at the trees and nearly knocked him from his feet. The dock stretched before him into the darkness. Fifty yards from shore the sailboat swayed at its mooring, mast swinging like a pendulum in the whitecaps, halyards screaming in the wind.

Michael Osbourne's voice, distant and metallic, ran through his head like recorded announcements in a train station.

I called you Nicolai Mikhailovich. It's your real name.

Delaroche thought, Goddammit! How could he know?

The KGB had made him one promise: His existence in the West would be so secret only a handful of people within the hierarchy would know the truth. So secret he had been permitted to kill his escorts to the West that night in Austria. Had they lied? Had someone betrayed him? Was it Vladimir? Or Arbatov? Or the traitor Drozdov? Had Drozdov found the truth buried in the files at Moscow Center and sold it to his new masters in the West? Delaroche vowed to kill Drozdov if he ever got off Shelter Island alive.

The revelation that the CIA had a dossier made Delaroche feel physically sick. Did they have a photograph, too? Usually, it was Delaroche who used the dossiers, Delaroche who leafed through the dark pages of a man's life until he found the weakness that would prove to be his undoing. Now, Delaroche knew his enemies had assembled a dossier on *his* life, and Osbourne had used it against him.

I called you Nicolai Mikhailovich.

Reflexively, the killings ran through his mind. He tried to shut it off, but the faces appeared one by one, first vibrant and alive, then burst by three bullet wounds. Hassan Mahmoud, the Palestinian boy. Colin Yardley and Eric Stoltenberg. Sarah Randolph. . . .

He could hear Michael Osbourne's screams echoing along the Chelsea Embankment.

It's your real name.

Some nights Delaroche had a dream, and the dream played out in his imagination now. The men he had killed would confront him, armed with silenced automatics, and he would reach for his Glock pistol or his Beretta and find only paint brushes. Then he would reach for his backup weapon and find only a palette. "We know who you are," they would say and begin to laugh. And Delaroche would raise his hands and shield his face, and the bullets would tear through his palms and bore through his eyes, and he would sit up in bed and tell himself it was only a dream, just a stupid fucking dream.

Delaroche charged across the sloping lawn, feet flying over the wet springy turf, until the smack of his feet along the wooden dock shattered the nightmare image of his own death. He could hear the dinghy banging against the pylons of the dock, but the engine was silent. A few seconds later he reached the end of the dock and looked down, gun leveled into the darkness.

The dinghy was empty.

"DROP THE GUN!" Michael shouted over the wind. "Lie flat on the dock, facedown, and do it very slowly."

Michael stood at the foot of the dock, October at the end, fifty feet away. His left arm hung at his side; his right arm was bent at the elbow, and the gun was near his face. He was motionless. By the sound of the sirens the police were on Shore Road now. They would arrive in a matter of seconds.

"Drop the gun now!" Michael yelled. "It's over. Just do what I say."

October lowered his right arm until it hung straight at his side. The police reached the front gate. Michael heard the cottage door swing open. He turned in the direction of the sound and caught a glimpse of Elizabeth's beige sweater, flashing through the darkness.

He shouted, "Stay back, Elizabeth!"

October dropped into a crouch and pivoted. The arm swung up. Michael fired several shots with the Browning but they all sailed over October's head. The assassin fired three times through the darkness. One shot found its mark, tearing into the right side of Michael's chest.

The Browning tumbled from his hand and clattered along the dock. Michael fell onto his back. His right arm went numb; then he felt an intense, searing pain in his chest.

The rain beat down on his face. Tree limbs twisted in the wind, and in his dementia Michael thought they were giant hands clawing at his body. He drifted toward unconsciousness. He saw Sarah walking toward him on the Chelsea Embankment, her long skirt dancing across buckskin boots. He saw her exploded face. He heard Elizabeth's voice, calling from a long way off, incomprehensible. Finally, it cut through the fog of shock.

"Michael! He's coming! Michael, please, God! Michael!"

Michael lifted his head and saw October slowly advancing toward him. The Browning lay on the dock, a few feet away. Michael tried to reach out with his right hand, but it would not obey his command to move. He rolled onto his right side and reached out with his left hand. He felt the cold metal of the Browning, the butt slick with rain. He grabbed hold of it, slipped his finger in the trigger guard, and fired down the dock.

DELAROCHE SAW THE MUZZLE FLASH of Osbourne's gun. He raised his Beretta as the first series of shots whizzed harmlessly past and took aim at Osbourne's prone body. He took a step closer. He wanted to shoot him in the face. He wanted to avenge Astrid's death. He wanted to leave his mark.

Osbourne fired again. This time a bullet ripped through Delaroche's right hand, shattering bone. The Beretta tumbled from his grasp and fell into the swirling water below the dock. He looked down and saw fragmented bone jutting from the ugly exit wound on the back of his hand.

He wanted to kill Osbourne with his one good hand—break his neck or crush his windpipe—but Osbourne still had his gun, and the police had entered the grounds. He turned, ran quickly down the dock, and leaped into the dinghy.

He pulled the starter cord four times until the little outboard motor turned over. He untied the line and guided the boat away from the dock into Shelter Island Sound.

Cannon Point was ablaze with flashing lights. Sirens filled the air. Above it all, Delaroche heard one thing—the screams of Elizabeth Osbourne, begging her husband not to die.

49. London

"IS OSBOURNE GOING TO LIVE?" the Director asked, from the library of his home in St. John's Wood.

"His condition stabilized this evening," Mitchell Elliott said. "There was some additional bleeding around midday, so the surgeons had to go back in. Unfortunately, it looks as though he's going to survive."

"Where is he?"

"Officially, his location is secret. My source in Langley confirms Osbourne is in the intensive care unit at Stonybrook Hospital on Long Island."

"I hope you realize Osbourne is untouchable at this point. For the moment, at least."

"Yes, I realize that, Director."

"He's survived two attempts on his life. Under no circumstances is there to be a third."

"Of course, Director."

"He is a very worthy opponent, our Mr. Osbourne. I have to say I admire him very much. I wish there were some way to entice him into working for me."

"He's a Boy Scout, Director, and Boy Scouts don't fit well into your organization."

"I suppose you're right."

"What's the status of October?" Elliott asked.

"I'm afraid he received a rather rude welcome from the extraction team."

"And the advance payments we made to his Swiss bank account?"

"All gone, I'm afraid. It seems October transferred the money from the account as quickly as it came in."

"That's a pity."

"Yes, but surely a man of your means isn't worried about a little loose change like that."

"Of course not, Director."

"There's still one target to be dealt with."

"I've already set those wheels in motion."

"Excellent. Do it skillfully, though. There's a great deal at stake."

"It will be done very skillfully."

"Mr. Elliott, I know I don't need to remind you that your first duty at this point is to protect the Society at all costs. You must do nothing that would place the Society in any harm whatsoever. I know I'll have your cooperation on that matter."

"Of course, Director."

"Very well. It's been a pleasure doing business with you. I only hope it wasn't all for naught. It's going to take all your considerable skills to ensure the survival of your missile defense contract."

"I'm confident that goal can be accomplished."

"Wonderful. Good night, Mr. Elliott."

"Good night, Director."

The Director replaced the receiver in its cradle.

"You're a very good liar," Daphne said.

She let her silk gown fall from her shoulders and slipped into bed next to him.

"I'm afraid it's necessary in this line of work."

She kissed him on the mouth and pressed her breasts against his body. Then she reached between his legs and took him in her hands. "Anything, my love?" she whispered.

He kissed her and said, "Perhaps if you tried a little harder, petal."

50. Washington, D.C.

PAUL VANDENBERG PARKED on Ohio Drive, overlooking the Washington Channel, and shut down the engine. He had come alone, in his private car, just as Elliott asked. The meeting was supposed to take place at 10 P.M., but Elliott was uncharacteristically late. Another car pulled in behind him, a large black four-wheel-drive vehicle, its tinted windows pulsating to the beat of gangsta rap music. Vandenberg started his engine and let it idle as he waited. The four-wheel-drive left at ten-fifteen. Five minutes later a black sedan pulled next to him, and the rear window descended.

It was Mark Calahan, Mitchell Elliott's personal aide.

"Mr. Elliott is terribly sorry, but there has to be a change of venue," Calahan said. "Come with me, and I'll bring you back to your car when the meeting is done."

Vandenberg got out of his car and climbed into the back of the black sedan. They drove for ten minutes—around Hains Point, across the Memorial Bridge to Virginia, then north along the parkway. Calahan remained silent the entire time. It was one of Elliott's rules, no small talk between staff and clients. Finally, the car pulled into a parking lot overlooking Roosevelt Island.

"Mr. Elliott is waiting for you on the island, sir," Calahan said politely. "I'll take you to him."

The two men climbed out.

The driver, Henry Rodriguez, waited behind the wheel.

Two minutes later, Rodriguez heard the snap of a single gunshot.

A JOGGER FOUND THE BODY at seven-fifteen the following morning. It lay next to a marble bench at the memorial to Theodore Roosevelt, which the media deemed fitting, since Paul Vandenberg had always admired TR. The gun had been placed in the mouth. A large section of the back of Vandenberg's head was gone. The slug was embedded in a tree trunk sixty feet away.

The suicide note was found in the breast pocket of his woolen overcoat. It bore the hallmarks of all good Vandenberg memos: concise, economical, to the point. He had taken his own life, the note said, because he was aware *The Washington Post* was preparing a devastating account of his fund-raising activities over the years on behalf of James Beckwith. Vandenberg admitted guilt. Beckwith and Mitchell Elliott bore none of the responsibility; Vandenberg had planned and executed everything. He had taken his own life, the note said, because death by gunshot was preferable to death by independent counsel.

A shaken James Beckwith appeared in the White House briefing room late in the afternoon, in time for the evening newscasts. He professed profound shock and sadness at the death of his closest aide. He then announced that the Justice Department would immediately commence a full and thorough investigation of all of Vandenberg's fund-raising activities on Beckwith's behalf. He left the briefing room without taking questions and spent a quiet evening with Anne in the family quarters of the mansion.

The following morning the *Post* devoted much of page one to the apparent suicide of Paul Vandenberg. The coverage included a lengthy account of the financial relationship between James Beckwith and Mitchell Elliott. The piece disputed the claim, made in Vandenberg's suicide note, that he alone was the architect of the complex web of financial arrangements that had enriched the Beckwiths over the years. It also implicated Mitchell Elliott's Washington attorney, Samuel Braxton, Beckwith's nominee to be secretary of state.

The piece had a double byline: Tom Logan and Susanna Dayton, *Washington Post* Staff Writers.

January

51. Shelter Island, New York

SOME NIGHTS were better than others. Some nights Elizabeth would see it all again in her dreams and she would wake up screaming, trying to rub the imaginary bloodstains from her hands. Some nights Michael would awaken, having dreamed that October shot him three times in the face instead of once in the chest. The guest cottage was repaired and repainted, but Elizabeth never went there again. Sometimes, Michael sat at the end of the dock and peered into the swirling waters. Sometimes, an hour would pass before he would awaken from his trance. Sometimes, Elizabeth would watch him from the lawn and wonder exactly what he was thinking.

OF THE AFTERMATH, Michael knew only what he read in the newspapers or saw on television, but like any man born to the secret world he generally regarded the news media as annoying background music. Each morning the new caretaker would drive to the pharmacy in Shelter Island Heights and pick up the newspapers—*The New York Times, The Wall Street Journal, Newsday*—and leave them on Michael's bedside table. By New Year's Day Michael felt strong enough to make the journey too. He would sit in the front passenger seat of his Jaguar and stare silently out the window at the water and the bare winter trees. His interest receded as January wore on, and by Inauguration Day he had stopped reading the papers altogether.

Beckwith successfully weathered the storm. Credit was given to his wife, Anne. Anne had become the President's most important adviser since the death of Paul Vandenberg. *Newsweek* put her on the cover Christmas week. Inside was a glowing article about her political acumen; Anne would have to play a critical role from the shadows if the second Beckwith term was to succeed. It was Anne, according to Washington's chattering class, who goaded the President into pressing for sweeping campaign finance reform. With the fervency of the newly converted, Beckwith called for a ban on unregulated contributions to the parties—the "soft money"—and pressed broadcasters to give candidates free airtime. By Inauguration Day his approval ratings had reached sixty percent.

Two of Beckwith's closest friends and supporters did not fare as well. Samuel Braxton was forced to withdraw his nomination to be secretary of state. He denied all wrongdoing but said he did not want to tie American foreign policy in knots by engaging in a long and divisive confirmation fight. It was Anne, according to the media, who pushed Braxton off the cliff.

Alatron Defense Systems voluntarily withdrew from the national missile defense project after Andrew Sterling, Beckwith's defeated rival and chairman of the Senate Armed Services Committee, promised to conduct "the congressional equivalent of a rectal exam" on Mitchell Elliott. The contract was awarded to another California defense contractor, and Sterling gave his reluctant support, ensuring the system would be funded and deployed.

Two days before the inauguration, the FBI and U.S. Park Police released the findings of their investigation into the death of White House Chief of Staff Paul Vandenberg. Investigators found no evidence to suggest his death was anything but a suicide. The investigation into the murders of Max Lewis and Virginia state trooper Dale Preston produced no arrests. The Washington Metropolitan Police Department quietly ended its investigation into the murder of Susanna Dayton. The case file remained technically open.

ELIZABETH SPENT LONG WEEKENDS on the island. She worked three days a week from the New York office of Braxton, Allworth & Kettlemen while she gradually shed her case load and auditioned new firms. Because of her record and her political connections, she had no shortage of suitors. The venerable New York firm Titan, Webster & Leech offered the most money and, more important, the most flexibility. She accepted their offer and faxed Samuel Braxton her letter of resignation that same afternoon.

MICHAEL HEALED FASTER than his doctors expected. Snow fell the first week of January, and the weather turned bitterly cold. But the following week the air warmed, and his doctors ordered him out of the house for gentle walks.

The first two days he gingerly strolled the grounds of Cannon Point, his right arm in a sling because October's bullet had shattered his collarbone and cracked his shoulder blade. On the third day he walked in the wind on Shore Road, a pair of Adrian Carter's security men trailing softly behind him. In a week's time he walked to the village and back in the morning, and in the late afternoon he would walk the long, rocky beaches of Ram Island.

In the evenings he wrote in Douglas Cannon's library overlooking Dering Harbor. After three days he showed the first draft to his father-in-law. Cannon edited with a red pencil, sharpening Michael's stiff bureaucratic prose, honing the logic of the arguments and conclusions. When it was finished he overnighted it to Adrian Carter at Langley.

"There's nothing I hate more than Washington on Inauguration Day," Carter said the following evening. "I could use some sea air and some of Cannon's wine. Mind if I come up for a couple of days?"

"HOW MUCH LONGER do I have to put up with these goons?" Michael asked the next afternoon as he bumped along the sixth fairway of the Gardiners Bay Country Club in a golf cart. A pair of CIA security officers in matching Patagonia parkas rode in a cart behind them, muttering into handheld radios.

"Shit, I trickled into the rough," Carter said, as he lurched to a stop next to his ball and climbed out of the cart. He pulled a nine-iron from his bag and prepared for a 140-yard shot to the green.

"Are you going to answer my question?" Michael said.

"Jesus, Michael, come on. Not while I'm addressing the ball."

Carter struck the shot. The ball plopped into the left bunker.

"Goddammit, Osbourne!"

"Go easy on yourself, Tiger. It's thirty-eight degrees out here."

Carter climbed into the cart and drove toward the green.

"Those *goons,* as you put it, are here to protect you and your family, Michael, and they'll stay until I'm satisfied your life is no longer in any danger."

"Right now my life is in danger because I'm riding in an open golf cart in the middle of winter."

"I'll take you home after nine and play the back alone."

"You're insane."

"You should take up the game."

"I have enough frustration in my life. Self-inflicted wounds I can live without. Besides, I'll be lucky if I can ever raise a beer with this arm, let alone swing a golf club."

"How's Elizabeth doing?"

"As well as can be expected, Adrian. Killing takes its toll, even when it's in self-defense. The fact that you were able to keep it from going public has made it easier for her. I can't thank you enough."

"She's a gem," Carter said. "I've always said you're the luckiest man I know."

Carter's chip rolled past the cup, leaving him with a ten-foot putt for bogie. "Fuck it," he said. "It's too goddamned cold for golf. Let's spend the afternoon by the fire getting drunk."

. . .

"DID YOU READ IT?" Michael asked, as Carter pulled the cork from an Italian merlot and poured two glasses.

"Yes, I read it. I had one of two choices—shit-can it or pass it up the line."

"Which choice did you make?"

"I chose the coward's route. Passed it up the line with no comment."

"You're a chicken shit."

"It's called the bureaucratic shuffle. Protecting one's flank."

"Protecting one's ass."

"Same thing. You could learn a thing or two from me. Your ass is usually fully exposed, hanging in the wind."

"I'm a field man, Adrian. Field men make lousy desk men. You always said so yourself."

"That's true."

"So how come you became such a great desk man?"

"Because I wanted a life, and I couldn't have a life if I was running from one shithole to the next, trying to remember what my cover name was that week."

"Who'd you give my memo to?"

"Monica Tyler, of course."

"Let me guess—she shit-canned it."

"In a New York minute."

"I didn't expect her to do anything else."

"So why did you write it?"

"Because I believe it to be true."

"You seriously believe Mitchell Elliott, with the assistance of a secret band of rogue operatives, brought down that airliner so he could build his missile defense system?"

Michael nodded. "Yes, I do."

"That falls into the category of a charge too dangerous to make—not without conclusive proof. Monica recognized that, and so did I. Frankly, what bothers me is why an officer of your experience can't see it."

Elizabeth knocked and entered the room. The senator had convinced her to take the *Athena* out on the bay with him for a couple of hours. Her face was bright red with the cold. She stood before the fire and warmed her backside against the flames.

Carter said, "I thought you were supposed to be taking it easy."

"Dad did all the sailing," she said. "I just drank herbal tea and tried to keep from freezing to death."

"Everything all right?" Carter asked.

"Everything's fine. The babies are perfect."

"God, that's wonderful," he said, and a large smile broke across his usually placid face.

"What were you boys talking about?"

"Shop," Carter said.

"Okay, I'm leaving."

"Stay," Michael said.

"Michael, some of this is—"

"She can hear it firsthand, or she can hear it later in bed. Take your pick, Adrian."

"Stay," he said. "Besides, it's nice to have something beautiful to look at. Make yourself useful, Michael, and pour me some more wine. Elizabeth?"

She shook her head. "I'm off booze and cigarettes for a while."

Carter drank some wine and said, "We received a report from the French service two days ago. They believe they've discovered the cover identity of October. He was living along the Breton coast under the name Jean-Paul Delaroche. A village called Brélés."

"Jesus, we've been there, Michael."

"He lived quietly in a cottage overlooking the Channel. It seems he was also a talented painter. The French are keeping it quiet, as only the French can do. We have a worldwide alert for him, but so far we've had no sightings. We've also heard from a number of different sources that he's actually dead."

"Dead? How?"

"Apparently, whoever hired him to kill you wasn't pleased that he failed to fulfill the contract."

"I hope they tortured him first," Elizabeth said.

Michael was looking out the window, toward the dock and the white-capped bay beyond.

Elizabeth said, "What are you thinking about, Michael?"

"I'd just like to see a body, that's all."

"We all would," Carter said. "But these things usually don't work like that."

He finished the wine and held out his glass for more. Elizabeth opened another bottle. The senator came into the room, face red, hair windblown. "I see you've raided the cellar," he said. "Pour me a vast amount, please."

Carter said, "I have one other piece of serious business before we get too drunk."

"If you must," Michael said.

"Monica has agreed to drop all disciplinary proceedings against you. She thinks they're inappropriate at this point, given what you and Elizabeth have endured."

"Oh, isn't that nice of Monica."

"Come on, Michael. She's serious. She thinks the whole thing got out of hand. She wants to put it behind us and move on."

Michael looked at Elizabeth, then back at Carter. "Tell her thanks, but no thanks," he said.

"You *want* the disciplinary proceedings to go forward?"

"No, I want out," Michael said. "I've decided to leave the Agency."

"You're not serious?"

"Dead serious," Michael said. "Sorry, poor choice of words. Okay, now we can get drunk."

Elizabeth crossed the room, leaned down, and kissed Michael's lips. "Are you sure, Michael? Don't do it for me."

"I've never been so sure about anything in my entire life. And I'm not doing it for you. I'm doing it for us." Then he touched her stomach. "And for them."

She kissed him again and said, "Thank you, Michael. I love you. I hope you know that."

"I know," he said. "God, I know."

Carter looked at his watch and said, "Oh, shit!"

"What?" Michael and Elizabeth said in unison.

"We missed Beckwith's address."

And they all burst out laughing.

EPILOGUE

Mykonos, Greece

IT WAS THE villa no one wanted. It clung to a clifftop overlooking the sea, exposed to the eternal wind. Stavros, the real estate agent, had given up on the idea of selling the property. He simply rented it each year to the same clan of young British stockbrokers who pillaged the island each August for three drunken weeks.

The Frenchman with the injured hand spent just five minutes in the house. He toured the bedrooms and the living room and inspected the views from the stone terrace. He paid particular attention the kitchen, which made him frown.

"I know men who can do the work for you, if you wish to undertake renovations," Stavros said.

"That won't be necessary," the Frenchman said. "I'll do the work myself."

"But your hand," Stavros said, nodding at the bandage.

"It's nothing," the Frenchman said. "A kitchen accident. It will heal soon."

Stavros frowned, as though he found the story unconvincing. "It's a popular rental," he continued. "If you wish to leave the island at the high season, I'm certain I can fetch a good price for it, especially if you make repairs."

"The villa is no longer for rent."

"Very well. When would you like to—"

"Tomorrow," the Frenchman said. "Give me an account number, and I'll have the money wired this afternoon."

"But, monsieur, you are not Greek. It's not so easy for a foreigner to buy property. There are forms to fill out, legal documents. These things take time."

"See to it, Mr. Stavros. But I'm moving in here tomorrow morning."

HE SPENT THE REMAINDER OF THE WINTER inside. When his hand had healed sufficiently he went to work, mending the villa with the devotion of a monk copying the ancient books. Kristos, the man from the home supplies store, offered to find good men to help with the work, but the Frenchman politely refused. He replaced the kitchen appliances and laid a new ceramic countertop. He repainted the entire interior. He carted away the old furniture—ghastly modern pieces—and filled the rooms with rustic Grecian chairs and tables. In March, when the weather warmed, he turned his attention to the exterior. He patched cracks in the walls and put down a coat of gleaming whitewash. He replaced the broken tiles on the roof and the broken stones on the terrace. By the middle of April, the villa no one wanted was the finest in the village.

THE ITALIAN RACING BICYCLE arrived that same week. Each morning he rode along the winding coast roads and up and down the steep hills in the center of the island. Gradually, as the days lengthened, he spent more and more time in the village. He dawdled over the olives and rice and lamb in the marketplace. A few afternoons each week he took his lunch in the taverna, always with a book for protection. Sometimes he bought broiled sea bass from the boys on the beach and ate the fish alone in a grotto where gray seals played. He ventured into the wineshop. At first he drank only French and Italian wines, but after a time he developed a taste for inexpensive Greek varieties. When the clerk suggested more costly vintages, the Frenchman would shake his head and hand the bottle back. The renovations, he explained, had put a dent in his finances.

AT FIRST HIS GREEK WAS LIMITED, a few staccato sentences, a vague untraceable accent. But remarkably, within two months he could conduct his business in passable Greek with the accent of an islander.

The village women made gentle advances, but he took no lovers. He had only one pair of visitors, a small Englishman with eyes the color of winter seawater and a mulatto goddess who sunbathed nude in the May sunshine. The Briton and the goddess stayed for three days. Each evening they dined on the terrace late into the night.

IN MAY he began to paint. At first he could hold his brushes for only a few minutes at a time because of the scar tissue in his right hand. Then, slowly, gradually, the scar tissue stretched and gave way, and he was able to work for several hours at a time. For many weeks he painted the scenes around the villa—the seascapes, the clusters of whitewashed cottages, the flowers on the hillsides, the old men taking wine and olives at the taverna. The villa reflected the changing colors of each passing day: a dusty pink at dawn, a filtered raw sienna at dusk that took weeks of patient experimentation to re-create on his palette.

In August he began painting the woman.

She was blond, with striking blue eyes and pale luminous skin. According to his cleaning lady, he worked without a model from a handful of crude pencil sketches. "Clearly," she told the other girls in the village, "the Frenchman is working from memory."

It was a large work, about six feet by four feet. The woman wore only a white blouse, unbuttoned to her navel, tinged with the raw sienna of the setting sun. Her long body was draped over a small wooden chair, facing backward. One hand rested beneath her chin; the other held something that looked like a gun, though no one would put a gun in the hand of a woman so beautiful, the maid said. Not even a recluse Frenchman.

He finished the work in October.

He placed it in a simple frame and hung it on the wall facing the sea.

ACKNOWLEDGMENTS

The events portrayed in this novel are entirely the product of the author's imagination, as are the characters that populate it. Still, several men and women similar to the people in this story gave me invaluable assistance, without which this work would not have been possible. The expertise is all theirs; the mistakes, simplifications, and dramatic license are all mine.

Several current and former members of the American intelligence community allowed me to peek behind the curtain into their world, and I wish to express my gratitude to them, especially the professionals at the CIA's Counterterrorism Center in Langley, Virginia, who patiently answered as many of my questions as they could and generously shared a few pieces of their lives along the way.

So much has been written about working in the White House, but several people from various administrations helped me fill in the blanks with their personal memories. Some of their insight helped shape this work, and some of it was just tucked away, but I am indebted to all of them.

In my previous life I was privileged to work with Brooks Jackson, who covers the intersection of money and politics for CNN and is one of the finest reporters in Washington. His wisdom was invaluable, though nothing written on the pages of a novel could ever do justice to the spirit and expertise of his work.

James Hackett and John Pike helped me decipher the Rubik's Cube of National Ballistic Missile Defense and also argued passionately for and against it. Obviously, I am to blame for the frightening oversimplification of missile defense contained in this book, not them.

I also wish to express my profound thanks to Dr. Zev Rosenwaks and Wally Padillo of the Center for Reproductive Medicine and Infertility at New York Hospital-Cornell Medical Center. Also, to Chris Plante, who helped me better understand Stinger missiles.

Over the years three dear friends, Tom Kelly, Martha Rogers, and Greg Craig, have given me a window on the world of Washington law, even though they never realized I was gathering material for a book. I thank them for their insight and, more importantly, their friendship.

As always, Ion Trewin, the managing director of Weidenfeld & Nicolson in London, gave me priceless counsel, as did his assistant, Rachel Leyshon.

A very special thanks to the team at International Creative Management: Heather Shroeder, Alicia Gordon, Tricia Davey, Jack Horner, Sloane Harris, and, of course, Esther Newberg.

And finally, to the talented and dedicated staff at Random House: Adam Rothberg, Jake Klisivitch, Sybil Pincus, Leona Nevler, and Linda Gray, and especially my editors, Brian DeFiore and Ann Godoff. There are none better.

ABOUT THE AUTHOR

DANIEL SILVA's first novel, *The Unlikely Spy,* was a *New York Times* and international best-seller and was sold as a major motion picture to Twentieth Century–Fox. A former journalist and television producer, Silva has covered everything from Washington politics to the conflicts in the Middle East. He lived and worked in Cairo, where some of *The Mark of the Assassin* is set. He now lives in Washington, D.C., with his wife, NBC *Today* show correspondent Jamie Gangel, and their two children. He is currently at work on a new novel.

(continued)

Puzo, Mario, *The Last Don*
Rampersad, Arnold, *Jackie Robinson*
Rendell, Ruth, *The Keys to the Street*
Rice, Anne, *Servant of the Bones*
Riva, Maria, *Marlene Dietrich* (2 volumes)
Salamon, Julie and Jill Weber, *The Christmas Tree*
Shaara, Jeff, *Gods and Generals*
Snead, Sam with Fran Pirozzolo, *The Game I Love*
Truman, Margaret, *Murder at the National Gallery*
Truman, Margaret, *Murder on the Potomac*
Truman, Margaret, *Murder in the House*
Tyler, Anne, *Ladder of Years*
Tyler, Anne, *Saint Maybe*
Updike, John, *Rabbit at Rest*
Updike, John, *Golf Dreams*
Whitney, Phyllis A., *Amethyst Dreams*

SEE THE DIFFERENCE

Random House Large Print Editions are available in bookstores throughout the country. For a complete listing of our wide selection of current bestsellers and timeless favorites write:

Random House Large Print
201 East 50th Street, Dept. CK, 23-2
New York, NY 10022

For Customer Service or to place a direct order call toll free: (800) 726-0600 or fax: (410) 857-1948

Our email address is audio@randomhouse.com

Visit our Random House Web Site at:
www.randomhouse.com